"You and your letters to the editor."

Everyone Should Have an
OPINION
... Here's Mine

By Dot Ward

Dot Ward
7/31/2010

First Edition

ILLUSTRATION: Marshall Ramsey, Editorial Cartoonist

Published by Thomson-Shore Publishers, Dexter, Michigan

Library of Congress Number: 2009935482

ISBN 978-0-9712424-1-8

Dedication

This book is dedicated to all those who have opinions – especially conservative ones – and are not afraid to express them;

to Erwin Ward, my loving husband of 52 years, who never once voiced an objection to having the family name used as a lightning rod for someone's opinions other than his own;

and to my grandchildren, Virginia and Brennan, with the hope that they will find within the pages of this book some bit of wisdom that will help them formulate sound opinions of their own.

CONTENTS

Chapter I
READER EDITORIAL BOARD OPINIONS

Chapter II
MORAL ISSUES

Chapter III
NATIONAL ISSUES

Chapter IV
STATE ISSUES

Chapter V
LOCAL ISSUES

Chapter VI
THE ARTS

Chapter VII
IMMIGRATION

Chapter VIII
CRIME

Chapter IX
THE NATCHEZ TRACE

Chapter X
EDUCATION

Chapter XI
THIS AND THAT ... and a Few Gripes

Chapter XII
PATRIOTISM AND CITIZENSHIP

Introduction

OPINIONS ... Everyone should have one! What you will find contained within the pages of this book are some of mine.

My forum has been local newspapers as a writer of letters to the editor or contributing columnist of opinion articles on a variety of subjects and issues. I have written for thirty-seven years, starting with a letter to the editor published in October 1972.

In the early years, I used a small, manual Royal typewriter which was highly work-intensive, requiring at least two or three re-types to get a clean copy for submission. I thought I had arrived when one Christmas my husband surprised me with a Smith-Corona 2200 electric typewriter with correction cartridge – and by 1990, I was beginning to hit my stride.

In the early nineties, I purchased my first computer with word processing software. Anyone who writes knows how the computer revolutionized composition. Having the ability to cut and paste, copy and print, and submit articles electronically provided the incentive to write more.

And write I did!

I had no idea that I had so much to say and how often I said it until I started compiling the articles for this book. I was astounded.

As with some writers, I can't take credit for every opinion contained herein because most of the columns came from research and reading of published materials that formulated my thought process as I wrote. In cases in which I borrowed extensively from others, I tried to credit the source. Where statistics were used, I tried to substantiate them from at least two sources.

The best writing comes from the need to express one's feelings and convictions. This need was evident in what I considered to be my best columns. Always much easier to write; the words flowed with little effort. Occasionally, I was asked by someone to write a letter or column on something they felt strongly about. I always refused but encouraged them to write it instead because the best expression comes from knowing the subject and having the passion for it.

The opportunity to be a member of the Clarion-Ledger Reader Editorial Board led to a regular column and the necessity to meet deadlines. For ten years I was a "contributing columnist," a position which required the discipline of saying what I wanted to say in a limited number of words. Since I have a tendency to be verbose, that requirement was a challenge.

I learned newspaper terminology such as op-ed (opposite editorial page) and above the fold (the top half of the page) a location reserved for articles of prominence. The editing and changes made when the piece was published taught me to use a set journalistic style – fewer commas, more paragraphing, and the preferred style generally prescribed by the newspaper. Style is usually dictated by *The Associated Press Stylebook and Libel Manual,* an invaluable resource and reference book that most journalists adhere to.

Lewis Grizzard said that when he turned out a compilation of his newspaper columns for a book, he'd throw them into the air, reach down and randomly pick them up. When the stack felt heavy enough to be a book, he'd send it to his publisher.

It certainly would be easy to do it that way, but my compilation is divided into twelve chapters, and the articles in each chapter are more or less in chronological order. I have not included every article or letter to the editor I've had published and you will find some are repetitious since I'm a "Johnny One-Note," especially on education and patriotism. I have included several unpublished pieces and noted some of the parts of articles that were edited out. (If you read between the lines, you'll understand why.)

I have misplaced many modifiers and left a few participles dangling, but I hope you'll have a good read and perhaps form an opinion of your own.

Heck, nothing wrong with being opinionated!

Dot Ward

Chapter I

Reader Editorial Board Opinions

"Opinion is ultimately determined by the feelings, and not by the intellect."

Herbert Spencer
1820-1903

"You tell me whar a man gits his corn pone, en I'll tell you what his 'pinions is."

Mark Twain

Reader Editorial Board Opinions

On Sunday, September 25, 1994, *The Clarion-Ledger* announced the formation of The Clarion-Ledger Reader Editorial Board. Made up of eight individuals ... four blacks, four whites; four males, four females; five liberals and three conservatives; the board was to be a forum for the exchange of ideas and opinions from members of the community.

I loved having the opportunity on a regular basis to express my opinion on a variety of issues. Topics were assigned by David Hampton, Editorial Director of *The Clarion-Ledger,* and were to be approximately 200 words.

Additionally, each member of the Reader Editorial Board was asked to submit a 500-word column every other month on a subject of his or her choice. The discipline that came from learning to write in newspaper style and column length with a specific deadline was invaluable training.

The assigned topics ended after two years, and several of the board members retired; but I continued to write columns on a regular basis for the next ten years.

After retiring, I continued to write, but only two or three columns or letters to the editor a year ... and those on subjects that stirred a little passion.

The short columns contained in this chapter are the assigned topics. The first one is a short essay that each board member wrote about themselves.

The Clarion-Ledger
September 25, 1994

Introduction of Editorial Board

I believe in God, home, and country ... in that order, and share the values and perspectives of many good, solid Americans.

I love fried oysters, dogs, long afternoon naps and my family ... not necessarily in that order.

I am very opinionated, and I'm sure that because I believe in the First Amendment right to express those opinions, and frequently do so, I have been given this opportunity to sound-off on a regular basis.

I recognize my weaknesses. I often speak before I think, I am rather authoritative. I am tolerant of some diverse opinions, intolerant of others. I think that I'm always right, and I've been told on numerous occasions that I'm not.

I love to write and my writing is based on solid research ... not just from one perspective, but a careful analysis of both sides of an issue. While I will always come down on the conservative side, my opinions are formed from in-depth reading, study, and a discerning spirit.

I believe in volunteerism – in fact, so much so that my husband has remarked on occasion, that as hard as I work, he wishes I'd take a job that would contribute to the family income.

As are you, I'm concerned about crime, drugs, education, disease, high taxes, jobs; those factors that affect us where we live.

I believe in the sanctity of human life ... the young, the old, the handicapped, and the unborn; the free enterprise system, a strong national defense, national sovereignty, and individual responsibility.

I am a traditionalist but am not opposed to change.

I believe that big government is encroaching into too many areas of our lives; that people too often look to "Big Brother" to solve our problems.

I know that our Founding Fathers gave us a democracy in a republic and as Ben Franklin predicted, we are having a hard time keeping it.

I am law-abiding except when I occasionally exceed the speed limit; I support the Constitution, respect the flag ... both Old Glory and the flag of Mississippi; and in spite of all that seems wrong with America, I still have a strong faith in her people and her future.

And a final disclaimer: the opinions of this writer soon to appear in *The Clarion-Ledger* will be mine and not necessarily those of this newspaper.

The Clarion-Ledger
Sunday, October 23, 1994

Term Limits

The petition to put the question of term limits on the ballot has my name on it. I support the concept, but I doubt that it will change much in government. It's more than just limiting terms; it's what's happening to our system of government.

Americans may be fed up with professional politicians looking for a lifetime job, but how do you turn out the un-elected bureaucrats and legislative staffers who are the entrenched micromanagers?

Americans may be tired of paying the salaries of people who don't represent their interests, but how will the influence of the PACs and perks of special interest groups be limited?

That which Americans really want is an end to government practices that are wasteful, inefficient, dishonest, and stupid.

Don't expect term limits to be the panacea for what ails us. With or without term limits, I predict it will be business as usual.

The Clarion-Ledger
Sunday, October 23, 1994

Contract with America

The American people have approved the Republicans' *Contract with America,* and the 104th Congress will have a historic opportunity to dramatically change federal policy-making.

The agenda, validated by the voters, is rooted in the core principles of accountability, responsibility, and opportunity.

The voters have said they want to change the way Congress does business and to change the business that Congress does. They want, among other things, reduced taxes, a strong national defense, welfare reform, and a balanced budget.

I just wish that the Contract had included a promise to kill GATT, repeal GOALS 2000, and replace Janet Reno and Joycelyn Elders. Guess we're never satisfied.

The Republicans have been handed a mandate not just for change, but also for restoration. They must answer the call to provide the leadership to reclaim society and save our culture.

In order to achieve the transformation, we must fulfill our part of the contractual agreement by looking beyond government solutions to the ultimate responsibility that rests with the people themselves.

The Clarion-Ledger
Sunday, December 18, 1994

State Tax Cuts Proposed

The income tax cut proposed by Gov. Fordice in his "Taxpayer Bill of Rights" is the fairest and most efficient way to cut taxes.

While I appreciate soon-to-be candidate for governor Dick Molpus' proposal to reduce the sales tax on groceries, his figures don't quite add up. He claims that Mississippi has the highest tax burden on groceries in America, but what he doesn't tell us is that we don't have added *local* sales tax as do most other states.

This means that when you combine state and local sales taxes, the "tax burden" averages 8 percent in Louisiana and Alabama and 8.25 percent in Tennessee compared to the 7 percent sales tax paid by Mississippians.

Gov. Fordice has accurately interpreted the desire of the people to *lower* taxes by *limiting* government. The question is will our legislators accurately gauge how serious the people are about cutting taxes. With an election year looming on the horizon, they'd better.

The Clarion-Ledger
Sunday, January 8, 1995

Crime and Accountability

It's the "A" word ... accountability. Without it, we won't stand a prayer of finding a solution to the crime problem.

There must be accountability on the part of parents "to raise up a child in the way he should go."

There must be accountability by our schools for teaching the basics, as well as returning discipline to the classroom where respect for authority can be learned at an early age. Sixty-five percent of felony offenses are committed by juveniles, and according to a U.S. Justice Department report, eighty-five percent of those offenders cannot read, write, nor do simple mathematics.

Elected officials must be held accountable for the leadership provided in solving our crime problems.

The judiciary must be accountable in bringing about swift and certain punishment for criminals who continue to make a mockery of our justice system.

As individuals, we must be accountable to a higher authority for our own actions.

There will be no accountability unless we unite, "roll up our sleeves", and become part of the solution.

The Clarion-Ledger
Sunday, January 29, 1995

1995 Session of Mississippi Legislature

Several beneficial education bills introduced in this legislative session merit a hardy "thumbs up" and strong constituent support.

HB-567 would require elementary schools to provide written notification to parent, guardian or custodian concerning their child's reading education. All schools would be required to provide at least one alternative reading program of approved, intensive, systematic phonics with in-service training for teachers in phonics instruction. Students would have to attain a minimum reading score at the third grade level and would be detained until satisfactory reading skills are achieved.

Individual freedoms would be protected by HB-1097 which would prohibit the use of "workplace competency tests" and the awarding of "certificates of employability" available to students only in Tech-Prep (state) programs as a requirement for college entrance or employment.

Believe it or not, there is a need to codify the nationally adopted Parental Rights Amendment. HCR29 would place a proposition on the November ballot to create a new section (31A) of the Mississippi Constitution to provide that "the right of parents to direct the upbringing and education of their children may not be infringed."

The Clarion-Ledger
Sunday, February 26, 1995

Welfare Reform

It's time, after 35 years and $3.5 trillion, to drastically reform welfare by developing a viable, dependency-breaking alternative.

The tax code should be changed to reward people for working.

Illegitimacy should no longer be subsidized, and virtue should be materially rewarded. Public policy should advocate responsible fatherhood. Marriage should be rewarded, not punished with a higher tax burden, and government-funded programs should stop giving preference to single-parent families.

Workfare should replace welfare with new, private-sector jobs created for the unemployed. Innovative employment programs should be implemented that utilize welfare, food stamps, and unemployment benefit funds to subsidize the initial wage costs of employers willing to hire welfare recipients unable to find regular jobs. State initiatives should not be stifled with federal mandates.

The truly needy should be cared for without creating government programs that make it easier to bilk the system than to earn an honest day's pay.

For the sake of the nation ... culturally and economically, the welfare state must be dismantled. Immediately!

The Clarion-Ledger
Sunday, March 19, 1995

Minimum Wage

Direct government intervention into the private business sector of a free enterprise society by mandating wage standards was unheard of in this country during its first 162-year history. It first came into existence under the federal Fair Labor Standards Act of 1938, adopted during the Roosevelt "New Deal" era.

Since that time, we've seen unbridled inflation. The minimum wage has increased more than 1,000 percent from 40 cents per hour in 1938 to $4.25 today.

Clinton's proposed increase would continue to fuel the unending inflationary spiral of the past 50 years. It would force thousands of small business employees to either close down or drastically cut back, eliminating thousands of minimum wage jobs, and would compel larger businesses to incorporate more automation or to make other job-displacing adjustments.

A decrease in minimum wage jobs would also be a detriment to young people just entering the workforce who are desirous of gaining income and initial work experience.

I oppose the Clinton proposal because I believe it is politically motivated rather than people motivated and not in this nation's best interest.

The Clarion-Ledger
Sunday, April 16, 1995

U.S. Judicial System

One needs only to view the history of the appointive process in the federal judiciary and the resulting, unchecked expansion of judicial encroachment into every facet of the daily lives of all citizens to realize that some form of direct accountability to the people must be maintained.

As Professor William Forrester, former Dean of the Cornell Law School noted: "The American people and their elected officials gradually have accepted the Court [U.S. Supreme Court] as the political instrument for law making."

The intrusive power of state appellate courts, without accountability, would likely follow the same trends.

The British historian, Edward Gibbon, in applying his observations to 2,000 years of history, wrote: "The discretion of the judge is the first engine of tyranny."

Since self-government by the people in the United States has literally been wrested from them by a legislating judiciary, it becomes even more imperative that citizens maintain the right to select or reject a judge by the direct power of their vote.

We must also insure effective oversight and removal authority for inadequate judicial performance and regulate political contributions to eliminate potential political influence over elected judges.

In the final analysis, necessary judicial independence must be balanced with necessary judicial accountability.

The Clarion-Ledger
Sunday, May 7, 1995

Teenage Pregnancy

The Mississippi Index of Leading Cultural Indicators, which measures social change in Mississippi, reports that teenage pregnancy has remained constant over the last 30 years. In 1965, about 70 percent of pregnant 15-19-year-olds were married; by 1990, only 35 percent were married. While 44 percent of Mississippi births in 1993 were to unmarried mothers, more than three-fourths of all births to teenagers were illegitimate.

The solution?

Men must make a commitment to marriage and fatherhood. Each generation should strive to restore to the family the role model of a committed father, with parents reinforcing the values of virtue and temperance in their children. Good parenting is learned through example.

Government must contribute to the solution by ending all economic support for single mothers. Rather than encouraging illegitimacy, incentives should be offered for raising children within marriage by making the tax code family friendly.

Just as many other cultural problems facing this nation are short on solutions, the ultimate answer to them all lies in individual responsibility.

To restore the family is to restore the nation.

The Clarion-Ledger
Sunday, May 21, 1995

Suburban Flight

Underlying causes of suburban flight? I think we all know the answers.

- Escalating crime
- Increased taxation without much to show for it.
- Better schools in the suburbs.

Having noted the downside, I believe an effective and cooperative effort is now under way to respond to some of these problems.

Citizens are working together to meet the crime problem head-on. The Metropolitan Crime Commission is coordinating efforts by taking significant steps to pass "get tough on crime" legislation, incarcerate criminals, hold judges accountable, monitor court room activity, and expand and improve jail facilities.

At least some city officials have taken note of the peoples' desire to streamline government with the best services for the tax dollars spent.

There is still hope for improving Jackson Public Schools if we can get an elected school board accountable to the people. The new JPS Superintendent needs our support. He also needs a directive to return to traditional (academic) instruction and a mandate to get rid of the bureaucratic freeloaders entrenched within the public school system.

Suburban flight can be curbed if a committed citizenry and a responsive city administration determine that Jackson will be a good place to live and pledge themselves to make it so.

The Clarion-Ledger
Sunday, June 18, 1995

Drunk Driving

In Mississippi, 813 people lost their lives in automobile accidents in 1993. Forty-seven percent of those deaths were alcohol related.If we're serious about reducing highway fatalities, DUI laws must be strengthened and strictly enforced.

There needs to be an open container law prohibiting any open container of alcoholic beverage in a vehicle.

The implied consent law allowing a minor to drive with .08 blood alcohol content is a contradiction and needs to be changed. Mississippi law makes it illegal for anyone under 21 to purchase or consume alcohol. Obviously, those under 21 should be driving with **zero** alcohol in their system.

Mandatory blood alcohol testing should be required in all accidents resulting in death or serious injury.

Loopholes that allow challenges to license revocation should be closed.

We need an educated judiciary, pledged to prosecute drunken driving violators to the full extent of the law. The law should be strictly enforced and the message made loud and clear, "IF YOU DRINK, YOU DON'T DRIVE!"

Whether you drink or not is your business. If you drink and drive, it becomes everyone's business. It is a question of safety on the road – yours and mine.

The law should be strictly enforced and the message made loud and clear, "IF YOU DRINK, YOU DON'T DRIVE!"

Whether you drink or not is your business. If you drink and drive, it becomes everyone's business. It is a question of safety on the road – yours and mine.

The Clarion-Ledger
July 9, 1995

Principal Issues in the Governor's Race

The most important and far-reaching issue in the governor's race is education. The two candidates for the highest office in our state have diametrically opposed opinions on how the children of Mississippi should be educated.

Mr. Molpus, who has garnered the support of the MAE (the Mississippi branch of the politically powerful NEA) was one of the architects of the failed education reform movement of the early 1980s. Molpus supports the concept of more money, more bureaucracy, and more control by state and federal agencies that would channel the future education of Mississippi's children in the same direction that has led to ever declining academic achievement.

The initiative proposal of Governor Fordice is called The People's Right to Initiate Model Education (PRIME). The governor's plan recognizes the people's right to govern and improve their local schools. It would also free parents, teachers, and school administrators to determine effective educational objectives for their children without the intervention of self-serving political unions or stagnated governmental bureaucracies.

While other issues, such as economic development, jobs, tax reduction, and welfare reform, rank very high in importance, effective leadership in the education of Mississippi's children is the key to Mississippi's future.

Gov. Fordice's plan would place Mississippi as a front runner in the nation to affect **real** education reform.

The Clarion-Ledger
Sunday, August 6, 1995

How Voters Can Become Informed on Upcoming Elections

An informed electorate is the key to effective government, but becoming informed takes time and energy.

First and foremost, the voter must know what will be on the ballot ... what races will be decided in his or her district. It's helpful to study sample ballots before going to the polls.

There needs to be a pre-determination of which candidate will receive your vote. To make that decision, find out all that you can about the candidate. Talk with people whose opinion you trust and who know the candidate personally. Don't base your choice solely on monied media campaigns.

Candidate issue surveys published in local papers are a good source of information to determine where office-seekers stand on issues that matter to you.

Attend public forums and ask questions.

Sometimes it's hard to find a candidate to support enthusiastically and once elected, some candidates may prove to be a disappointment. Don't let this be a deterrent to your voting.

In the words of George Mason, "Public office is a public trust, and public officials are the people's trustees".

Institutions and governments do not preserve themselves. They can be preserved only by the vigilance of an informed citizenry.

The Clarion-Ledger
Sunday, August 20, 1995

Should Casino Gambling Be Legalized in Jackson?

Will Jackson succumb to the "something for nothing" trap by bringing institutionalized covetousness (gambling) to our Capitol City? I hope not!

Jacksonians deserve more than glitzy casinos promoted by over-eager developers and cash-starved politicians to sustain the life-blood of this community, especially in light of recent developments indicating gaming overkill – too many casinos and not enough gamblers.

According to Michael Rose, casino executive with Harrah's Hotels and Casinos, "Half the casinos in Atlantic City are bankrupt. Half the casinos in Nevada are earning less than 3 percent profits."

When the President Riverboat Casino closed last year in Tunica County, officials said losses were more than $2.7 million with nearly 800 people losing their jobs.

And in New Orleans, first month figures from the lavish new casino in the "Big Easy" were shockingly below expectations, causing severe cutbacks and reassessment.

What makes us think that Jackson would be different?

Any benefit derived from casino gambling is heavily outweighed by the negative consequences: the cultivation of compulsive gamblers and teen addicts (eighty percent of adult compulsive gamblers start betting at 14 or under); the adverse impact on local businesses; the havoc heaped on families; and the detrimental effect on the lifestyle of the community.

The future of Mississippi's capital city is just too important to wager.

The Clarion-Ledger
September 24, 1995

Should Candidates Be Required to Release Income Tax Information?

Absolutely! As Harry Truman said, "If you can't stand the heat, stay out of the kitchen." In other words, if you've got something to hide, don't get into politics.

Running for public office indicates a desire on the part of an individual to become a public servant, thereby granting the public the right to know a lot of things that life outside of politics allows one to keep private.

Tax returns are an example. They tell a lot about candidates ... whether they're financially successful, what their sources of income are, how much is owed in taxes, and to what extent tax loopholes are utilized.

Tax return revelations can cause a lot of grief ... just ask Bill and Hillary.

Aside from what the tax return may reveal, failure to make public disclosure raises the perception that there must be something to hide, and a negative public perception can be deadly to an election bid.

There is no law requiring candidates for public office to open their tax returns for scrutiny, but with the present day's jaundiced view of politicians held by the voting public, the wise candidate would be quick to do so.

The Clarion-Ledger
Sunday, October 7, 1995

Should Mississippi Go to An Open Primary System?

Hardly an election goes by that dissatisfaction is not expressed by some voters regarding Mississippi's closed primary law. This law requires two ballots (Democrat and Republican), with voters restricted to voting one or the other.

Only three states, Hawaii, Washington, and Louisiana, have blanket (open) primaries, and Louisiana has held hearings to consider closing its open primary. The reason: David Duke and Edwin Edwards – two not-so-hot choices for governor.

In an open primary, the top two vote-getters, usually those with the highest name recognition and most campaign dollars, are declared the winners and face each other in the general election. A primary race with 15 candidates, as in Louisiana, can produce the worst of extremes, often providing less than desirable choices for public office. Of all votes cast, 25 percent or less can elect your top officials in a blanket (open) primary.

A public hearing held last year by the Mississippi House Committee on Elections evidenced no consensus for change. In fact, according to Bill Denny, Elections Chairman, no one bothered to show up.

Mississippi's system is not perfect, but it certainly has more pluses than minuses. Closed primaries are necessary to strengthen the two-party system in Mississippi and to provide the best candidates from each party to face-off in the general election.

The Clarion-Ledger
Sunday, November 12, 1995

Instilling Values and Deterioration of the Family

"Out of the heart come evil thoughts, murder, adultery, sexual immorality, theft, false testimony and slander." (Matt. 15:19) The cultural morass of present-day America can best be traced to the "heart" condition of man.

As we have sought more and greater personal liberty, flinging off one restraint after another, we have been unable to restrain ourselves. As a nation, we have lost our moral compass. Our culture has suffered; our families have deteriorated.

It's always easy to blame someone or something – parents, poverty, lack of education, socio-cultural influences – for our condition, but we're only deceiving ourselves.

Unless we are willing to take personal responsibility for our actions, make commitments to strengthen and nurture the family, and recognize that "man is not right in his own eyes" but needs to be in submission to a higher authority, our health will continue to deteriorate.

As with other great civilizations that have declined and fallen ... our nation's demise would come not from external conflict, but from internal moral decay.

To instill values and heal the family, we should begin with a heart catheterization. We may be so far gone that major surgery is necessary, but with the Great Physician writing the prescription, a good diet of virtue and exercise of temperance will provide the best hope for a full recovery.

The Clarion-Ledger
Saturday, December 17, 1995

Advice for the Governor

I don't know how well qualified a few amateur newspaper pundits are to presume to advise a governor on affairs of state, but here goes nonetheless:

Obviously, the people of Mississippi are satisfied with the job Gov. Fordice is doing or he wouldn't have been re-elected by such a substantial vote of confidence.

The Governor has been on target with his proposals to downsize government, cut taxes, reform welfare, market Mississippi through tourism, initiate pro-business reforms, and develop a sound economic environment for the state. Too bad the legislature didn't always go along.

On education, his PRIME Initiative would give parents more power and genuine options for the education of their children. I would suggest that he say "NO" to GOALS 2000 money which further federalizes our public schools and helps implement much of the Clinton agenda to micro-manage American lives.

In his 1994, "Mississippi Can Do Anything Now" State of the State address, Gov. Fordice showed an attitude of positive thinking that is vital to effective leadership. His enthusiasm for and his belief in the Great State of Mississippi is a confidence builder for the people he leads and goes a long way in reinforcing faith in the future.

All Mississippians should take his advice and speak "Only positive Mississippi!"

My advice .... Just keep on keeping on, Gov. Fordice!

The Clarion-Ledger
Sunday, January 14, 1996

Should Jackson Schools Institute Corporal Punishment?

JPS Superintendent Dr. T. C. Wallace, Jr. stated at a recent meeting of the Metropolitan Crime Commission that 16,000 questionnaires were circulated to parents, teachers and administrators on the subject of re-instituting corporal punishment in Jackson Public Schools. Of the 8,000 questionnaires returned, 70 percent of parents, 90 percent of teachers, and 95 percent of administrators favor corporal punishment. The results reflect an obvious belief among those who must deal directly with disciplinary problems that strong, corrective action is needed.

There is no question in my mind that there is an urgent need for children, especially in the lower grades, to learn respect for authority. Children who are not taught to respect authority will not be receptive learners and will suffer later in life when the stakes are greater and the punishment harsher.

Dr. Wallace also stated that three disciplinary infractions will initiate corporal punishment which will involve parents who must be "on site" when the spanking is administered. Good luck on that one.

Regrettably, parents who haven't taught their children proper behavior will be the very parents who won't be available to back up school authorities.

The key ingredient in regaining the upper hand is for school personnel to have the *full support of all parents* in disciplinary procedures.

The Clarion-Ledger
Sunday, February 11, 1996

Who Is To Blame for the Federal Budget Impasse?

The federal budget impasse rests ultimately at the feet of the American people.

Beginning with the New Deal, we allowed a socialistic seduction to take place, resulting in what has become a staggering \$4.9 trillion national debt and a current \$1.6 trillion budget that has ransomed our children's future.

We allowed ourselves to be deceived into thinking that government could do more for us than we could do for ourselves.

We forgot that the Government has no money except that which it takes from us, and we looked on the largess of grants, entitlements, and welfare programs as "free" gifts from some wealthy benefactor. We all share the blame for jumping on the bandwagon to get our share.

Big benefit programs, particularly Medicaid, Medicare, and welfare, have been growing faster than 10 percent a year. With the economy growing at only half that rate, the government will, by early in the next century, consume every penny of taxes it takes in just to support these programs.

As a people, we can no longer expect the federal government to supply not only all our needs but also all our wants.

If the "impasse" can't be resolved by our present national leadership, it's incumbent upon the American people to elect leaders who can get the job done.

It's time the piper is paid.

The Clarion-Ledger
Sunday, February 18, 1996

"Commuter" Income Tax?

Read my lips. No new taxes!

Like bringing casinos to Jackson ... a "commuter tax" is a bad idea.

In my opinion, such a tax imposed on those who live in the suburbs but commute to work in Jackson, would force more businesses to exit the city. No business owner wants his workforce pool limited only to those who live inside the city nor do they want to raise salaries of employees to offset the imposed penalty of this inane idea.

Has any thought been given to how this "commuter tax" would be levied and administered? How much would it cost in administration?

How would employee tracking be done to determine who is a commuter? What penalty would be imposed on those businesses and employees who fail to comply?

Would state legislators be considered "commuters"? After all, they work in Jackson but live elsewhere.

It would behoove the City Fathers to spend their time making Jackson a better place in which to live. The needs of our city are great: better schools, clean water, and crime-free streets.

At some point, our elected leaders should understand that primary to our republican form of government is individual freedom ... and that freedom includes the right to choose where to live and work without government influencing that decision with a "penalty tax."

After all, wasn't that what the Boston Tea Party was all about?

The Clarion-Ledger
Sunday, March 9, 1996

The State's Image and What Should Be Done to Improve It

I've lived in other parts of the country, and I know people from almost every state in the Union, including Alaska and Hawaii. If I'd never left Mississippi, I'd probably believe that we are pathetically backward and don't hold a candle to the other forty-nine. 'Taint so, Magee!

Most of the time when something negative is said about Mississippi it's being said by Mississippians. We're paranoid about "being 50th" or "being last". We need a good dose of "accentuating the positive, eliminating the negative, and latching on to the affirmative ...."

We've all seen the Southern stereotype on television or in the movies. We're made to look like a bunch of backwoods Bubbas.

But I look at it this way ... We should be glad if the stereotyping keeps outsiders from discovering the good things about Mississippi.

If the truth were told, it would mean a whole lot of folks moving in, trying to make us #1 (whatever that is) .... That would ruin the state for sure. I haven't seen anything that **they've** got that's better than what **we've** got.

So the next time someone starts poor-mouthing about our state, just take stock of those things that are never measured ... the natural beauty of the Magnolia State, the strength of our churches, and the goodness of our people.

It'll go a long way to help you forget about "being 50th!"

The Clarion-Ledger
Sunday, April 14, 1996

How Did the Mississippi Legislature Perform in Its 1996 Session?

It could have been worse. Legislators could have legalized cock fighting.

At least three significant bills supported by the Metropolitan Crime Commission made it to the Governor's desk. The bills would make auto theft a felony, provide funding for additional state prosecutors, and increase the amount of money that can be seized under the state forfeiture law.

Too bad the bill to revise Mississippi's Youth Court system failed to make it. Further restrictions were placed on the initiative and referendum process, and no consideration was given to a tax cut.

I would give thumbs up to the passage of bills regulating abortion providers, increasing the speed limit, closing the loopholes in DUI laws, suspending privilege licenses of parents who refuse to pay child support, improving water safety by regulating boat and jet-ski operators, and providing an advance-payment college tuition plan.

A major disappointment was the failure to pass a phonics bill that would have provided an alternative, cost effective phonics curricula for public schools.

With reading scores at an all-time low because of the failed Whole Language curricula, many children are being passed from grade to grade without acquiring the reading skills necessary to function as literate adults. The lame excuse of a few legislative leaders that "we can't dictate curriculum" is one that can't be justified.

The Clarion-Ledger
Sunday, May 19, 1996

What is the #1 Issue in the Presidential Race?

Returning integrity to the office of the presidency may not be the No.1 issue of the campaign this year, but in my opinion it should be.

The American people need a credible leader in the White House who will return the office of president to one respected both at home and abroad. The president of the United States should be highly principled, commanding personal respect and admiration from those he leads and with whom he deals. He should be honest, courageous, trustworthy, and morally sound in all respects.

Acting presidential should be second nature and not a charade. At all times the president should conduct himself with the demeanor becoming the office he holds. To that end, there should be no public discussions about the kind of underwear he wears or repeated allegations of marital infidelity or shady business dealings.

The well-being of the nation depends upon the president being held in high esteem. It is incumbent upon the people to elect a leader who will provide an exemplary example of the best this nation has to offer. If those in authority have genuine personal attributes of honor, character, and integrity, the trust placed in them by the American people will be rewarded and respect restored to the office of the Presidency.

The Clarion-Ledger
Wednesday, June 19, 1996

Governor Fordice's College Board Appointments

Gov. Fordice has appointed four eminently qualified men to the State College Board.

Three senators – Johnnie Walls, Alice Harden, and David Jordan – have blocked the confirmation process by raising objections. Objections based not on qualifications ... but on race.

This outrageous scenario is occurring more and more frequently ... especially in consideration of appointments by our present governor. There's no doubt that he has few friends in the Black Caucus; some of them even rudely walked out on his State of the State address in his first year of office.

Instead of working for the betterment of the state, to these color-blinded individuals black is the only color they know. Thus they try to block appointments that do not meet their litmus test: liberal, black, female, and Democrat.

In their opinion it's all right for the Democrat Party with Senator Walls as party chairman, to elect only Blacks to leadership positions at the state convention, or for the Jackson Public School District to have created an overwhelming racial imbalance in the administrative staff; after all, some would reason, it's just making up for past inequities.

Forget qualifications. Forget what's best for the state.

If racist attitudes continue to dominate the confirmation process, Mississippi's future does not bode well.

Gov. Fordice is right to stand behind the men he has appointed to the College Board. They should be confirmed by full vote of the Mississippi Senate, and our "conservative" Lt. Gov. Ronnie Musgrove should make sure that happens.

The Clarion-Ledger
Sunday, August 4, 1996

Same-Sex Marriage

The basis of society is found in the strength of its families, and any move to legitimize or legalize a "union" that is morally wrong and socially harmful should be vigorously opposed.

The legalization of same-sex "marriage" is opposed by 68 to 72 percent of Americans. President Clinton, forever sitting on the political fence and with his usual double-talk, announced that he does not "personally" support full legal sanctioning of homosexual marriages (while seeking ways to satisfy the demands of the homosexual community for limited "administration" approval of same-sex marriages").

A Hawaii Court decision has created the potential for this court-imposed cultural revolution by the possibility of requiring every state to recognize same-sex "marriages" licensed in Hawaii under the U.S. Constitution's "full faith and credit" clause (Article IV, Sec. 10.)

The fact that marriage could be transformed by the action of a few judges in Hawaii has prompted the introduction of the "Defense of Marriage Act" in the U.S. Congress which would protect state sovereignty and define for all purposes of federal law, marriage as a "union between one man and one woman."

While Defense of Marriage Act frees states from having to recognize same-sex "marriages," it would not prevent a judge from ruling in favor of recognition of a marriage license legally obtained in Hawaii if there is no state policy clearly stating the type of marriage recognized by the State.

To guard against this possibility, there need to be changes in Mississippi statutes, a constitutional amendment defining marriage ... and a vocal populace expressing themselves to their elected representatives.

CHAPTER II

Moral Issues

Our ancestors established their system of government on morality and religious sentiment. Moral habits, they believed, cannot safely be trusted on any other foundation than religious principle, nor any government be secure which is not supported by moral habits.

Daniel Webster

FIRST LETTER TO THE EDITOR
The Northside Sun
Letter to the Editor – Wednesday, October 18, 1972

Asks That Movie Ads Be Toned Down

You have asked your readers to express themselves concerning your policy of advertising X and R rated films. Since you asked for it, here's my opinion.

If you feel an obligation to all of your readers to advertise the films presently showing at the local movie house or drive-in, can't you do so with a little more candor and good taste? Wouldn't advertisements for X and R rated films get the message across to those who are interested by using smaller, less conspicuous ads that are in keeping with the family newspaper that you have so successfully provided for Jackson Northside residents – such as the movie ads you have run for the last two Sun issues.

I have been told that each film comes with a choice of newspaper "cuts" and the editor or advertiser can choose advertising copy best suited to the general reader. You should also consider that a large number of your readers are under the age of 17 and would not be admitted to the movies you advertise.

Don't let the question of censorship bother you. I've never seen an ad for a house of prostitution or published information where illegal drugs can be obtained in your paper. It's just assumed by you and me that such things are unadvertiseable.

Why, then, low-cost production "sexploitation" films whose own rating board classifies them as undesirable for those under 17 years of age?

You may be interested to know that presently there are some 13 major newspapers – including papers in San Diego, Dallas, and Detroit, which have banned advertisements for X rated moves. I'm glad to know that there are still folks who are willing to place principle before profit, and I don't call it censorship!

The Clarion-Ledger | Jackson Daily News
Sunday, September 30, 1984

Porn Laws "Ounce of Prevention"

Your editorial policy is astounding! One day you are promoting good education and the next day you are opposing the city ordinance to restrict pornography.

The "danger" you point out in the editorial ("What's obscene: Dangers abound in proposed ordinance," Sept. 25) is that an ordinance could lead "to an emotional new campaign" against legitimate booksellers and magazine outlets.

If the booksellers are legitimate they have nothing to fear. If they are falsely accused of selling pornography, then the authorities or courts can so decide. That's why we have laws. An ordinance dealing with pornography is as important as ordinances dealing with the accumulation of garbage on the streets. Both are needed.

And since in your opinion Jackson has a "pittance of smut dealers" and "there's been no sign of real escalation," why does Jackson has an adult theater and a number of bookstores selling hard-core pornography by anyone's standards?

Your editorial sets forth the premise that as long as we have just a little sleaze, its okay. When does a little become too much? Where should the line be drawn? No law, no line.

In my opinion, an ounce of prevention is worth a pound of cure.

The Clarion-Ledger
Saturday, September 4, 1993

McKenzie's Right: Moral Values in Decline

Danny McKenzie's column of Monday, August 30, "Are we trading our values for casinos and stadium beer?" made some good points about our values system.

His questions, "Do you ever get the feeling our values are a tad bit askew? Or just downright warped?" can be answered with an unequivocal YES.

It's not just casinos and beer but the whole sordid state of our national morality.

While Mr. McKenzie points to two specific areas affecting the public sector, casinos and beer, I can point to other cultural indicators such as the "free" R.S.V. P. "personal" ads published by this paper. The R.S.V.P. disclaimer states that "this publication reserves the right ... to edit or refuse to print advertisements it deems detrimental to its public image or unsuitable for readers" but in truth the $1.99 per minute charge for respondents – the average call being $8.00 – places profit above values.

Could be that *The Clarion-Ledger* should be taking "a long hard look at what we're doing".

William J. Bennett provides an analysis of the moral, social and behavioral condition of modern American society in his *Index of Leading Cultural Indicators.*

The index is a comprehensive statistical portrait of 19 social indicators showing a substantial social regression over the last thirty years ... a 560 percent increase in violent crime; more than a 400 percent increase in illegitimate births; a quadrupling in divorce rates; a tripling of the percentage of children living in single-parent homes; more than a 200 percent increase in the teenage suicide rate; and a dramatic increase in child abuse.

What has caused the decline? The hard truth is that in a free society the ultimate responsibility rests with the people themselves.

Indeed, it is our beliefs, our behavior, and our philosophy that have in many instances changed for the worse.

Arthur Gordon, in his book *Touch Of Gold*, said it best: "We begin to tolerate, then accept, then condone, and then openly endorse ... so subtly ... we have lowered the flag of righteousness."

The burden to reverse America's cultural decline rests in individual responsibility. These responsibilities, replicated through the generations, are among the constitutive acts of civilization ... the values of faith and family: discipline, self-control, chastity, fidelity, honesty, fortitude, frugality, civility, and respect for authority.

Our social and civic institutions – families, churches, schools, neighborhoods and civic associations – should share the responsibility by nurturing cultural values through moral education of the young.

Danny McKenzie's long, hard look should begin with a check-up of the health condition of our own values.

The Clarion-Ledger
Letter to the Editor
Wednesday, June 24, 1998

Every Day Brings More Bad News

Each morning when I open the paper, I brace myself for the graphic descriptions of the day's news.

The reports have become commonplace ... parents killing their children, in one case an 18-month-old's body parts were cooked and fed to dogs; a man dragged behind a truck until his body comes apart; a baby being cut from its mother's womb; students shooting classmates and teachers; an airline crash where "body parts are strewn for miles."

There is no doubt that Satan is loose in the land!

But is it necessary to bombard readers with in-depth details that deny any common decency?

Are such reports becoming so commonplace that we're slowly desensitized to such horror?

Is there any line drawn as to what is acceptable for publication in a family newspaper?

And if so, where is the line?

Are the large number of copycat incidents a result of too much press being given to such abominations?

Does the news media bear any responsibility for planting ideas in the minds of the depraved?

In a world gone mad, my daily prayer:

"Come quickly, Lord Jesus. Come!"

The Clarion-Ledger
Tuesday, October 13, 1998

America Deserves Moral Leadership, Not A Bill Clinton

America deserves better than William Jefferson Clinton.

America deserves a resident in the White House who recognizes the importance of telling the truth; not a con artist skillful with half truths and stratagems of deceit.

America deserves a leader who is governed by a higher authority; not just a Bible-carrying fraud who uses religion to cloak a corrupt and barren spirit.

America deserves a President who is a role model; a possessor of high morals and principles, an honorer of marriage vows, a protector of family, a respecter of persons.

America deserves a President whose private life is as exemplary as his public life, who places the public good over personal gratification, and who has the courage to assume responsibility for wrongdoing.

While America deserves all of the above, the American people must share some of the responsibility for having elected William Jefferson Clinton in the first place.

It's not like we didn't know Bill Clinton, the candidate. The "character thing" surfaced early and the "scandal-a-week" campaign revealed important aspects of a personal life and political record that should have had a direct bearing on his suitability for the office of President.

Nation's future at risk

Random polls and on-the-street interviews have indicated that some of the general public believe that the President's personal life doesn't affect his ability to govern; that, after all, we should expect no more of the President than we expect of ourselves.

If those being polled really believe that we should mind our own business and move on to the "important business of the country," that a healthy economy takes precedence over a virtuous leader, and that they "just don't care," the future of this nation is in peril.

If we say that character doesn't count and choose to elect corrupt, dishonest, and immoral leaders, it is a reflection of our own principles and values. As a nation, we proclaim to be "one nation under God;" yet, as a people, we seem to have forgotten that "righteousness exalts a nation, and sin is a disgrace to any people."

We are at a pivotal point in history. The impeachment question before Congress will either raise or lower the level of personal character that we are willing to accept in the highest elective office of this country.

Integrity of highest import

The American people must recognize the importance of electing a person with the highest level of personal integrity, a leader highly respected and beyond reproach. The President of the United States should be the role model for all that's best in manhood or womanhood. If we don't recognize the importance of electing a moral leader, we fail ourselves.

When *Hail to the Chief* announces "Mr. President," eyes should not have to be averted or snickers suppressed.

Clinton's violation of his oath of office, heinous acts, perjury and abuse of power, not to mention the disgrace brought to the office of President, in sum total should leave no question that he is unfit to continue as America's leader. Alexis de Tocqueville, French historian and statesman, recognized the truth when he said, "America is great because America is good ... and if America ever ceases to be good ... America will cease to be great."

Let history record that Congress, the representative body of the American people, did the right thing in removing Bill Clinton from office.

The Clarion-Ledger
Letter to the Editor
Thursday, May 27, 1999

Shame Missing from McRae, Protectors

Shame – there doesn't seem much of it around today.

State Supreme Court Justice Chuck McRae should immediately resign, but he won't because he knows no shame.

He believes he's above the very law that he has sworn to uphold. He can break that law with no remorse because he knows no shame.

As a judge, he sits in judgement of others while he himself is accused of breaking the law. He does so because he knows no shame.

And then there's the lack of shame on the part of those who have the ability to remove McRae from office but probably won't because of politics. They'll let Mississippi bear the shame.

Shame on us for electing men and women who know no shame.

The Clarion-Ledger
Tuesday, October 24, 2000

Scouts' Assault Illustrates "Evil" of Our Culture

Nothing more vividly illustrates the struggle between good and evil in our culture than the assault being made on the Boy Scouts of America; nor is there any better example of how political correctness has warped the minds of the American people.

For more than 90 years, the Boy Scouts has taught boys to do their duty to God and country, to help other people, to keep physically strong, mentally awake and morally straight.

It is a private organization made up of local troops led by parents and neighbors who come together to impart traditional moral and religious values held by a majority of Americans.

Why Public Enemy No. 1?

The organization is quite rightly not open to those who want to destroy those values and impart different ones.

So, why has the Boy Scouts become Public Enemy No.1? Why have they been vilified by major corporations and charities who have cut funding; booed at the Democratic National Convention (definitely not your father's Democrat party); denied use of public facilities by city councils and public schools; and investigated by the Interior and Justice Departments of the federal government?

In today's politically correct world, tolerance has become synonymous with goodness and open-mindedness and has arisen as the sole virtue of Western culture. Tolerance has been so cleverly promoted that when anyone advocates moral values, he/she is criticized and accused of opposing personal rights.

In the name of tolerance, intolerance abounds and appeals for diversity end up as demands for conformity.

Five days before the Supreme Court handed down its decision upholding the First Amendment rights of the Boy Scouts, President Clinton, whose legacy is immorality in the Oval office, issued Executive Order 13160 banning discrimination on the basis of "sexual orientation."

In doing so, Clinton has tried to usurp the authority of Congress by broadening existing non-discrimination legislation to include sexual orientation.

The inherent danger in Clinton's executive order is that if it's allowed to become law, eventually every other private group, private school, church, business and social group would be forced to accept the notion that "sexual orientation" is a "right" that cannot be opposed.

Issue reveals much more

The vendetta against the Boy Scouts is not just about discrimination, intolerance, or inequality, but about constitutional questions affecting individual and collective freedoms.

It's about whether we, the people, want a government not much different from Nazi Germany in which the beliefs of one group can be imposed upon another by the government.

The Boy Scout issue tells us something about ourselves, too.

Have we become indoctrinated by political correctness to the point that we remain silent as the Boy Scouts are summarily destroyed through lawsuits and by financial and social intimidation? Where is our righteous indignation?

Understand that it's not generating hate toward any group of people to uphold the tenets of an organization that teaches traditional moral values.

After all, isn't character development the most important lesson taught our children?

We would be wise to heed the words of Edmund Burke when he said, "All that is necessary for evil to triumph is for good men to do nothing."

The Clarion-Ledger
Letter to the Editor
Friday, September 6, 2002

"Christian Values" Belong in Schools

In her letter ("Values' shared via many religions," Aug. 28) Jan Hampton was critical of Madison Middle School Principal Ted Poore's promise to uphold "Christian values" in remarks at the ribbon-cutting ceremonies for the new school.

I would like to know what "Christian" values Ms. Hampton objects to.

Surely, it can't be the Ten Commandments, which the Mississippi Legislature recently approved for posting on the walls of every public school in the state; or the Christian values of loving one's neighbor more than one's self, being wise in the way to act, developing self-control, speaking truthfully, being quick to listen, slow to speak and slow to become angry.

All children would profit from being taught these values.

Ms. Hampton expressed disappointment that Mr. Poore mentioned "Christian" when other religions share many of the same values and there are students of other faiths attending the school.

This is a blatant attack on Christianity and a clever ploy often used to rid our schools and public life of any religion.

Of the 1,200 students at MMS, I would guess that the overwhelming majority embraces Judeo-Christian beliefs.

Ms. Hampton, who states she is "a newcomer to the area and to public schools," should realize that she now resides in the Bible Belt.

~ ~ ~ ~ ~ ~ ~ ~ ~ ~ ~

As a daughter-in-law, sister-in-law, wife, and mother of attorneys, I've included this unpublished article as a guide for those who would seek to uphold the dignity of the profession.

The Ideal Lawyer

The ideal lawyer is described in the prison memoirs of Alexander Stephens, a lawyer, a U.S. congressman, and the vice president of the Confederacy. Stephens actually lived up to these ideals. He was so well-liked that when the southern states seceded, a move Stephens had opposed, he was the only departing Southerner whom the northern congressmen wanted to honor with a farewell dinner. He remained a personal friend of Abraham Lincoln. One of Stephens' slaves who chose to stay with him after emancipation said of him that Stephens was kinder to dogs than most people were to people.

Imprisoned like all Confederate officials after the war, Stephens said this of lawyers in his prison diaries:

> No pursuit in life is more honorable or useful than that of the law, when followed as it should be. None requires more rigidly a stout adherence to all the precepts and principles of morality, or the possession and practice of the highest and noblest virtues that elevate and adorn human nature.
>
> Not even the office of the holy minister opens up such a wide field for simply doing good to one's fellow man. The lawyer's province is to aid in the administration of justice, to assist the oppressed, to uphold the weak, to contend against the strong, to defend the right, to expose the wrong, to find out deceit, and to run down vice and crimes of all grades, shades and characters.
>
> A good lawyer is ever a peacemaker. The tangled web of most private controversies can be better unraveled and straightened by bringing the parties together in private conference than by carrying them into court. But with what intense regard for truth, for right and justice, does the lawyer investigate facts and pore over his books, preparing himself for such occasions.
>
> In the Temple of Justice, he glories in the fact that everything is weighed in her scales. Reason and wisdom are his necessary weapons. The materials to be handled are human acts colored with human passions, prejudices, and infirmities. What a field here for exhibition of the noblest virtues in exposing knavery, fraud, villainy and falsehood of every sort and of securing to honesty, right and truth, their just reward.
>
> He sits as it were in the marketplace and on the highways; not a day passes in which

> he may not and should not dispense with a liberal hand the Christian charities of his counsel in the succor of the needy, the destitute, the wronged, the widow and the orphan. There should be nothing mean or low about him. He should have no ambition but to serve his fellow man and to do good. In doing the greatest possible good to others, he achieves the greatest good for himself.

The practice of law is an honorable profession, but like many other professional standards, lawyers and judges have allowed the standards to become passé.

What a better world this would be if every attorney would strive to uphold the ideals of Alexander Stephens.

Chapter III

National Issues

I don't make jokes. I just watch the government and report the facts.

Will Rogers

The Clarion-Ledger
Letter to the Editor
Friday, November 9, 1979

Stop SALT

This is an open letter to Senator John C. Stennis:

A recent report from Washington indicates that you are undecided about how you will vote on the Strategic Arms Limitation Treaty (SALT II), now being debated in the United States Senate.

This indecision is a surprise to me because of your past leadership and ability to convince others of the importance of a strong national defense. I cannot imagine how you, as Chairman of the Senate Armed Services Committee, having been briefed by top military leaders, the majority of whom are opposed to SALT II, could ever vote to lock the United States into a militarily inferior position with the USSR.

Aside from this fact, you are the elected representative of the people of the State of Mississippi and, as such, represent in your vote the views of Mississippians. You and I know that the majority of the people of this state would be diametrically opposed if fully apprised of the facts to agreeing to any treaty that would weaken this nation militarily or give the Soviets a strategic advantage.

I know that a vote against SALT II would not be an easy one politically with the present Carter administration pushing so adamantly for its passage. But we, here at home, are looking to you to exert the leadership and statesmanship that you have exhibited in the past. The challenge of responsible leadership is one that must be met – with political interests laid aside!

Please don't wait any longer to make your position known. Vote NO on Salt II!

The United States must maintain its stance as a world leader for peace and freedom through strength.

The Northside Sun
"As I See It"
Sometime in 1987

ACLU – Writer Tells "Rest of the Story"

The following data on the American Civil Liberties Union (ACLU) was compiled by Phoebe Courtney, managing editor of the Independent American, Littleton, Colorado.

On January 12, 1920, the American Civil Liberties Union was founded. Among those who created the ACLU were the following: William Z. Foster, Elizabeth Gurley Flynn and Louis F. Budenz. All of the three ACLU founders later became prominent leaders of the Communist Party USA, although Budenz broke with the Communist Party in 1945 and became a militant anti-Communist.

The ACLU has never deviated from the philosophy enunciated in its first official publication, *The Challenge*, published in January 1920, in which appeared the following: "There should be no prosecution for the mere expression of opinion on matters of public concern, however radical, however violent."

Report No. 2290 of the U.S. House of Representatives' Special Committee to Investigate Communist Propaganda, (Jan. 17, 1931) states: "The American Civil Liberties Union is closely affiliated with the Communist movement in the United States.

The ACLU held a dinner on October 17, 1970, celebrating its 50th anniversary. The dinner honored long-time Communist Paul Robeson, and three others, who were given "50th Anniversary Civil Liberties Awards." The award to Paul Robeson, was presented by identified Communist Pete Seeger.

The ACLU defends the Communist Party of the United States as if it were a legitimate political party whose members are entitled to all the rights, liberties, and privileges enjoyed by loyal American citizens.

Among the "civil liberties" defended by the ACLU is the burning of the American flag during protest demonstrations. In 1967, Lawrence Speiser, the ACLU's Washington director, called flag-burning "a part of free expression protected by the First Amendment" of the U.S. Constitution.

When teachers or students refuse to salute or pledge allegiance to the flag of the United States, the ACLU defends their "right" to do so.

The ACLU has defended the "right" of Communists to speak on campuses and the "right" of student groups to hear Communist speakers. On the other hand, the ACLU has opposed the use of public schools for anti-Communist seminars.

The Communist Party and the ACLU for many years expended their efforts to abolish the House Committee on Un-American Activities, which was one of the last remaining obstacles to unimpeded Communist infiltration in the U.S.

The ACLU claims that voluntary, non-denomination prayer in public schools is a violation of the First Amendment prohibition against the establishment of an official religion, and that all such public expressions of religion are against the guarantees of the separation of church and state in the First Amendment.

The ACLU's position is not only absurd, it is also a deliberate misinterpretation of the First Amendment of the U.S. Constitution which stipulates: "Congress shall make no law respecting an establishment of religion, or prohibiting the free exercise thereof ...." and does not mention 'separation' of church and state.

What the First Amendment forbids in government isn't religion, isn't prayer, but an "establishment" of religion, by which the authors of the Amendment meant a national church.

In its campaign against religion in this country based on the doctrine of separation of church and state, the ACLU purposely avoids cognizance of the fact that the First Amendment expressly states that Congress may not "prohibit the free exercise" of religion. But what Congress, representing the people of this country, cannot do, the Leftwing-extremist ACLU has been doing for years.

The fact is that the Constitution does NOT ban religious expressions in public affairs. Sessions of Congress open with prayer. Presidents and other officials take the oath of office on a Bible. Our money is imprinted with "In God We Trust." Many of our national buildings and monuments are inscribed with references to God.

Additionally, some proposed state legislation aimed at reducing crime is immediately opposed by the ACLU. Such legislation includes automatic increases in penalties for crimes committed with guns; removal of bail for second offenders; removal of probation and parole, longer sentences for certain offenses, and the use of voluntary oral confessions. It is difficult to find any threat to "civil liberties" in any of the foregoing except the "liberty" to commit crime without punishment.

The ACLU ridiculously claims that obscenity and pornography are indefinable and therefore protected by the First Amendment's provision of free speech. The ACLU has defended the publication, distribution, and sale of pornography, objectionable pictorial materials and films, and has been a major obstacle in efforts to combat the propagation of pornography or enforce the laws that deal with such material.

For a decade the American Civil Liberties Union has been engaged in a nationwide legislative campaign aimed at the repeal of all criminal laws pertaining to marijuana. In this campaign they have joined forces with a radical organization for the Reform of Marijuana Laws, which not only seeks the removal of all criminal penalties for the use or possession of marijuana, but favors "making it available through sellers licensed by the State."

Incredibly, in spite of the nature of its activities, the ACLU is tax-exempt. This exemption was acquired through its affiliate, the Roger Baldwin Foundation. The ACLU also has another tax-exempt arm called the ACLU Foundation, Inc.

Before contributions to the ACLU were ruled tax-exempt by the Internal Revenue Service, nearly 90 percent of its work consisted of supplying "amicus" briefs in civil liberties cases and only 10 percent in actual litigation. However, after the IRS ruling, the percentages were reversed, with ACLU lawyers filing an avalanche of harassing lawsuits against local and State officials and school boards to carry out the various phases of its anti-American campaign.

According to an article in the New York Times, February 13, 1972, the ACLU and its affiliates and chapters and the ACLU Foundation, its tax-exempt arm, spent about $5 million in 1971. That was 16 years ago; so you can imagine what with current inflation, the ACLU is now spending each year as it works to destroy constitutional safeguards for law-abiding citizens, to undermine internal security against subversive forces, and to destroy the moral and religious foundations of our country.

While the history of the ACLU is well documented, it takes local issues that affect our daily lives to wake most of us up to the real purpose of the ACLU. The recent challenge to the lighted cross on the state Sillers Building and the opposition to optional prayer at Flora Elementary earlier this month have caused Mississippians to realize that the ACLU can affect change through the weapon of threatened lawsuits ... all supported by tax-free dollars.

I think that this fact was brought home to me most clearly when I attended, as an interested parent, a meeting of the State Textbook Selection Committee held in Jackson several years ago. There were two observers ... Jan Lewis, executive director of the state ACLU from 1981-1984, and I. It was obvious that the presence of the ACLU was an intimidating factor to the committee in textbook selection.

How many Mississippians are aware that the textbook selections for the school children of our state and paid for with our tax money are being monitored by the ACLU?

It's a nice name, The American Civil Liberties Union .... Who can be opposed to something that sounds so good? And believe me, it was planned that way.

But the facts speak for themselves. The ACLU's primary goal is to use all facilities at its command to undermine the American way of life and the religious and moral foundations of this nation.

And as Paul Harvey would say, "Now you know the rest of the story!"

The Clarion-Ledger
Voice of the People
Sometime in 1989

Statutory Changes Are Preferred to Adoption of ERA Amendment

Not all women – in fact the greater majority of women, if they know the facts – could possibly favor the Equal Rights Amendment. Certainly obsolete state laws that discriminate unfairly against women, especially in employment, can and should be appealed upon demand.

The most eminent lawyers in America advocate the elimination of discrimination against women by the statutory method, thereby permitting legislative bodies to proceed in an orderly way, and thus avoid constitutional and legislative chaos which adoption of the ERA would bring this nation.

Time and space do not allow me to enumerate all of the many far-reaching consequences and social upheaval that the "opening of Pandora's Box" by the passage of this amendment would cause. All women, and men, should inform themselves by studying excerpts from the minority report by Senator Sam J. Ervin, Jr. of North Carolina and also a complete analysis of the ERA from the April 1971 issue of the Yale Law Journal.

Passage of the ERA would wreak total havoc of our military system. Women would become eligible for the draft and the supposition that an all-volunteer Army is forthcoming holds no validity – because we don't have it yet.

Under the ERA:

If unmarried women are excused from military service because of pregnancy, men shown to be fathers of children born out of wedlock would also be discharged. Presently male officers are provided a dependent's allowance based on their grade and number of dependents. ERA passage would have to recognize the husband and children of a female officer as dependents.

Segregation by sex in public institutions such as prisons, hospitals, and schools would be outlawed – as well as separate public restroom facilities.

Our judicial system would be totally disrupted. Criminal laws which apply to only one sex, because of different physical characteristics and health considerations, would have to be invalidated or rewritten. The ERA would forbid any legal distinctions between men and women.

Common law and statutory rules requiring name change for the married woman would become legal nullities. States could conform by allowing selection of the name of either spouse or the selection of a third name satisfactory to both.

Impossible? As long as there are Madeline O'Hares around, it's not. The greatest concern, in my opinion, is the radical effect of the Equal Rights Amendment on the American social structure. Family life and foundation of mental health and happiness in the home will be greatly damaged.

When God created man and woman, he made physiological and functional differences between them. Certainly this does not make either sex superior to the other. Men and women complement each other in the relationships and undertakings on which the existence and development of the human race depends. Our country has established laws protecting the institution of marriage, the home, and the family – realizing that the American way of life would deteriorate without them.

It's time to wake up! Twenty states have ratified the ERA with 38 state approval necessary for passage. The bill has been defeated, at least temporarily, in Illinois, Louisiana, Connecticut, Oklahoma, and Vermont. When it is brought before the governing body of Mississippi, let's see it defeated by a resounding NO!

The Clarion-Ledger
Letter to the Editor
Sunday, March 4, 1990

Supports Those Who Voted Against Mail-in Registration

Just as you suggested in your "Voting" editorial of Sunday, February 25, I have contacted my representative whom you've labeled one of the "nine good ol' boys" who voted against a bill allowing mail-in voter registration. I told him that I wholeheartedly supported his vote against this preposterous legislation.

I not only oppose mail-in voter registration in Mississippi, but I hope that Mississippi representatives and senators will vote against the National Voter Registration Act (Bill S.74), which would make it easier for illegal aliens and repeat voters to vote.

There is no question that such an act would facilitate fraud in the election process. *The New York Times* reported in 1989 that a man in New York registered 84 times by mail, each time using a different name. He then voted 33 times in the election.

Another provision of this legislation would permit private groups to register voters without the supervision of trained election officials. And as your editorial pointed out, voter registration is what our circuit clerks get paid to do.

Please, tell us how our elected representatives vote, but refrain from telling us how you think they should vote. I, for one, hope that our elected representatives will never become lackeys for the editorial board of *The Clarion-Ledger*.

The Northside Sun
Thursday, March 15, 1990

Mail-In Voter Registration – Do We Need It?

Bill S.74 known as the National Voter Registration Act (H.R. 2190), passed by the U.S. House of Representatives in mid-February, would allow mail-in voter registration. A similar proposal was recently rejected by the Mississippi House.

This legislation was designed to help boost voter turnout in federal elections but in effect would end the last safeguards against voter fraud and political degeneration by ordering states to open their registration rolls to post-card or driver's license applicants and to cease periodic purges of registration rosters for non-voting.

Supreme Court rulings and the Voting Rights Act already ensure easy registration by citizens. Literacy tests are banned; registration practices with a discriminatory impact on minorities are outlawed; registration must generally be permitted until 30 days before an election.

This is the law, and while I cannot say with certainty that some irregular registration procedures don't still exist, registration guidelines have been adopted state wide to facilitate easier voter registration.

In 1984, the Mississippi Legislature approved a plan that would broaden the registration process by allowing circuit clerks to have satellite registration – thus making registration available in locations easily accessible to the general public.

In Hinds County, officials from the Circuit Clerk's office go into the field at least twice a year to conduct registrations in local courthouses, city offices, and local precincts.

Upcoming registrations are scheduled for Saturday, April 28 and Saturday, May 5, from 9:00 a.m. until 12 Noon.

In presidential election years, registration drives are conducted on two consecutive Saturdays prior to the 30-day deadline, thereby adding additional hours to the 9-5 weekday schedule and enabling those who work a five-day week to register.

In addition, the 1984 legislation provides that if a person is physically impaired and unable to go to a place of registration, a request can be made of the circuit clerk to send someone to the person's residence to complete registration forms.

I'm afraid that I don't agree with the premise that making registration as easy as mailing in a postcard will produce a larger voter turnout. Statistics prove that easier access to voter registration does not create a larger participation in the voting process.

In the 1980 election, 65 percent of registered voters participated; in 1984, 61 percent voted and in 1988, only 59 percent voted. If a person doesn't have enough get up and go to get registered, I doubt that he'll ever make it to the polling place to cast a ballot.

A registration plan instituted by some states, allow for "instant registration," which permits Election Day registration. Oregon found that such a plan proved to be an open invitation for abuse when, in an in-state election, Bagwan Rajneesh bussed in 4,000 homeless people to vote him into office on Election Day. Soon afterward, the Election Day Registration law was repealed.

Another provision of the National Voter Registration Act would permit private groups to register voters without the supervision of trained election officials. Any special interest group could thereby register ineligible voters in droves.

Voter-registration rules, entrusted by the U.S. Constitution, prevent fraud and divisive disputes over electoral outcomes. Democracy is endangered by electoral disputes stemming from fraud allegations.

I believe that one of the primary reasons for the decrease of the American populace's participation in the electoral process is a failure of the American educational system to teach patriotism and responsible citizenship. Thomas Jefferson warned: "If a nation expects to be free and ignorant – it expects what never was and never will be." Voter registration practices requiring modest mental alertness – namely, the location and time rules for registration – shields states and the nation from the dangers of ballots cast with ignorance.

It has been said that decisions in America are made by the majority of the people. This could not be further from the truth! Decisions are made by a majority of those who vote.

We, as Americans, should recognize that the full measure of our responsibility is the privilege of participating in government through the ballot box – a privilege paid for with blood and sacrifice and still denied to many in other parts of the world. Apathy and indifference threaten the future of this representative Republic, and if democracy fails, it will be because of a lack of vigilance on the part of those whom it serves and protects.

(The charges of voter fraud that arose during the 2008 presidential election stemming from fraudulent and multiple registrations – using such names as Mickey Mouse, Dick Tracy and Mary Poppins – is evidence that those who know how to work the system can influence election outcomes. Massive voter registration drives in "swing states" by the Association for Community Organizations for Reform Now (ACORN), while not illegal, brought chaos and confusion to the process.)

The Clarion-Ledger
Letter to the Editor
Tuesday, February 19, 1991

National Defense System Needs Immediate Funding

The success of the Patriot missiles in the Persian Gulf conflict points up the importance of having a defense system in place in the event of enemy attack on the United States.

The Strategic Defense Initiative (SDI) is a non-nuclear, space-based defense system which would pose no threat to people of any nation and would give the United States the ability to intercept deliberately or accidentally fired strategic ballistic missiles.

From the initial funding of "Star Wars," scientists have developed an even more cost effective defense system dubbed "Brilliant Pebbles," which could be developed and deployed in two to five years. It would provide the U.S. with a "peace shield" against mass destruction from conventional, chemical, biological, or nuclear warheads delivered by ballistic missiles.

It is imperative that the United States Congress approve adequate funding for this advanced technology, deploy SDI at its earliest availability and insist it may not be bargained away in any arms control negotiations.

U.S. senators and representatives should hear from those who support the president's initiative in providing a defensive system for our country.

Any money expended for protection of our homeland is money well spent!

The Clarion-Ledger
Friday, October 23, 1992

Will State Voters Find the Grit to Turn Whitten, Espy Out of Congress?

Presidents come and go, but committee chairmen stay on to control the funding and the legislative agenda.

New faces are needed in the United States Congress.

It is not surprising that 2nd District U.S. Rep. Mike Espy came to the defense of 1st District U.S. Rep. Jamie Whitten and has jumped into the fray with Governor Kirk Fordice on the question of term limitation. Espy and Whitten, like other pork-barreling politicians, are interested in perpetuating their lucrative positions of power and influence.

Lest we forget, Mr. Espy wrote 191 overdrafts on his account at the House Bank from July 1, 1988, through October 7, 1991. That averages about five checks a month which, even with "sloppy bookkeeping," should be just cause for dismissal.

The Council for Citizens Against Government Waste (CCAGW) has just released the ratings of U.S. senators and congressmen based on votes taken between August 1, 1991 and August 3, 1992. The votes rated include appropriations for unauthorized programs, spending for local projects without national significance and procedural votes that in effect hide government spending practices.

These votes had a significant impact on eliminating or reducing government waste or decreasing costs to taxpayers. The higher the rating, the better a senator or representative did in fighting waste.

Of the 435 members of the House of Representatives, five (all Democrats) had 00.00 ratings. Members whose scores were zero to 19.99 percent were described as "hostile" to taxpayers. One of the five was Mississippi's Whitten. Espy rated a 10.00. By comparison, Ted Kennedy had a 17.65 rating for Senate votes.

Several cases in point: while the other three Mississippi Congressmen voted against an amendment to cut $21 million from Congress's "free" mailing budget (Congress spends between $80-$90 million annually on "free" mail), Whitten and Espy voted for the congressional perk.

On the question of term limits, Mississippi's five congressmen (all Democrats) voted for a motion to table a resolution preventing Congress from using tax dollars and government lawyers to fight congressional term limit measures in the states. (November 6, 1991). The motion was adopted 265-160, which means our tax money will be used to help the rascals keep their jobs.

Taxpayers have been picking up the tab for Whitten's boondoggles since he became chairman of the House Appropriations Committee in 1979.

According to an article in Reader's Digest, Rep. Whitten bestows gifts of taxpayer money on his district almost at will. Colleagues rarely challenge his decisions. As one who was afraid to be identified put it, "Why run the risk of his retaliating against your own projects? Whatever the chairman wants, the chairman gets."

During Whitten's 41 years as chairman of the House Appropriations Subcommittee on Agriculture, he has dispensed hundreds of billions of dollars in federal largess. The nine presidents and ten secretaries of agriculture who have served during that time have had only transitory control. Whitten, notes *Congressional Quarterly*, is the "permanent secretary of agriculture." Presidents come and go, but committee chairmen stay on to control the purse strings and the legislative agenda.

Whitten is a prime example of why the American people are fed up with the "Imperial Congress".

With the focus on winning term after term, lawmakers have pandered to special-interest groups that finance their campaigns. Fearful of offending their supporters, some members of Congress have continued to feather their own political nests and refuse to make the tough decisions required to curb government spending.

But the real question is whether the recipients of Whitten's and Espy's pork barreling – the 1st and 2nd Congressional Districts of Mississippi – have the intellectual honesty and courage to turn their congressmen out.

Jamie Whitten was elected to the House in 1941, a month before Pearl Harbor. The saddest part of his 51 years is that he didn't know when it was time to come home. To have served fifty years in the Congress was, at one time, considered a distinction, but today, it's more of a disgrace.

There is certainly something to be said about the value of long experience. But is that experience being put to the best use? A $4 trillion national debt which equals nearly $30,000 for every American taxpayer is, according to U.S. Sen. John Danforth, "giving our children a legacy of bankruptcy."

Vicksburg Sunday Post
Letter to the Editor
Sunday, November 6, 1994
(Also published in *The Clarion-Ledger*, October 27, 1994)

Sovereignty At Stake

Mississippi's Attorney General Mike Moore was one of 44 state attorneys general to sign a letter to President Clinton raising serious questions about the new General Agreement on Tariffs and Trade (GATT) preliminarily approved by Congress this month.

What concerns the state attorneys general is that passage of GATT would put the United States in a foreign organization called the World Trade Organization (WTO) which will make laws and trade rules that override U.S. laws and trade practices, bypassing all local, state and national governments.

As the persons designated by law to defend state laws, the state attorneys general have good reason to be concerned. They asked:

- How will states be able to defend their laws against challenges from foreign governments, since only national governments will have standing before WTO panels?
- Can the states count on the U.S. Government to protect them from being forced by WTO to rewrite their state laws?
- How can any due process guarantees be put into the WTO dispute resolution system, since all the WTO dispute tribunals will meet and make their decisions in secret?

GATT has been submitted to the Congress under a newly-invented procedure called "fast track," which forbids amendments and calls for only a simple majority in both Houses of Congress for passage. This audacious "executive agreement" bypasses the U.S. Constitution that requires that treaties be ratified by two-thirds of the U.S. Senate.

If GATT-WTO passes, the U.S. will have only one vote out of 117 nations and no veto. We'll have the same vote as Haiti or Cuba or Somalia or Rwanda or Korea or Antiqua (population 64,000). Third World countries can make the trade rules, but they won't have to obey the rules they make for us.

Of course, we'll be assessed the biggest share of the costs, with no say as to how our money is spent. The Office of Management and Budget warns that WTO will cost an estimated $14 billion over five years and $40 billion over 10 years.

The Clinton Administration is floating the idea of waiving the Congressional pay-as-you-go budget requirement and adding the cost of this deal onto the national debt.

With your congressional delegation at home asking for your vote, ask THEM whether they've even read this 22,000 page bill.

If America is to remain an independent nation with the sovereign power to write our own laws and make our own decisions about our own livelihood, Mississippi U.S. senators and U.S. congressmen must vote *no*.

Immediate action is needed. Debate is set for Nov. 30 with final vote scheduled in both chambers for Dec. 1.

The Clarion-Ledger
Tuesday, March 14, 1995

Beware A "Convention" That Could Damage U.S. Constitution's Fabric

Unfortunately, a Conference of the States could lead to a Constitutional Convention, and a flawed Constitution.

Glowing reports fill the pages of our newspapers about the "rebirth of America." The American people seem to be euphoric with the idea that states may break the shackles of the federal government and regain their sovereignty.

Capitalizing on this enthusiasm, resolutions proposing a Conference of the States (COS), "an action plan to restore balance in the federal system," are being approved by state legislatures.

On the surface it sounds like a good idea – a plan to support states' rights within our federal system. However, statements made by its chief sponsor, Governor Mike Leavitt of Utah, indicate that COS may take us down an uncharted road to a U.S. Constitutional Convention (Con-Con) and/or basic structural changes in our form of government.

The Council of State Governments (CSG), in conjunction with the National Governors' Association, and the National Conference of State Legislatures have designated themselves "convenors." The American Legislative Exchange Council (ALEC), one of the principal promoters of a Constitutional Convention, has also endorsed COS.

Through the efforts of these private, intergovernmental groups, identical COS resolutions are being introduced in most state legislatures and, if passed by 26 states, the Conference will be convened this Fall.

While the "convenors" claim that the Conference of the States will not be a Con-Con, they plan to emulate the historic convention of 1787 that drafted the U.S. Constitution by holding the Conference in Philadelphia, Pennsylvania.

Mississippi's COS Resolution, (SCR 567), passed by the Senate and presently awaiting action by the House Rules Committee, states that COS bylaws shall "specify that the conference agenda be limited to fundamental, structural, long-term reforms."

I don't know about you, but I'd like to know what "structures" and "fundamentals" of our government would be targeted for change.

I'm also concerned about a group of governors and "a number of legislators not to exceed six" (from each state) acting as un-elected delegates to a conference where they will tinker with our federal system. Last time I looked, I didn't see any Washingtons, Franklins, or Madisons in the group.

Article V of the U.S. Constitution provides two ways to amend the Constitution: amendments proposed by a two-thirds vote of each house of Congress and then ratified by three-fourths of the states; or through application to Congress by two-thirds of the states for a Constitutional Convention.

The U.S. Constitution has been amended 27 times but never by a Con-Con. The most recent effort to call a convention (in the name of a balanced budget amendment) failed to gain the necessary 34 states.

There are people who would like to change our system of government. They view the convention route as a means by which to achieve their objective ... a new U.S. Constitution. The "checks" of Article V and the obvious lack of enthusiasm for a convention by the American people have prevented this from happening.

Soooo ... by necessity, there arises a need to provide an alternative method to bypass the safeguards of Article V in order to accomplish their goal.

One "idea for change" suggested by state task forces and "scholars" as a possible "constitutional remedy" would circumvent Article V. A clause would be added to put states on equal footing with the federal government by allowing three-fourths of state legislatures to propose amendments to the U.S. Constitution that would become valid unless rejected by a two-thirds vote of Congress.

If the intergovernmental agencies now circulating "participation resolutions" for the Conference of the States can do so without the general public having any knowledge of it, the same thing can be done by special interest groups with proposed amendments to the U.S. Constitution.

I would like to believe that right motivations are behind the proposed Conference of the States, and that such a meeting would never jeopardize the U.S. Constitution. I also don't want to be guilty of chasing ghosts but, realistically, we live in an age of appalling ignorance of the constitutional role of government and our responsibilities regarding it.

The Constitution is not flawed. All a state has to do to cast aside the unconstitutional shackles of the federal government is to "return checks paid out of the federal treasury for activities that the federal government has no constitutional authority to engage in or to impose upon the states as set forth in the Tenth Amendment of the U.S. Constitution."

Colorado State Senator Charles R. Duke, the author of the Tenth Amendment legislation, says: "Our present Constitution gives us all the rights we need for states to reclaim their sovereignty. There is no need for a new Constitution. Calling a Conference of the States is a constitutionally dangerous act to take. A meeting of states, fully sanctioned by state legislatures, has the power to turn such a conference into a Constitutional Convention by resolution. It would mean the death of our present Constitution."

Senator Duke is right! The United States Constitution has served this nation well for more than two centuries. It has endured longer than any other constitution in the world and has provided a unique system of government known as a Constitutional Republic – a government of law and not of men.

The American people must not lose sight of our nation's founding principles. We must oppose any effort to call a Constitutional Convention and recognize the possible dangers in the proposed Conference of the States.

Let's not open Pandora's box.

The Clarion-Ledger
Sunday, July 21, 1996

Hillary Clinton's "Chat" Sessions Just the Tip of the New Age

The movement has infiltrated almost every facet of American life – especially education.

It has been interesting to see the spin the press has put on recent revelations that Hillary Clinton has conversations with ghosts. "Much ado about nothing," "an intellectual exercise done by many business corporations," just "peccadilloes (a slight offense) of the rich and famous" is how the press tells it.

It is not surprising to learn that occultist and mythic ritualist Jean Houston, who calls herself "an intellectual," moved into the White House for three weeks to help Hillary in the preparation of her book on child rearing. You know the old saying, birds of a feather ....

What is shocking and rarely covered by the press is the scope of influence that Jean Houston and other New Agers have with policy makers. According to one of Houston's promo sheets, she is a featured speaker and chairperson for many major academic, scientific, and government meetings.

The New Age movement has infiltrated almost every facet of American life – especially education.

Hillary and Jean share the same "vision" of changing society to shape a new social character and "a new partnership with the whole Earth." They believe that the change agent (government or government agencies) should become the custodians of the children, the main regulator of the community, coordinating education with mental-physical health, acting as conflict managers, thus determining the future culture and affecting all sectors of society – economic, social and political.

That's what GOALS 2000 is all about.

Change, instituted in schools, with "goals" and "performance outcomes" dictated by the U.S. Department of Education and the education gurus who think like Hillary and Jean.

I have followed the trend away from academics over the last twenty years and have witnessed firsthand how the change masters are succeeding in redefining education.

In June, 1989, a friend sent me a transcript of the keynote speech at the 44th Annual Conference of the Association for Supervision and Curriculum Development (ASCD). The conference had been held in March of '89 in Orlando, Florida, and the speaker was none other than Jean Houston. The title of her presentation was "Whole System Transition, The Birth of Planetary Society."

The seminar featured sessions on how to plan and restructure the whole (education) system transition; how to educate for a new world; how to program for a global network for improvement, and how to build a model for teacher change. Other seminar topics included "humanizing students and using whole brain thinking and higher order thinking skills" (the current jargon for incorporating occultic activities and altered states of consciousness in learning – like talking to Eleanor Roosevelt.)

I know what you're thinking. That's Florida! Our Mississippi schools don't have stuff like that! My child's textbooks and learning materials are sound; our teachers would never be taken in by New Age religion!

I thought so too until just after receiving the Jean Houston transcript, I was dismayed to hear the 1989 Jackson Public School Board approve payment of expenses for school personnel and board members to attend the ASCD meeting in Orlando at which Jean Houston delivered the keynote address. The real outrage was that when a question was raised about the conference, the budget director jokingly said that it was "after the fact" because the conference had already been held, JPS personnel had attended, the money already paid.

This kind of irresponsible use of tax-payer money is just another example of how JPS thumbs its nose at any sort of accountability.

Additionally, the JPS director of curriculum for a number of years, who now holds an education position in another Mississippi town, was the state president of ASCD.

The next year, in June, 1990, Global Mississippi - International Education for Economic Survival in the Emerging Global Village was held on the Mississippi Gulf Coast. Its focus was "to chart the general directions for social studies and humanities curriculum reform in Mississippi's public schools for the next decade."

The conference was sponsored by the Mississippi Department of Education, the Mississippi Association of Educators, corporate "partners in education" and received major funding from the Mississippi Humanities Council and the National Endowment for the Humanities.

Some topics addressed: Our future in a changing world and getting the curriculum reform process started.

One of the speakers was Sister Miriam McGillis, a "futurist, who lectures widely on educating 'our children' to deal creatively and positively with current global challenges." According to conference literature, Sister Miriam "works extensively with religious congregations as they integrate global spirituality and world order into their ministries."

Think again if you don't believe that the influence of education change masters like Sister Miriam, Jean Houston and Hillary Clinton, and curriculum developing organizations like ASCD do not impact Mississippi classrooms.

When do we take off the blinders and admit that we have lost the education system because of disbelief coupled with inaction?

The Clarion-Ledger
Thursday, April 10, 1997

U.N. Chemical Weapons Convention Must Be "Overwhelmingly" Rejected

No previous treaty has ever subjected U.S. industry or citizens to such inspection

In the next few days the United States Senate will vote on ratification of the Chemical Weapons Convention (CWC).

This United Nations treaty is being promoted by the Clinton Administration as a prototype for a whole list of "global initiatives" – addressing everything from imposing new "international" taxes for social engineering, to controlling the world's climate, to creating international gun control agreements.

The CWC purports to be a global means to ban chemical weapons and forbid their production, stock-piling, and use. Strategists, concerned about national defense, believe that ratification of CWC would increase, not eliminate, the risk of chemical weapons use, and would seriously damage U.S. national security interests.

As in the case of most U.N. plans, CWC would cost American taxpayers and companies dearly. The U.S. tab is expected to be as much as $20 million annually – just like the $6.6 *billion* bill we picked up for U.N. military/peacekeeping operations from 1992 through 1995. Uncle Sam is the U.N.'s number one soft touch.

A massive new, U.N.-style international inspection bureaucracy (the Organization for the Prohibition of Chemical Weapons is already headquartered in The Hague) will have the right to inspect any site in the United States – government buildings, factories, and even homes of individuals on demand.

No previous treaty has ever subjected U.S. private industry or U.S. citizens to international inspection.

CWC would impose a regulatory and reporting burden on U.S. companies that produce, process, or consume a scheduled chemical. U.S. manufacturers of paint, varnish, dyes, nylon, electronics, insecticides, textiles, ceramics, and pharmaceuticals would be affected. Once implemented, Americans would no longer have Fourth Amendment rights which prohibit unlawful search or seizure without probable cause or judicial search warrants.

Does anyone really believe that U.S. intelligence can verify a world-wide ban on chemical weapons? If we've learned anything from experiences with the Kremlin, it's that they violate treaties. Currently they have refused to implement the 1990 Bilateral Destruction Agreement on chemical weapons.

While Russia is among those who have signed the CWC, it is unlikely to be ratified unless the U.S. pays billions in U.S. aid to destroy Russia's vast arsenal.

Former CIA Director James Woolsey testified on June 23, 1994, that "the chemical weapons problem is so difficult from an intelligence perspective that I cannot state that we have high confidence in our ability to detect noncompliance, especially on a small scale."

Rogue nations know full well that even militarily significant stockpiles (i.e., one agent ton) will be undetectable.

Many volatile nations, such as North Korea, Libya, Syria and Iraq, have not signed the convention. Who for a minute believes that a piece of paper will deter China or Iran, which have significant chemical weapons programs, from continued development of chemical arsenals?

And what about the many dangerous chemicals that CWC would *not* ban such as phosgene and hydrogen cyanide that were employed with deadly effect in World War I?

Bad guys are deterred by force, the threat of force, or by their calculation that aggressive action is not worth the risk.

The lesson learned from World War II is that the best way for civilized countries to prevent the use of chemical weapons is for the good guys to have their own deterrent arsenals of chemical weapons.

It will be interesting to see how the "most conservative" Senate in history votes on this dangerously flawed U.N. Convention.

It should be overwhelmingly rejected.

The Clarion-Ledger

Tuesday, May 6, 1997

Lott "Deal" On Chemical Weapons Treaty Harms Sovereignty, Security

If Sen. Lott wants to make a deal, I wish he'd work on getting us out of the United Nations

In 1777, George Washington, embroiled in a critical battle during the Revolutionary War, wrote his regimental commanders to "Put none but Americans on guard tonight." Wise words from the Father of Our Country, who knew the importance of having trustworthy men on watch.

The heirs of the men and women who won American Independence would be wise to heed Washington's warning as United States sovereignty and security are whittled away by U.S. Senate passage of United Nations treaties.

Mississippi's own, Senate Majority Leader Trent Lott, announced his support for the U.N. Chemical Weapons Convention (CWC), claiming that his concerns had been satisfied with a letter from President Bill Clinton promising to pull us out of the treaty if it adversely affected U.S. interests.

It was an outrage to have two Mississippians, Senators Lott and Thad Cochran, and a "conservative" GOP Senate hand President Clinton a significant victory on an unverifiable treaty that sets up a massive new U.N.-style international inspection bureaucracy, funded by U.S. taxpayers, and which, according to four past Secretaries of Defense, poses a danger to our national security.

Let's not forget that Cochran voted for the treaty; but it was Lott, as Majority Leader of the Senate, who was recognized as the key player in the chemical weapons treaty debate. It was he who could steer it to passage or marshal the votes for defeat. Days before the vote, there were predictions that Lott would facilitate the passage of the treaty because of a deal made with the Clinton Administration.

What kind of deal?

In my opinion, Trent Lott should have listened to the American people, and certainly the folks back home in Mississippi, instead of making a deal that binds us to a U.N. treaty that undermines our national security and sovereignty and is a sell-out to a President who loathes the military and doesn't keep his word.

If Sen. Lott wants to make a deal, I wish he'd work on getting us out of the U.N.. Now that would be a deal worth making!

Just think of the dollars it would save. Presently, the U.N. General Assembly requires the U.S. to pay 25 percent of the U.N. operating budget. They want us to pay 31.7 percent (now limited to 25 percent) of the "peacekeeping" budget compared to Russia's 8.5 percent, France's 7.6 percent and the United Kingdom's 6.3 percent. The peacekeeping budget has expanded from $700 million in 1990 to *$3.5 billion* today.

With passage of the chemical weapons convention, pressure is being exerted by the Clinton Administration for Senate approval of additional U.N. treaties such as the Convention on Biological Diversity, the Convention on the Rights of the Child, and the Convention on the Elimination of Discrimination Against Women.

The American people should understand that all U.N. treaties are bad because the U.N. concept embodied in covenants and treaties creates an all powerful international control that restricts and eliminates individual rights granted by the United States Constitution.

Some in the media are praising Lott for his great flexibility, his ability to work cooperatively with liberal members of the opposition party, and for his skillful dealing and broad-mindedness in steering to passage the chemical weapons treaty.

Why then, do I feel so betrayed?

It's probably the realization that Lott is not a true conservative and that he has turned a deaf ear to those who have gotten him where he is today.

I've felt a wide range of emotions – from anger on one hand to sadness on the other. Anger, at what was viewed as betrayal, and sadness to see a bright and shining star on the political horizon begin to fade.

Personally, I could have overlooked Lott's lack of Republican leadership and even forgiven the deal-making with Clinton, but I'll never forget that Lott's vote on the chemical weapons treaty jeopardized our national security and undermined American sovereignty.

There seem to be fewer and fewer statesmen around, and I've concluded that it really doesn't matter whether we're represented by Republicans or Democrats – what we generally get for our votes are office holders seeking a lifetime career of power and influence.

A true statesman does not compromise principle when it comes to the sovereignty of this nation, nor does he forget that to be prepared for war is one of the most effectual means of preserving the peace. The statesman loves independence more than interdependence; he values American citizenship over world citizenship; he remembers his oath of office to uphold and defend the United States Constitution, and he recognizes that our form of government is far superior to World Government dictated by the United Nations.

While the United States Senate is given the right to approve or disapprove United Nation treaties, it is we, the people, who pay the bills, run the risks and suffer the consequences. And on this one, the American people deserved better.

The Clarion-Ledger
Letter to the Editor
Wednesday, August 20, 1997

U.S. Leaders Knew NAFTA Would Cost Workers' Jobs

I was saddened to read that another U.S. company was heading to Mexico with the loss of MagneTek, Simpson County's largest employer; but I wasn't surprised.

A report prepared by the U.S. Commerce Department during the Bush administration, but never released to the public, estimated the United States would lose 40 percent of jobs in autos, steel, textiles, and apparel with the ratification of the North American Free Trade Agreement (NAFTA).

At the time of NAFTA ratification, it was estimated that 500,000 U.S. jobs would be lost, but our illustrious leaders thought more of the *global* economy than the economy of Simpson County and the 857 employees of MagneTek when they put their stamp of approval on it.

The Clarion-Ledger
Tuesday, October 28, 1997

UNESCO Confiscates, Regulates U.S. Land Without Congressional OK

Can it be long before American independence is replaced with global interdependence?

The United Nations – 52 years old last week and still kickin' – us!

For years the United States has been suckered by the "community of nations" to pay the bills and police the world while serving as the whipping boy of member nations. (The 10 nations most often opposing the U.S. at the U.N. received nearly $313 million in aid from American taxpayers in 1993.)

Are we crazy, or what?

If you like self government and independence, take note that the U.N. is expanding its powers to a new and formidable role in making U.S. policy and legislative decisions. The vehicle is U.N. treaties – many of them dealing with the environment and land use and being promoted as solutions to "global warming," ozone depletion and concerns about biodiversity.

Practitioners of environmental apocalypse have mapped a plan to establish a bureaucratic system to protect humanity's common "environmental assets" and "fragile ecological systems." Globalists have captured the issue, seeing it as the uniting cause that can bring about one-world government and control of the earth's resources and economy.

Springing from the Rio "Earth Summit" of 1992, numerous environmental treaties and agreements called "memorandums of understanding" and implemented by the State Department have set in place the framework to control human activity and property to protect the environment.

The latest is scheduled for approval by U.S. representatives in Kyoto, Japan, next December when voluntary restrictions on U.S. energy consumption become legally binding commitments.

The Clinton administration has pledged to reduce greenhouse gas emissions below the 1990 level, and if the Kyoto treaty is signed, regulations imposed by the treaty will result in higher energy costs through taxes, add an estimated 50 cents a gallon to gasoline, double home heating oil costs and raise electric rates by 30 percent.

And don't be surprised if you wake up one day to discover that the global neighborhood includes your back yard.

Currently 47 "Biosphere Reserves" (an area set aside for the purpose of conservation and scientific study) total almost *50 million acres* in the United States. That's more land than Maine, Rhode Island, Massachusetts, Vermont, New Hampshire and Connecticut combined!

Biosphere Reserves are the brain child of the United Nations Educational, Scientific and Cultural Organization (UNESCO). The U.S. severed official ties with UNESCO in 1984; yet the Clinton administration is allowing UNESCO to confiscate and unfairly regulate our own land without congressional approval and using our tax dollars to do it.

Another U.N. treaty, the World Heritage Convention, ratified by the U.S. Senate in 1973, designates our most important historic landmarks, monuments and scenic natural heritage areas as "World Heritage Sites." Twenty-two U.S. sites – including the Statue of Liberty, the Grand Canyon, Independence Hall, Yellowstone National Park and the Great Smokey Mountains – are now U.N. "protected areas."

On Oct. 8, four Mississippi congressmen (all except Out-of-Step Bennie) wisely voted in favor of the "American Sovereignty Protection Act" (HR901), a bill to prohibit federal officials from nominating U.S. lands for "protection" under UNESCO conservation programs without previous congressional approval.

The bill passed by a vote of 236-191, but Clinton has promised a veto.

With the national media continually raising our consciousness to the importance of meeting our "global" responsibilities, school children being taught that it's up to them to save the planet by being good citizens of the "global village," and our national leadership binding the U.S. to one U.N. treaty after another, can it be long before American independence is replaced with global interdependence?

The scariest aspect of U.N. encroachment is how little the American people know about it – and how little they seem to care.

The Clarion-Ledger
Tuesday, April 1998
Reprinted in the *NSDAR National Defender*, Vol. 40, No. 2, October 1998

U.S. Senate Should Oppose Expanding NATO Membership

George Washington warned the American people "to steer clear of permanent alliances with any portion of the foreign world."

Yet, Bill Clinton's primary foreign policy objective is the NATO Expansion Treaty, which *The Washington Post* calls "the most ambitious expansion of U.S. global commitments since the end of the Cold War."

The North Atlantic Treaty Organization (NATO) was created in 1949 at the end of World War II when an alliance of Western nations signed a treaty known at the North Atlantic Pact.

Article 5 of the treaty obligated each NATO member to "forthwith" go to war to defend any NATO member against attack.

By signing, the United States, for the first time, accepted military commitments in Europe.

Expansion a change of mission

NATO served its purpose during the Cold War to keep the old Soviet Union from invading Western Europe. But the NATO Expansion Treaty now before the U.S. Senate is a profound change in that mission.

The New York Times calls the treaty a "commitment to use American soldiers and weapons, including nuclear arms, to defend new members in Eastern Europe."

Madeline Albright testified before the Senate Foreign Relations Committee that this treaty commits us to defend not only the borders, but also the NATO-defined "interests" of Eastern Europe. She urged that NATO extend its geographic reach *beyond* Europe to "the Middle East to Central Africa."

Can the U.S. afford a permanent interventionist policy that would keep U.S. troops stationed in Europe, committing them to every conflict that arises?

Sen. John Ashcroft, R-Mo., who opposes NATO expansion, worries that NATO could become a "mini-United Nations with a standing army to be deployed in peacekeeping operations all over the world."

NATO expansion would institutionalize Clinton's Presidential Decision Directive 25 to put U.S. troops under foreign command, not to mention the billion-dollar cost to U.S. taxpayers.

A still higher price would be paid in lost American lives, sacrificed to a foreign conflict under NATO.

Why are we giving a foreign organization (NATO) the power to commit the United States to war when it is clearly unconstitutional?

The U.S. Constitution gives the power "to declare war" to Congress – that doesn't mean

NATO, and it doesn't mean just the U.S. Senate.

'What's in it for me?'

Passage of the NATO treaty is considered a tremendous political asset for the Democrats. There are large blocks of ethnic votes, Poles, Hungarians, Croats, Lithuanians, Estonians, etc, in the big cities of the North who want U.S. foreign aid for their homelands.

If the Democrats stand to gain from passage of the NATO Expansion Treaty, why do so many Republicans (including newt Gingrich and Trent Lott) support it?

It's the same old story – what's in it for me?"

What's in it is $32.3 million in campaign contributions funneled to congressional candidates from U.S. defense contractors who expect to make billions of dollars selling arms and military equipment to the new NATO nations.

The U.S. Senate should not commit the United States to an expanded military alliance.

A far better plan would be to press our allies to address the needs of eastern European countries by opening the markets of Western Europe to them and admitting them to the European Union, an organization much better suited to nation-building.

With the vote on NATO expansion expected in the Senate early this week, I hope that Sen. Lott won't say (as he did with the Chemical Weapon Treaty) that he "hasn't heard from a single Mississippian" who opposes NATO expansion.

The NATO Expansion Treaty would be a terrible and costly mistake, and both Mississippi senators, Lott and Thad Cochran, should be told so.

The Clarion-Ledger

Tuesday, June 23, 1998

Senate Republican Majority No Bar to Clinton Judgeships

In recent months, there has been considerable talk in the media about an alleged "judicial vacancy crisis." Claims of a "judicial system on the verge of collapse" have spurred the Senate to confirm a record number of federal judicial nominees in the first quarter of 1998.

The present "crisis" is merely a subterfuge by liberals to confirm activist judges who reflect the leftist ideology of the Clinton administration. When the Democrats controlled Congress, the confirmation process was impeded because the nominees happened to be conservatives. Remember Robert Bork and Clarence Thomas?

Consider that President Clinton appointed 202 federal judges in his first term. This compares with 189 appointees by President Bush and 164 appointees by President Reagan during their respective first terms.

The Senate did not reject any first-term Clinton judicial nominees. In fact, just four roll call votes were taken, with 198 nominees approved by "unanimous consent" without a roll call vote or floor debate. President Clinton has appointed more than 26 percent of currently active federal judges. More than 170 federal judges will become eligible to retire during his second term. President Clinton thus has the potential for naming more judges than any other president in history and could pick nearly 60 percent of all active judges by the end of his second term ... a lot of them straight from Hillary's Rolodex.

Typical Clinton appointee

Typical of the Clinton activist appointees is Margaret McKeown. She was confirmed on March 27 to the U.S. Court of Appeals for the 9th Circuit and received a "yes" vote from both Mississippi senators.

As lead counsel for the ACLU, McKeown went to court to deny the citizens of Washington state the chance to vote on a ballot initiative that would deny special legal status to homosexuals; she signed a report to successfully lobby the American Bar Association to abandon its neutral position on abortion and embrace the entire pro-abortion agenda; and was a member of a task force that sparked a movement to impose feminist political correctness on the judicial process.

In 1996, the Judicial Selection Monitoring Project published a 48-page report describing and analyzing the activist decisions by a majority of Clinton's appointees to the U.S. Court of Appeals. Rarely reported in the establishment media, the report unmasked the overwhelming liberal bias of judicial activists among Clinton nominees.

The Republican-controlled Senate, in an effort to be more than a "do-nothing" Senate, has confirmed twice as many Clinton nominees in the first quarter of 1998 than GOP Senates have confirmed Republican nominees in the first quarter of the past 20 years.

On May 23, Majority Leader Trent Lott stated on the Senate floor, "Should we take our time on these federal judges? Yes. Do I have any apologies? Only one: I probably moved too many already."

'Proper attention' urged

If that's true, why were eight more judges, six of them by unanimous consent, rushed to confirmation in the 10 days following his pronouncement? This brought the number of Clinton nominees confirmed in the first quarter to 12, compared to an average 6.2 GOP nominees confirmed by GOP Senates since 1979.

Sen. Lott, in a statement to *The Washington Post* and reprinted in *The Clarion-Ledger*, said: "It's about time proper attention was given to these unique government officials, who are appointed for life, paid salaries that can run to nearly $145,000 and are provided facilities and staff costing American taxpayers many millions of dollars annually," and "if the cost of these judgeships and the judiciary bureaucracy isn't enough to cause concern, consider that many such lifetime appointed judges attempt to make law from the bench ... seek to impose taxes on the public or turn criminals loose on society."

Maybe Sen. Lott should read his own press releases.

Maybe Lott and Sen. Thad Cochran should be reminded that no judge is better than a bad judge.

The Clarion-Ledger
Tuesday, January 9, 2001

Advice to Bush: Don't Appease, Restore Dignity

Memo to George W. Bush:

It won't be long now! January 20 and the Oval Office is yours.

It was a long, arduous, and expensive campaign, but soon you'll be directing the affairs of state. What an awesome responsibility, and how overwhelming it must be to realize that you are now a world leader.

You're off to a good start by surrounding yourself with men and women who will provide the needed experience and expertise to fill cabinet positions to help guide the ship of state.

You know the territory

It's not like this White House thing is new to you. You've been in the wings as your father held the Presidency. But now it's your turn.

You won't get much of a honeymoon.

Even before you take the oath of office, there are those who are plotting against you. They'll be like hounds nipping at your heels, hoping you'll stumble and fall. The media will be leading the pack; critical, unforgiving, eager to move in for the kill.

There will be the hate mongers and the race baiters; the Jesse Jacksons creating frenzied chaos. There will be the partisan politicians…the Democrats and Republicans, vying for power by promoting personal agendas. There will be the special interest groups bringing tremendous pressure to bear.

During the next four years, there will be crisis, hardship, indecision, heartache. There will also be times of triumph, gratification, and joy.

Whatever comes, I'm confident that you are capable of handling it because you have been brought to this time and place for a reason.

While there are many who want to see you fail, there are far more who want you to succeed.

These Americans want you to be a leader with a clearly defined agenda who can stay true to the principles upon which you were elected, clearly articulating your beliefs.

And a few suggestions:

Bipartisanship must not be defined by appeasement and concession. Republicans have been duped into believing that they must "build bipartisan coalitions" to succeed. Give the Democrats as much bipartisan consideration in this administration as they gave Republicans during the eight years they controlled the White House.

We don't need "a New World Order." The sovereignty of the United States should be of primary importance. We won our independence in 1776, and we don't need to lose it to the interdependence of World Government and the United Nations.

Rebuild our national defense. Lift the morale of our armed forces.

Overturn Clinton orders

Overturn many of the more than 350 Executive Orders of Bill Clinton who, in an unprecedented power grab, created law (a constitutional right that belongs to Congress) designed to restructure our governmental system, invent new powers for the executive branch, make broad policy changes and spend non-appropriated dollars.

Restore dignity to the office of the President. We don't need to know whether you wear boxers or briefs.

Honor commitment to family. Your family, as well as every other family in America, needs to be strengthened and nurtured.

Above all, trust in God. Make your motto Coram Deo, "living a life pleasing to God". And may God bless you as you lead our nation.

The Clarion-Ledger
Letter to the Editor
Tuesday, January 16, 2001

Don't Let Liberals Railroad Ashcroft

Confirmation hearings on the nomination of former U.S. Sen. John Ashcroft as U.S. Attorney General are scheduled to begin. The confirmation is shaping up to be an all-out fight with no holds barred.

The radical feminists, leftist organizations, and liberal columnists have gone on a rampage to defeat the nomination.

Tells me that Ashcroft is the man for the job.

His qualifications are impressive. He is the first attorney general-designate in U.S. history who has served as a state attorney general, governor, and U.S. senator. He is known as a man of impeccable character and integrity. His experience as a lawyer and public servant has prepared him for cleaning up the Justice Department and restoring America's confidence in the rule of law. And as one liberal columnist branded him, "He's a good ol' boy in the Old South tradition." The bottom line is that his only "sin" is that he's conservative.

Mississippi's U.S. Senators Thad Cochran and Trent Lott, because of their seniority and positions of leadership in the Senate, should publicly support John Ashcroft for attorney general and condemn the radical attacks on his character.

The Clarion-Ledger
Letter to the Editor
Monday, May 28, 2001

Say Thank-You to a Vet By Taking Action

Today is the day set aside to honor veterans. It's important that we honor the men and women who have served in the Armed Forces of the United States, for without their sacrifice and service we would probably not have the freedom we enjoy today.

While we honor veterans of all wars, an outrageous situation continues in Washington where construction of the National World War II Memorial has been delayed indefinitely, pending resolution of a lawsuit brought by a small group of malcontents.

The memorial, funded almost entirely by private contributions, will be built. But sadly, the ones to be honored, the members of America's WWII generation, won't be here to see it. Of the 16 million servicemen and women who served in World War II, it is estimated that only 5 million are still alive, and every day approximately 1,100 pass away.

To expedite construction, the U.S. House of Representatives voted overwhelmingly, 400-15, on May 15, to direct the American Battle Monuments Commission to "expeditiously proceed with the construction of the World War II Memorial at the dedicated Rainbow Pool site in the District of Columbia". The legislation also would make all previous decisions regarding the memorial "final and conclusive" and not subject to judicial or administrative review.

The bill, H.R. 1696, now moves to the U.S. Senate for action. If passed by the Senate and signed by the President, the legislation would allow construction to finally begin. I'm confident that Mississippi's senators, Cochran and Lott, support this legislation, but they need to know that you do, too.

The National Capital Planning Commission (NCPC) has scheduled a public hearing on June 13th and 14th to review all previous decisions on the memorial which could result in reconsideration of the memorial site and design.

To express your support for the memorial+, please write:

Richard L. Friedman, Chairman
National Capital Planning Commission
401 9th Street, NW
North Lobby, Suite 500
Washington, D.C. 20576
Or e-mail to info@ncpc.gov.

Honor our veterans by voicing your support for the World War II Memorial!

The Clarion-Ledger

Thursday, October 17, 2002

"Big Brother" Has a Smallpox Vaccine for You

The Department of Health and Human Services (DHHS) has announced that an estimated 500,000 first responders, 5000 of them medical workers in Mississippi, will receive smallpox vaccine.

The multi-phase smallpox vaccination program is being developed by the federal government as a response to the possible threat of a biological terrorist attack.

Once recommendations are received from the Centers for Disease Control (CDC) and approved by Tom Ridge and the Bush administration, preparations will be made for possible mandatory vaccination of the general public.

Sounds good? Not everyone thinks so.

Some in the medical community believe that we are setting the stage for a health disaster unlike anything we have seen before in America, and it will be our own doing.

Recipe for new disaster?

Here's why:

The smallpox vaccine has not been given in the U.S. since 1972. When Dryvax, the first vaccine made available thirty years ago, was pulled out of storage, there were serious questions surrounding its safety and efficacy. In 1999, *Science* reported that one-fourth of the vials "were suspect" because their rubber seals were deteriorating.

New smallpox vaccine will be genetically engineered. Many scientists believe that genetically engineered vaccines may be responsible for the global epidemic of auto-immune disease and neurological dysfunction.

The U.S. government apparently intends to forego double blind studies on the safety of the new smallpox vaccine. It has ordered 286 million doses, one for every man, woman and child in the nation at a cost of $428 million.

According to the American Medical Association, for each million people vaccinated with the smallpox vaccine, as many as 250 could die. Multiply 250 times 285 (millions of Americans) and the possible deaths from universal smallpox vaccination could equal 71,250.

Shots worse than disease?

Dr. Steven Black, co-director of the Kaiser Permanente Vaccine Study Center in Oakland, Calif., said in a commentary for ABC News, "Vaccinations may be more dangerous than the disease itself."

He points to the fact that the smallpox vaccine was developed at the end of the 18th century when medical technology was limited. But because of the high risk of smallpox disease, people accepted the dangers associated with routine smallpox vaccination.

Dr. Black doesn't believe that there is a need to expose the entire U.S. population to the risks of smallpox vaccination when the real risks of severe reactions and death must be balanced against what is currently only a theoretical risk of smallpox being introduced by terrorists.

Dr. Joel Kuritsky, director of the National Immunization Program and Early Smallpox Response and Planning at the CDC in Atlanta, has stated that smallpox has a slow transmission and is not highly contagious.

So, it appears that fear, not disease, is the problem.

Vaccination is a procedure that has the ability to cause injury and death. Full disclosure of the risks and benefits of vaccination must be made available to the general public so that every citizen will be free to make the ultimate decision on smallpox vaccination without government force or sanctions.

George W. Bush has said of smallpox vaccination: "One of my concerns if we were to have universal vaccination, some might lose their life."

Don't let it be yours.

The Clarion-Ledger

Thursday, November 4, 2004

Advice for a Solid 2nd Term: "Hold Fast" Now

Thank goodness it's over!

Like most Americans, I don't think I could have stood much more campaign babble. This Presidential campaign consumed way too much time and money and has left most of us feeling as if we've been dunked, run through the wringer and hung out to dry.

In spite of it all, we elected George W. Bush to a second term as president.

Four years ago, just before Bush was inaugurated, my column was a "memo to George W. Bush." In it, I said, "During the next four years, there will be crisis, hardship, indecision, heartache."

9-11 defined the 1st term

No one could have imagined the crisis that would come eight months later. The hardship, indecision, and heartache of 9-11 united the American people behind a forceful leader. Too bad, that unity didn't last.

The terrorist attack on our country was to define the Bush presidency and change forever our comfort level here at home.

George W. Bush is an honorable man and, no doubt, sincerely believes in the course he set as president. And while it's easy to be a sideline quarterback, I don't question for a minute that the nation is better off today with George W. Bush than it would have been with Al Gore. The same holds true of a Kerry presidency.

While the election outcome suggests that most Americans support the war on terrorism, many feel that Bush should have finished business in Afghanistan before going into Iraq, especially with no clear exit strategy.

In my opinion, one of Bush's greatest failures was his refusal to protect our borders (an estimated 12 million illegal immigrants have entered the U.S. since Bush took office). He also enlarged the role of Big Brother in education, health care, and homeland security.

To his credit, Bush supported a strong national defense and lifted the morale of our armed forces, cut taxes and boosted the economy, defended the lives of the unborn, and restored dignity to the office of president. And he definitely gets an A+ for giving us Laura Bush as First Lady.

So, here's to four more years, Mr. President, and my Memo No. 2:

Stay the course in Iraq

Stay the course. From all reports, democracy is taking root in Afghanistan and Iraq. Once the plant begins to grow, allow the Afghan and Iraqi people to tend the garden.

Immediately institute a strong immigration policy. Close U.S. borders to illegal aliens who are overloading our healthcare facilities, penal institutions, and schools.

Protect American sovereignty. The U.S. may have to compete "globally" but Americans shouldn't have to learn a second language to be able to place an order or get information by phone from an out-sourced American company ... and believe me, it's just about to that point. Customer service representatives in India, Bangladesh, or Timbuktu don't speak good Southernese.

Continue to appoint conservative, constitutionalist judges to the federal bench to restore a balance to the courts of our land. We have suffered a half-century of activist/liberal court decisions that seriously threaten to undermine our rule of law.

Above all, keep the faith; hold fast to your principles; and talk often with God.

The Clarion-Ledger
Letter to the Editor
Tuesday, July 4, 2006

"Sovereignty" of USA Must Survive

The plan for a "North American Union" which would erase our borders with Mexico and Canada, should strike fear in the heart of every United States citizen who believes in the sovereignty of our country.

Unthinkable? Never happen? Don't count on it.

President George W. Bush is following a blueprint laid out in a 2005 report published by the left of center Council on Foreign Relations which sets forth a five-year plan for the "establishment by 2010 of a North American economic and security community."

George Bush is a globalist and is of the same ilk as his father who called for "a new world order" when he was president.

This probably explains why Bush has so stubbornly rejected the advice of his supporters even though that advice is consistent with the thunderous message from public opinion surveys showing that an overwhelming number of U.S. citizens want our borders controlled to stem the flow of illegal aliens.

At a meeting in Waco, Texas in March of 2005, Bush, Mexican President Vicente Fox, and Canadian Prime Minister Paul Martin committed their governments to a path of cooperation and joint action. The plan called the Security and Prosperity Partnership of North America (SPP) would create a free trade zone protected by a common security perimeter, within which goods, people, and capital would move freely across what once were established international borders.

A follow-up meeting in Cancun, Mexico, in April of this year, celebrated the first anniversary of the "partnership."

In a nutshell, the plan would integrate the United States with wildly incompatible cultures and political systems and permit migration, which unlike immigration, would allow free flow of whole peoples within national borders. It would essentially require U.S. citizens to surrender their citizenship in the independent constitutional republic founded in 1787.

Aside from the question of national sovereignty, why would anyone in their right mind even consider merging the United States of America with Mexico and Canada?

**Mexico is ruled by a corrupt political system intimately connected to that nation's narcotic-terrorists syndicates, while Canada, with linguistic and regional conflicts, has become a haven for Muslim refugees, some with possible terrorist connections.*

This Independence Day, we would do well to remember the tremendous sacrifice of the men and women who fought and died to preserve this nation.

**Those patriots of the American Revolution who gave us independence from Great Britain; the 180 fearless men who died fighting Santa Anna's two thousand Mexican troops at the Alamo to make Texas a part of the United States; the gallant men and women who answered the call in World War I and World War II, in Korea, in Viet Nam, and now in Afghanistan and Iraq.*

Their service and sacrifice haven't been for the North American Union, but for the United States of America!

Before it's too late, we should rise up and encourage all our public officials to be very zealous defenders of American sovereignty.

*Omitted when published.

Chapter IV

State Issues

The root of the kingdom is in the state. The root of the state is in the family. The root of the family is in the person of its head.

Mencius
372-289 B.C.

The Clarion-Ledger
Letter to the Editor
Tuesday, February 3, 1987

Dangers Involved In Constitution Rewrite

To read your editorial page, one might get the impression that a constitutional convention is the only way to revise the state constitution. In the Jan. 28 editorial, "Critical vote: Constitutional reform at stake," readers were urged to "bestir themselves, to let (constitution) committee members know that they want to replace an antiquated document…that stifles economic development and helps hold Mississippi in last place." Baloney!

The old worn out tune of "Mississippi in last place" makes me tired! I doubt that a new constitution will do much to improve our ranking among the 50 states.

As to stifling economic development – prove it. According to the Mississippi Manufacturers Association, not one state industry has ever stated that the constitution had any effect on the location or expansion of a manufacturing plant nor that its provisions had any adverse effect on a company's manner of operation.

Granted, the 1890 Mississippi Constitution needs some limited revisions. It can be done by the existing amendment process and not a costly and dangerous constitutional convention which could jeopardize our legislative, judicial, and executive laws under which we presently operate.

There are many dangers involved in a complete rewrite of the state constitution. Special interest groups are chomping at the bit to see that a constitutional convention takes place so that their policy can be written in. The delegates who will be elected to such a convention could be easily manipulated by such groups whose money could help see them elected.

Any constitution rewrite will have to be approved by the U.S. Justice Department under the Voting Rights Act of 1965. While the constitutional changes and revisions submitted to the Justice Department by other states have met with general approval, I would hate to risk having it dictate the document that will be the foundation of Mississippi government.

I believe that the people of this state, as proved in the past, can, through the existing amendment process, make the necessary changes in those sections of the constitution that should be repealed or amended, are outdated, or have been ruled unconstitutional.

I hope that our legislators will take the leadership in saying NO to a constitutional convention. Bestir yourselves, Mississippians, and say NO to your representatives on the question of a constitutional convention.

On the surface a new constitution sounds wonderful. But beware – new is not always better.

The Clarion-Ledger
Undated, sometime in 1987
Letter to the Editor

Constitution Panel "Cutting Its Own Throat"

Well, it looks like Gov. Bill Allain's Constitution Study Commission is right on course. It has opened the proverbial Pandora's Box and started tampering with things best left alone, specifically the Equal Rights Amendment (ERA) and the reading of the Bible in public schools.

Special interest groups have managed to propose changes with which the general populace disagrees, thus jeopardizing any legitimate revisions in the state's constitution.

With only about 80 of the committee's 350 members present at the recent meeting (and that vote split 30-44 on Bible use) it looks as if the commission is cutting its own throat. Let us hope that the full 350-member commission will have the wisdom to override these recommendations before the "baby is thrown out with the bath water!"

The Clarion-Ledger
Sunday, June 12, 1988
Letter to the Editor

Denial of DAR Use of Mansion Protested

On Bert Case's *Inquiry* television program of Sunday, May 15, Gov. Ray Mabus stated that the Governor's Mansion was for the enjoyment of the people of Mississippi and as governor he intends "to wear it out."

If this is true, how can he justify the refusal of its use to the 6000 Mississippi members of the Daughters of the American Revolution?

For many years the Magnolia State Chapter of Jackson has used the mansion as part of its Christmas pilgrimage. This year the chapter was told by the mansion secretary that its request for its use had been denied by the Mabuses because the mansion would be used *only* for occasions when economic development would be stressed and jobs brought into the state.

This does not seem to agree with Gov. Mabus' public statement about use of the mansion or justify the increased staff and financial expenditures for entertaining by the Mabuses.

If the Christmas pilgrimage were just a social function, I might understand why use of the mansion was denied. However, proceeds from the pilgrimage, which is open to the public, go to support DAR projects such as the maintenance of Rosalie, our beautiful antebellum home in Natchez and a major tourist attraction for the state; providing flags and flag codes to the schools and presenting National Defense Medals to outstanding ROTC cadets in state high schools and colleges; support of Kate Duncan Smith and Tamassee DAR Schools; and maintaining an outstanding genealogy collection at the Eudora Welty Library. (The DAR library is now housed at Rosalie.)

The DAR has always been warmly received at the Governor's Mansion – as well as at the White House during Continental Congress (the national DAR annual convention). Many of Mississippi's first ladies have been DAR members. Carroll Waller is a member of my chapter and played a key role in the restoration of the beautiful home Mr. Mabus now enjoys as governor.

I hope that Gov. Mabus will carefully review the decision to refuse the DAR use of the mansion. The many members and guests from Mississippi and from out of state who attend Magnolia State's Pilgrimage will be highly insulted by a governor who intends to "wear the mansion out" but refuses its use once a year to the DAR.

I will be interested to see just who will be guests at our mansion and whether it will truly be used ONLY for economic development and bringing jobs into the state. This policy seems to limit its use by Mississippians who are asked to foot the bill.

The Clarion-Ledger
Letter to the Editor
Friday, January 5, 1990
Companion articles *The Northside Sun*, July 20, 1989
The Sun Herald, August 6, 1989

Constitutional Convention for U.S. Seen as Perilous

Many important issues will be considered in the 1990 session of the Mississippi Legislature.

Among them is an effort to recall a resolution passed by the legislature in 1975 petitioning the U.S. Congress to call a U.S. constitutional convention in order to consider a balanced budget amendment.

Until last year, most Mississippians, including legislators, were unaware that Mississippi was on record as favoring a U.S. constitutional convention.

While most would favor a balanced budget amendment, a convention, in the opinion of many, would be a crisis of divisive, destructive dimensions and if called, could place the U.S. Constitution in jeopardy.

Gerald Gunther of the Stanford Law School, who is recognized as a constitutional authority, states emphatically in an article published in the American Bar Association Journal that state legislatures should not endorse the balanced budget constitutional campaign on the basis of over confident answers to unanswered and unanswerable questions, or of blithe statements that inadvertently or intentionally blind us to the genuine hazards.

What are some of those unanswered questions? Could a convention be limited to consideration of just a balanced budget amendment?

How would delegates to a convention be selected? Would they be appointed or elected and would they be answerable to the will of the people? Who would conduct proceedings? What would the agenda be? How would a convention be funded and how much would it cost the taxpayer?

Why subject the U.S. Constitution to a convention – a Constitution that has served this nation well?

We are dangerously close to having a U.S. constitutional convention called. To date, 32 of the necessary 34 states have called on the U.S. Congress for a convention, Mississippi being the first state to do so!

Last year, the Rules Committee of the Mississippi House refused to take action on this important question, and it was allowed to die in committee.

If nothing else, Mississippians should demand that Mississippi's constitutional convention resolution be reconsidered by bringing it to the floor for a vote.

The recall resolution would put Mississippi on record as favoring a balanced budget amendment but would cancel the call for a constitutional convention.

The Northside Sun
Thursday, May 24, 1990

It's Time to Salute State's National Guard

MAY 20 was celebrated nation-wide as Armed Forces Day. Americans from all walks of life pay tribute to those men and women who have served their homeland by military service in the United States Army, Navy, Air Force, Marines, and Coast Guard.

I was privileged to join a group of civic leaders in Mississippi for a series of briefings on the defense structure of this nation and the role played by the National Guard in the military order of the United States. It was a rare opportunity for a civilian to travel aboard a C-141V transport aircraft of the 172nd Military Airlift Group of Jackson, to the National Guard Bureau at the Pentagon in Washington, D.C. to learn firsthand of the common goal of the Mississippi National Guard in protection of country, state and hometown.

THE NATIONAL GUARD is a volunteer organization with both a state and a federal mission. This two-fold mission is to provide units that are manned, trained, equipped, and ready on short notice to perform their national defense assignments as part of the nation's Total Force military system; and to respond to the Governor's request to protect life and property and to preserve peace, order, and public safety.

The Mississippi National Guard is one of the state's major employers with 653 state employees and 2600 federal employees. Nearly 200 Army and Air National Guard units and activities exist in approximately 100 communities within Mississippi. Guard personnel are highly trained and motivated.

There are three training sites in the state: Camp Shelby (the largest state operated military training site in the nation with 136,000 plus acres); Camp McCain at Grenada and the Air National Guard Training Site at Gulfport.

DURING THE PAST four years, the Mississippi Army Guard has received new equipment valued far in excess of $300 million. The equipment includes M-1 Abrams tanks, the Bradley Fighting vehicle, and state-of-the-art engineering equipment. This figure does not include the value of the RF4C Phantom jets flown by the Air Guard at Meridian nor the C-14B Start Lifters at Jackson nor the new, $27 million Aircraft Combat Maneuver Instrumentation (ACMI) facility at Gulfport.

Direct federal funds to support the Mississippi National Guard amounted to more than $212.8 million during fiscal year 1989. A portion of the funds went to every community in Mississippi. Of the federal total, $155.8 million went to support the Army National Guard and $57 million to the Air National Guard.

UNDER THE TOTAL Force Concept, the Army National Guard is an integral and full-fledged partner in the Total Army. In fact, the Army could not respond to any major conflict without the significant and immediate response and support of the Army National Guard, which represents the eleventh largest army in the world.

Today's Army national Guard accounts for almost half the Army's combat units and more than one-third of its overall strength. Army Guard units account for half the Total Army's infantry and field artillery battalions, almost half its armor battalions, more than half its armored cavalry regiments, more than one-third of its combat division, and two-thirds of its separate brigades.

The Air National Guard provides 92 percent of the Air Force's air defense interceptor force; 50 percent of the reconnaissance force, 24 percent of the tactical fighter force, 37 percent of the tactical airlift, and 11 percent of the electronic combat capability. It provides 19 percent of the air refueling tankers, 29 percent of the rescue and recovery capability, 55 percent of the tactical air support, and six percent of strategic airlift forces.

THE MISSISSIPPI National Guard is actually older than the State of Mississippi. Governor Winthrop Sergeant, the first territorial governor of Mississippi, issued an official order dated September 8, 1798, calling for the militia to be organized. The first regiment was mobilized January 20, 1806, making the Mississippi Guard the seventh oldest in the United States.

The facts and figures which I gleaned from participation in the National Guard Civic Leaders Tour do not begin to tell the full story of the 16,000 men and women in Mississippi, from hundreds of backgrounds and professions, who serve our state and nation in war and peace.

As we honor those who have served in the U.S. Armed Forces, I hope that you will join with me in saluting the Mississippi National Guard for its dedication and commitment to home and country.

The Clarion-Ledger
Letters to the Editor
Tuesday, March 19, 1991

House Rules Committee Dragging Feet on HCR 44

The old saying "that's politics" is evident in how much of the business of the Mississippi Legislature is transacted. It is vividly portrayed by the inability of the average citizen to overcome "the system" in working to effect legislation.

One would be led to believe that an issue, properly researched, introduced by a member of the Mississippi House and supported with the signatures of 94 of the 122 members of the House would certainly be passed out of committee for a vote on the floor – sailing to smooth passage. Right? Wrong!

As is so often the case, the committee to which the resolution was referred failed to take action, allowing the issue to die. The issue, to be more specific, was the simple desire by some Mississippians to rescind Mississippi's resolution petitioning the U.S. Congress to call a federal constitutional convention in order to consider a balanced budget amendment.

Back in 1975 when the resolution was passed by the Mississippi Legislature, the idea seemed like a good one. But as time passed and more people became acutely aware of the dangers of a U.S. constitutional convention, it became evident that reconsideration was in order.

The issue was all but dead already, with no state since 1983 approving resolutions for a convention and four states (Florida, Alabama, Louisiana, and Nevada) rescinding previously passed resolutions.

The resolution (HCR 44) introduced to rescind, continued Mississippi's support for a balanced budget Amendment but memorialized its call for a federal convention.

When the House Rules Committee allowed the resolution to die in the 1989 session, it was reintroduced in 1990, this time in both the House and the Senate. It was passed by the Senate but the House Rules Committee again refused to take action, allowing the recall resolution to meet the same death as in 1989.

The year is 1991, and again the House Rules Committee is dragging its feet in passing House Concurrent Resolution 44. I wonder if the full House will ever have the opportunity to vote on this important question.

How can a few individuals, for whatever reason, deny another vote by the full House? Why does this happen? Your guess is as good as mine. Just call it politics.

The Northside Sun
"As I See It"
Thursday, September 3, 1992

Does Mississippi Really Need A Lottery?

MISSISSIPPIANS will have the opportunity to consider several important questions in the November 3 general election ... namely, who the next president of the United States will be and if the Mississippi Constitution will be amended to remove prohibitions on a state lottery.

Having secured the right to decide whether to remove the prohibition from the Constitution, Mississippians should exercise the good judgment to reject the proposal.

Proponents of a state lottery say that a lottery is the reasonable way to provide the state with the needed dollars to fund education. Their reasoning is that everyone has to pay taxes but not everyone has to play the lottery.

True, lotteries raise money for states, but not nearly on the scale that we're led to believe.

Researchers claim that for an average state's budget dollar, a lottery raises about two cents. That profit is weak in comparison to the 29 cents for each state budget dollar usually raised by sales tax or the 24 cents generally provided by federal aid.

The LOTTERY IS a very inefficient means of taxation. Ordinarily, it costs the state one or two cents to produce a dollar in sales tax revenues. With the lottery it costs $1.50 to produce a dollar – 60 cents to raise 40 cents of revenue. No state has ever reduced its taxes because of the lottery and in fact, statistics reveal that 22 states with lotteries have had more tax increases than non-lottery states.

California is one of the best examples of how the people of the state bought into the lottery idea with great expectations of additional funds for school coffers. But according to a July 6, 1992,

McClatchy News Service article from the Marin County *Independent Journal,* some educators have found that the California lottery has created a sort of "addiction" to an unreliable source of funding. In 1986, when the California State Lottery was instituted, educators were warned to use the money wisely. When lottery sales peaked at $2.6 billion in 1988-89, schools received just over $1 billion ... a pretty good sum. The next year, sales fell and schools got $980 million. A year later, schools received $804 million. This past fiscal year, the education money was expected to be an estimate $480 to $500 million. Now, there's trouble in the Gold Rush State.

The PAINFUL lesson learned is that balancing education funding on an unstable and unreliable source of income, such as a lottery, is risky business.

Tom Watson, Jr., in his book on gambling and lotteries titled *Don't Bet On It,* asserts that the most disconcerting issue concerning lotteries and taxation is what he calls "regressive taxation" and unfair redistribution of wealth.

He explains: "State lotteries as funding devices, unlike traditional tax formulas, tend to produce income for the state in reverse proportion to the earning levels, and thus the tax liability, of its citizens. As an alternative to tax revenue, lotteries are regressive and, therefore, unfair."

Watson adds: "Poor people outnumber rich people wherever we go, and the lotteries show us that less affluent citizens are the ones willing to risk what little they have against the possibility of lasting freedom."

COLORADO HAS far fewer poor than Mississippi, but according to an editorial in the Colorado Spring *Gazette Telegraph,* the lottery "has been a bad bet, for both players and public policy. The fiscal promises made to taxpayers and voters almost never come true. It is bad enough that poor families invest scare resources in such a wasteful activity as gambling; it's downright awful that the state of Colorado spends millions urging them to do so."

Thrilling accounts of "rags to riches" stories always make the news.

I'm reminded of the recently reported story of the winner of the Florida Lottery – a homeless family, living in a car, whose last dollar was spent on the winning lottery ticket. Or the glowing reports from the local papers of the happy winners who have hit it big in the casinos of the Gulf Coast.

Tragically, what we don't hear is how much money is lost and the misery of many of the losers.

What are your chances of holding a winning lottery ticket?

The mathematics department at Miami's Barry University says that the odds against winning with any single lottery ticket in Florida are 7.25 million to one.

RETAIL MERCHANTS in lottery states are often appalled at the flow of dollars away from their merchandise to lottery tickets. Wage earners cannot spend money twice.

A lottery takes money out of the economy which would be used to pay for rent, utilities, food, clothing, and furniture. It creates an increase in unpaid bills, embezzlement, bankruptcy, and absenteeism from work.

Do we want to sell our children the idea that gambling is good? Experts are concerned that such easy access to gambling will create new gamblers, some of whom will become pathological betters who bring painful and expensive havoc on themselves, their families, and society.

Do we really want to teach Mississippi young people that gambling is okay by instituting a state lottery? Instead of destroying the work ethic, we should be teaching them that wealth and success in life come through discipline, sacrifice, and hard work.

LOTTERIES ARE economically unsound, socially disintegrating, and morally dangerous.

The lottery can be defeated on November 3 if concerned, caring, and convinced people become knowledgeable and take action to preserve integrity in our system of government and avoid exploiting its most vulnerable citizens.

It is impossible for Mississippi to gamble itself rich and unconscionable for a state to make losers of its people. Vote NO to Constitutional Amendment number one.

The Clarion-Ledger

Monday, January 18, 1993

This "Johnny Come Lately" Republican Is No Leader

In a front page article from the Sunday, January 10, *Clarion-Ledger*, ("Briggs rises fast despite long odds"), our lieutenant governor is quoted as saying, "I want more people to know about Eddie Briggs".

What I know about Eddie Briggs is that he doesn't possess the leadership ability needed in the Mississippi Legislature.

A "Johnny come lately" to the political scene, Mr. Briggs, a Democrat at the time, first won election to the Mississippi Senate in 1983 by a mere 105 votes.

His lackluster years in the Senate did nothing to distinguish him as a leader. His election as lieutenant governor was only because it was time for Brad Dye to go. His election was by less than a 50-percent majority and was helped by Henry Kirksey, who ran as an independent.

They say that in politics, timing is everything, and Mr. Briggs positioned himself to be at the right place at the right time.

Obviously, Mr. Briggs is politically astute, as demonstrated by his switch to the Republican Party in 1991 as a way to win election. I'm convinced that almost any viable candidate running a "it's time for a change" campaign would have been as successful as Briggs.

Conspicuously absent from the "TEAM Mississippi" meeting in which Gov. Fordice outlined his legislative agenda, Briggs has distanced himself from any team involvement and has his own agenda, a campaign for the governorship in 1995.

If Gov. Fordice is having trouble developing a consensus and coalition with lawmakers, much of the blame should rest on the shoulders of the lieutenant governor who, as second in command, should be guiding the governor's legislative initiatives to passage.

And as to Mr. Briggs' "leadership" on the issue of a state lottery ... doesn't he know that lotteries won't solve the state's fiscal woes?

If a state lottery is instituted, the big money makers will be the out-of-state gambling equipment providers who stand to gain millions of Mississippi dollars – hard-earned tax dollars that will leave the state coffers and never provide one dollar of sales tax for Mississippi.

A leader? Not in my book.

The Clarion-Ledger
Letter to the Editor
Tuesday, March 15, 1994

Constitutional Convention No Way To Balance Budget

What's a state representative from Mississippi doing testifying before a legislative committee in New Jersey?

According to an article from an 1987 American Legislative Exchange Council (ALEC) publication, David Halbrook, of Belzoni, was there, and in other states as well, persuading the New Jersey Assembly to pass a resolution calling on the U.S. Congress to hold a federal Constitutional Convention (Con-Con) to consider a Balanced Budget Amendment.

Come again? Don't we have enough pressing issues here at home to keep him busy? Apparently not. **This Mississippi lawmaker's position with ALEC, a private organization of state legislators, has placed him on a larger playing field with big time players. He hob-nobs with the likes of U.S. Senator Orrin Hatch. He likes Washington so much, he even made an unsuccessful run for the U.S. Congress last year.*

Representative Halbrook is given credit by ALEC for sponsoring the first successful constitutional convention call (for a Balanced Budget Amendment) when in 1975 he steered a resolution to passage in the Mississippi Legislature. **It could prove embarrassing if his own state decided a federal convention is a bad idea and rescinded that resolution, so he has wielded his influence to prevent that from happening.*

When 32 state legislatures passed resolutions for a constitutional convention (it takes 34 for it to happen), Americans began to wake up to the dangers a federal convention posed. Many are convinced that it could lead to constitutional damage from which our republic may never recover.

These concerns led Alabama, Florida, and Louisiana to rescind their convention resolutions.

In Mississippi, the rescission resolution was referred to the House Rules Committee which has refused for *six years* to take any action. This year, the Rules Chairman, Rep. Glenn Endris, of

Biloxi, told me, "As long as I'm chairman, the issue will not be brought up."

What has happened to our representative form of government? What recourse does the average Mississippian have when one person can make the decision that "his" committee will not take action?

These two legislators have been in the Mississippi House for 26 and 22 years, respectively. If ever there is need for term limits, this is it!

Some might say that this is the very reason a convention is necessary ... to force Congress to pass amendments to limit terms or balance the budget.

In my opinion, no matter how worthy, the real issue is not term limits or a balanced budget, but the integrity of our United States Constitution.

A federal convention could bring about a constitutional crisis of divisive, destructive dimensions.

The full Mississippi House should be given the opportunity to reconsider whether Mississippi supports a U.S. Constitutional Convention.

*Omitted when published.

The Clarion-Ledger
Letter to the Editor
Tuesday, May 31, 1994

Parker, His Congressional Office Really Responsive

Several recent letters highly critical of the responsiveness of 4th District U.S. Rep. Mike Parker to his constituents and the courtesy of his office have prompted me to write.

I write letters to *all* congressional offices about as often as I write letters to the editor. If the subject of my correspondence is on a current issue before the United States Congress, I know that the response I receive will be a "form letter," signed by the representative, and sent to each and every person who writes on that issue. This is generally the way constituents hear from a congressional office and comes from a legislative assistant who is knowledgeable on that issue and has prepared a "position statement" based on the representative's or senator's position.

Every time I contact Congressman Mike Parker's office, whether by phone, by mail, or in person, he and his staff are always responsive and most helpful.

Last fall, I wrote Mr. Parker asking him to vote against the GOALS 2000 – Educate America Act. In a two-page response, he told me why he was supporting this legislation and enclosed an eight-page summary of the bill for my information.

Several weeks ago, I visited Parker's Washington office. I knew prior to my arrival that the Congressman would not be in because it was Monday, the House was in recess, and most representatives were in their home districts.

I was graciously received, talked separately with two legislative aides on specific issues of concern, and received a letter upon my return home, thanking me for my visit.

Though I am no particular lover of Democrats, it is to counter unfair charges being leveled at Mike Parker and his office that I feel a response is in order, especially in light of the fact that a recent candidate survey I mailed one-month ago to Marshall Bennett has not to date received a response.

The Clarion-Ledger
Tuesday, April 18, 1995

Let's Visit "Our" Crown Jewel –The Mississippi Governor's Mansion

Sometimes one can almost hear the walls of the Mansion reverberating with the sounds of Mississippi past

The 153-year old Governor's Mansion, nestled in the very heart of Mississippi, shaded by giant oaks and surrounded by stately gardens, is one of the State's greatest treasures and unquestionably the crown jewel of Mississippi's heritage.

The Mississippi Governor's Mansion is the country's second oldest executive residence that has been (except for time of war, renovation and restoration) continually occupied by governors and their families. The oldest? Virginia's Mansion, built in 1813.

In 1842, architect William Nichols completed a plan for "a suitable house for the governor in the town of Jackson" at an approximate cost of $50,000. It was of the Greek or Classic Revival style with "plain republican simplicity, as best comporting with the dignity of the state."

Following the Civil War and Reconstruction, the Mansion fell into such disrepair that Gov. Edward Favor Noel (1908-12) refused to reside in the house, and it seemed doomed for demolition.

But through the efforts of patriotic women's organizations whose rallying cry was "not to destroy what Sherman would not burn," the Mansion was saved. In 1908, state funds were provided for renovation of the historic portion of the house and to add a two-story family annex to the back of the building.

Sixty-three years later, the Mansion was once again in dire need of attention. Gov. John Bell Williams and his family were forced to move out in 1971 when the Mansion was declared unsafe by state building inspectors.

During the administration of William L. Waller (1972-76), a $2.7 million project restored the "rich home of our heritage" to a close approximation of its original form. First Lady Carroll Waller worked with consultants to investigate original construction details and to oversee the purchase of

19th century furnishings. It was largely because of her efforts that the Mississippi Governor's Mansion was designated a National Historic Landmark in 1975.

Since Gov. Tilghman Tucker first occupied the Mansion in 1842, forty-three Mississippi governors have called the Mansion home.

Confederate and Union soldiers, heads of state, entertainers, artists, sports figures and just plain folk have crossed the threshold of the stately mansion at 300 East Capitol Street.

As a Mansion Docent (a volunteer who conducts tours), I have had the pleasure and unique opportunity to open the door to many of these visitors.

When meeting guests – a Japanese businessman, honeymooners from Texas, Russian legal journalists, retirees from Florida, a visiting diplomat from Nigeria, "snowbirds" from up north, tour and convention groups, and hundreds of school children – I'm always filled with pride to hear the "oohs and ahhs" in appreciation of the beauty of "our home".

School children hear the story of "The Voyage of Life", as they view four paintings from the school of Thomas Cole and presently on loan to the Mansion; they press together with unrestrained curiosity to get a look at the geometric design stenciled on the original pine floor and hidden under the carpet of the Back Rose Parlor.

Young and old alike enjoy hearing that former President and Mrs. George Bush were honored with a dinner in the State Dining Room just before Christmas and in 1992, Arnold Schwarzenegger enjoyed healthful oatmeal with brown sugar, skim milk, and fresh fruit as the breakfast guest of Gov. and Mrs. Fordice.

Antique buffs are shown some of our priceless treasures: the three "signed" pieces in the Mansion collection and the irreplaceable, circa 1800, Worchester cachepots on the mantle in the Front Rose Parlor, among others.

Sometimes one can almost hear the walls of the Mansion reverberating with the sounds of Mississippi past.

If you listen closely, you too, might hear:

- The laughter of some of the twenty-one children of Gov. William McWillie (1857-1859) or the marriage vows being recited by his daughter, Ann, the first Mansion bride.
- The cry of the first baby born in the Mansion to Ann McWillie.
- The strains of "Army and Navy Forever" sung by General William T. Sherman and his men, as they dined in the Governor's Mansion in July of 1863, following the Siege of Vicksburg.
- The weeping of the servants in the upstairs bedroom at the death of Gov. Thomas Bailey (1943-1946), and the voice of Fielding Wright as he took the oath of office in the Gold Parlor just below.
- The magnificent voice of Leontyne Price as she sang `God Bless America' following a

dinner party hosted by Gov. and Mrs. William Winter (1980-1984).

If you haven't stopped by "our house" lately, now is the perfect time for a visit. Relish the beauty of the house and gardens; listen for the voices of the past; and take advantage of a tour conducted by a knowledgeable docent and free to anyone who calls at the West Street Gate between the hours of 9:30 and 11:00 A.M., Tuesday through Friday.

The Clarion-Ledger
Tuesday, October 15, 1996

Rep. Thompson Out of Step with Mississippi Congressional Delegation

What 2nd District U.S. Rep. Bennie Thompson reflects in his votes can't possibly be what the majority wants.

In 1993, when 2nd District U.S. Rep. Bennie Thompson was elected to fill the seat of Mike Espy, he arrived in Congress just in time to vote for President Clinton's tax-and-spend budget plan. That vote was to be the first of many votes by Thompson designed to pour more and more dollars into government programs that are bankrupting this nation both financially and morally.

Thompson voted to use federal funds to (unconstitutionally) deploy U.S. troops to Bosnia. He voted against Medicare revisions that would reduce the out-of-control growth of Medicare over the next seven years and would save the average household $2,692; he voted for an amendment to kill new limitations on lobbying by groups that receive federal grants; and he voted "present" on a bill that would prohibit the secretary of the Treasury from robbing federal retirement or Social Security trust funds to pay public debts.

If you read *The Clarion-Ledger's* Congressional Roll Call that reports the votes in Congress, you've probably noticed how often Mr. Thompson is out of step with Mississippi's other four representatives. If they vote "yes," he votes "no;" if they vote "no," he votes "yes." Fellow Democrat Gene Taylor is the next most liberal Mississippi congressman and occasionally votes along party lines with Thompson.

According to political columnist Bill Minor, Bennie Thompson "frightens a lot of white people because of his bluntness and tough talk that has the sound of black power rhetoric." It ought to scare many of his black constituents as well, because what Thompson reflects in his votes can't possibly be what the majority of blacks in his district support.

Thompson voted "yes" on a bill to reject the automatic death penalty for drug kingpins; he voted "yes" to lifetime prison sentences rather than new death penalties in the House crime bill; and voted "no" on a bill that would provide more money for prisons and police and less money for liberal "crime prevention: social programs like "midnight basketball leagues" and "dance classes." This in the face of public outcry to remove drug dealers from our streets and get violent criminals behind bars.

On issues critical to the family, he voted against the balanced budget bill that dramatically cut taxes for working families and provided a $500 per-child tax credit; he voted against an amendment to provide vouchers to low-income students in the District of Columbia that would permit parents to decide where to send their children to school; he voted against an amendment to prohibit Washington, D.C. from giving homosexual couples and other unmarried "domestic partners" the same health care and benefits normally reserved for married couples; and his most heinous vote was against the bill that would prohibit partial-birth abortion. That means Bennie Thompson thinks it's all right to kill a baby as it is being born.

The people of the 2nd Congressional District are not fairly represented in Mr. Thompson's Washington office. His employment practices fail to meet the black/white litmus test of today's political correctness.

On a recent visit to the office, I didn't see a white face there. If a white congressman failed to have proper black/white quota, he'd be so maligned he'd probably have to resign. But for some reason, when a racial imbalance exists in favor of blacks, it goes unnoticed and unreported.

My interest in education issues has prompted me to visit most Mississippi congressional offices when I'm in Washington to lobby for or against specific legislation. I'm often asked, "Who do you represent?" I always say, "Myself." I don't like that question because it makes me feel like the individual citizen doesn't count, that it's only the special interest groups that have the ear of our representatives.

I've learned the routine. On Monday, things are slow in the office; the congressman is rarely in. That's true of most Fridays, too. If the congressman is not available to see you, you'll talk to a legislative assistant who is generally knowledgeable about the topic that you wish to discuss.

On this particular visit, a Monday, I had a pleasant 20-minute chat with a legislative assistant. Upon my departure, I signed the guest register.

Several days after arriving home, I received a very nice letter from Bennie Thompson thanking me for my visit, expressing great appreciation for my views, noting the fact that I had taken time to express them personally, and saying that it had been a pleasure to meet me.

Meet me? He wasn't even there!

Every congressional office uses form letters, prepared on just about every subject, ready to be mailed. But to have a staff member so inept that a personal letter of this sort goes out over the congressman's signature when the congressman wasn't even in the office is inexcusable.

Bennie Thompson is out of step with the Mississippi congressional delegation. He rates a zero on almost all conservative voting score cards, with even his closest Democratic counterpart, Gene Taylor, scoring 75 percent or higher. He's a slick politician, manipulating and using many of his own people to build a political power base and providing little or no representation for the minority white population of his district.

In my opinion, the people of the 2nd Congressional District of Mississippi deserve better.

The Clarion-Ledger
Monday, November 11, 1996

This is a Special Time to Visit the Mississippi War Memorial Building

A DAR centennial project brochure now preserves the history of the War Memorial Building in printed form.

Sometimes there's a special place, "a hallowed place" that stirs the memory of the sacrifices of stalwart men and women. These memorials, erected as physical reminders of war, can be found at the Vietnam Memorial in Washington, the Tomb of the Unknown Soldier in Arlington National Cemetery, the Confederate Battlefield in Vicksburg, and the Mississippi War Memorial Building Jackson.

It was February, 1995, in the quiet, solitude of the courtyard of the War memorial Building at 120 North State Street that Wanda Fowler, of Gunnison, received the inspiration that would result in the publication of a brochure that would preserve the history of the War Memorial Building in printed form.

Fowler, in recounting that day, marveled at her experience in the courtyard. "I was absolutely enthralled. There wasn't a soul there. I felt in awe ... like there was a presence there. It was just a great experience."

Her special interest was in the doors to the building. "I came upon the doors with amber glass panels and 26 different etchings. They were magnificent. I just stood looking at the doors and really marveled at what was on them, and what it took to make them," Fowler said.

As Wanda Fowler related her experience to the members of her Mississippi Delta Chapter of the Daughters of the American Revolution (DAR), her enthusiasm led to a year-long project. Since 1996 marked the centennial of DAR in the state of Mississippi, the chapter enthusiastically embraced the idea of a brochure as a centennial project that would further the objectives of the society in promoting education, history and patriotism.

Intensive research provided information.

The War Memorial Building was designed by E. L. Malvaney and built by the crews with the Works Progress Administration (WPA) in 1939 and 1940 at a cost of approximately $285,000. It was remodeled in 1973 at a cost of "several million dollars."

The tall, stately, square concrete columns of the facade mark the entrance of the courtyard where the American flag flies at half-mast as the official memorial tomb to the state's war dead.

Inscribed on the tomb are these words: "May this symbol stand guard over the ideals and purposes for which Mississippians suffered and may it serve as inspiration to us to shield forever the fragile quality of liberty."

Three sets of identical ornate aluminum doors, each portraying 26 etchings of war implements, surround eight octagonal amber glass windows.

The etchings range from 400 B.C. Greek war shields and swords to American bombers and battleships of 1940. The 26 etchings include depictions of a Roman warship, Saracen crossed swords of 750 A.D., the Nina, Pinta, and the Santa Maria, Indian tomahawks, and a "Whistling Dick" cannon from Vicksburg.

To Fowler's amazement, no records were uncovered to disclose the names of the talented artisans who did the etchings or how the scenes depicted were selected.

Portraits of Indian fighter Samuel Dale, Confederacy President Jefferson Davis, and John A. Quitman, a general and early governor of Mississippi, are carved in stone over the entrance portal.

A lintel border of aluminum panels portrays three versions of Miss Liberty with battle scenes to her side. The battles depicted include: Ackia, 1736, where the Chickasaws defeated the French; Buena Vista, 1847, where Zachary Taylor defeated Santa Anna of Mexico; New Orleans, 1815, where Andrew Jackson defeated the British; Vicksburg, 1863, where Grant defeated Pemberton; San Juan Hill, 1898, where American troops defeated the Spanish; and Belleau Wood, 1918, where American Marines defeated the Germans.

Inside the foyer is a marble wall engraved with a concise history of Mississippi. Aluminum panels depict lumbering, agriculture, Beauvoir – the home of Jefferson Davis – and the Old Capitol topped with cornices of shocks of grain.

Wanda Fowler's hope, shared by the members of Mississippi Delta Chapter DAR, is that *The Doors of the Mississippi War Memorial Building* will be distributed to schools for use by students studying Mississippi history. Brochures are available, free of charge, from Fowler at P.O. Box 74, Gunnison, MS 38746 or can be picked up at the American legion Office in the War Memorial building.

Each year on November 11, Veteran's Day, Mississippians gather at the memorial to remember those Mississippians who gave their lives ... 704 in World War I, 4,185 in World War II, 409 in Korea, and 637 in Vietnam, "to shield forever the fragile quality of liberty."

If you have never visited the War Memorial Building, Veterans Day may be a good time to go. Take your children with you so that they, too, may experience the awe and wonder of a hallowed place and learn first-hand the lesson that "peace shall come to those who strive for peace".

The Clarion-Ledger

Tuesday, February 17, 1998

Maybe We Should Just Start Fresh On Voter Registration

The Clarion-Ledger editorial board and several liberal columnists have had a field day beating up on Rep. Bill Denny for his tenacious stand against Motor Voter.

Denny's "diabolic scheme" isn't about "disenfranchising individual voters, erecting barriers to registration or discriminating against the poor, the young and the elderly".

Instead, Denny's crusade is about the integrity of the voting process and the protection of the ballot against fraudulent or fictitious voter registration.

If we're serious about modifying voter registration procedures to allow for ease of registration while at the same time maintaining the integrity of the voter rolls, I'd like to propose that we start from scratch.

Throw out all previous registrations.

Establish registration sites at drivers license bureaus, schools, social service centers, the local Wal-Mart.

Require proper identification of all registrants. The year 2000 would be a good time to start ... a new year, a new century, new voting rolls.

Remove name if not voting

To counter low voter turn-out, if after two years, the registrant has not cast a vote, the person's name would be automatically removed from the roll.

If registering is easy, no one should mind doing it again.

I can't understand why there's so much fuss about showing identification.

Do "Mississippi poor folks" never cash a check, sign-up for Social Security and welfare assistance, or catch a plane?

If these folks don't have identification, it would be to their advantage to get some.

Everyone should be prepared to produce identification before being given a ballot.

For a number of years, I worked as the manager of my local precinct.

The poll books were full of deceased residents, former neighbors who had moved away, and young adults who had left the nest to establish residences elsewhere.

With more than 1500 registered voters in the precinct, it's virtually impossible for precinct workers to personally know each voter.

In the general election of 1978, Charles Evers was a candidate for the U.S. Senate, and Mississippi was inundated with federal voting officials.

Local polling places were filled with poll watchers, and my precinct was no exception. A poll watcher from the Ever's camp had done her homework.

Just by using the telephone book and checking the addresses of those registered in the precinct, she successfully (and legally) challenged a large number of voters who no longer resided in the precinct.

Easy to tip balance

The incident made me aware of how someone with knowledge of the voting system could tip the balance in favor of a particular candidate and by reversing the process, corrupt individuals could use the system to vote the dead or some unknown whose name has been on the precinct books for 20 years.

If I had my way, all voters would be required to be literate. Oops! Sounds like discrimination.

Common sense dictates that if a voter can't read the ballot, his ability to vote accurately is severely diminished and certainly subject to manipulation by unscrupulous individuals.

Rather than focusing on ease of voter registration, we need to begin an educational process to stimulate voting as a civic duty.

With Americans staying away from the polls in record numbers, I doubt that adding more names to the voting rolls will produce more voters, especially qualified ones.

The right to vote is one of the highest privileges granted to American citizens. Like education, if we continue to devalue it as something that everyone has and obtainable with no effort, voting could soon become a futile and worthless exercise and the ballot not worth the paper it's printed on.

The Clarion-Ledger
Letter to the Editor
Sunday, September 20, 1998

Mississippians Are Deserving of a Cut in State Taxes

Read my lips: Mississippians are entitled to be on the receiving end of a tax cut.

If the two legislative appropriations committee chairmen, Sen. Dick Hall and Rep. Charlie Capps, don't think hard-working Mississippians deserve a tax break, they have been in office too long and have lost touch with the people they represent. An income tax cut should receive top priority.

If, as Sen. Hall stated, "there is not any serious consideration, that I know of, of any kind of a tax reduction," then there should be.

And if Rep. Capps sees no great public demand for a tax cut based on the reaction he received when he mentioned a tax reduction to a civic club in Cleveland, I'd like to invite him to a few civic clubs to which I belong.

If early estimates are correct that a record high budget of $3.4 billion is on the table for Fiscal 2000, the least the 10 elite members of the Joint Legislative Budget Committee could do is throw a few crumbs from the table to those who deserve and need it the most.

Those crumbs – a proposed 10 percent income-tax rebate estimated at up to $100 million – would be an across-the-board refund to every working Mississippian.

And please spare us the cliché that more money is needed for education because "If we don't take care of them they'll end up on welfare or in Parchman." Government involvement in education, which began approximately 40 years ago, has done nothing but contribute to public education's downward spiral.

It's time for the taxpayers of the state to let their elected representatives know that a tax cut is long overdue. And, at the same time we should remind our esteemed public officials that it's not their money that they're spending, but ours, and that *we* the people know better than *they* how best to spend *our* money.

Much gratitude is owed Gov. Kirk Fordice for the leadership he has provided in continuing to work for a tax cut for the people who are the most deserving – hard-working Mississippians.

The Clarion-Ledger
Tuesday, June 6, 2000

Archives Building Exciting Addition to the Capital City

The recent ground breaking for the new Mississippi Archives and History building in Jackson initiated a new chapter in the history of Mississippi's Department of Archives and History.

It couldn't have come at a better time.

Mississippi's archival collections have expanded beyond the storage facilities in the Charlotte Capers Building.

Because of storage problems, valuable and significant collections are being lost to other states whose institutions can provide the room to house them.

For years, archival staff has lacked adequate workspace and researchers using the Search Room facilities, are frequently frustrated by cramped quarters and their inability to access research documents.

Recognizing the Department's critical needs, the Mississippi Legislature passed legislation in 1998 to fund a major expansion project.

Greatly expanded

The new Archives and History Building will measure 140,575 square feet and contain greatly expanded and modernized archival storage and work space.

The Search Room will be approximately four times the size of the current facility and will accommodate a large open-stack area.

The new building will also house new programs, including an Electronic Records Project and the Local Government Records Office.

The total budget for the new building is $25,588,252.

Appropriately, the new facility will be named for former Gov. William F. Winter, who was elected to the Board of Trustees of the Mississippi Department of Archives and History in 1957, and has served as its president since 1969.

The Legislature has also authorized planning for the renovation and restoration of the War Memorial Building, the Charlotte Capers Building and the Old Capitol and for construction of new museum space behind the Old Capitol Museum.

Mississippi can take pride in having the second-oldest archives and history department in the nation. The independent, non-political agency was created in 1902.

Over its 98-year history, the department has had five directors: Dunbar Rowland, William D. McCain, Charlotte Capers, R. A. McLemore and Elbert R. Hilliard, the present department director, who assumed the position in 1973.

Good time to visit

The state's archival collections have been housed in many locations. First placed at Concord, the former residence of the Spanish provincial governors at Natchez in 1798, the archives were moved a total of 10 times before being placed in a building designed specifically as an archival repository.

That building, named for Charlotte Capers, has housed the collections since 1971.

The next move to the William F. Winter Archives and History Building, projected to be completed by spring of 2002, will assure that Mississippi's archival facilities are adequate for many years to come.

If you've never seen the "Egyptian" mummy, the museum's most popular attraction for four decades before being deemed a fake, or the size 20 shoes worn by a soldier during World War I, there's no better time than now to visit the Old Capitol Museum.

Until June 30, and free to the public, an outstanding exhibit, *Preserving the Past, Planning for the Future,* provides visitors an insight into the evolution of the department and documents its many noteworthy events, exhibitions, and personalities of the past century.

The Clarion-Ledger
Tuesday, August 8, 2000

Reinstate Term Limits for House Speaker's Post

The three most powerful positions in Mississippi government are governor, lieutenant governor, and speaker of the House. The governor and lieutenant governor are chosen in state-wide elections with limited terms in office, while the speaker of the House is elected by his peers in the Mississippi House with no term limits.

In 1987, a reform movement led by the "House 26" brought a change in House rules to limit the speaker's term to two four-year terms, thus weakening the speaker's authority.

C.B. "Buddie" Newman, who held the position of speaker for twelve years – from 1976-1988 – was ousted.

Two terms promised

Claiming the need to replace the "old guard" and citing the importance to keep the House's balance of power from tipping toward the speaker, Tim Ford was elected largely on his promise to uphold the two-term limit.

But how soon campaign promises are forgotten. Ford's enthusiasm for a limited term quickly faded once he was enthroned as speaker and in 1993, the two-term limit rule was lifted.

Many legislators believed that Ford quietly orchestrated the switch back to the "old guard" regime.

There is no question that Tim Ford has been a good speaker of the House. He brought in some needed changes, providing a "democratized" chamber far more open than the Newman era. During his twelve years as speaker, he has provided leadership and presided capably.

Why then should his term as speaker be limited?

There is a fine line between leadership and dictatorship. Some believe that the House speaker is the most powerful person in MS government because he appoints committee chairmen and assigns bills to committees – powers that can mean life or death for a bill.

He also shapes debate on the House floor and can prove to be a stumbling block to getting things done. It's a well-known fact that staying in the speaker's good graces is a wise move.

Retirement perk example

A case in point is the recent retirement perk debacle. Don't think for a minute that Tim Ford was not fully aware of what was going on and gave his support to the stealth legislation.

And you don't have to look far to see how many of Ford's cohorts who keep the speaker in power, have profited with key committee chairmanships.

This year, Ford was elected to his fourth term as speaker. He will have been speaker 16 years by the time his term is up. That's four years longer than the "old guard" regime of Buddie Newman.

If the terms of the governor and lieutenant governor are limited, then why not the position of Speaker of the House? It is obvious that another revolution to limit the term of the House speaker is in order.

There were enough shenanigans in this year's legislative session to sound a wake-up call for a leadership change. As the old saying goes, "Power tends to corrupt and absolute power corrupts absolutely."

In a 1993 interview, Tim Ford was quoted as saying: "You certainly can get stagnant in the same place. I certainly don't think I'll be speaker forever, I can tell you that."

I hope you're right, Tim, I hope you're right!

The Clarion-Ledger
Tuesday, March 27, 2001

Motor Voter Bill Helped to Create Election Turmoil

The 2000 presidential election added some new words like "chad" and "dimpled ballot" to our vocabularies and caused Americans to recognize the need for addressing election reform.

Let's hope that the comically inept situation that arose in Florida will prove to be the wake-up call for long overdue reform of our election process.

Congress helped create the current mess with the "Motor Voter" bill.

Some Mississippi legislative leaders, Rep. Bill Denny in particular, had the wisdom to oppose Motor Voter until it was literally forced upon us.

Motor Voter helped create the most inaccurate voting rolls in our history.

It provided a means by which citizens can register in multiple jurisdictions at the same time but lacked effective procedures to ensure that those registered are even American citizens.

Registration lists flawed

Easier sign-up provisions and overworked or incompetent election supervisors have contributed to often grossly inaccurate lists sent to local polling places to determine who is eligible to vote. In the last election, many Mississippians who registered under Motor Voter found that their registration was never recorded when they showed up at the polls.

According to a study by Scripps Howard News Service, official registration lists in the United States have become so flawed that scores of counties claim to have more voters than actual adult population.

The study based on election records in 3,189 counties and voting districts found that at least 167,968 people in these areas were still eligible to cast ballots even though they had died or moved away.

The most over-registered county in the country, according to Scripps Howard, is rural Issaquena County in west-central Mississippi.

Issaquena had 1,669 registered voters four years ago, even though census estimates put the adult population at only 1,102 people, giving the county a 151 percent registration rate.

According to Circuit Clerk Erline Fortner of Mayersville, who oversees the voter rolls, "I've never looked into this to analyze it. I just don't have the time to do that. I know some people who have family here but no longer live here do come back to vote."

Excuse me? What happened to the voting regulation that requires voters to *live in* the precinct in which they are registered?

And that's not all.

Mississippi and Michigan are tied for having the largest number of counties with impossibly bloated voter lists. Each has 28 countries that report more than 100 percent registration rates.

Not all eligible to vote

And what about the large number of voters who are non-citizens and those disenfranchised by state law because they are convicted of various crimes?

There is substantial evidence that felons voted in large numbers in some counties in Florida and Wisconsin where the presidential vote was extremely close.

The question of how best to reform the registration and election process is complex, but it is one that must be addressed in order to insure the integrity of the ballot.

Secretary of State Eric Clark, who is responsible for assuring fair and honest elections in Mississippi, should move forward immediately to restore confidence in the voting procedure.

Surely something can be done to assure that each person who votes is alive, is a United States citizen and not a convicted felon, is registered in the precinct where they live, and is allowed to vote only once.

The Clarion-Ledger
Tuesday, December 31, 2001

Why Should Anyone Oppose ID Law?

While enjoying the bowl games and downing a second helping of black-eyed peas, consider this question .... Should voters be required to produce identification before being allowed to vote?

And then ask yourself why Secretary of State, Eric Clark (D), charged with the responsibility of overseeing Mississippi elections, squashed any efforts to include Voter ID as part of the report of his hand-picked Select Task Force on Election Procedures and Technology.

The report of the Task Force isn't worth the paper it's printed on if it doesn't address Voter ID, the simplest and most cost-effective means of guarding against voter fraud.

Not a hardship

When Mr. Clark charged the Task Force to concentrate on "Florida issues" arising from the presidential election debacle, he deftly sidestepped the possibility that Voter ID would be part of the recommendations to the Mississippi Legislature. By assigning Voter ID to a subcommittee dominated by Democrats, the issue was dead-on-arrival because it was "not part of their charge".

The fallacy is that Voter ID wasn't a problem in Florida because Florida already has a Voter ID statute in place, as do 21 of 50 states, six of them being our southern neighbors.

In its August 2001 report, the National Commission on Federal Election Reform points to one of the most serious problems in America's elections – identifying who can vote. The commissioners believe that those who register and vote should be expected to identify themselves.

Those who oppose Voter ID claim it places a hardship on the poor or minority groups who may not have identification. They assert that producing identification could be intimidating to some voters or racially discriminatory.

How long are we going to fall for that ploy?

The national commission estimated that a small percentage of adults, perhaps 5 to 7 percent, do not possess a driver's license or other photo identification.

With so few people lacking identification, wouldn't it be logical to assist them in obtaining identification? Who knows? There may come a time when they need ID to cash a check or take a trip on a plane.

Arizona has a good plan. Their driver's license bureau waives the fee for a non-operating identification license.

And don't tell me these unidentified persons can't get to the driver's license bureau. They seem to be able to get to the polls to vote.

Safeguard against fraud

Or, Mississippi could take Georgia's lead by adopting a broad definition of proper identification, accepting an employer ID card, passport, birth certificate, or social security card as identification.

And as for disenfranchisement, voters are not stupid. With a little education, most will arrive at the polling place prepared to show identification. It is universally accepted in the United States that using proper ID is a safeguard against fraud and theft and most Americans want the ballot protected. If the law required uniform application for all voters, even your mother, how could anyone feel intimidated?

Voter ID shouldn't be a Democrat-Republican issue, a black-white issue, or a rich-poor issue. It's a means to eliminate voter fraud in Mississippi and assure that the election process is fair to everyone.

Legislation will be introduced in the next session to require Voter ID. Let your representative know what you think.

The Clarion-Ledger
Thursday, October 6, 2005

Lawsuits Over Flood Insurance Not the Answer

What in the world is the State Attorney General, Jim Hood, thinking? Suing insurance companies to force payment of claims outside of their legal contractual obligation is ludicrous.

If the Mississippi Coast is to rise from the devastation of Katrina, it must have a viable insurance market. Contractors must have insurance to build, and lending institutions must have insurance on mortgaged homes in order to protect their investments.

If insurance companies are forced to retroactively rewrite policies to cover any or all risks, they will either leave the state or raise insurance premiums to such an exorbitant rate that homeowners' insurance will be out of the question for many Mississippians.

Just ask your local insurance agent how many insurance companies have already left Mississippi because of the large number of claims resulting in staggering losses.

Policy a legal contract

Homeowners' policies are clearly written and most people living along any coastline in the United States cannot help being aware that they could possibly suffer property loss from storm surge when a hurricane comes ashore. That's why, in recent years, flood insurance is required for new construction in flood zones.

A policy is a legal contract between two consenting parties, in this case, the insurance company and homeowner. Before entering into any contractual agreement, the homeowner should have a full understanding of what the insurer agrees to pay if a loss is incurred. Ignorance of policy terms is no excuse.

Flood and earthquake insurance are generally not included in basic homeowners' policies and comes at an additional cost.

Most homeowners who live in areas not prone to flooding, choose not to carry flood or earthquake insurance so as to keep premiums lower. At least that's true at my house.

Mr. Hood must not have thought of those homeowners who have paid through the nose for flood insurance. How fair is it for those who didn't pay for the coverage to receive the same benefits as those who did?

Before the days of insurance, FEMA, and MEMA, hurricanes battered the southern coastline of the United States. People living in coastal areas, lacking today's early warning system and means by which to evacuate, suffered unbelievable loss of life and property. Yet the people endured.

Not having any disaster relief to put them back on their feet, and expecting none, they were self reliant. And they persevered.

'Can-do' spirit aids Coast

There is no way words can express the sorrow felt for those who suffered such devastation from Katrina, but placing blame and suing insurance companies for uninsured losses is not the way to go.

Some have proposed that the federal government offer emergency assistance for those flooded homeowners or reimburse insurance companies for water damage claims.

Sounds plausible, but we must stop expecting the "nanny state," created over the last forty years, to continually solve our problems and cure all our ills.

No matter what the risk, people will continue to build in coastal areas and flood zones; hurricanes and floods will continue to wreak havoc and destruction.

The lifeblood of a community is its people and knowing the "can-do" spirit of Mississippians, I'm confident the Mississippi Gulf Coast will weather the storm.

The Clarion-Ledger
Saturday, November 10, 2007

Excesses in Campaigning Demean Politics

That sound you hear is the collective sighs of relief from Mississippi voters worn to a frazzle by television and radio appeals, campaign mailouts, emails, phone calls, and thousands of political signs of every size and description.

With each passing election, campaigns are becoming more and more excessive and downright distasteful. It's taking obscene amounts of money to mount a campaign and keeping good folks from running for public office.

Just think of the junk mail that fills our mailboxes; the millions of dollars spent on print material and postage ... most of which is never read but dumped in the closest trash can; the millions spent on television commercials to defame an opponent's character; and the huge expense of thousands of political signs that are an eyesore to our communities.

A widely used method of reaching voters in this election that proved to be particularly irritating was the use of recorded phone messages to voters from candidates, friends, family members, or well known elected officials.

Haven't they heard of the "Do Not Call List?" My phone number is on the list because I don't want nuisance calls. Yet in the final days before the election, I received recorded messages from Benny Thompson, (I haven't spoken to him in years); Madison County Supervisor, Tim Johnson, identifying himself as "yo friend Elvis"; and at least a dozen other calls with some inane campaign message from a variety of candidates.

So hear this! In future elections, all recorded campaign messages will be duly recorded on my "Do Not Vote For List". I don't care if it's my favorite candidate or one who really needs my vote. NO candidate who insults my intelligence, disturbs me when I'm busy, wakes me from a nap, or interrupts a meal with annoying and unwanted phone calls, will get my vote.

And why is it necessary to put up so many signs?

I know that name recognition is important in political campaigns, but how many people determine who gets their vote based on 50 signs for that candidate at the polling place?

In the campaign prior to the primary, one Madison County candidate even had kids lining the streets waving signs and shouting at passersby.

Campaigns are not only excessive; they've gotten even more low-down and dirty. It's not just the mudslinging and personal attacks, but the corrupt practice of elected officials who use their office to influence the race of a particular candidate.

Political endorsements are one thing, but direct involvement and conniving to influence an election is wrong.

How sad that our election process has evolved to the crass commercialism, manipulative tactics, and personal attacks evident in almost every candidate's campaign. But the saddest reality is that campaign strategists use these techniques because they have proven effective in winning elections.

When the electorate is lazy and apathetic, too busy, or just doesn't care to make the effort to cast a ballot based on an intelligent, informed opinion, they can be easily influenced by recorded phone calls, cute TV ads, and the candidate who has the most yard signs.

Chapter V

Local Issues

The noblest service comes from nameless hands, and the best servant does his work unseen.

Oliver Wendell Holmes

The Clarion-Ledger
Tuesday, December 14, 1982

More People Need Help This Year

Each year the Salvation Army does an outstanding job of seeing that may families and individuals in the Jackson area have a happy Christmas. Through the Christmas Clearinghouse, which screens applicants referred by social welfare agencies, those who are in need of assistance can be matched with someone (group or individual) who can meet their needs.

Recently, while volunteering a few hours at the Clearinghouse, I was conscious of the large increase of applicants seeking assistance. Because of high unemployment and bleak economic times, there are more people in need of help this year than ever before. And, for the same reasons, there are fewer people volunteering assistance. With more than 1,000 cases on file, only four calls came in while I was there to "adopt" a family.

There are always good excuses to ignore the poor and needy among us. I'll deal with a few of them as follows:

- "I don't have anything to spare."
  But the needs in many cases are so small – food for an elderly couple; clothes for a toddler; or toys for children in a family with little or no income. Items supplied don't have to be new things. Any item in good condition is welcomed, and the Clearinghouse can supply the sizes and specific information on a family's needs to match what a person may have to give.

- "I don't have time and don't want to get personally involved."
  The Salvation Army will gladly accept a check or donation of clothing, food, or toys for distribution. But if you don't get personally involved, you miss a lot of the joy in helping others less fortunate than yourself. Truly, it is more blessed to give than to receive!
- "They're all on welfare and not really needy."
  All applicants are screened to determine true need. However, invariably, there will always be some who manage to cheat. The government, through funding of welfare programs, has caused charity to become obsolete – robbing us in more ways than one. Perhaps the answer is to let God be the judge of the motives of both the giver and the recipient.

What a wonderful service the Salvation Army provides for our community and state through its many projects – the Clearinghouse, the thousands of gift boxes taken to the elderly in hospitals and nursing homes at Christmas, the Toy Store where needy parents can pick several new and used toys for their children; the meals and lodging provided at the Salvation Army shelter and the help provided in disaster relief.

The Salvation Army needs our help. Please receive the joy of helping someone this Christmas by calling the Clearinghouse (948-2244 or 948-2246) to adopt a family. Or the next time you pass a bell ringer on the street, drop in a donation for the Salvation Army Christmas Relief Program.

You'll be glad you did!

The Clarion-Ledger
Letter to the Editor
Undated – (1988)

Jackson No. 1 Nationally In Daily Bible Readings

Mississippi can't be too bad a place to live. A recent nationwide marketing study by Standard Rate & Data Service of Wilmette, Ill., ranking the top 100 markets of Bible readers, shows that the state's Capitol City of Jackson is No. 1 with 36.14 percent of households reading the Bible daily. The national average is 18.2 percent.

Mississippi may be considered the third least desirable state in which to live by the business executives recently surveyed by the Marketing Research Institute, but in the things that really count, Mississippi is No.1!

The Clarion-Ledger
Tuesday, March 14, 1989

Finds Much to Be Desired in Cleanup After Ice Storm

More than a month after the ice storm, Jackson looks like a disaster area! The handling of storm debris pick-up has been a disgrace.

I think that the citizens of Jackson are entitled to the following explanations:

- Whose idea was it to divide the city into zones for cleanup? This plan provided service for some residents but denied it to others. If regular scheduled pick-ups had been continued (even if only six blocks a day could be serviced,) then at least area residents could see some progress in cleanup efforts. I haven't seen a trash truck anywhere since the storm.
- Whose idea was it to use parks as a collection point? Parham Bridges Park is used and enjoyed by many people as a walking trail. To allow a public park to become a public dump is inexcusable.

A well-managed program would have designated centrally located disposal sites not used by the general public where minimum damage would be done and daily trash removal would be provided.

When I read the article in the March 8 edition of *The Clarion-Ledger* containing the comments of Buford Clark of Waste Management, I was disgusted. If the "carrot" of adequate trash pick-up is an enticement for extending a three-year contract with the city, I'd tell Waste Management to pack its bags.

Almost everyone suffered financial losses from the storm – the utility companies, local businesses and property owners. If waste disposal can't be handled efficiently by the company presently employed, the city fathers should initiate a cleanup contract elsewhere and terminate the one with Waste Management.

Mr. Clark needs to learn the old work ethic that doing a good job at the present task is the best way to assume a job for the future.

The Clarion-Ledger
Letter to the Editor
Tuesday, January 7, 1992

Will Our Children's Children Handle Legacy We Leave?

I used to be proud to say that I was from Jackson until it became the murder capitol of Mississippi and the home of topless bars.

I used to leave my doors unlocked and felt safe in my home until I became afraid of being robbed or raped.

I used to go to evening cultural and civic events and shop the malls at night until I became afraid to venture out after dark.

I used to trust our elected officials to do what was best for our city, state and country until I saw that they do what is politically expedient and in their own best interests.

I used to go to football games until I saw a drunken student physically and verbally assault his date in the parking lot.

I used to enjoy going to the movies until the violence, foul language, and explicit sex of the films made it disgusting.

I used to watch television until my intelligence and sensitivity was insulted by the programming.

I used to enjoy shopping until inefficiency and incompetency filled the marketplace.

What has happened to law and order?

When did we allow promiscuity to replace decency?

Why has laziness and incompetency replaced a "job well done"?

Where have all the heroes gone?

And what kind of legacy do we leave our children and our childrens' children?

~ ~ ~ ~ ~ ~ ~ ~ ~ ~

In the early 1990s, I became interested in the Jackson Public Schools and the programs that were being used in the classrooms.

Quite truthfully, I was astounded at the mismanagement and outright education malpractice that I found. I attended school board meetings, studied curriculum and annual budgets and while Jackson Public Schools mirrored the larger problems in public education, I was outraged at the misuse of tax dollars and became greatly concerned for the children who were stuck in failing schools.

I have included articles written during that time that address specific issues.

The Clarion-Ledger
Sunday, June 2, 1991

Should Jackson Voters OK Public School Bond Referendum? NO!

On June 4, taxpayers of the city of Jackson are being asked to approve the Jackson Public School's $74.9 million bond referendum, adding more funds to an already staggering school budget.

Last year, the 1989-1990 JPS budget was $140 million plus, an increase of almost 300 percent over the school budget of 10 years ago. This year, the budget is over $145 million. Yet, once again, the taxpayer is asked to provide the funds for an array of "critical needs" to the tune of $74.9 million.

To put these figures into perspective, taxpayers are presently assessed a 68.15 millage rate which goes into the coffers of the Jackson Public Schools compared to 50.12 mills for the City of Jackson.

If voters approve all 10 bond issue projects, the 17.5 mill tax increase will bring the tax burden for the school budget to 85.65 mills or 1-1/2 times the taxes that go for the cost of city government.

Add to this astronomical increase the fact that the Mississippi County Supervisors Association, in March of 1989, implemented, with legislative approval, an up to 7 percent automatic annual tax increase in ad valorem taxes which can be applied to each school district without voter approval.

These drastically increased education expenditures might be tolerable if the taxpayers got their money's worth.

According to a February 25 *Clarion-Ledger* article, reporting 1988-89 American College Test (ACT) scores, Jackson students averaged a 14.1 overall score (15.1 for students enrolled in a college preparatory core curriculum.) Jackson students' average ACT score is almost one point below the *minimum* required for admission to any Mississippi university.

The article reported that Jackson, the largest public school district in the state, with the highest paid and most well-educated teachers, and with one of the highest local education tax levies and the largest operating budget in the state, was ranked 127th out of Mississippi's 152 districts.

If more money were the answer, we should have been off the top of the charts in comparative education achievements!

In my opinion, one example of extravagant spending is the $1.6 million in salaries paid to 29 "administrative officials."

How do these salaries compare to salaries paid to our police and firemen who are asked to put their lives on the line every day?

Another glaring extravagance is the $483,820 budgeted this year for travel by local school board members and school employees. It's difficult to envision how a local school board could reasonably justify annual travel expenditures of this magnitude while asking the taxpayers to underwrite an additional $74.9 million upon claims of "critical" financial needs.

Instead of being told by school officials that all but 18 of 57 Jackson schools are already air conditioned and that money has been set aside to air condition seven more this summer, leaving only 11 of 57 schools without air conditioning, individuals who compose the public must ferret out this information for themselves.

Rather than succumbing to the intensive campaign being waged for the bond issue, the taxpayer should be asking how money already allocated to the Jackson Public Schools is spent. With an appointive school board answerable to no one, especially the taxpayer, those answers are hard to come by.

With our city's tax base rapidly crumbling, with more citizens fleeing the city every day to escape escalating taxes, and at a time when the country is in a recession, voters should say enough is enough!

Until the education bureaucracy is required to become accountable to the public for the product they produce – a well-educated student – and provide a dollar's value for every dollar spent, the taxpayer should not support "a bond with our schools."

If we vote for the $74.9 million bond issue, we pay twice for education ... with our taxes and by our failure to provide Jackson students with the high educational standards necessary to become responsible and productive citizens.

The Clarion-Ledger
Monday, March 2, 1992

Jackson Public Schools Students Don't Need Multicultural Education

Multiculturalism is a prescription for dividing students into ethnic and racial groups by teaching a separateness.

The Jackson School Board recently approved a 10-point plan to ensure the active role of multicultural education for Jackson students.

Those of us who try hard to support the public school system of Jackson question the "social engineering" programs that have replaced mastery of knowledge with the latest educational fad.

In my opinion, the emphasis that is being placed on "global education" and other unessential programs is one of the primary reasons Johnny can't read, write, or do arithmetic.

Even liberal historian, Arthur M. Schlesinger, has attacked multicultural education. In his most recent book, *The Disuniting of America*, Schlesinger states strong opposition to the growing trend of emphasizing ethnic differences rather than American unity.

He notes that "the new ethnic gospel in its militant form rejects the unifying concept of a unique American identity, rejects the ideal of individuals from all nations melted into a new race, rejects the ideals of assimilation and integration, rejects the common culture and underlying philosophy that America is not a nation of individuals at all but a nation of groups, that ethnicity is the defining experience for most Americans."

Multicultural curriculum and textbooks threaten Western civilization, Judeo-Christian morals, and cultural values by rewriting language to include "Language Sensitivity", emphasizing conformity of thought, and excluding comparative judgments.

Regarding the controversy over curriculum and the idea that we should replace the study of Western culture, Schlesinger states, "It's not that Western culture is superior to other cultures, it is that it is for better or worse our culture, and we better master it."

He also criticizes those who want to revise history: "It may be lamentable that dead white European males played a large part in shaping our history, but that's the way it was, and to pretend otherwise would be to falsify history."

Schlesinger is disturbed to see multiculturalism making its way into the nation's system of public education, one of the primary modes of assimilation into the American mainstream.

One part of the bond referendum taxpayers approved last June included $1.3 million for library books to bring all school libraries up to accreditation standards. JPS stated at the time that the money was needed "to purchase books for all schools to reflect multicultural curriculum". For that reason, I voted NO! I don't want the money that I pay in taxes for education to be used by the JPS School Board "to ensure the active role of multicultural education."

I also don't appreciate the "financially strapped" public schools sponsoring paid newspaper ads promoting Black History Month. I hope I live long enough to see February designated as American History Month – where the achievements of ALL great Americans – both black and white – are recognized.

I, along with many others interested in quality education, oppose the plan for this five-year initiative which, according to Dr. Ben Canada, JPS Superintendent, would "increase awareness of different learning styles, both in the curriculum and in the classroom, which are related to cultural differences in areas such as race, sex, language and socioeconomic status".

In a nutshell, multiculturalism is a prescription for dividing students into separate ethnic and racial groups by teaching separateness rather than American unity and reverence for our common heritage.

The goal of public education should be the mastery of information rather than emphasizing a "politically correct" social policy that promotes ethnic separatism and heightens racial tensions.

If, as Dr. Canada has stated, Jackson does have "a nationwide reputation for multicultural education", then shame on us!

The Northside Sun
"As I See It"
Thursday, July 15, 1993

JPS Should Be Accountable to Taxpayers

ONE OF THE major problems facing the Jackson Public Schools is accountability to Jackson taxpayers on the part of the JPS administration and JPS Board of Trustees.

Having recently attended three meetings of the board when a series of budget hearings were held, I can attest to the fact that the accountability factor is very much in question.

On February 17, 1993, the Jackson School Board in a closed executive session increased the base salary of the district superintendent by 10 percent effective April 1, 1993, with no announcement to the public of their action.

With the raise, Dr. Ben Canada, Jackson's superintendent, now receives an annual base salary of $110,000 which is supplemented by $5,000 a year from local businessmen and another $20,000 annually placed in an escrow account and will be paid (plus interest) to Dr. Canada if he remains superintendent until 1997.

Add $1,000 per month travel allotment ($12,000 annually) for wear and tear on his car (for which he doesn't have to record mileage) and it adds up to $127,000 a year plus – the plus is for all of the hidden perks that I don't know about.

Dr. Canada oversees the administration of 56 district schools with 33,500 pupils.

BY COMPARISON, the state superintendent receives an annual salary of approximately $92,000 and has the oversight of 149 school districts in the state (including Jackson) with 500,000 pupils in grades K-12.

It makes one wonder why Dr. Canada continues to interview for out-of-state positions with pay much less than his present salary. He announced at the conclusion of the budget hearings that his latest withdrawal from consideration as superintendent of the Montgomery County, Alabama schools came after "a lot of soul-searching" and that his "commitment to Jackson and the children compelled me to withdraw."

If Dr. Canada truly has a commitment to Jackson, what's he doing interviewing for a job in Montgomery with a reported annual salary of $73,000 or more than a 40 percent decrease in income?

A recently conducted performance audit on operations of JPS by the state auditor's office showed that money could be saved by trimming administrators and improving fund management. It also pointed to the need for department heads to justify each spending request during the budget process and that board members should have more responsibility for budget amendments while the director of finance should have less.

THE NORTHSIDE Sun reported in a July 9, 1992 article that the public relations office of JPS has a budget more than twice that of public information offices in three larger school districts in neighboring states. At that time the PR office had a staff of 15 and a budget which had increased from $425,081 in 1991-92 to $586,815 in 1992-93, a jump of $161,734.

During budget hearings, Dr. Canada explained that a "mistake" had been made last year by lumping pupil placement and the "partners in education program" with public information, thus reflecting large staffs and budgets that in effect were three different programs.

Well, this year the budget breakdown has public information at $435,053, partners in education $97,614, and pupil placement $127,969 for a total budget of $660,636. What cost us $586,815 last year has gone up $73,821. Take that, Mr. and Ms. Taxpayer!

One of the JPS Board members suggested that in the future any misinformation published in local papers should be immediately corrected by school officials.

Please prove my information incorrect! It's difficult for us common folk to follow budgetary decisions, and to tell you the truth, it would take a genius to follow the money trail.

To sit in on the marathon budget sessions is an experience in itself. I was told by a school official who attended such sessions for years, that it is almost impossible for anyone to gain an insight into how dollars are actually spent. I can see why.

I APPLAUD the "No" vote on the budget by two of the board members, Tim Medley and Mona Weber. To Mr. Medley's credit, he continually questioned department expenditures and asked why many departments did not expend the budgeted amount for 92-93 but requested the same amount, or in many cases, more funding for 93-94.

Parents raised questions concerning budgeted items such as the Reentry Program that spent $3,270 when $640,620 had been budgeted for 92-93 and was included in the 93-94 budget at $72,830, or the student activities fund which spent $177,531 of $337,401 budgeted, but was in the 93-94 budget at $325,698. This type of pyramid budgeting invites increased spending.

I continually heard that budgetary increases were due to mandated programs and regulations. This is an example of what has happened in public education.

When government becomes involved, expect "mandates" that result in more bureaucracy and increased spending. Never, at any of the budget hearings, did I hear anyone ask who mandated these requirement or question if any effort has been made to reverse edicts that place a burden on the school system.

THE FINAL outcome is that the JPS Board approved a $171.8 million budget for 1993-94 that will result in an estimated two mill tax increase.

The current millage rate for school taxes is 72.55 mills. With the increase, the district's levy will be about 74.82 mills. That's more than one and one half times the taxes that go for the total operating budget of the City of Jackson!

The increase will generate $7.5 million for capital improvements that voters approved in a 1991 bond issue. While school officials claim that the two mill increase is for bonded indebtedness that taxpayers have already approved and is not a result of the budget, the bottom line is that taxpayers will be paying more.

Not reported in news coverage of budget hearings were the reasons given by Tim Medley for voting against the budget. He stated concern for depleting reserve funds and supports deeper cuts in budgeted amounts to avoid a shortfall next year that would produce an even greater tax increase. He pointed out that any businessman, when faced with reduced revenue, adjusts his budget by cutting expenses. Regrettably, his reasoning fell on deaf ears.

IN MY OPINION, taxpayer outrage is justified. The school administration must be reined in.

As long as they are allowed to feed unrestrained at the public trough, costs will continue to rise, more programs will be instituted, and the tax base of Jackson will continue to erode.

Jackson school administrators should recognize that they are not exempt from the same cut backs that are taking place nationwide. With the passage of the bond issue and the infusion of the one-cent state sales tax earmarked for education enhancement, it is unconscionable to continually increase the budget and even worse to use the threat that any reduction in spending "will adversely impact our children."

Jackson's corporate leaders should stop feeling good about themselves for continuing to throw more money at the problem. Instead of achieving the goal of improved education, they in effect exacerbate the situation. It's pure folly to think that more dollars will result in any sort of significant change when the money goes to the education bureaucrats who control the schools and maintain them the way they are.

I THOUGHT that when my family put down roots here more than 30 years ago that Jackson would be home for the rest of my life. But every day we come a little closer to joining the exodus to the suburbs.

Property owners of this city who are directly affected must become actively involved in achieving a change. The 1993-94 JPS budget will not be a done deal until approved by the City Council prior to the August 15 deadline. Mr. Medley has indicated that he plans "to revisit" the budget with recommended amendments.

If more streamlining is not forthcoming, I intend to be at that City Council meeting to voice my concern and I would encourage others to do the same.

The future of Jackson and responsible public education depends upon it.

The Clarion-Ledger

Monday, August 2, 1993

"Whole Language" Reading Program Failed in Jackson Public Schools

The program doesn't work because it fails to give students the key to unlock the names of unknown written words

A July 14 headline in *The Clarion-Ledger* proclaims "State students read below U.S. average" and a Sunday, July 25 edition announced that "Jackson scores drop below state's in Stanford tests."

Why can't our students read? The answer is tough medicine to swallow. Education professionals have been engaged in a form of education malpractice. They have foisted upon our school system a failed reading program called "whole language".

When it was reported by *The Clarion-Ledger* in March 1991 that JPS was instituting "a radical change in how they teach reading to elementary and middle-school pupils", I knew that we were in trouble. What I didn't know was how rapidly the failure of "whole language" would show up in test scores.

Three of the "best elementary schools" in Jackson had test scores plummet. Casey dropped six percentile points from 54.8 in 1992 to 48.3 in 1993; Spann dropped eight percentile points from 53.0 to 45.1; and Boyd dropped five percentile points from 48.4 to 43.7.

The whole language method (also known as "look and say") teaches reading by memorizing or guessing at words in context by using initial letter or picture clues. Whole language doesn't work because it fails to give a student the key to unlock the names of unknown written words by phonetically sounding out and blending the letters that make up the approximately half a million words of the English language.

This "new method" was developed in 1837 by Horace Mann based on the work of Thomas A. Gallaudet who used "look and say" to teach deaf children to read. Since deaf children have no ability to "sound out" letters, syllables or words, the constant repetition of "sight" words from a controlled vocabulary seemed to be an efficient way to teach reading.

In 1930, with the help of the father of progressive education, John Dewey, and normal schools to train teachers springing up around the country, intensive, systematic phonics (the method used successfully in the schools of this country since 1655) was debunked in favor of the whole word "look and say" method of teaching reading.

Today, the "basal reading" series developed in the 1930s is used by nearly 85 percent of American school children ... most of whom can't read.

The result?

Statistics cited in a 1989 U.S. Senate Republican Policy Committee Report, show that the number of functionally illiterate adults is increasing by approximately 2-1/2 million persons each year. As much as a quarter of the American labor force, anywhere from 20 to 27 million adults, lack the basic reading, writing, and math skills necessary to perform in today's increasingly complex job market. One out of every four teenagers drops out of high school, and of those who graduate, one out of every four has the equivalent of an eighth grade education.

Schools using intensive, systematic phonics report high scores on the Stanford Achievement Test. Instead of averages at the 50th percentile, reading scores are at the 90th percentile. Examination of test scores at a local private elementary school show that less than one percent of the students were on grade level or below and that 50 percent of the pupils were four levels above grade level.

Why do our public schools continue to embrace a failed reading program? In his book, *Preventing Reading Failure: An Examination of the Myths of Reading Instruction*, Dr. Patrick Groff gives some of the reasons:

- Interlocking relationships between basal reader publishers and reading experts.

- Refusal of reading experts to accept outside criticism.
- Lack of knowledge about phonics teaching, negative biases toward phonetic instruction, and fear that phonics advocacy equals political conservatism.
- Negative attitudes toward phonics by teachers' organizations.
- Refusal to admit that there is a literacy crisis.
- Establishment of public schools and teacher education as a monopoly.

In promoting phonics to local and state educators, I frequently hear, "But we do teach phonics" – The truth is that if phonics is taught, it is a combination of "phony phonics" and look/say and not intensive, systematic phonics.

**Not all children can learn by the phonics method" – False! Few children fail to learn to read if phonics is properly taught. There are always a small percentage of children who have learning disabilities and are dysfunctional students, but why penalize the majority?*

And the sorriest excuse of all from our state legislators, "I don't know anything about education" and have to leave curriculum decisions up to the educators.

The overwhelming evidence from research and classroom results indicates that the cure for the "disease of illiteracy" is the restoration of the instructional practice of intensive, systematic phonics in every primary school. It is imperative that the teaching of reading – a prerequisite for everything done not only in school but in life itself – receive highest priority.

I refuse to give up on public education! *Open Court*, far and away one of the best phonics programs ever developed (and also cost effective) has been placed on the approved list for Mississippi schools. What are we waiting for?

*Omitted when published.

The Northside Sun
Thursday, December 9, 1993

Money Could Be Spent to Defend Opposing Position

THE BUNGLED handling of the prayer controversy at Wingfield High School by the JPS administration points out once again the need for drastic changes in Jackson school leadership.

The actions taken by school officials – placing Bishop Knox on administrative leave, the demeaning of Knox by requiring one-hour call-ins to administrative offices, and the culmination of Knox's firing on Thanksgiving Eve – leaves no doubt that there is a need for wisdom (the kind that comes from God) in the handling of school affairs.

It is my hope that the JPS Board will exhibit some leadership in reversing the firing of Bishop Knox if a hearing is requested. Otherwise, I have no doubt that thousands of tax dollars will be expended to defend the firing ... probably all the way to the U.S. Supreme Court.

The saddest part of the whole scenario is that my money will be spent to defend a position I do not support. If the percentage of other Jacksonians (who will be footing the bill) is reflected in the national numbers – that 85% of American citizens support prayer in school – then this is a sad situation indeed.

Two hundred thousand dollars for legal fees was cut from the proposed JPS budget this year, but you can forget that. If legal action is pursued the $650,000 figure budgeted for legal services will be a drop in the bucket.

IF PAST ACTIONS of the JPS Board are any indication of whether they will uphold the firing, I bet they'll side with the school administration. The administration of JPS seems to be "the tail that wags the dog".

Board member Louis Wright has already come out in support of Dr. Canada saying, "The law is very clear on that (school prayer) ...I'm in support of the decision the district has made". This is the same man who stated at a JPS board budget meeting last summer, "We're not in the business of saving money".

Also revealed in the prayer controversy is the obvious link to public schools and government funding. Ollye Shirley, past school board president, came right out and said so in her letter to the editor of Wednesday, November 24: "What will we do when every school begins to have prayer each day and the government withdraws all federal money? The majority of the children in the Jackson Public School District get a free or reduced price meal. Many participate in other programs which are federally funded."

How well Mrs. Shirley knows the value of feeding at the public trough. I won't even venture a guess as to how many tax dollars have gone into projects, including school based "health clinics", developed by Mrs. Shirley and her husband.

THE BOTTOM line to "educators" is money and power. In my opinion, the very best thing that could happen to our schools is to get the federal government out of education.

I have no doubt that the vindictive termination of Bishop Knox sent a message to other JPS employees who may be intimidated to silence in fear of losing their jobs. Make no mistake, the hierarchy of JPS wields a big stick. Spy techniques abound to assure tight control by the authoritarians and woe be to any employee who may step out of (administration) line. That's why a lot of school business, which should be public business, is done behind closed doors.

There's something terribly unsettling when a good man, obviously of fine character and moral conviction and respected and supported by his students, can lose his job over prayer when on the other hand, incorrigible and dangerous thugs, who terrorize teachers and their fellow students, are coddled with alternative schools, special re-entry programs, expensive security and hall monitors.

What kind of lesson does that teach children?

The Clarion-Ledger
Letter to the Editor
Wednesday, May 18, 1994

The JPS 2005/2010 Plan Won't Improve Education

A recent editorial on the first community meeting to unveil plans formulated by a task force working on Jackson 2005/2010 (a planning process for the future of Jackson Public Schools), reported a disappointing turnout by the community.

Having been one of the few attendees at the meeting who was not working for the school district or directly involved with the task force, I can share the concern of this paper that "the No. 1 need in education is participation" ... participation from those of us who foot the bill.

The general public needs to be fully apprised of plans for Jackson Public Schools that, in my opinion, will do nothing to improve the quality of education instruction provided Jackson students.

While the goals of the task force addressed community needs, curriculum, facilities, human resources, and technology, the "vision for the future" involves restructuring schools to become "community centers," increasing community use of school facilities for pre-school child care and extended day care centers, health centers, sites for senior citizen activities and "special interest" meetings and "recreation" centers.

I'm sorry, but until the Jackson Public Schools are accountable for the product they turn out – a well educated individual who can read, write, and do arithmetic – even the suggestion of turning schools into community centers should raise the ire of each citizen of Jackson.

Data from the Mississippi Report Card, a compilation of budgetary, academic and demographic information for all of the state's districts, show Jackson was the eighth highest in the state in spending per pupil ($4,199), ranked second in the state for teachers who have advanced degrees and has a comparatively low teach/pupil ratio.

Add to these statistics, our schools are now air-conditioned, Jackson's school superintendent is paid more than the state superintendent and travels all over the country to get "recharged with new ideas" and "get the money."

And Jackson holds the distinction of ranking 110 out of 149 school districts on overall standardized test scores.

How long will non-participation by the citizens of Jackson allow this to continue?

The Jackson Public Schools can best meet "community needs" for 2005/2010 by providing a program of academic excellence for our children.

The Clarion-Ledger
Letter to the Editor
Friday, June 24, 1994

Lawsuit Over School Board Taxation Definitely "Proper"

There is no question that the suit brought by Representative John Reeves is proper and in order.

The Jackson School Board is an appointed, autonomous Board of five individuals who has been given the authority by the Mississippi Legislature to impose a 3 percent annual tax increase without referendum. They are answerable to no one: not the mayor, not the City Council, and certainly not to the voters.

Actually, the JPS Board adopted the 1994-95 budget with only three of the five board members voting for it. That means that three people – Mark Bailey, Doris Bridgeman, and Louis Wright – are increasing our taxes.

If we don't like it can we vote them out of office? No. That's called taxation without representation and should be challenged in court.

As far as Mr. Reeves's "crass political opportunism," I say it was a wise move. May his tribe increase!

The Clarion-Ledger
Letter to the Editor
Monday, November 28, 1994

Elected School Boards Can End "Tax-and-Spend" Ideas

During the upcoming session of the Mississippi legislature in January, the citizens of Jackson should demand, and vigorously support, passage of legislation to establish elected school boards in every school district in the state.

At present the Jackson Public School Board is dominated by "rubber stampers" who approve just about anything the school administrators bring before them. With the replacement of Tim Medley, the only board member who ever raised a question about how money was spent, it's a sure bet that things will get worse before they get better.

Last spring, the JPS Board raised taxes by approximately $1.7 million because it lacked the resources to adequately fund the needs for the 1995 fiscal year.

In September, JPS received an unexpected bonus of some $1.2 million from the city from sale of tax delinquent property.

An accountable board would have held faith with the citizens of Jackson by at least considering a roll-back of the tax increase.

A roll-back could have been achieved by simply revising the 1995 budget to include the new revenues and advising the taxing authority (city of Jackson) of the action. The taxing authority would adjust the millage rate accordingly so that only the revenue needed to fund the new budget would be extracted from the taxpayer.

But, you guessed it: $800,000 of that unexpected bonus was spent, with plans to spend the remaining $400,000 as soon as administrators bring their recommendations to the Board.

It looks like new board member, Dr. Acie Whitlock, Jr., will fit right in. It took him no time at all to learn how much fun it is to spend tax money.

No matter how much money the school district has, it will never be enough. They'll spend all they have and then want more. Taxpayer be hanged!

Without the ballot box, the taxpayers of Jackson have no recourse; tax and spend, spend and tax, and tax and spend, spend ....

The Clarion-Ledger
Thursday, June 22, 1995

Can JPS Budget Be Cut? Let Me Count the Ways!

It has been difficult to obtain facts and figures to suggest specific budget savings.

About this time every year, the public is treated to the usual tale of woe from Jackson Public School officials. We're told that teachers are being terminated and programs slashed and that "the children" are going to suffer because of tight budget restraints.

In the past, JPS has been accused of being less than honest with the public in how business is conducted and funds expended. In 1993, the state auditor questioned the way district funds were handled.

While budget figures have been hard to come by (I made at least six trips to the JPS District Office before getting final budget figures), there is a glimmer of hope that the Board of Trustees is making an effort to reign in the highly inflated JPS budget. Adding to this perception is the leadership that I hope will be exerted by incoming Superintendent T. C. Wallace, Jr.

While JPS personnel have been extremely cordial, a change from experiences in the past, it has been difficult to obtain facts and figures to suggest specific budget savings.

Why should this situation exist when advertisements have run in the local papers for over a month announcing the opportunity for the public to present comment on the budget to the Board of Trustees? How can the public have input when accurate budget figures are not available?While JPS still operates under a veil of secrecy, it is my hope that future budgets will offer full disclosure of all JPS business operations. Other public agencies are required to do so, so why should JPS be exempt?

One of the most egregious misuse of funds can be found in the travel budget of $92,475.00.

Granted, this figure is down from the '94 budget by about $50,000, but travel expenditures remain too high, especially when $26,475 for conference registration fees is added to the pot.

I don't have a problem with school officials traveling, but let them do it at their own expense. If the taxpayer is footing the bill, **full** disclosure should be required of who's going where for what and how much it's costing.

All travel at JPS expense should be approved prior to the trip and not after the fact.

While the perception of the Board of Trustees is that they serve in the public interest with small pay, the truth is, they spent $18,025.34 on travel last year. Acie Whitlock, the newest board member, and Louis Wright, the next board president, spent $4,458.52 on a trip to San Francisco in early April. Registration for the two was $1,040; airfare $933; with $2,485.52 spent on hotel, food, etc. How can this be justified when charges are being made that some local schools don't have materials and supplies?

Our previous superintendent was probably the most-traveled of the 149 local superintendents, spending $26,000 on travel during his final year. He also instituted some 21 new programs during his tenure, adding millions of dollars to the budget.

One of the best things that could happen to our schools is to keep our school folks at home. The conferences are planned by educationists who have an agenda to promote. Attendees learn to perpetuate the myth that education failures are from inadequate funding and how to fend off criticism by labeling anyone who raises questions from the outside as "anti-public education".

There are other education conferences (never attended by JPS people) which would be truly beneficial to board members and school personnel. These conferences offer a broad spectrum of education issues, with registration fees under $150, and would provide school personnel with a balanced outlook and maybe a balanced budget.

To illustrate how over-budgeted certain items are, the board allowed themselves $5,000 for postage last year. They only spent $43.84, but $5,000 remains in the 1995-96 budget.

The public information office had a 94-95 postage budget of $10,000; spent $273.95, but has a 1995-96 postage budget of $8,000.

The superintendent's office also over-budgets for postage. Last year, $20,000 was budgeted, $934.31 spent. This year, so as "not to tie the new superintendent's hands," the budgeted amount is $5,000 – $4,065.69 more than was needed last year.

Looking at the total amount budgeted for postage, I have concluded that JPS Central Office has an identity crisis. They must think they're a branch of the main post office just across the street from Central Office.

Because personnel contracts are entered into in closed board meetings, the public will probably never know if our new superintendent will have a life insurance policy of $300,000 with his family as beneficiaries; a credit card issued in the joint names of JPS and the superintendent, with charges paid for by JPS; an automobile allowance of $1,000 per month; or a $3,000 computer for home use ... all perks enjoyed by Ben Canada.

And then there's the money expended in legal fees, with $200,000 in the 1995-96 budget for legal services. I applaud the effort to make a significant cut of $125,000 in the budget for legal fees, but paying an attorney legal rates to lobby the legislature should be curtailed.

The board attorney attended the 2-1/2 hour Senate Education Committee confirmation hearing of my appointment to the State Board of Education. I wonder if he was being paid with my tax dollars to lobby against the confirmation.

Whatever happened to the watchdog group promised by Ben Canada to ensure the public that their tax investment would be spent wisely?

The JPS Board and school officials should make every effort to uphold the public trust. This means lean, efficient administration and full accountability to the citizens who pay the bills.

The Clarion-Ledger
Letter to the Editor
September 1995

If City's Student Test Scores So Low, We Must Ask Why?

In the September 20 article ("Public school curriculum declared in 'state of emergency' ") it was reported that school officials have declared that Jackson schools' curriculum is outdated and that "we're behind national standards".

Heaven help us! With national standards at an all-time low, we must be in worse shape than I thought.

I can't help wondering where Parents for Public Schools has been to allow this "state of emergency" to occur.

Several years ago, I attended a meeting of this group to hear a discussion on JPS curriculum. During the question and answer period, I raised some pointed questions about the source of some of the district's curriculum. From their reaction, you would have thought I had tread on the sacred education cow.

**Several hostile parents confronted me following the meeting and indicated that I was not welcome at their meetings. They claim to want community support and input, but only with unconditional, blind allegiance to an inadequate public school system.*

Obviously, from the present "state of emergency" their energies would be best spent supporting **good** education rather than just public education.

And then there's the JPS Board who worshipped at the altar of Ben Canada. Whatever Ben wanted, Ben got ... and he got plenty!

Excuse me if I seem cynical, but while Dr. Canada was superintendent, he pulled the wool over more than one person's eyes.

I've always thought that a board was to oversee and direct the activities of the entity for which it is responsible. This is not the way it works with our un-elected school board.

JPS administrators and department heads bring recommendations before the board and they receive (almost always) tacit approval for their proposals and expenditures. Even when questions are raised, very seldom is any definitive action taken that is contrary to what school officials prescribe. It's the case of the tail waggin' the dog.

And in the case of Ben Canada, it was only after he'd "done us wrong" by accepting a higher paying job in Atlanta that any criticism was raised. Where were the Parents for Public Schools and the JPS Board when we were being ripped off?

With a consultant to be hired to "audit the district's courses" and our new superintendent hinting at a school bond issue, my advice is to hang on to your wallets.

Let's just hope that test scores go up as fast as taxes.

*Omitted when published.

The Clarion-Ledger
Wednesday, June 12, 1996

Can Jackson Public Schools Board Meetings Take Any "Public" Input?

In the past, there has been intolerable arrogance on the school board – an insider's club that reeks of elitism.

In the editorial from the May 21, 1996, The Clarion-Ledger, "School Board: Parents should speak up about ideas," the Jackson Public Schools Board (JPS) was cited as being "fairly lenient about letting people speak their minds".

And who from *The Clarion-Ledger* Editorial Board has ever spoken before the School Board to know what that experience is like?

Having attended JPS School Board meetings over the past five years, I can assure everyone that speaking before the board is not a pleasant experience.

It's so unpleasant, in fact, that most people won't do it.

If you hold a differing view on education policy or if you raise questions about how the district is spending money, you'll be about as popular as a muddy dog on a new white couch.

The JPS School Board meetings, which are usually televised, take place in an over-crowded room filled with school administrators, principals, and central office personnel. They're there by direction, to present proposals, answer questions, and provide information for the Board.

The problem with the meeting format is that the Board very rarely hears an opinion that is contrary to that of the educationists. Pomposity abounds. Diversity is non-existent. Rarely is an action taken that is not pre-determined or controlled by those who like the status-quo.

When someone from outside the education establishment raises any question or makes a proposal contrary to the authoritarian position of the "professional" educators, he or she is usually met with contempt and hostility from the audience and indifference from the board.

I've spoken before the board and felt the animosity. I've heard the derogatory comments from the audience. I've seen how people who are "school people" are received compared to others who are non-public school patrons.

On one occasion, when a state senator, who had been asked by some of his constituents to attend a JPS Board meeting, requested a school department head in the audience to stop making snide remarks about one of the speakers during the 3-minute "public comment" time, the senator was invited outside to "duke it out".

In fairness to the present School Board, I have not attended a board meeting since the appointment of the last two new board members. With consideration of the 1996-97 JPS budget close at hand, it won't be long before I'll be making numerous trips to central office. I hope that the board will closely question exorbitant budget items and hold school administrators accountable. We'll see.

In the past, there has been intolerable arrogance on the School Board – an insider's club that reeks of elitism. Because the JPS Board is appointed rather than elected, board members feel secure in being able to turn a deaf ear without fear of losing their jobs.

Attendance at out-of-state "educational" conferences provide an excellent opportunity for administrators and board members to learn effective ways to counter any criticism and "control the environment."

The National Education Association (NEA) conducts seminars such as "Combatting The New Right," a training program developed by Western States Regional Staff NEA to teach school administrators and boards to counter parental objection by blasting them as part of the "right wing movement." The manual calls right-wingers "the barefoot and pregnant coalition – the politics of the so-called pro-family movement." (p.16, "Combating The New Right Participant's Manual")

The attitude of the education elite is that if you don't have a child in the public school system, you are "anti-public schools." It's just another way to duck accountability by avoiding the question of whether "public" education is "good" education.

Since public schools are public institutions supported by public funds, every citizen, whether a parent or not, has the right to be heard. School boards should listen with the same non-prejudicial receptiveness and cordiality accorded school administrators and give serious consideration to academic proposals of merit.

And quite frankly, there's room in the marketplace of ideas for "far-right" suggestions. Can't be any worse than some of the far-left, politically correct, non-academic junk already in the public schools.

The Clarion-Ledger
Tuesday, December 10, 1996

Will 3rd Time Be a Charm for Filling Job of JPS Superintendent Well?

Here are a few suggestions to the Jackson Public Schools Board members to help them get it just right.

The search is on ... again. The Jackson Public School Board is looking for a new superintendent, the third in six years. It took three police chiefs before Jackson finally got a good one. Let's hope that the third time proves to be the charm for a good superintendent for our city schools.

The selection of a superintendent will be made by a relatively new JPS Board. No one from the five-member board that hired Ben Canada is presently on the board, and only Doris Bridgeman and Aycie Whitlock remain from the board that hired T. C. Wallace.

At least this time no money is being expended to hire a consultant to find a school superintendent for Jackson; the selection process seems a little more open; and the general public is being asked for recommendations. I've made mine.

I don't have children in Jackson Public Schools, but that doesn't mean that I'm not interested in improving our educational system. Since my tax dollars help pay the JPS superintendent's salary, I want the best that money can buy ... within reason.

And I'm also particular about qualifications.

While there are some prerequisites for employment that I haven't listed, I hope the JPS Board won't mind if I make a few suggestions.

- First and foremost, the superintendent must make our schools safe. Schools are not meant to be juvenile detention centers. Any student who is convicted of a crime, is disrupting classes, or brings a weapon to school should be immediately expelled or suspended.

Forget the bleeding hearts that say it isn't fair. An effective disciplinary policy must be maintained, and principals should be fully supported in actions to remove troublemakers from schools.

- The superintendent should raise expectations. Expect the best from everyone: parents, teachers, administrators, board members and students.

JPS teachers are among the highest paid in the state and should be masters of the subject they teach. Teachers should be unencumbered by paperwork and reports, freed from worthless "in service" training programs, and fully supported by the superintendent when they refuse to pass a student whose work is unsatisfactory.

Additionally, the new superintendent would be wise to turn a deaf-ear to teachers' unions. Their interest is more money rather than quality education.

- Forget the year 2000 or 2010! While it sounds wonderful to be far-sighted about educational goals, we need a superintendent who is a little more near-sighted about the classroom needs of *today*.
- Require more of students rather than less. Stop treating students as though you expect them to have problems, and start treating them like they're bright and capable. As William Raspberry wrote in a 1994 column on the success of "Paideia" schools, "Young people will rise to our higher expectations of them. Why should we doubt that they will sink to our lower ones?"

Former JPS Superintendent, Ben Canada, who missed his calling as an actor, would frequently speak, with knitted brow and fervent plea, of "the children" and how "he would never do anything to impact the children."

In my opinion, Dr. Canada had it wrong. We need to impact the children!

- Jackson needs a superintendent who will place more emphasis on basic academic subjects. Junk the whole language method of teaching reading and return to the tried and true systematic, intensive phonics method of reading instruction. Enable students to grasp *all* subject matter by making them good readers. Elevate the reading scores of JPS students to the highest in the state.
- Jackson needs a superintendent who is not an "educationist." We've had enough of "higher order thinking skills," "inventive spelling," and "behavior modification."

Individual excellence should be recognized and encouraged rather than leveling the achievement standard for the sake of "self esteem."

- We need a superintendent who will clean house; unload all the unnecessary personnel and staff on the JPS payroll; cut wasteful spending; and see that the money spent on "education" gets to the classrooms where it belongs.

The superintendent needs to heighten fiscal responsibility, beginning with central office and extending to every school within the district.

And finally, a few suggestions to the JPS Board to help them get it just right ....

Tell that well-paid school board attorney to put a clause in the employment contract to assure that under no condition or circumstance will the superintendent sue the Jackson Public Schools or the JPS Board; and above all, don't hire a superintendent who wears a ring on every finger!

The Clarion-Ledger
Letter to the Editor
Wednesday, November 17, 1999

School Tax Increase Is Not Avoidable?

The five-member Jackson Public Schools (JPS) board has voted to let the taxpayers of Jackson pick up the tab for last year's \$2.8 million budget shortfall and cough up an additional \$5 million to cover the expected shortage next year.

The vote increased the millage rate (a mill is a unit of taxation equal to \$1 for each \$1,000 of assessed valuation) as much as the law allows. That means that a home assessed at \$70,000 will have a \$70 increase in their tax bill this year. Next year that same property will be assessed a whopping \$210 to cover the shortage.

The situation was created when some incompetent city employee miscalculated, for two consecutive years, how much tax revenue was owed the school district. As if that were not bad enough, the JPS budget office failed to catch the mistake at the outset.

And the JPS Board has hired a public relations firm at \$50-\$150 per hour to help them make us feel better about the situation?

Once again, the JPS board is being told by their high-priced attorney that some programs may have to be cut permanently. Good! Let them do what the rest of us have to do when there's a budget crunch: tighten the belt.

I would question why the shortfall can't be covered by the JPS' \$15.7 million reserve fund. If the fund is earmarked for cash flow problems, seems to me a serious one exists.

Is this a permanent increase, or will the millage rate drop after the shortage is covered? I think I know the answer to that one.

What about the unidentified city employee who is costing the taxpayers of Jackson millions of dollars? Have any heads rolled?

Is there no oversight or checks and balances in place to be sure that million-dollar errors don't occur? And where are the PEER Committee and the state auditor's office when we need them?

I've contended for years that Jackson should have an elected school board. We couldn't be any worse off.

The Northside Sun
Publication date unknown

Why Jackson Public School Pupils Can't Read

The news is out.

Jackson Public School pupils are scoring below the state level. This is especially bad news since the state scores on the Stanford Achievement Tests (ACT) are below the national average.

The national average of 50 percentile is nothing to brag about.

My particular concern is how Jackson students scored in reading. The tests were administered to 4th, 6th, and 8th graders.

Of particular interest to Northsiders is how public schools in our area fared. In one year, Boyd dropped 5 percentile points from 48.4 to 43.7; Casey dropped by 6 from 54.8 to 48.3; Spann dropped by 8 points from 53.0 to 45.1; and McLeod by 2 1/2 points from 57.2 to 54.8.

Of the 37 schools tested, 25 showed decreased reading scores while only 12 showed an increase and several of these by less than 1 percentile point.

Something is terribly wrong and I believe I know what it is. The public schools are using a failed method of reading instruction.

In March of 1991, the Jackson Public Schools instituted "a radical change in how they teach reading to elementary and middle-school pupils". This was done without School Board approval but received enthusiastic support from then board president, Ollye Shirley. The program the district put into action is the "whole language" concept of teaching reading.

Actually, whole language or the "look and say" method is not new. It was originated in 1837 by Horace Mann based on the work of Thomas A. Gallaudet who used "look and say" to teach deaf children to read. Since deaf children have no ability to "sound out" letters, syllables, or words, the constant repetition of "sight" words from a controlled vocabulary seemed to be the most efficient way to teach a child to read.

In 1930, John Dewey, the father of progressive education, embraced whole language and with teachers being trained in normal schools that sprang up around the country, intensive, systematic phonics was debunked without any research to support the new teaching method.

The debunked system of intensive, systematic phonics was invented by one of the most towering mathematical and scientific geniuses in history, Blaise Pascal. It worked successfully in the schools of this country from 1655 until 1837.

The "basal reading" series with rigidly controlled vocabulary and emphasis on memorizing whole words before the letter of sounds are learned was introduced in the 30s; and today's basal reading books used by nearly 85 percent of American school children are essentially the same as the 1930-31 books.

The problem with whole language is that it fails to provide the key to unlocking the English language. The student is limited to only the words which he is able to memorize or guess in context by using initial letter or picture clues.

But what happens when the volume of words needed for reading more difficult material, in science, literature, history, or math cannot be memorized quickly enough? Usually by the middle and upper grades, real problems begin to develop.

The result? According to current estimates, the number of functionally illiterate adults is increasing by approximately two and one quarter million persons each year. As much as a quarter of the American labor force, anywhere from 20 to 27 million adults, lack the basic reading, writing, and math skills necessary to perform in today's increasingly complex job market. One out of every four teenagers drops out of high school, and of those who graduate, one out of every four has the equivalent of an eighth grade education. (Statistics from a 1989 U.S. Senate Republican Policy Committee Report)

Try as I may, I can't figure out why the parents of public school students continue to accept the poor performance record of reading instruction when there are other reading programs available.

Take, for example, a local private elementary school with SAT reading scores ranking in the 90th percentile. The school uses Open Court, probably the best phonics program ever conceived. An evaluation by the Southern Association of Colleges and Schools showed that less than 1 percent of the school's pupils were on grade level or below and that 50 percent of the pupils have reading skills 4 levels above their grade level. So don't let anyone tell you that phonics doesn't work.

Open Court was started by the Carus family, German immigrants who came to the U.S. at the turn of the century. In 1940, concerned with the quality of reading instruction in the U.S. schools, the Carus family (now successful owners of Carus Chemical Company) hired consultants to develop a reading program that uses intensive, systematic phonics and good literature. Their goal was to teach the decoding of the English language.

Open Court is available for use in any state school, having been placed on the "approved" list by the State Department of Education. Open Court provides consultants, who must have taught in the classroom, to train teachers to use the program. Educators have nothing but the highest praise for Open Court educational instruction and materials, and test scores seem to prove them right.

Naturally the question of cost is raised. Cost of reading instruction can be reduced while at the same time improving reading scores. One Massachusetts school superintendent reported that the cost of reading materials to implement phonics was eighty-eight percent less per pupil than the "look and say" reading program previously used in his district. A Mesa, Arizona, principal reported that in 1978 his school spent $23.42 per student on reading materials, but by 1981, expenditures had dropped to $8.50 per student with a phonics program.

I contend that with the budget of the Jackson Public Schools we can afford the best. Forget the cost!

In his book, *Preventing Reading Failure: An Examination of the Myths of Reading Instruction,* Dr. Patrick Groff lists some of the reasons educators fail to accept research finding that prove that intensive systematic phonics is far superior to "whole language":

- interlocking relationships between basal reader publishers and reading experts; (A lot of money is involved.)
- refusal of reading experts to accept outside criticism;

(What do parents know?)

- negative attitudes toward phonics by teacher organizations;
  (They might have to work harder.)
- refusal to admit that there is a literacy crisis;
  (I wonder if they're reading the same test scores I am?)
- establishment of public schools and teacher education as a monopoly.
  (Have you ever heard of NEA, the largest, most powerful union in the country?)

The most disillusioning aspect of this whole scenario is that most educators refuse to accept the fact that they have failed in their most important objective ... the teaching of reading, a prerequisite for everything done not only in school, but in life.

Education leaders can no longer be excused from what amounts to education malpractice. If parents really care about the education of their children, they will insist that intensive, systematic phonics replace the whole language approach to reading instruction.

And one final word .... When you approach your school administrators you will probably be told "But we teach phonics." What Jackson Public Schools teach is "whole language" with "phoney phonics" thrown in. Ask for a tried and true program such as OPEN COURT.

You may also be told that "Not all children can learn phonics."

There will always be a small percentage of children who have learning disabilities and are dysfunctional students, but why penalize the majority who can learn to read phonetically? Few children don't learn phonics well if properly taught.

The Clarion-Ledger
Letter to the Editor
Friday, September 26, 1997

How Can Anderson "Live the Message" Host Farrakhan?

The lead article ("Council inflamed over Farakhan gesture") in the State/Metro Section of *The Clarion-Ledger* on Sunday, reported Nation of Islam leader, Louis Farrakhan, called "the white man" the "anti-Christ" to rousing applause from the estimated 1,200 people at Anderson United Methodist Church.

Is this the Anderson United Methodist Church that is a participating church in Mission Mississippi ... the organization that encourages and expresses unity in the Body of Christ across racial and denominational lines?

Are those who applauded Farrakhan's remarks church members who support Mission Mississippi's goals to "live the message" by striving to love one another in greater ways and to work for unity in Christ and true reconciliation?

Need I say more?

The Clarion-Ledger
Letter to the Editor
Unpublished

The Mayor, Crime, and the Bold New City

I'm glad that something finally got Mayor Johnson's attention. If he thinks the anti-crime commercial produced for the Metropolitan Crime Commission is an unfair characterization of downtown Jackson, he's in a state of denial about the magnitude of the crime problem in the Bold New City.

Most Jackson residents won't leave their homes after dark, much less go downtown after sunset. And it's not just after dark. Downtown is not always safe in the middle of the day.

Case in point: After leaving the previewing of the *Welcome to the Bold New City* press conference held in the heart of downtown Jackson at 2:00 P.M. in the afternoon, I was approached by a street vagrant seeking a handout. I was alone, the street deserted.

While the incident was non-threatening, it could have been otherwise. It brought into sharp focus that all of us are just a breath away from being a crime statistic.

The quote from the front page piece by Butch John quoting the manager of the Iron Horse Grill, "I feel safer here because we have an armed guard than I do going home" was certainly paradoxical. He doesn't feel safe going home and only feels safe at his downtown workplace because of an armed guard.

Statistics don't lie. The Bold New City is blighted by crime. The video is a portrayal that lasts 60 seconds. Experiencing the real thing lasts a lifetime. Just ask a victim.

If the vivid pictures from the video produced for the Metropolitan Crime Commission serve as an unpleasant reminder to city leaders and complacent citizens, it has achieved its goal.

The Clarion-Ledger
Thursday, March 14, 2002

Please, JPS, Do Not Recruit a Canada Clone

Once again, Jackson Public Schools is looking for a new superintendent.

It's hard to say good-bye to Dr. Jayne Sargent because she's been good for Jackson's schools.

She has brought stability to the district and has conducted business efficiently and with far less turmoil and controversy than was experienced with some of her predecessors.

As I thought about the prospect of a new superintendent, I began to think back about former JPS superintendents. One in particular came to mind.

Remember Ben Canada? He was JPS superintendent from 1990 until 1994.

Credibility squandered

He was the affable guy with the big grin who loved to travel. He was also the superintendent who bungled the handling of the Bishop Knox (school prayer) controversy.

To his credit, Canada garnered support for passage of most of the $74.9 million Jackson Public Schools bond referendum for "critical needs" in 1991. But about halfway into his three-year stint in Jackson, Canada began to lose credibility with the JPS board.

Excessive administrative spending and bureaucratic waste coupled with Canada's lack of knowledge in handling the budget process and his threat to close down APAC, caused his effectiveness to come into question.

In spite of the fact that some in the Jackson business community tried to use "golden handcuffs" (monetary incentives and perks) to keep Canada in Jackson, he left for Atlanta, where greener pastures and bigger bucks beckoned.

In Atlanta, while Canada was viewed as a "top educator," he was considered by some members of the Atlanta Board of Education to be a weak administrator who lacked the follow-through necessary to achieve the goals of the Atlanta Public Schools Strategic Plan.

In 1998, Canada was offered a second three-year contract as Atlanta's superintendent, but four months into the contract he accepted an offer to assume the helm of the public schools in Portland, Oregon.

Who knows why Dr. Canada left Atlanta. According to one newspaper account, Canada was feeling tremendous stress created by some board members who had lost confidence in his ability to administer the school system.

Perhaps he saw the handwriting on the wall.

Portland problems

And while the explanation for leaving Atlanta to return to the Pacific Northwest, where he had worked for fifteen years as a teacher and principal, sounded plausible, his failure to purchase a home in Portland appeared to be a lack of commitment.

In Portland, 85 percent of the city's children attend public school, and there is a lot of parental and community involvement.

In a good school system, it doesn't take long to spot mediocrity, and it soon became apparent that Portland's new superintendent never said or did anything of substance.

As one letter to the local paper put it, "Canada has been an unmitigated disaster for Portland's schools."

In May of 2001, Ben Canada was fired and left Portland with a settlement worth more than $200,000. Reportedly, he headed for Georgia with plans to enter divinity school.

This leads me to the search underway in Jackson.

I hope the dollars expended to find just the right superintendent will produce a Jayne Sargent and not a Ben Canada.

The Clarion-Ledger
Letter to the Editor
Monday, January 13, 2003

Treacherous Roadway a "Death Trap"

The four-vehicle accident that occurred Monday night on I-55 at Ridgeland, leaving one person dead and another in serious condition, is just the latest tragedy to occur in what some are calling Death Alley.

Road construction from the intersection of north I-220 to just north of the Ridgeland exit has produced a very treacherous stretch of roadway.

Concrete barriers line one side of the road with a soft gravel median bordering the other.

The roadway is narrow, poorly striped, scarcely lit, and heavily traveled. The speed limit is 60 mph, entirely too fast for motorists who are unaware of the danger that negotiating the road presents.

Those of us who travel the road daily can testify to the fact that the graveled median does not provide a safe shoulder.

If an inattentive motorist drops off the pavement or an emergency situation arises that would require leaving the highway, little could be done to control the vehicle or prevent it from crossing the narrow median into on-coming traffic.

Since construction began, with serious accidents occurring almost daily, three lives have been lost.

The recent accident blocked the interstate for more than two hours. And both north and southbound lanes have frequent lane closings – backing up traffic for miles – when no obvious work is being done that would require lane closure.

As motorists become impatient, the likelihood of additional accidents increases.

Central Highway Commissioner, Dick Hall, and Mississippi Department of Transportation officials should take immediate action to correct the death trap that has been created and closely monitor this highway project to a rapid and satisfactory completion.

Unpublished – Written sometime in 2004

What Happened To the "Bold New City?"

Jackson, that Bold New City, the Crossroads of the South, the Capitol City of the State of Mississippi. What happened?

The city that held so much promise just thirty years ago when my family chose Jackson to call home is in cardiac arrest.

The signs of urban decay are everywhere. Boarded up houses, iron bars on windows and doors, streets full of potholes, once good public schools languishing in low test scores and discipline problems, and residents fleeing the high crime rate and unsafe areas that have spread like an unchecked cancer.

Add to this a police force in total chaos, a City Council who fight among themselves, spending more time on removing flags than addressing the serious problems facing the city, and a mayor who has exhibited little leadership ability and who seems unable to make decisions without hiring costly consultants.

Pretty strong words, but they need to be said.

My portrait of Jackson has been painted with a broad brush, but just ask any long-time residents of Jackson how they see it and I think they'll agree. Jackson has major problems.

But problems, no matter how large, can be solved.

Jackson's demise didn't occur overnight, and Jackson mayor, Harvey Johnston, inherited many of the problems facing the city today. But as the urban decay continues, he has failed to provide the forceful leadership and resolve to initiate solutions and push them through. In my opinion, a major mistake was made early in his administration when he replaced police chief, Robert Johnson, with Bracy Coleman.

According to recently released census data, Jackson now has a 70.64% African American population. Future leadership will likely be from this racial and ethnic group.

Harvey Johnson was the first African American elected as mayor. The question needs to be raised as to whether future elected officials, be it Johnson or any other candidate who seeks the office of mayor or councilman, can provide the leadership to solve the myriad of problems that need urgent attention.

It seems that just a few short years ago the shoe was on the other foot, with black citizens screaming about racial imbalance and expressing the need for more representation. Now that they have the leadership role, what are they doing with it? Can racial differences be set aside in the interest of a better Jackson or will the Bold New City become the City That Was?

Jackson needs decisive leadership and accountability from its leaders. With a broad field of candidates offering for election, it should be incumbent upon each citizen to listen and question all candidates to determine which can best provide that leadership. Take advantage of every opportunity to attend public forums and rallies where candidates will be seeking your vote.

And those with a vision for Jackson should become involved, perhaps offering for public office next time around. The job description is for public servants, not self-important people who seek power and influence; smart, honest people with business acumen who know how to set goals and reach them; unifying office holders who seek the best for all Jacksonians rather than just their constituency.

Casting a ballot should not be based on the color of a candidate's skin, but the mettle of the person.

Until all citizens of Jackson, especially within the black community, recognize this fact, the future of Jackson, as a bold, new city, hangs in the balance.

The Clarion-Ledger
Thursday, September 9, 2004

Allow the Old Farmers Market to Remain Open

In an effort to promote and provide a new market for Mississippi fruit and vegetable growers, the state Department of Agriculture and Commerce has gone to meddlin'. Just let Big Brother get involved and you can bet your bottom dollar that things are going to get worse rather than better.

Such is the case with the controversy that has arisen over rules and regulations governing the new $2.4 million farmers' market being constructed at the Mississippi State Fairgrounds in Jackson.

New market is different

The new market prototype was developed after spending $12,000 on a study of farmers' markets in California, North Carolina and Alabama.

The plan – proposed by the Mississippi Central Market Board and still not finalized – is to provide Mississippi farmers a central location for selling their produce, but on a come and go basis.

Once produce is sold, they can close up shop and go home.

As proposed, priority would be given to those farmers who sell only Mississippi grown produce and vendors would adhere to weekly, semi-weekly or monthly drawings for space to promote equity in the market

Market operation would be limited to Tuesday afternoon, and all day Friday and Saturday. Walk-in coolers would not be available for produce unless provided by vendors, and pea and bean shellers would no longer be allowed

This is not at all like the operation at the Farmers' Market at Woodrow Wilson and West Street that operates seven days a week with permanently leased stalls that are much larger in size than the ones proposed for the new market, and where a full variety of produce has been available.

Needless to say, the vendors are not happy with the plans for the new market. In fact, they say it will put them out of business.

They ask, and rightfully so, how they can survive when a six and a half-day workweek is cut to a two and a half-day week? And how can a wide selection of produce be made available if vendors are frequently shuffled from stall to stall?

Consumers could be hurt

Also, what about the consumer?

If present proposals were implemented, shorter hours of operation would severely limit a consumer's shopping time. Consumers would also be limited by Mississippi's growing season and yields. Out-of-season crops, not available in Mississippi, or produce such as peaches from Georgia or Chilton County Alabama, would be in short supply.

Officials of the Department of Agriculture have all but turned a deaf ear to the expressed concerns of the vendors and on more than one occasion have derogatorily referred to them as "peddlers".

Many long-time customers of the Farmers' Market have had their ire raised by the short shrift given these hard-working "peddlers" who, for some 56 years, from daylight to dark, in good weather and bad, have provided a wide-selection of produce to Metro area consumers.

But all may not be lost ....

At the Market Board's meeting last Friday, it was announced that a 2-4 year lease agreement might be in the works that would allow the Woodrow Wilson Market to stay open – coolers, pea shellers and all!

If change is to come, let it not be at the expense of those who made Farmers' Market a success – or at the expense of the consumers, who have enjoyed its produce.

Madison Country Journal
Letter to the Editor
(Unpublished)

Mannsdale Heritage Foundation

When my husband retired, we moved to Madison County. That was before Nissan and road construction.

I guess we've contributed to the problem, driving one of the many cars now traveling the small, rural back roads of the county. But when we chose to make Madison our home, it was for that very reason ... small, rural, and away from city problems.

As my husband recently observed, "If I had wanted to live in an automotive capitol, I would have moved to Detroit City."

That being said, I applaud the recent uprising of citizens on the west side of I-55 who want to protect the aesthetics of their neighborhood and who don't want a four-lane road to destroy its beauty and historic significance.

The Mannsdale Heritage Foundation, an organization composed of citizens, developers and church members of the Mannsdale community, was organized to protect as much as possible of the rural character of their area.

The Chapel of the Cross, built in 1848 and one of only ten remaining structures in Madison County listed on the National Register of Historic Places, and at least ten other historic homes and sites, are in the Mannsdale area situated along Highway 463.

While the Mannsdale Heritage Foundation recognizes the need for a portion of Hwy. 463 to be four-laned, they oppose the four-laning of Hwy. 463 from the proposed Reunion/Annandale Parkway to Mississippi Highway 22.

The Mississippi Department of Transportation (MDOT) is asking for public input on the issue. I hope that those of us who love Madison and want to preserve as much of its integrity as we can, will let our voices be heard.

The Clarion-Ledger
Thursday, June 24, 2004

Hospice: Place of Shelter for Life's Travelers

All of us are travelers on the road of life. And just as every journey has a beginning, it also has an end.

I recently helped my mother make that journey, and as we traveled along the way we found a hospice – a place of shelter for travelers.

For anyone who has to say good-bye to a loved one, the time for final farewells can be painfully difficult. Often the pronouncement, "nothing more can be done" has a devastating effect on the individual and family members.

In a terminal illness, the emotional roller coaster of despair, fatigue, fear, and anxiety can be overwhelming.

Place of peace, respite

What we found at Hospice Ministries, Inc., were friends who understood.

From the time we walked in the door, Hospice Ministries provided professional care and loving support. Its primary mission is to treat each patient with respect, dignity and compassion and to provide quality end-of-life care.

Hospice Ministries serves thirty-five counties with in-home care available through offices in Brookhaven, Southaven, Forest, Natchez, and the Ridgeland facility that offers inpatient care as well.

In-home care allows the patient to remain in the familiar surroundings of home with nurses and highly trained volunteers working with the supervising physician to meet patient needs.

When expectations have changed from "cure" to "comfort" Hospice Ministries provides needed medication, supplies and equipment, and holds a hand, lends an ear, and offers a shoulder to lean on.

For us, inpatient care at the Ridgeland facility, with its immaculately kept grounds, lovely gardens and soothing fountains, gave a weary traveler a place of peace and rest and a respite from the journey.

We arrived when the inner courtyards were ablaze with color from the abundance of flowers lovingly tended by June Stevens and her crew of volunteer gardeners. June's husband, Dr. Tom Stevens, served on the Hospice board before his death, and "Dr. Tom's Rose Garden," dedicated to his memory, can only be described as spectacular when in full bloom. On a regular basis, volunteers take vases of cut flowers from the gardens to each patient's room.

Support is needed

And the hospice chapel – built with funds contributed through the efforts of the Chamber of Commerce of Ridgeland, Harris Constructors, Inc., and other generous benefactors – provides a quiet place for prayer and reflection.

Any family or caregiver who has been blessed by Hospice Ministries can testify to what this service has meant in their lives and in the life of a terminally ill loved one.

Hospice Ministries, Inc. is a not-for-profit, community based organization. For it to continue to provide and expand its ministry, Hospice depends upon the generosity of many supporters who sustain their mission; from individuals who designate Hospice Ministries as the charity of choice, through major gifts from corporate and business partners, and with the help of many dedicated volunteers.

One day soon, I plan to return to Hospice Ministries as a volunteer.

But who knows? Perhaps someday, at the end of my journey, Hospice will provide this traveler a shelter and the care and support of many loving friends.

Jackson Christian Family Magazine
March, 2006

THE GARDENS OF HOSPICE MINISTRIES, INC.

"Blooms from the happy heart's garden
Plucked in the spirit of love;
Blooms that are earthly reflections
Of flowers that blossom above.
Words cannot tell what a measure
Of blessing such gifts will allow
To dwell in the lives of many,
So give them the flowers now!"

The words from the poem by Leigh M. Hodges sum up the ministry of dedicated gardeners who provide the blessing of flowers to the patients at Hospice Ministries, Inc., in Ridgeland. Hospice Ministries, Inc. is a not-for-profit, community based hospice providing care in the patients' homes or as resident patients at the Ridgeland facility.

The Hospice Gardens are lovingly tended by Master Gardener, June Stevens, and a team of dedicated volunteers who work year round to till, plant, cultivate and nourish flower gardens that bring beauty to the eye of the beholder and provide a place of quiet repose to patients, family members, friends and staff.

Dedicated to the memory of Dr. Tom Stevens, June's husband, the Hospice Garden concept was first started at Whispering Pines Hospice where, in retirement, Dr. Tom assisted in making rounds of those in hospice care at the facility on Raymond Road. In 1998, Whispering Pines, an inpatient facility, and Hospice Ministries of Central Mississippi, an in-home hospice, merged and a new facility was built on Towne Center Boulevard in Ridgeland.

It is customary for the Hospice chaplain and staff to hold a simple memorial service for family members when a patient dies. A rose is placed on a memorial table to symbolize the life of the deceased. In the early days, no fresh flowers were available so an artificial rose was used. Because of Dr. Tom's love of roses and the fact that he wanted each life represented by a "real rose," he determined that the new facility would have a rose garden.

With the help of Charles Wright, Dr. Tom tilled the stone-hard earth and prepared a rose bed. The first rose bushes were contributed by Karen McKie; Miriam Etheridge lent her expertise as a consultant.

Because the facility in Ridgeland was designed with two inner courtyards, the Hospice gardeners created flower beds that were planted with flowering trees and many varieties of bedding plants. The profusion of colorful blossoms can be seen from the windows that opened onto the courtyards from patient rooms and hallways. Not only is the visual effect pleasing, but wind chimes and fountains add soothing sound effects. Birds in abundance visit the gardens to feast on the birdfeeders attached to the windows of each room.

When Dr. Tom died in 2002, the Stevens family erected a pergola (a vine arbor) in his memory. The pergola was designed by John Weaver and built by the Stevens children, Tom, Jr., Tricia, Carney, and their friends.

Other friends made contributions to the gardens as well. Bob Jones designed and built the rose trellises and garden benches that now grace both courtyards.

Today, June Stevens continues the work first envisioned by her husband and with the help of Tom Harris, Rebecca Allen, Jo Jones, Sara Elam and other volunteers, the Gardens of Hospice continue to flourish.

Christian ministries come in many forms and fashions ... some in faraway places, and some just around the corner. It's truly a special ministry that brings comfort and pleasure to those who are in the final days of life by showing them God's love through a profusion of colorful blossoms, the sound of a bubbling fountain, the touch of a gentle breeze, and the warmth of a bright and sunny garden.

Submitted to *The Clarion-Ledger*
Thursday, April 24, 2008
Unpublished

Capitalizing on Death

In case you haven't noticed, there is a war being waged between *The Clarion-Ledger* and the funeral homes over the display advertising listing area deaths on the obituary page.

The Clarion-Ledger claims that the "modest increase of 2 to 4 percent" is no more than the costs passed on to families by local funeral homes. The bottom line is that the funeral homes have drawn the line on advertising rates which, in my opinion, have become exorbitant. And I say more power to 'em!

I have noticed for some time how *The Clarion-Ledger* is capitalizing on death.

In its obituary advertising policy, the paper states that it publishes "basic" obits "free of charge." Basic means name, date and place of death, and a number to call for information. If you want a list of survivors, visitation or funeral services added, there is a "typical charge" of $89 (if you can get it done in 25 lines.) Each line over 25 costs $5.

Now that sounds like a minimal charge until you count the number of lines.

I did just that and was shocked at the cost of some obituaries. Granted, I counted longer ones, but the average obit ran about $300 with some running as much as a $1,000.

I think that *The Clarion-Ledger* is more than covering increased operating costs considering that before 2001 obituaries were run free of charge.

And have you noticed the increase in font size?

Don't be fooled. If they really cared about old folks finding the obits easier to read because the print is larger, they would be printing the entire paper in large type. The reason the print is larger on the obituary page is that it uses more lines and more lines is more MONEY.

I have no problem with *The Clarion-Ledger* making a profit. After all, they're in business like everyone else. However, in considering the rates charged for block ads used by funeral homes to list funeral arrangements, the paper should recognize that mortuaries are providing a public service to the readers of this paper.

If, indeed, *The Clarion-Ledger* "prefers to continue this invaluable service" they will reconsider their position on the price increase and reach an agreement that is in the best interest of the funeral homes and the families they serve.

Chapter VI

The Arts

To further the appreciation of culture among all the people,
to increase respect for the creative individual, to widen
participation by all the processes and fulfillments of art –
this is one of the fascinating challenges of these days.

John F. Kennedy

The Northside Sun
"As I See It"
Thursday, August 16, 1990

Jackson Really Is a Ballet City

THE RECENT SUCCESSFUL conclusion of the IV International Ballet Competition (IBC) is indeed a worthy tribute to many people in Jackson, both past and present, who have contributed to the cultural life of our city and state by participating in and supporting ballet as one of the major performing arts.

Jackson has always been considered a "ballet town". In early days, ticket sales to performances of touring ballet troupes were brisk and the reception visiting ballet companies received was warm and enthusiastic.

But it was not until the early 1960's that professional ballet in Jackson took an important turn. How could anyone have guessed that the opening of a dance school in a tiny studio behind the old Wright Music Center on North State Street by Rex and Albia Cooper would eventually result in bringing to Jackson world-wide recognition as a major ballet center?

As dancers and choreographers, Rex Cooper and Albia Kavan (Mrs. Cooper's professional name) had many professional performances to their credit. They had danced leading parts with the American Ballet, Ballet Theatre, Ballet Caravan, Markova-Dolin Theatre, Metropolitan Opera

Ballet and the Ted Shawn Group.

THE COOPERS WERE the only dancers and instructors in Mississippi who were listed in Antole Chujoy's "Dance Encyclopedia" and "Dance Magazine's Annual Dance Index".

Cooper had been soloist with the Strawbridge Ballet and his Broadway shows included "Seventeen," "High Button Shoes," "Gentlemen Prefer Blondes" and "By the Beautiful Sea." His performances in the Dallas production of "Annie Get Your Gun" had become a tradition. He choreographed 35 musical productions in theatres across the country.

For the first time Jackson had its own ballet masters in residence.

So it was only natural that in 1964, Paula Cazenave and Clara Allison, who were ballet enthusiasts, approached the Coopers with an idea for a regional ballet company. Albia and Rex were receptive to the idea and gave their time and talents without pay, working tirelessly to organize and train the new company.

The Jackson Ballet Guild was organized to provide the backbone support for the fledgling troupe with Cazenave and Allison being the co-founders and advisers.

LOCAL BALLETOMANES worked in various capacities to assure the success of the organization. Their goal was to keep alive the best traditions of classical ballet, enrich the cultural life of the city and state, and to give talented young people an opportunity to perform.

Their efforts were rewarded with the first performance of the Jackson Ballet in April of 1966 at the Millsaps Christian Center.

In 1967, the Guild's fall membership luncheon featured noted writer and dance critic, Walter Terry. He shared guest honors with Eudora Welty whose children's book, "The Shoe Bird," would be produced as a world premier for the opening of the new Municipal Auditorium the following spring.

Quite an undertaking for the three-year old ballet company made up of some twenty, very young, female dancers! Among them, Kathy Denton (Thibodeaux), who was to become, in 1982, a silver medal winner in the International Ballet Competition.

THE EXCELLENT training by the Coopers, combined with many hours of hard work and rehearsal by company members, made "The Shoe Bird" a resounding success and the Jackson Ballet, to the rave reviews of many critics, was launched as a genuine civic ballet company.

In the years that followed, the Jackson Ballet provided production support for the Jackson Opera Guild, participated in youth concerts with the Jackson Symphony Orchestra, and toured the state with special ballet performances.

A milestone was reached when the company traveled to Atlanta to participate in the 17th Annual Southeastern Ballet Festival, sponsored by the Southeastern Regional Ballet Association (SERBA).

After the death of Rex Cooper in 1970, Albia Kavan Cooper continued as the artistic director of the Jackson Ballet and continued in that capacity until her retirement. She was succeeded by Gayle Parmelee as artistic director and in 1975, by Thalia Mara, who brought with her the idea of a professional company and the dream of staging international competition in Jackson.

For the first time, dancers were salaried and the Jackson Ballet took on the status of a professional company. Thalia Mara's vision of hosting the International Ballet Competition in Jackson was realized when she went to Varna, Bulgaria, as Governor Cliff Finch's representative to extend the invitation from the state of Mississippi for the 1979 competition. Mississippi Ballet International was established to host the IBC events.

Ms. Mara was succeeded by Charles Dickson as artistic director of the Jackson Ballet and as 1982 drew to a close, ballet in Jackson took another step forward with the consolidation of the Jackson Ballet with Mississippi Ballet Theatre and the founding of Ballet Mississippi with Charles Dickson as artistic director. The 1983-84 season of Ballet Mississippi saw four exciting performances produced by the company.

TODAY, WITH International Ballet Competition IV a monetary and artistically acclaimed success; Ballet Mississippi, under the artistic direction of Alan Woodard, planning an exciting season with two extra-seasonal performances by IBC Grand Prix winner, Jose Carreno and partner Ana Lobe; Ballet Magnificat, a professional Christian ballet company founded in 1986 and directed by Kathy Thibodeaux, continuing to flourish; and several excellent ballet schools operating year round, with dance workshops and seminars being conducted locally; the ballet picture for the future is bright indeed.

Because of Rex and Albia Cooper's love and dedication to dance, Thalia Mara's brainchild of having Jackson the site of the prestigious International Ballet Competition, and the efforts of many civic minded individuals – too numerous to name – Jackson's reputation as a center of culture and refinement will continue to grow and with that growth we'll see bigger and better things coming our way.

The Clarion-Ledger
Letter to the Editor
Thursday, July 5, 1979

Vision Came to Rapturous Life

What a memorable two weeks! From the first arrival on June 15 until our last guest departed on the 30th, the International Ballet Competition has taken Jackson by storm!

When Thalia Mara, artistic director of the Jackson Ballet Guild, said that she wanted to see Jackson audiences as enthusiastic over ballet as they were football, she had a vision that was to come true. From the appearance in April of Baryshnikov, Martins and McBride, to the smashing success of the most exciting artists of the world participating in the first world competition to be held in the United States, Jackson has truly had ballet fever.

My hat is off to every person who had a part in bringing Jackson what, in my opinion, has been the greatest cultural event in our city's history. The many, many hours of work by a host of people has paid off in national attention and a superior display of professional skill that has brought credit to everyone.

However, the person who has received the least credit and deserves the most is Thalia Mara, who had the vision and saw it become a reality. Congratulations!

The Clarion-Ledger
Letter to the Editor
Thursday, July 10, 1990

International Ballet Competition IV

Now that the International Ballet Competition IV is history, it's time for the thousands of people who have worked to assure its success to take a bow!

Certainly, the Mississippi Ballet International, Inc. Board of Directors is due the lion's share of the recognition for the four years of planning that went into the competition.

Businesses and government benefactors deserve recognition for acknowledging through their participation, the importance of aiding economic development by support of the arts.

The Mississippi Ballet International staff, Sue Lobrano, as executive director, handled every aspect of the Competition with a high degree of professionalism.

And to the Friends of IBC, the statewide corps of volunteers who manned the various projects sponsored for the benefit of the Competition, a special thanks for a job well done.

Hundreds of volunteers worked as host families, interpreters, transportation personnel, dance school and dormitory monitors, and in scores of jobs to assure that things ran smoothly and that our guests got a good dose of Southern hospitality.

The thousands who supported the competition by purchasing the tickets to assure that almost every performance was a sell-out made it all worthwhile!

And our lasting gratitude is due Thalia Mara who had the vision that someday Mississippi audiences would be cheering the athletic ability of ballet dancers just as they do their favorite football team.

Without Albia Kavan and Rex Cooper and their love and devotion to dance, the success enjoyed by the IBC would probably have never been realized, at least not in Jackson.

The Coopers, who returned to make their home in Jackson in 1960 after outstanding professional dance careers, gave their time and talents without pay to keep alive the best traditions of classical ballet, to enrich the cultural life of the city and state, and to give talented young people an opportunity to perform.

One of those talented young people was Kathy Denton Thibodeaux who won a silver medal in 1982 for her performance in the International Ballet Competition II, and who credits the Coopers with the initial ballet training that brought her to that point in her career. She is now the director of Ballet Magnificat, a professional Christian ballet company founded in 1986.

So to all who have enriched our lives by bringing the best young dancers in the world to Jackson and making ballet a truly viable performing art: BRAVO!

The Clarion-Ledger
Letter to the Editor
Monday, April 2, 1990

Says "Censorship" Does Not Apply in Arts Endowments

The editorial staff of *The Clarion-Ledger* is again provoking readers to wrath by raising the question of "censorship" when it comes to the funding of obscene art by the National Endowment for the Arts.

There is no difference in the federal government paying a defense contractor $7,000 for a hammer and an "artist" being funded $15,000 for a photograph of a crucifix submerged in a jar of urine. Both are monumental rip-offs of the American taxpayer, and perpetrators of such madness should be tarred and feathered. The question of censorship does not even apply.

If creativity begets creativity, let it be at its own expense.

The Clarion-Ledger
Letters to the Editor
Saturday, November 29, 2003

"Robinson and Friends" a Celebration

Robinson and Friends, billed as a celebration of the centennial of Walter Anderson's birth, was a celebration indeed! The performance not only celebrated the life and work of the Ocean Springs artist, but captured the essence of Anderson's work with music, dance, and humor.

Lester Senter, who created and starred in *Robinson and Friends,* was outstanding, particularly in her performance of "Contemplations" and Robinson the Cat." Colman Pearce's music was so appropriate with his skilful instrumentation that captured the vibrant colors of Walter Anderson's Realizations – now delicate, now robust.

And if that wasn't enough, the Belhaven Dance Department presented a musical palette-full of splendid dancing; Dr. Tim Coker provided a moving setting of Psalm 104 for unaccompanied men's chorus and mezzo; and William Fulton gave a stirring narration about Anderson, all enhanced by striking projections of Anderson's art and family photographs.

And to think that this was just the send-off performance for the Discovery Theater at the

Smithsonian in Washington, D.C. on January 9 and 10, 2004. What a great way to showcase the talent that is ours in Mississippi.

The Clarion-Ledger
Letter to the Editor
Saturday, January 14, 2006

Piano Extravaganza Wowed Crowd

Wow! The concert of Eighty-Eight (the number of keys on a piano) Times Eight (the number of pianists at eight grand pianos) was outstanding.

The sensational piano concert rivaled anything to appear on a Jackson stage in recent memory. ("Pianists keyed up for MSO benefit concert," Jan. 4).

Billed as a piano extravaganza, the concert showcased the talents of metro area pianists under the baton of Crafton Beck.

Lester Senter charmed the audience in her recitation of poems by Ogden Nash set to *The Carnival of Animals* by Saint-Saens. Senter, with Tim Coker as co-producer, brought Phil Pletcher, music director of St. Cecelia Music Society, of Grand Rapids Michigan to Jackson as music consultant.

By audience demand, an encore of the finale, *The Stars and Stripes Forever,* nearly brought the house down. It featured eight additional pianists.

Best of all, the concert was to benefit the Mississippi Symphony Orchestra. Wow!

The Clarion-Ledger
Letter to the Editor
Saturday, January 3, 2009

Holiday Offerings Provide Pleasure

Christmastime in the metro area offers a surfeit of entertainment with talent that rivals the best anywhere. Considering that most performances are free or offer reasonably priced tickets – there's a wealth of pleasure to be had by the audiences who attend.

Probably the most well-known and widely-attended event is First Baptist Jackson's *Carols by Candlelight.* Every year the program spotlights outstanding soloists, vocal ensembles, and musicians, and this year's *Home for Christmas 2008* was no exception. The personal dedication and sacrifice by members of the choir, cast and crew at a busy holiday time, not to mention the physical drain of rehearsals and four performances, is laudable and greatly appreciated by the community.

Equally enjoyable is First Baptist's *Keyboards for Christmas.*

Jackson's First Presbyterian Church's annual music program, *A Christmas Service of Lessons and Carols,* has always been a personal favorite, and I seldom miss Ballet Magnificat's annual performance of *A Christmas Dream* directed by Kathy Thibodeaux, Jackson's premier ballerina and 1982 Silver Medalist at the II USA International Ballet Competition.

Exceptional in this year's performance was Jiri Sebastian Voborsky, who choreographed the Battle Scene and danced the lead as Beelzebub.

The performances of New Stage Theatre's classic *A Christmas Carol;* Ballet Mississippi's *The Nutcracker;* Belhaven College's *Singing Christmas Tree*, (in its 76th season!); and the many churches and schools that present outstanding music programs add up to an exceptional holiday smorgasbord.

I hope everyone who enjoyed the offerings of so many talented individuals will join me in expressing heartfelt thanks and appreciation to each and every one of them for their time, talent and hard work to give us all the Christmas spirit.

CHAPTER VII

Immigration

Mexico President Vicente Fox is in the United States. He's been here three days and already has a job and a social security number.

Conan O'Brian

The Clarion-Ledger
Thursday, March 6, 2003

U.S. Border Protection Vital to Our Defense

The United States is being invaded!

Illegal aliens are sneaking into our country at the rate of approximately a half-million each year. In 2001, the U.S. Census Bureau set the number of illegal aliens in the U.S. at 8 million, but some analysts have set the number as high as 11 or 12 million.

Of primary concern is the U.S.-Mexico border where civilian patrol groups are being forced to take up arms to stem the flood of migrants illegally crossing into the United States.

For years, border states have been overwhelmed with illegals who are depleting available funds for education, healthcare, housing, social services, and police protection.

Terror, drugs, disease ….

Many illegal aliens are trafficking in drugs, and some illegals bring exotic diseases and new strains of old diseases across the border. And still others enter the country illegally to engage in terrorist acts.

Border Patrol agents have confirmed that large numbers of Middle Easterners are illegally crossing our southern border. The trial in El Paso of an Iraqi smuggler produced evidence that he alone brought more than 1,000 Middle East illegals into the United States via that route.

Mexico's president, Vicente Fox, has attacked current U.S. immigration policies and in a five-year development plan presented to the Mexican Congress, he called for the elimination of the U.S.- Mexican border. He has demanded amnesty for illegal aliens and wants U.S. laws rewritten to allow illegal aliens to obtain U.S. driver's licenses (even though they don't have insurance and are unable to read road signs).

Mexican consulates in the U.S. are issuing an identification card called "matricula consular" to Mexicans illegally living in the U.S. The cards are part of Fox's plan to establish "illegal status" for undocumented immigrants and access U.S. privileges and benefits to which they are not entitled. In some states, driver's license offices, banks, and law enforcement officials are already accepting the matricula consular as though it were a valid I.D. card.

And now, Washington bureaucrats have hatched a "Totalization" program to provide illegal immigrants with Social Security benefits. This shocking proposal is projected to siphon some $345 billion from the Social Security "trust fund" over the next couple of decades, mostly to pay benefits to Mexican citizens who work illegally in the United States.

Fox is playing politics

Vicente Fox is playing U.S. politics to achieve his goals and it seems that the Bush Administration is being "out-Foxed" and willing to give away the whole enchilada. That is, unless the American people wake up and demand an immediate stop to this foolishness.

The Republican National Committee is hard at work trying to wrest the Hispanic vote away from the Democrats. This is a huge mistake.

A study from the nonpartisan Center for Immigration Studies confirms that as immigrants naturalize, they swing even further to the left and support the core position of the Democrat Party.

If the Republicans want to see George W. Bush reelected, they'd be wise to do what is right for the country rather than what they perceive as being right for the party.

If the tide of immigrants entering the U.S., both legally and illegally, is allowed to continue unchecked, our country will bear no resemblance to the United States that the Founders fought so hard to establish.

The Clarion-Ledger
Sunday, June 4, 2006

Just Say No to Senate's Immigration Legislation

When George W. Bush sides with Ted Kennedy on an issue and gets accolades from Jimmy Carter, you know we're in trouble!

The Hagel-Martinez amnesty bill (S.2611) that was passed May 25 by the U.S. Senate has been called "abominable," "incomprehensible," "a disaster" and "a betrayal," among other things.

It is probably one of the worst pieces of legislation ever foisted on the citizens of the United States.

Thank goodness, Mississippi's two senators, Thad Cochran and Trent Lott, had their heads on straight and voted against it.

The bill grants amnesty to more than 15 million illegal aliens, putting them on the "path" to U.S. citizenship.

Amnesty bill misguided

If this weren't bad enough, the Senate bill would admit 66 million new foreigners over the next 20 years, and loads them onto our entitlement benefit programs, including Social Security – a program already heading for insolvency for the next generation of Americans.

The amnesty bill would also allow illegals to have the privilege of bringing in extended family members, which could double or triple the projected 66 million new immigrants.

Every poll shows that an overwhelming majority of Americans want our borders secured. Yet, employers who hire illegals are let off scot free, exempting employers from any civil or criminal liability prosecution or penalty.

The Basic Pilot Verification Program, which requires employers to check the legality of workers, was scrapped.

Worst of all, while a token 370 miles of border fencing won approval, (half of the fencing proposed by the House), the Senate bill contains no meaningful enforcement to stem the flood of illegal aliens crossing the southern border – an open invitation to terrorists.

Consider the unfairness to American agricultural laborers, who can be fired for any reason, while "temporary guest workers" cannot be fired by their employers except for what the bill calls "just cause." Additionally, guest workers must be paid the prevailing wage while American workers have no such guarantee.

Many parents make huge sacrifices to give their kids a college education. But the Senate bill provides for in-state tuition for illegal aliens. With public education costs skyrocketing, just imagine what it will do to our education system when we have to add untold numbers of immigrants, both legal and illegal, who don't even speak English.

Taxpayers bear burden

Taxpayers are already bearing the burden of medical care for those who cross our borders illegally and for incarceration of illegal criminals who currently make up one-third of the prisoner population in the federal prison system.

And the outrage of having Mexico's President, Vicente Fox, dictate to us what we should and should not do with those who have broken our laws, should make American citizens' blood boil. Even the immigrant-rights groups are rewarded under the bill with taxpayer dollars being provided them to help illegal aliens "adjust."

What ever happened to national sovereignty? This is a nation that once was governed by the rule of law.

The 62 senators who voted for amnesty for those who have broken our laws should be tarred and feathered and run out of Washington on a rail.

My prayer is that as the senate bill goes to conference with the House border security first bill (H.R. 4437), that House members will hold firm to their resolve and say no to any report that includes guest-worker/amnesty or increases legal immigration.

The Clarion-Ledger
Letter to the Editor
Sunday, September 3, 2006

Illegal Immigration Foe Not Necessarily a Bigot

The editorial ("Immigration: Mississippi caught in the puzzle," Aug. 22) accuses those who have expressed concerns over the massive influx of illegal aliens into this country as exhibiting a "backlash of xenophobia and bigotry against illegal immigrants."

Xenophobia – with its connotation of a personal, unfounded hatred or fear of strangers; and bigotry, with its connotation of an unfounded personal prejudice against a particular person or class of persons; are both highly inflammatory and blatantly degrading labels.

When you paint with a sweeping brush, you have unjustly branded thousands of Mississippians who have genuine concerns about illegal immigration and the aliens who have openly violated the laws of this nation with impunity and without accountability.

And how can you suggest that our supposed dependency on immigrant labor and the "benefits" it affords qualifies lawbreakers for amnesty and future U.S. citizenship? Does it benefit this country to have a servant class of low-wage, non-English-speaking immigrants unable to climb up the economic ladder?

The editorial, while making a few positive points, rings hollow with the plea "to address issues without rancor" while at the same time publicly pinning the unwarranted and provocative labels of "xenophobe" and "bigot" on those having opposing views.

The Madison County Herald
Fall of 2006

Enforce Immigration Laws Now

The guest column by Trent Lott ("Senate must focus on Iraq, energy, illegal immigration," Sept. 7) sounds as if he's planning a compromise on the illegal immigration issue.

The article states that Lott has "voiced support for a temporary worker program where foreign nationals wanting to work here would be allowed to do so, but only for a short time and under close watch before being required to return home."

I would like to know how this would be accomplished.

What new governmental agency would be created to keep "a close watch" on "foreign nationals," (I call them illegal aliens) and just how would the tens of thousands already here be registered? And how, "after a short time," would they be rounded up if they decide they don't want to go home?

**And why should law abiding American taxpayers be asked to foot the bill for yet another unworkable bureaucratic plan when the effort to keep hoards of illegal aliens from crossing our borders has been a miserable failure?*

Trent's right about one thing: Americans do want action! Not the action of compromise, but action such as Congressman Tom Tancredo is proposing.

Since Trent's decisions on illegal immigration will be based on what is best for America, may I suggest beginning with securing our borders? Along with that, grant no amnesty for those who have entered this country illegally. Enforce the law dealing with employers who hire illegals. Protect U.S. sovereignty by refusing to erase our southern and northern borders to integrate the U.S. with Mexico and Canada. **Support legislation designating English as the official language because a bi-lingual society will divide our country. Do whatever is necessary to stop the overburdening of our prisons, schools, and medical facilities with people who are not American citizens and are in this country illegally.*

That, Senator Lott, is what's best for the United States of America!

*Omitted when published.

The Clarion-Ledger
Monday, January 29, 2007

Legislators Must Address Illegal Immigrations' Impact

Will Mississippi be last again? I hope not. Those in the know seem to think that the Mississippi Legislature will once again turn a blind eye to the problem of illegal immigration.

Hardly a mention has been made by the news media of any bills, even though 13 have been introduced, that address constituency concerns about the thousands of illegal aliens pouring into Mississippi.

Rising education costs, job losses, escalating crime rates, and soaring costs of medical care are issues that directly affect the taxpaying citizens of this state and are impacted by those who have entered our country illegally.

With the federal government refusing to protect our borders or enforce the laws already on the books, states have been forced to take the initiative in addressing the problem.

More than 500 bills were introduced in state legislatures last year with 57 being passed. The State of Georgia approved a bill, described as the "strongest single bill in America dealing with illegal immigration," that would require adults seeking benefits to prove U.S. citizenship, sanction employers who hire illegals, and require police to verify the legal status of anyone arrested.

Bills passed by other states deny health benefits, in-state college tuition, drivers' licenses and voter registration to anyone who cannot prove U.S. citizenship or legal immigrant status.

It's a crying shame that Mississippi lawmakers have thus far been unable to pass any Voter ID bill – much less one that would require proof of citizenship to become a registered voter.

According to a *Clarion-Ledger* article ("State has the highest percentage increase in immigrants, Oct. 5, 2006), the Center of Immigration Studies (CIS) reports that in terms of the percentage of immigrant population growth, Mississippi led the nation with an increase between 2000 and 2005 from 29,000 to 72,000 immigrants or 148.7 percent.

That's the highest rate of immigrant population growth in the nation and more than eight times the national average – and most of these immigrants are illegal aliens entering the United States across our southern border.

The study, titled *Immigrants at Mid-Decade: A Snapshot of America's Foreign-Born Population in 2005*, authored by CIS director of research Steven A. Camorota, shows that of adult immigrants, 31 percent have not completed high school, three and a half times the rate for natives.

Also, according to the study, the poverty rate for immigrants and their U.S.-born children (under 18) is 18.4 percent, 57 percent higher than the 11.7 percent for natives and their children. Immigrants and their minor children account for almost one in four persons living in poverty nationally.

The state auditor's office reported that illegal immigrants cost the state an estimated $25 million in 2005.

If Mississippi had 72,000 immigrants, according to the March 2005 CIS report, just imagine how those numbers and costs to the taxpayer have skyrocketed with the influx of illegal aliens seeking work on the Gulf Coast in the wake of Katrina.

Mississippi lawmakers can no longer ignore a problem that is rapidly escalating. It's up to us, who elected these legislators to office, to hold them accountable for passing significant legislation to deal with the problem.

The Clarion-Ledger
Sunday, December 9, 2007

Support English-Only Workplace Allowance
(or as I titled it, "Press One for English!")

I don't know about you, but I do a slow burn when I get a recorded telephone message telling me to "press 1 for English." I can't understand why so many businesses are quick to jump on the bandwagon of bilingualism and compromise the language of this country. Don't they realize that it's an affront to customers who speak the language of the United States, which is ENGLISH?

Early immigrants were assimilated into American public life because they learned to speak English. Today we seem determined to make it as easy as possible for immigrants and aliens NOT to have to learn English.

This is a prescription for disaster.

Richard Lamm, former governor of Colorado, nailed it when he said, "If you want to destroy America, turn it into a bilingual or multi-lingual and bicultural country. History shows that no nation can survive the tension, conflict and antagonism of two or more competing languages and cultures."

Yet we have people quick to accommodate *their* language. Bilingual recorded telephone messages are more the norm than the exception; ballots and government documents are printed in multiple languages (Los Angeles taxpayers footed the bill for $3.4 million to print ballots in seven languages); employment is based on whether an applicant can speak a 2nd language (many school districts are requiring prospective teachers to be able to speak Spanish); packaging directions and information on labels and advertisements are almost always printed in more than one language; and 38 states offer drivers license exams in a language other than English.

In the year 2000, 11.9 million U.S. residents were "linguistically isolated." This reflects an increase of more than 53 percent from 7.7 million in 1990. (Source 2000 Census)

And now this outrage ....

When the Salvation Army required employees to speak English while on the job, the Equal Employment Opportunity Commission (EEOC) sued the Salvation Army because it believes requiring employees to speak English violates their civil rights!

Thanks to Senator Lamar Alexander R-TN an amendment to the Commerce, Justice, Science (CJS) Appropriations Bill (H.R. 3093), to prohibit federal funds from being used by the EEOC to sue employers for requiring English on the job has passed the Senate. When the House and the Senate met in a conference committee to reconcile their CJS bill, the House voted 218-186 to instruct the House conferees to agree with the Senate and keep the Alexander language.

However, Speaker Nancy Pelosi, Majority Leader Steny Hoyer, and Senate Majority Leader Harry Reid ordered that negotiations be indefinitely halted because they oppose allowing the Alexander English amendment to be included in the bill.

The CJS conference committee should reconvene immediately, and Senator Thad Cochran is one of the conferees. The Democrat leadership, Senator Cochran and your representatives should be contacted ASAP via Capitol Switchboard (202) 224-3121 and told that you want English spoken in the workplace. Ask them to support the Alexander English amendment to prevent businesses from being sued if they require employees to speak English on the job!

The Clarion-Ledger
Letter to the Editor
Sunday, February 3, 2008

Barbour Priority Must Be Illegal Immigration

Gov. Haley Barbour's priority during the next 4 years should be addressing the problem of illegal immigration.

Based on his State of the State Address, nary a word on illegal immigration was mentioned and his campaign promises to the people of the State of Mississippi were just that ... campaign promises – once elected, soon forgotten. By comparison, Gov. Tim Kaine of Virginia dedicated 14 of 131 paragraphs to the subject in his State of the Commonwealth Address.

Surely Gov. Barbour knows that illegal immigration impacts every aspect of the issues he considers important: education, health care, jobs, crime, and taxes; and that the drain on state resources will continue to increase until significant state legislation is enacted.

The federal "immigration reform" bill to grant amnesty to millions of illegal aliens who continue to cross our borders in droves, failed miserably last year when the American people rose up to oppose it.

With Congress unable to close our borders or strengthen immigration laws and President Bush making deals with Mexico and Canada to erase our borders, states have been forced to enact laws to deal with the problem.

Last year forty-three states enacted 182 immigration-related laws. This year, Missouri Gov. Matt Blunt, Minnesota Gov. Tim Pawlenty, and Nebraska Gov. Dave Heineman, along with legislative leaders in almost every state in the Union, are supporting legislative initiatives to crack down on illegals and those who break the law by employing them.

Georgia, Arizona, Colorado, and Oklahoma are seeing illegals immigrants leave their states because of the laws they have enacted. And where do they go? Either back to their homes south of the border or to states that do not have immigration laws – like Mississippi.

But being the good Republican that he is, Barbour marches to the drum of the commander-in-chief who has tried to destroy the Republican Party with his open-border policy. Barbour is also beholden to big business that profits from cheap labor and fills campaign coffers with big bucks.

From 2000 to 2005 Mississippi had the greatest increase (148.7 percent) in immigrants – most of whom are illegal – than any other state in the Union. If the Mississippi Legislature once again fails to act and Gov. Barbour fails to provide the leadership to get the job done, Mississippi will become, by default, a sanctuary state for even more illegal aliens, and the taxpayer will be expected to pick up the tab.

CHAPTER VIII

Crime

The law is not a "light" for you or any man to see by; the law is not an instrument of any kind. The law is a causeway upon which, so long as he keeps to it, a citizen may walk safely.

Robert Bolt
A Man for All Seasons, Act II

The Clarion-Ledger
Tuesday, September 5, 1995

An Inefficient, Part-Time Court System Won't Work

Citizen volunteers in MCC's Court Watch project have revealed major problems.

The Metropolitan Crime Commission (MCC), founded in 1994 by citizens concerned about escalating crime in the tri-county area, has initiated projects and identified problem areas in the criminal justice system in an effort to make the Jackson area a safer place to live and work.

For the criminal justice system to work effectively, there are certain steps that must be taken:

- An arrest must be made.
- Prosecution must be undertaken.
- A court trial must be held and conviction obtained.
- Appropriate incarceration facilities must be available.

Each one of these steps is essential or the system will fail.

Chief Justice Warren E. Burger observed that to work effectively, it is important that society's criminal process satisfy the appearance of justice ... and the appearance of justice can best be provided by allowing people to observe it.

Observing is just what citizen volunteers in MCC's Court Watch project do. Through on-site monitoring, they are able to gauge the effectiveness and responsiveness of judges, prosecutors and law enforcement personnel and report their findings to the general public.

A shocking report on the Hinds Circuit Court system, buried on page 2B of the Aug. 30 edition of *The Clarion-Ledger* should have made the front page. During testimony by Hinds District Attorney Ed Peters, before MCC's Task Force on Criminal Justice, the following came to light through an ongoing MCC study:

- The average time between arrest and trial of a drug trafficker is 437 days, with most spending the vast majority of that time out on bond.
- Of 210 cases examined which were finally adjudicated during the first six months of this year, a total of 25,226 days were lost to continuances that had been granted – at the rate of seven-to-one in favor of defense attorneys – during the life of the cases.
- Hinds County Circuit Court judges spent only two of every five working days, about 16 hours each per week on the bench.

This jibes with what Court Watchers continually report: that courtrooms are under-utilized and that judges are on the bench too infrequently.

It would seem that overcrowded court dockets and high criminal caseloads would generate a sense of urgency. Not so. In June, judges lost 160 hours of potential court time during the Mississippi Bar Association convention in Florida and lost 32 hours celebrating a two-day Memorial Day holiday.

Jackson Police Chief Robert Johnson, confirmed to MCC's Task Force on Criminal Justice, that "Our judges here are *under-worked* when compared against similar jurisdictions."

Judges do hear preliminary matters, review legal motions and write opinions outside of the courtroom, but from all reports, there's still approximately 60 percent of unaccountable time.

And then there are administrative problems ....

According to Chief Johnson, there is a definite need for better communication among judges and prosecutors. He states: "we have four courts that don't talk to each other. Things as simple as a common court docket would alleviate a lot of that."

The "need" is echoed in a June 1994 Task Force report to the Hinds County Board of Supervisors, stating that each of the four (Circuit Court) judges handles only his cases, independently of the others, without even a common court administrator and there is no system to assure uniform sentencing for similar offenses.

It was reported that the system is "unnecessarily complex and fragmented and needs administration from a person or agency with the authority and responsibility to ensure that all parts within the system work effectively together."

That report, virtually ignored by public officials, called for the following:

- The courts to adopt some broad latitude in sentencing guidelines for uniformity.
- The establishment of a county-wide computer system connecting all court dispositions.
- Creation of a special court for the prosecution of drug cases exclusively.
- Passage of legislation to allow Circuit Court and state prosecutors to concentrate on major felony and major drug violations and provide adequate space for city and county courts to handle misdemeanor cases that are presently clogging the Circuit Courts.
- Speeding up the process of explaining constitutional rights to those entering guilty pleas, thereby saving hours of waiting by jurors, victims, witnesses and attorneys.

An inefficient judicial system operating at only "part-time" capacity does nothing to expedite the administration of justice, and fails to instill confidence in either our court system or in our judges' determination to fulfill their responsibilities to the community.

The breakdown in the "court trial and conviction" step, necessary for the system to work, should be remedied immediately to assure that when arrests are made the criminal will be expeditiously prosecuted to the full extent of the law, given the maximum sentence and put behind bars.

We've just celebrated a holiday that honors labor and the laborer. If we really mean business about crime, it's time to turn on the lights in the courtrooms, address and resolve the dysfunctions in the criminal justice system, and make the administration of justice more effective and more responsive to the needs of our communities.

Criminals will never be removed from our streets unless the court system works ... and works well.

The Clarion-Ledger
Tuesday, January 9, 1996

Oakley Training School Has Become a Success Story in the Making

No wonder professionals from around the nation have come knocking at the door to learn Oakley's secret.

Just south of Raymond, on 2,714 acres that was once the site of a state penitentiary farm, is a success story in the making.

It's called Oakley Training School, and it is receiving world-wide recognition as a model juvenile correctional institution.

I have visited the campus on two occasions, and both visits reinforced the opinion that something is being done right at Oakley.

Call it enthusiasm or *esprit de corps* – it's there and it's contagious. You catch the feeling as you walk the campus or visit a classroom. You see it in the faces of the young cadets.

Much of Oakley's present day success can be attributed to Don Taylor. Taylor, director of the Division of Youth Services in 1992 and now director of the Department of Human Services, provided the vision, the know-how, and the leadership to give Mississippi an outstanding juvenile correctional institution.

In the words of Dr. Nanolla Yazdani, administrator of Oakley, Don Taylor has the brain, the heart, and the intestinal fortitude for the job.

The military program developed by Taylor in 1992, and carried forward by Walter Wood, present director of the Division of Youth Services, proffers Spartan living conditions, a structured daily routine and rigorous physical fitness in directing the rehabilitation process.

The core component of the program is the boot camp regimen of inspections and military drills. Each cadet learns at the outset that (1) he is at Oakley, (2) there are others in charge, and (3) he's going to get his life together.

A typical day begins at 4:30 a.m.

Upon arrival, the cadet is given a military style haircut and learns the correct military response to commands. "Yes sir" and "no sir" become a part of the cadet's vocabulary early in the Oakley experience.

Following a complete medical evaluation, assignments are made to a receiving unit where each individual is screened to assess educational, psychological, vocational, and recreational needs. Tests are administered to determine academic and aptitude levels.

After team evaluation, the cadet begins a three-week period of basic training which is designed to develop leadership, creative thinking, and a more focused individual.

A 100 percent performance is required in basic training to qualify for graduation to an advanced unit.

Contributing to the success story are Oakley's 155 staff members who become the authority figures in the lives of some 250 juvenile males, 15-17 years of age. The staff, working as a team, is dedicated to professionalism combined with tough love. They are trained to deal with young men, some of whom, through no fault of their own, are in need of the kind of guidance that will give them a step up in gaining self control, self confidence, and necessary skills for responsible adulthood.

Statistics tell much of the success story. Most impressive is the rate of recidivism at Oakley. Of the 2,382 graduated since the military program began, only 246 have been returned. This 10.32 percent recidivism is truly exceptional.

In comparison, before the program was instituted, the recidivism rate was 55 percent, which is about the average for juvenile correctional institutions.

Ten years ago, the training school averaged 70-80 escapes a year. (Oakley has no walls or fences; so the term "escape" means leaving without permission.)

Since the inception of the military program, that number has declined dramatically. In 1995, only one cadet went AWOL, giving Oakley the lowest "escape" record in the United States. No wonder the American Correctional Association and other professionals have come knocking at the door to learn Oakley's secret.

Foremost in Oakley's success story is the recognition that juveniles incarcerated in correctional and detention facilities have had poor elementary and secondary education experiences. For many, difficulties in reading underlie their poor academic achievement, and most have been pushed through school on the basis of age rather than achievement.

According to an October, 1994 Juvenile Justice Bulletin published by the U.S. Department of Justice, the average reading ability of youth confined in correctional institutions is at the fourth-grade level. To address this deficiency, an intensive, systematic phonics reading program, developed by a 1991 competitive grant awarded to Mississippi University for Women, has been introduced at Oakley.

The results of the project have been dramatic with increased skills in composition, vocabulary, mechanics, and spelling reported in 75 percent of participants. Moreover, students demonstrate newly found self-esteem and improved self-image.

At a time when many troubled young people find correctional institutions a revolving door, the effective military program and team effort of a caring and dedicated staff make Oakley Training School the best kind of success story – a story not just of incarcerated juvenile delinquents, but of young lives being molded into productive, law-abiding citizens.

The Clarion-Ledger
Monday, July 7, 1997

New City Council's Priority: Move Quickly on Youth Detention Center

The long overdue final argument between the city and county is still up in the air.

Today is a historic day for the city of Jackson. Great expectations for effective leadership rest on the new city administration elected to lead Jackson into the 21st century.

There are many pressing issues demanding immediate attention. High on the list is the building of the new youth detention center.

I don't know about you, but my patience is beginning to wear thin as I see the years slip by with the long overdue final agreement on the facility still up in the air.

By now, everyone knows the facts and figures – approximately 60 percent of the crime in Jackson is committed by juveniles; the present juvenile detention center is unfit and grossly inadequate; and after years of costly studies and reports, we still don't have the desperately needed juvenile detention center.

The buck has been passed so many times from the Hinds County Board of Supervisors to the Jackson City Council and back again that the 1995 cost estimate of $8 million for the facility is now $9 million. The architect estimates that if construction begins next May, it will take a full year for the facility to be completed. That means that we are still two years away, barring any future delays.

In January of 1996, George Smith, then president of the Hinds County Board of Supervisors, told the Metropolitan Crime Commission that a new juvenile detention center could be open in 1 1/2 years. That would have been this month.

What happened?

Disagreements arose between the city and county over who would pay for building and operating the juvenile detention facility.

Does it really matter? It's taxpayer money, whether city or county. And in the meantime youth offenders are either freed under judges' orders to stalk more victims, or else they are farmed out to other facilities around the state at $80 a day per youth – quite a hefty bill for taxpayers to pay.

I attended the Hinds County Board of Supervisors meeting several weeks ago when plans for the new youth detention center were scheduled to be approved. Instead of that being top priority, Doug Anderson, president of the board, didn't want to take time from the agenda to hear from the architects who were present to submit final design plans. Doesn't the board realize that until plans are approved, construction bids can't be let?

While the Board of Supervisors did approve the estimated cost of $9 million, they failed to approve the architects' plan. At least, at a snail's pace, the board began the process by authorizing action to secure right-of-way access to the proposed detention center's nine-acre site off McDowell Road and South Gallatin so that construction on sewer lines can begin.

Although on several occasions informal agreements have been reached, none has resulted in a final binding agreement between the city and county that would meet all requirements of state and federal law.

The city and the county have been given notice that the current juvenile detention facility fails to meet standards required by law. Such failure could subject the public officials responsible to legal action.

If city and county officials do not act promptly, this matter could be placed in the hands of a federal court by the Justice Department, a Youth Court judge, a city or county official, the parent or guardian of a detainee, a non-governmental organization, a taxpayer, or some other person, organization or public official with standing to sue.

The citizens of Jackson and Hinds County expect and deserve to have their tax dollars spent on building an adequate facility and not on defending public officials in lawsuits.

And now the ball is in the court of the new Jackson City Council, being put there by the former city administration who delayed action until the new officials are sworn in.

A test of the leadership of Mayor Harvey Johnson and the effectiveness of the new city administration is how rapidly they can move ahead with the county to finalize plans and begin construction.

A new juvenile detention center should be the first priority of the new city administration.

CHAPTER IX

The Natchez Trace

Earth has not anything to show more fair:
Dull would he be of soul who could pass
by a sight so touching in its majesty.

William Wordsworth

THE NATCHEZ TRACE PARKWAY

The Natchez Trace Parkway, begun in 1937 and finished in 2005, runs 444-miles from Natchez, Mississippi to Nashville, Tennessee. It is one of about 365 units in the system of national parks and monuments supervised by the United States National Park Service. The Parkway is unique in that while it is a roadway, it was designed more as a park where leisure travelers could experience its scenic beauty, rich history, and varied recreational activities.

The Natchez Trace Parkway runs through the northwest tip of Alabama for 33 miles and crosses the Tennessee River 102 miles into Tennessee before reaching the northern terminus just south of Nashville. Mississippi's 309 miles cuts diagonally across the heart of the state and because Tupelo, Mississippi, is about the halfway mark between the northern and southern terminus, the Parkway Headquarters and Visitors Center is located there.

I love the Natchez Trace, and it concerns me that so many Mississippians seem to know little of its historical significance and the great benefits the Parkway provides for our state – both financially, from tourism dollars – to the recreational opportunities for our citizens.

I began addressing some of the issues in the press when I saw the protective laws being weakened with exemptions by the Mississippi Legislature.

It's not rocket science to know that if exemptions are granted for building and commercial development in one locale along the Trace, it will be difficult to deny the same exemptions for building in other locales. The domino effect that will be created will destroy the scenic viewshed and threaten the esthetics that makes the Parkway one of America's most-visited national parks.

With more than five million people a year visiting the Natchez Trace, how short-sighted we would be to allow special interest groups to bring pressure to bear on legislators to further weaken the laws that have protected the Natchez Trace Parkway for the past 40 years.

The Clarion-Ledger
Sunday, May 17, 1998
Reprinted in *The Coffeeville Courier*, August 6, 1998

Slow Going on the Natchez Trace

After 60 years, it is time to complete the Natchez Trace

Sixty years ago, on May 18, 1938, the Natchez Trace Parkway was established by an Act of Congress. In exchange for conveyance of lands for parkway construction, the federal government committed to timely completion of the roadway.

Timely?

Sixty years and approximately $397.7 million dollars later, 20 miles still remain to be completed in the state of Mississippi. Eight miles of parkway have been partially funded and construction is under way. Left to be funded are the last 12 miles, and Congress is dragging its feet on appropriating the estimated $72 million cost.

Uncompleted parts of the Trace include a segment from Ridgeland to Clinton around Jackson, parts of which are now under construction, and another 8-mile section at the end of the Parkway at Natchez from U.S. 61 at Washington to Prentiss Street.

With open support from the Natchez Trace Parkway Association, numerous civic groups and communities, the congressional delegations from Mississippi, Alabama and Tennessee, and a U.S. Senate resolution supporting the continuation of funding for the parkway, why in the name of Ned can't we get it finished?

One major reason is that the National Park Service feels it has higher priority projects than the Natchez Trace Parkway. Even with the House and Senate directing the department to commit $10 to $25 million per year, only $5.1 million was appropriated for fiscal year 1998.

At that rate and with a price tag of $72 million on the remaining 12 miles, it will take 15 years to complete the parkway. Theoretically, that means less than a mile a year will be constructed and that the 2003-2006 projected completion date is merely a figment of a federal bureaucrat's imagination.

The historic Natchez Trace Parkway is more than 400 miles long, cutting a diagonal path across Mississippi, the northwest corner of Alabama, winding to an end in Nashville, Tennessee.

Beginning as a timeworn buffalo path thousands of years ago, the scenic roadway has been trekked by Indians, Kaintuck boatmen, frontiersmen, missionaries, bandits, and fortune seekers.

In 1909, the Mississippi Society Daughters of the American Revolution spearheaded the initial campaign to mark the Old Trace, seeing its work culminated with the development of the modern Natchez Trace Parkway. The vision of those early activists came to fruition when Congress authorized the survey of the Old Trace in 1934 and began construction on the roadway in 1937.

No one would have dreamed that 60 years later the Natchez Trace Parkway would still be under construction.

The present day parkway is one of this country's longest and most beautiful recreational drives, enjoying tremendous popularity with national and international visitors. In 1997, approximately 12.9 million people traveled the parkway, enjoying its scenic beauty, abundant wildlife, and recreational facilities.

What will it take to finally see the Natchez Trace Parkway completed? Oil! The oil that makes the "squeaking wheel" stop squeaking.

And that's where we come in. We are the "wheels" that have to start "squeaking".

In addition to each person in the Mississippi Congressional delegation, especially Trent Lott, who enjoys a catbird seat, you need to contact Vice President Al Gore.

The beauty of the parkway should rank high on his environmental agenda, and its completion should be a plus for his home state of Tennessee.

Ask, no, demand, that the full estimated amount for funding be appropriated and that the target date for completion be no later than the year 2003.

I don't believe that this is an unreasonable request. Sixty years is ample time to build a road. According to Sen. Thad Cochran, "It is taking us longer to complete the Natchez Trace Parkway than it did for the Romans to build the Appian Way."

It will take a concerted effort by every interested Mississippian.

The 4,700 plus members of the Mississippi DAR will once again become actively involved to get the job done. Every Mississippian who values the beautiful Natchez Trace Parkway as one of our state's great natural resources should join the campaign.

The Natchez Democrat
Letter to the Editor
Friday, July 17, 1998

Natchez Trace Deserves a Terminus Near the River

The National Park Service held hearings the second week of June for public input on the southern terminus of the Natchez Trace Parkway. I attended the meeting held in Jackson to learn of the plans being proposed for the completion of the Parkway and read with interest the article from the June 19, *Natchez Democrat* "Extending Natchez Trace to the downtown called `ideal'."

In 1908, the Mississippi State Society Daughters of the American Revolution spearheaded the initial campaign to develop and preserve the old Natchez Trace by placing the first marker on the Trace Road in Tishomingo County. The second marker, which stands on the Mississippi River bluff in Natchez, was placed in 1908. A total of 14 markers were placed as Mississippi Daughters campaigned to have the Natchez Trace paved. Their efforts were rewarded when Congress passed an act on May 21, 1934, to authorize a survey of the "old Indian Trail" known as the Natchez Trace with a view toward constructing a national road.

In February 1937, a historic event took place when dignitaries gathered at the original marker on the Mississippi River bluff to sign the receipt of the first government check to begin the paving of the Natchez Trace. In 1938, President Franklin Roosevelt signed an act making the Natchez Trace Parkway a part of the National Park Service.

The reason I've given this brief history of the parkway development is to stress the importance of having the southern terminus end at the Mississippi River, where historically the Natchez Trace began.

Three plans were presented by the Park Service, none of which terminated at the Mississippi River. Of the proposals presented, "Alternative 2" extends the Parkway nearest the river and the new Intermodal Center. According to the article in *The Democrat,* once that phase of the project is completed, city and national officials can start working on bringing the Trace all the way to downtown Natchez.

My question is why wait? If the Illinois Central Railroad is "eager to relocate" and the railroad right-of-way is the perfect route from Liberty Road to the bluff, why can't the completion of the southern terminus include bringing the Trace to its original beginning?

Each day that goes by, each mile of the unfinished roadway costs more. The decision should be made to extend the Parkway to the Mississippi River, finalize plans for construction, and seek full funding from Congress to bring this project to conclusion.

In May, the U.S. Park Service celebrated the 60th anniversary of the Natchez Trace Parkway. Sixty years is long enough to wait for the scenic and historic roadway from Natchez to Nashville to be completed.

The Clarion-Ledger
Tuesday, March 16, 1999

Funding, Repair Are Critical Needs for Natchez Trace

It will have taken 67 years, if all goes well, to finally complete the 444 miles of the scenic national roadway known as the Natchez Trace Parkway that connects Natchez to Nashville.

The Parkway, including related facilities such as visitor centers, campgrounds, picnic areas, trails, interpretive exhibits, maintenance areas, ranger stations, and administrative facilities, now serves approximately 12 million visitors annually. It is one of Mississippi's greatest natural resources.

While the funds for completing the Parkway were appropriated last year by Congress, there is a critical need for additional funding to operate and maintain the roadway and to construct needed facilities.

As part of the National Park Service, the Natchez Trace Parkway has fared worst than average for operating funding. Since 1986, the relative operating dollar increase for units of the National Park Service has averaged 52 percent while the Natchez Trace Parkway received only 12 percent.

This difference has resulted in a drop of the Parkway's operating funding from $13,000 per mile to $8,600 per mile, a decrease of 34 percent.

Since 1980, 138 additional miles of Parkway and related facilities have been constructed, representing a 48 percent increase in physical plant.

When devalued for inflation, the Parkway's operating funding increased by only1 percent over this same period.

In order to cope, operations on existing sections of the Parkway have been severely reduced, including a 20 percent reduction in operations overall.

Road maintenance hurt

This lack of funding has greatly affected road maintenance. If 25 miles of roadway were resurfaced each year, it would take 20 years to complete a full cycle of resurfacing. But in the past 20 years because of decreased funding, only 41 miles of existing parkway have been resurfaced.

The seventeen comfort stations/restrooms along the Parkway have been serving visitors for more than 35 years. They are old, small, and cannot be remodeled to meet the Americans with Disabilities Act (ADA) standards. The comfort stations need to be replaced at the rate of five per year in order to meet the targeted roadway completion date of 2005.

Mississippi's congressional delegation, the Natchez Trace Parkway Association, and numerous municipalities and civic groups have campaigned for completion of the Parkway. Because the public is unaware that this critical need exists, there has been little interest expressed in providing the related funding for operation and maintenance of Parkway sections and facilities.

Funding needs twofold

The parkway's funding needs are twofold: First, there is a need to achieve a corresponding funding increase to cover the 48 percent increase in physical plant added since 1980. Second, there is a need to achieve a funding increase to cover the additional maintenance needs on the rapidly aging pre-1980 physical plant.

While I strongly support cuts in federal spending, in the case of the Natchez Trace Parkway I think that an old adage applies: "When a task has once begun, never leave it till it's done. Be the labor great or small, do it well or not at all."

With the Parkway nearing completion, an increase in operating and maintenance funding is essential.

In the next few weeks, the dogwoods will be in full bloom and the springtime beauty of Mississippi will begin to unfold. What better place to see it than on the scenic Natchez Trace Parkway?

The Clarion-Ledger
Tuesday, January 18, 2000

Construction Law Exemption Threat to Beauty of Trace

Various bills will be passed during the current legislative session that will have long-range and lasting effects on Mississippi and its people.

One such proposal is being pushed by Tupelo school officials who want legislators to approve an exemption to a law that limits the height of structures within 1,000 feet of the Natchez Trace Parkway to no more than 35 feet high.

The Mississippi Code of 1972 set in place certain restrictions to protect the scenic and historic integrity of the Natchez Trace Parkway.

The wisdom shown in passing protective legislation has made the Natchez Trace Parkway one of Mississippi's greatest natural resources. An estimated 14 million visitors annually travel the Trace to enjoy the beauty of our state and to utilize the various recreational facilities offered visitors and homefolk alike.

Churches, silos first

When state Rep. Steve Holland, from the Tupelo area, introduced legislation in 1996 to exempt churches and silos from the 35-foot height limitation, it was approved by the Legislature without even a dissenting vote.

This year, Rep. Holland has filed a bill to exempt schools from the 35-foot limit.

According to an article in the December 14 edition of the *Tupelo Northeast Mississippi Daily Journal*, Mr. Holland would support doing away with all "viewshed" restrictions, which no doubt will follow.

Mr. Holland is quoted as saying: "The Natchez Trace folks don't like it, but it's not like you're going to have something every 10 feet. If it gets out of hand we can come to our senses." Mr. Holland needs to be brought to his senses now. Does he really believe that if protective provisions are removed from the Natchez Trace Parkway, allowing expanded public and commercial encroachment, we can "come to our senses" and restore the beauty that has been destroyed?

And then there's Rep. Billy Bowles, of Houston, who also supports removing the viewshed restrictions.

He says it's because of "property rights", but according to the *Journal*, "many view it as retribution for a speeding ticket on the Parkway."

If this report is true, we've got a law "maker" who is a law "breaker" using his power of public trust to gain personal revenge at the expense of the public welfare.

It's already begun

It is paramount that Mississippians understand what is happening to the scenic quality along the entire route of the Natchez Trace Parkway. New plans to invade the Parkway's viewshed surface almost daily.

Already the construction of a Wal-Mart Supercenter near Tupelo has altered what was once one of the most appealing agrarian vistas along the Parkway.

A sign more than 35 feet high was allowed to be erected adjacent to the Parkway due to a technicality in the existing law, and numerous proposals have been sent to the Federal Communications Commission (FCC) for construction of cellular communications towers adjacent to and within view of the scenic route.

Concerned Mississippians should tell their state representatives to veto further viewshed exemptions.

Ask them to support legislation that will be introduced this session to clarify and strengthen the law protecting the scenic beauty of the Natchez Trace Parkway.

Act now because the camel already has its nose under the tent.

The Clarion-Ledger
Saturday, May 27, 2000

Natchez Trace's Beauty Is in Jeopardy

Tupelo school
exemption opened door
for more scenic clutter

When Mississippi Congressman Jeff Busby introduced legislation in 1934 to construct a national road to follow the route of the historic Natchez Trace, it set the stage for a partnership between the State of Mississippi and the National Park Service to assume shared responsibilities for the Natchez Trace Parkway.

Early leaders of the Mississippi Legislature knew the importance of establishing legal provisions to protect and preserve the natural beauty and historical significance of the Natchez Trace.

The Mississippi Code of 1972 outlined "viewshed" restrictions that would prohibit construction above 35 feet within 1000 feet of the roadway. This law assured that the quality and integrity of the landscape would be protected and the scenic view would remain unencumbered by visual clutter of our modern day world.

In 1996, state Rep. Steve Holland, of Plantersville, (near Tupelo) introduced and steered to passage a piece of "stealth" legislation that was to become the first crack in the law.

The bill which exempts silos and churches from the height restrictions was unanimously approved by both houses.

Confident in his previous success, Holland introduced a bill this session to exempt schools from the viewshed restrictions. The precedent of gradual dismantling of the Parkway's viewshed protection was thus established.

Despite the fact that other options were available, Tupelo school officials moved forward with plans to construct a performing arts center on the Tupelo High School campus adjacent to the Parkway.

The proposed building would be 65 feet at its highest point, 30 feet over the maximum height permitted by law. Additionally, the school board had purchased 55 acres of land adjacent to the high school campus with plans to construct athletic fields. Lighting for the fields also would exceed the 35-foot height limit.

As the public became aware that these exemptions would apply along the full length of the parkway, opposition began to mount.

The Senate was far more level-headed in recognizing the threat to the beautiful, historic roadway. Unanimous approval was given to a Senate bill that would have prohibited any building within the scenic viewshed except for a church steeple already under construction.

Despite slight modifications to the bill in conference and strong last-minute public protest, Holland, along with other powerful legislative leaders from his area, including House Speaker Tim Ford, greased the wheels to make a second assault on the Natchez Trace a "done deal." Governor Ronnie Musgrove concurred by signing the bill into law.

What irony! With the completion of the 62-year old Natchez Trace Parkway just a few years away and our congressional delegation successfully garnering the federal dollars to complete the project, the Mississippi Legislature is dismantling the laws that protect its scenic beauty.

The Natchez Trace Parkway is one of Mississippi's greatest natural resources, attracting approximately 16 million visitors a year to enjoy the aesthetic and recreational experience that is uniquely ours. Cash registers of communities along the parkway jingle with tourism dollars.

Wake up Mississippians! We have a treasure in our state that has been designated a "National Scenic By-way." If the scenery along a scenic parkway is ruined, what's left?

The Clarion-Ledger
Thursday, April 21, 2005

Natchez Trace Parkway Finally at "Completion"

Natchez Trace Parkway enthusiasts and dignitaries from across the country will gather in Natchez in a few weeks to celebrate the completion of the Natchez Trace Parkway – 67 years after construction began.

U.S. Senator Thad Cochran once remarked that it has taken longer to complete the Natchez Trace Parkway than it did to build the Appian Way.

A 67-year national project

But hey ... What's 67 years when you look at the results?

The 444-mile long, Natchez Trace Parkway is the seventh most visited destination in the National Park System, attracting some 12.6 million visitors in 2003. Parkway officials expect to see that number increase to at least 15 million once the roadway is completed.

The Parkway's natural beauty and scenic vistas offer travelers a landscape of wetlands, prairie landscapes, agricultural croplands, abundant wildlife, and historic sites.

The Parkway has 52 nature, hiking, and horse trails.

The Parkway has been designated an All-American Road and one of America's 75 National Scenic Byways.

Regrettably, when the ribbon is cut on May 21 to open the last twenty plus miles of the Natchez Trace Parkway, some of the visionaries who saw the importance of preserving the historic Natchez Trace for future generations and the possibility of creating a scenic national parkway from Natchez to Nashville are no longer alive to witness it.

Two women, Elizabeth Blanton Jones and Roane Fleming Byrnes, members of the Daughters of the American Revolution, played important roles in the development of the Natchez Trace Parkway and will be honored during completion ceremonies with a marker placed at the Trace's southern terminus in Natchez.

DAR marked historic sites

In 1905, Elizabeth Jones, of Holly Springs, first proposed to the Mississippi State Society DAR, that historic sites along the Natchez Trace be commemorated by erecting granite boulders with appropriate inscriptions. By 1933, the DAR had placed fifteen markers from Natchez to the Mississippi-Alabama state line telling the story of the historic pathway.

In the fall of 1933, a movement was begun in Mississippi for the organization of a Natchez Trace Association to memorialize the Trace and work for a single aim – "a paved road from Nashville, Tennessee, to Natchez, Mississippi."

Roane Byrnes, of Natchez, was elected president of the Natchez Trace Association in1934 and served in that capacity until her death in 1970. For more than 30 years, this remarkable woman used her influence, unique talent for friendship, and organization skills to gain support for developing the Natchez Trace into a national parkway. Her influence was so far-reaching that she became known as "Queen of the Natchez Trace."

Recognition should also be given to former U.S. Rep. Jeff Busby of Mississippi, who, in 1934, steered to passage legislation that authorized a survey of "the old Indian trail known as the

Natchez Trace" that would result in the 1935 allocation of federal funds.

In those early days, three other association members joined Mrs. Byrnes to assure that the movement succeeded. They were Ralph Landrum of Kosciusko and Jackson, P.M. Estes of Nashville, and Paul Coburn of Tuscumbia.

Wendell Simpson, Natchez Trace Parkway superintendent, has provided capable leadership and, with the enthusiastic support of Senators Thad Cochran and Trent Lott and other elected officials, the task has been accomplished.

To each one, past and present, we owe a great debt of gratitude.

The Clarion-Ledger
Thursday, May 26, 2005

Let's Protect, Preserve Trace Parkway Now

The Natchez Trace Parkway – all 444 miles of it – is now complete from Natchez to Nashville. How fortunate we are to have 309 of those miles traversing Mississippi.

I think that sometimes we take the Natchez Trace Parkway for granted. Will it always be a beautiful, historic roadway, a showplace of our state, a recreational and cultural resource for Mississippians, and a tourist Mecca that is an economic boon to local coffers?

Recently as I traveled the Trace, enjoying the dogwood trees and early spring wildflowers, I thought about the efforts of hundreds, if not thousands, of people who over the years have worked to preserve the historic Old Trace.

These people of vision were successful in arousing local interest in creating a national parkway. They lobbied for federal funding to survey and start construction and worked to secure state appropriations to purchase rights of way.

Old threat resurfaces

After 67 years, their efforts have been rewarded, their task completed. The torch has been passed to the next generation to protect and preserve the Natchez Trace.

It is essential that adequate federal funding for maintenance, resurfacing, and improvements of the Parkway be generated. In recent years, allocations of federal dollars from the National Park Service have been directed to projects other than the Natchez Trace. Our U.S. senators and representatives can have an impact on funding and should be encouraged to keep the Parkway as a top priority.

But a more immediate and ominous threat has surfaced.

In 1972, the Mississippi Legislature wisely passed legislation that established "viewshed" restrictions to protect the quality and integrity of the landscape on the Natchez Trace and assure that the scenic view would remain unencumbered by visual clutter and commercial development. This same legislative body is now granting exemptions to that law.

In 1996, Rep. Steve Holland introduced a bill to exempt churches and silos from the 35-foot height limitation. In 2000, Rep. Holland again steered to passage an exemption for schools and was quoted in an article from the *Northeast Mississippi Daily Journal* that he would support abandoning all "viewshed" restrictions.

Assault via exemptions

In 2004, another attempt to exempt newly erected buildings and structures in the Ridgeland area of the Trace was introduced. Fortunately, to the credit of the House Transportation Committee, with chairman Bill Miles, the effort died in committee.

If exemptions are granted for one individual or municipality, how in good conscience can other municipalities or individuals be denied? Once exemptions are granted, a domino effect will be created and commercial and residential construction along the Trace will quickly destroy its scenic beauty.

This assault on the Natchez Trace Parkway must be stopped.

It should be incumbent upon local officials and building permit offices in the counties through which the Trace runs to be knowledgeable about the "viewshed" laws and refuse to issue any permit that would be in violation.

New state legislation should be drafted to eliminate ambiguous language in the 1972 MS Code, so as to strengthen the law to establish stiff penalties for any violation.

It is up to each Mississippian to protect and preserve the Natchez Trace Parkway for ourselves and our posterity.

Unpublished

Written in May 2005 in response to Bill Minor's syndicated column in the *Sun Herald*. Before it was published in *The Clarion-Ledger*, Mr. Minor must have been told that his original column was in error and it was edited accordingly.

Bill Minor Column in Error

A marker missing from the Natchez Trace? Hardly!

Bill Minor's column ("A marker is missing from Natchez Trace", June 2) is a wonderful tribute to Roan Fleming Byrnes, but is sorely lacking in factual content.

Obviously, Mr. Minor did not attend the Natchez Trace completion ceremony on May 21, but depended on "some who were there" to tell him that "shamefully no mention was made of Mrs. Byrnes." His sources would have to be both blind and deaf to have missed the unveiling of a historic marker placed by the Mississippi Society Daughters of the American Revolution as part of the completion ceremony or not to have heard the many tributes paid to Mrs. Byrnes.

In fact, the front page of the *Natchez Democrat*, on the day of the completion ceremony, featured a large picture of the covered 2-1/2 ton granite boulder and a story about Mrs. Byrnes and her contribution to the development of the Natchez Trace Parkway from Nashville to Natchez. Not only does the marker recognize the accomplishments of Mrs. Byrnes, but also commemorates the work of Elizabeth Blanton Jones, who, in 1905, led the DAR in a historic preservation project to mark the old Natchez Trace, saving it from extinction.

The beautiful granite boulder bearing the bronze plaque is in a very prominent place at the gateway to the Natchez Trace Parkway in Natchez for all to see ... especially you, Mr. Minor.

The Clarion-Ledger
Letter to the Editor
Monday, November 17, 2008
Reprinted in *The Madison County Herald*, December 4, 2008 (*Trail Funds Not There*)

Natchez Trace Parkway Can't Be Widened for Bikes

The editorial ("Bikeways: lanes provide health and safety" Oct. 13) missed the mark in suggesting that the Natchez Trace Parkway be widened. At the cost of asphalt today, no telling how much it would cost to widen 444-miles of parkway or where the funding would come from, especially in dire economic times.

The Natchez Trace Parkway (NTP) was not created as a highway, but as a scenic by-way. In fact, the entire length of the parkway is designated a bicycle trail and has received national attention in major cycling and travel magazines, bringing thousands of cycling enthusiasts to enjoy the Trace each year.

Because bikeways provide health and safety, Congress directed the NTP, which is controlled by the National Park Service, to design and construct multi-use trails in conjunction with new segments of the parkway to separate the non-vehicular users from the vehicular traffic. And typical of much that Congress does, they said "do it" but didn't provide the funds to do it with.

The problem stems from the large volume of vehicular traffic that uses the parkway as a feeder or connector road to major traffic arteries such as I-55. There is a greater need of off-road, multi-use trails in high volume traffic areas, such as Tupelo, Jackson and Natchez.

Long-range plans include constructing a 22-mile trail from the Ross Barnett Reservoir to Clinton at an estimated cost of $35 million. The city of Ridgeland completed one section of the trail, and the next phase will be construction of the trail from Old Canton Road to the reservoir.

Also planned is a 9.4-mile trail along the parkway in Natchez at an estimated cost of $20 million, but the estimates of costs made in 1999 have increased dramatically. With federal budget cuts across the board, national parks have been strained just to maintain park facilities.

The lack of funds has placed a hardship on parkway officials to provide road maintenance, patrol and staffing, not to mention upkeep and renovation of an aging physical plant.

As an example, the old Crafts Center at Ridgeland, which was originally used as a visitor and information center and later used by the Mississippi Craftsmen's Guild, has been closed for more than a year when the crafts center was relocated to a new and larger facility.

Plans are underway for the 57-year old dogtrot log cabin, which is a landmark on the Trace and adjacent to the multi-use trail, to be renovated and reopened next spring or early summer.

The Natchez Trace Parkway Association, a support group of the parkway, is contributing $7,500 toward the project, but like every other project on the Natchez Trace Parkway, funding is the major issue.

The Clarion-Ledger
Saturday, February 14, 2009

Join Advocacy Group, Help Promote Natchez Trace Parkway

The history of the Natchez Trace Parkway Association is as colorful and interesting as the old Natchez Trace itself and tells the story of a unique organization of dedicated men and women from Mississippi, Alabama, and Tennessee who banded together with the single aim of "a paved road from Nashville, Tennessee, to Natchez, Mississippi."

The first meeting of the Association, originally known as the Natchez Trace Association, was held in Jackson, Mississippi, in January 1934, with Trace enthusiasts joining the new organization. Four exceptional individuals emerged to lead the group for the next 35 years:

- Mrs. Ferriday Byrnes of Natchez was elected president, and her extraordinary gifts for friendship and hospitality, coupled with unequalled organizational skills, earned her the title, "Queen of the Natchez Trace."
- Ralph Landrum, an influential Jackson attorney, who conducted a never-ending letter writing and personal contact campaign to arouse interest and support, was executive secretary.
- P.M. Estes, of Nashville, TN, a wealthy insurance company president, highly respected by the movers and shakers in politics on the state and national levels, induced the State of Tennessee to join in a cooperative development program.
- Paul Coburn, of Tuscumbia, AL, editor and publisher of *The Tuscumbia Reporter* and a member of the Alabama Legislature, steered to passage parkway legislation for land acquisition in Alabama.

The activities of these four activists, laid the groundwork for the completion, in 2005, of a 444-mile-long national scenic parkway. Without their untiring efforts and continually lobbying, it is doubtful that the federal funds for road construction would have been appropriated or the land acquired by the state for road right-of-way.

"Colonel" Jim Walton, an unconventional and flamboyant itinerant journalist, had promoted the idea of "a military highway" and solicited memberships in the Association. Walton suggested to Mississippi Congressman Jeff Busby that he sponsor legislation to fund the initial survey leading to construction appropriations and the eventual signing of the bill by President Franklin D. Roosevelt that established the Natchez Trace Parkway as a permanent part of the National Park Service.

With the deaths of Mrs. Byrnes and Landrum in the 1970s, the work of the Association slowed with several segments of the Parkway left unfinished.

The Bicentennial year of 1976 brought renewed interest for the three state associations, and a "Finish the Trace" committee was organized by the Tupelo Community Development Foundation that put the Natchez Trace Association under one umbrella, making it the present-day, non-profit, Natchez Trace Parkway Association with representatives from Mississippi, Alabama, and Tennessee serving on the board of directors.

Now and then, exceptional people with extraordinary foresight and vision set goals worthy of a life-long commitment. What greater tribute to one's perseverance than the Natchez Trace Parkway!

With the 75th anniversary of the Association being celebrated this year, there is still work to be done to preserve, protect, develop, and enhance the Natchez Trace Parkway.

There is also a need to maintain a strong advocacy group for the Parkway and to encourage a new generation of Natchez Trace enthusiasts to become members. Anyone wishing to join can send $25 annual dues to "NTPA", P.O. Box 156, Franklin, TN 37065.

CHAPTER X

Education

The benefits of education and of useful knowledge, generally diffused through a community, are essential to the preservation of a free government.

Sam Houston

The Northside Sun
"As I See It"
Thursday, October 12, 1989
Companion article, *The Clarion-Ledger*
Monday, October 16, 1989

Too Many Questions Left Unanswered

THE TOWN MEETING held at Murrah High School recently left me wishing that Governor Mabus had been a little more specific about his education reform proposals. What I failed to hear was ....

How much will it cost and will the money produce literate students and a better school system?

Will requirements for high school graduation be upgraded and higher standards required for college admission?

Will teachers be tested for competency and will teacher salaries bc commensurate with their performance?

Will academic excellence be encouraged and rewarded or will there be a "dumbing down" of students to meet the education level of the lowest common denominator?

WILL THE Governor's education reform produce a "Class of 2001" culturally and morally literate with graduates possessing the ability to reason, equipped with the intellectual discipline to become productive citizens in whatever field of endeavor they undertake ... whether it be the road to higher education or a trade?

Will Mississippi's educational system continue to be dictated to by the national Education Association (NEA) with its agenda of political indoctrination; the ACLU, which watchdogs textbook selection and makes sure that prayer and religion are prohibited in the classroom; the Carnegie Corporation, which is involved in restructuring curriculum and establishing a nationwide system of teacher certification in cooperation with the Soviet Union's Academy of Sciences; Planned Parenthood with its sex education message; or by the New Agers and Global Educators, who plan to restructure the educational system with "Higher Order Thinking Skills" (the current jargon for incorporating occult activities and altered states of consciousness in learning)?

THESE QUESTIONS and others were not addressed by Governor Mabus.

What I would have liked to hear Governor Mabus propose is a visionary and revolutionary plan called "choice" or "denationalization of the education industry." The idea was presented at the national Governors' Conference by those who are much more knowledgeable than I, but basically here's how the plan works:

The plan would allow the state to accredit schools and enforce school attendance and standards through some kind of voucher system in which parents would be free to patronize privately owned schools of their choice.

THE SYSTEM would be similar to the G.I. Bill of Rights, which in effect issued education vouchers to veterans.

This method would encourage competition, discourage collectivism, and champion the individual. It would be a system effective in rewarding merit and would attract teachers with ability. It would increase variety, innovation, and academic excellence.

Workable? Maybe, but certainly with the track record of the public schools, it won't hurt to try something new.

I wish that money could answer our education woes, but in recent years expanded financial expenditures for education have produced no noticeable gains in knowledge.

NEW JERSEY spends more per pupil than any other state ($6,901 compared to Mississippi's $2,716 – these figures are based on 1987-88 information from the NEA for elementary and secondary schools).

During the last six years alone, such outlays have surged by more than 50% faster than either the cost-of-living or per capita GNP. School budgets currently are rising at a record-breaking pace, but facts do not seem to indicate that money is the answer to our education dilemma.

Many parents across the country are turning to home schooling as an alternative.

The public school system of this nation has become an insulated state monopoly of mediocrity. In many instances, local school boards and administrators have closed out parents and teachers (as in the case in Jackson) and have established imperialistic fiefdoms from which to pontificate.

I DO NOT MEAN to indict all associated with public education, for there are many outstanding and dedicated teachers and administrators who continue to work effectively in deplorable conditions against unbelievable obstacles.

True reform must begin at home. Until parents accept their responsibility to instill in their child the desire to learn ... making education fun and desirable, and until the school and teacher accept their role as an extension of the home and parent, no amount of money on earth will accomplish the goal of education reform.

Education has continually declined since the introduction of "progressive" education by Socialist John Dewey. Until we are willing to try some new revolutionary idea, hope for better education will remain a dream.

OBVIOUSLY Governor Mabus wants to be The Education Governor, but if education reform is no more than I heard presented at the Town Meeting, he'd better get ready for a disappointment.

Sadly, the real losers are the children of Mississippi.

The Clarion-Ledger
Letter to the Editor
Wednesday, February 17, 1988

Stressing Black History Injustice to Students

I see that *The Clarion-Ledger/Jackson Daily News* is promoting Mississippi black history with a $50 sponsorship of a historic tabloid to be distributed in the schools. What a shame!

Your paper continually praises the 1982 Education Reform Act as a step in the right direction and supports more pay for teachers. All well and good. But in promoting the study of black history, you have missed the real key to literacy. It's not black history that you should be advocating, but American history.

According to a 1985 Foundations of Literacy study, two-thirds of the 17-year-old students tested could not place the Civil War in the correct half-century; a third did not know that the Declaration of Independence was signed between 1750 and 1800, and a third did not know that Columbus sailed for the New World before 1750.

With your paper adamantly pushing for a new constitution for Mississippi, saying that those of us who oppose a complete rewrite are "chained to the past," I think your promotion of black history is chaining the students of this state to the past by not stressing the importance of ALL history as essential for a well-educated individual.

It's no wonder that the NAACP is threatening to sue the state Department of Education unless the functional literacy examination mandated by the 1982 Education Reform Act is dropped. True education is more than black history, and the students of this state are being done an injustice by stressing it.

I doubt that the 46 percent black students who were unable to pass the literacy exam last year will be helped much by your black history tabloid. Sponsors should think twice about what they are promoting.

The Clarion-Ledger
Letter to the Editor
Thursday, June 14, 1990
Companion Article *The Northside Sun*, July 5, 1990

It's Time to Ask Question on Education Reform Plans

It's time that taxpayers begin to ask some pointed questions about the type of education being touted by the Mississippi Department of Education and the Mississippi Association of Educators.

A conference held in Biloxi, May 31 through June 2, called "Global Mississippi – International Education for Economic Survival in the Emerging Global Village" shows that the brand of education espoused by our education leaders is so far removed from the basic curriculum needed in our schools to produce literate individuals that it's high time taxpayers revolt.

Global Education is a coordinated attack on traditional education and an instrument for social and political change.

Rather than emphasizing American history, **the values set forth in the Constitution of the United States of America, and pride in our culture and our national heroes,* global education teaches equivalence or even a preference for the **cultural, economic, legal, and political* systems of other governments. It substitutes pluralism, world government, disarmament and fear of nuclear holocaust for freedom, patriotism and faith in the future.

The stated purpose of the global education conference was "to chart the general direction of kindergarten through 12th grade social studies and humanities curriculum reform in Mississippi's public schools for the next decade."

**Major sponsors were the Mississippi Department of Education, the Mississippi Association of Educators, Gulf Coast Community College, with major funding from the Mississippi Humanities Council and the National Endowment for the Humanities. (Other patrons and supporters included the Phil Hardin Foundation, Hancock Bank, Blossman Gas, Peoples Bank, Deposit Guaranty National Bank, South Central Bell, AT&T, Alcan Cable, Leaf River Forest Products, Inc., Close-Up Foundation, Bradley Commission on History in the Schools, the National Geographic Project, Auto Discount Glass of Gulfport and Valley Brook Farm, Hammonton, N.J.)*

Featured speakers included Gov. Ray Mabus, Hodding Carter, Marjorie W. Longley, chairman of the American Forum for Global Education; Dr. Jesse White, former executive director of the

Southern Growth Policies Board, (presently serving as a Fellow in the Institute of Politics, John F. Kennedy School of Government, Harvard University), and Sister Miriam MacGillis, "futurist" of Genesis Farm in Blairstown, N.J.

Having read the transcript of Sister MacGillis's address, which was nothing but New Age hocus pocus, and hearing reports from some in attendance, I am amazed and appalled that so many Mississippians can be taken in by such preposterous "education" garbage.

I hope that the Mississippi Legislature will think long and hard before funding the "Mississippi BEST" education reform bill. I would be hesitant to support any education proposals that make Mississippi schools experimental laboratories and our children the guinea pigs.

*Omitted when published.

(The primary emphasis of the letter to the editor was to show the type education initiatives being pushed by the MS Department of Education and how easily well-meaning companies and foundations can be hood-winked in the name of 'education'. These deletions graphically illustrates how the press can control the people's right to know.)

Unpublished

Educators Are Not Supposed to Be Social Engineers

I was astounded to read the "global education" op-ed piece by Vincent R. McGrath, assistant professor of Education in the College of Education at Mississippi State University.

Mr. McGrath's premise that as educators, we must bring new ideals to the classroom (not ideas, but *ideals*, emphasis added) which will guide the way people will behave is exactly why we are turning out teachers who can't teach and students who are ill-prepared to function in the "disorderly world" in which they live.

While I recognize that students need to understand their place in a "global community," I have problems with a system which "reshapes" children's attitudes and beliefs and indoctrinates them to accept Global Government and citizenship, and international control of our resources and population while failing to provide a firm foundation in American history, government, geography, culture, and appreciation of the unprecedented and unparalleled religious, political, and economic freedoms and successes of our country.

Rather than being instructed on "classroom strategies" and "learning theory," the real foundation for a teaching career ought to be the knowledge of something to teach – cell biology, the mythology of ancient Greece, the Renaissance in Europe, the U.S. Constitution and the Bill of Rights, or the mathematical concepts that underlie computers. Emphasis should shift from emphasizing *how* to teach to learning *what* to teach.

Rita Kramer's most recent book, *Ed School Follies: The Miseducation of America's Teachers*, which is recommended reading for anyone interested in education, lays much of the blame on school failures to the politicization of the schools in general and of teacher education in particular.

According to Kramer, "The function of the schools is no longer perceived as the transmission of the common culture and the acquisition of those skills necessary to understand it, participate in it, and extend it. Instead, the schools have been transformed into agencies of social change with their primary goal being the attainment of equity at all costs and their emphasis consequently on the therapeutic and the remedial in place of the quest for knowledge and excellence."

Social engineering has become so entrenched in the education establishment that I'm convinced most "educators" wouldn't recognize it if they saw it.

As long as educators promote fads such as globalism, multiculturalism, bilingualism, and self-esteem – in which elementary school teachers are taught to concern themselves with children's feelings of self-worth and not with the worth of hard work or of realistically measured accomplishment – our schools will continue to fail.

I'm also convinced that the strangle hold of education unions must be broken before any education reforms can be achieved.

Interestingly, the same issue of *The Clarion-Ledger* contained "concerns" expressed by spokesmen from the Mississippi Reading Association and Mississippi American Federation of Teachers about Mrs. Fordice's reading program "Earning for Learning." Some educators are guilty of the misconception that they are the final authority on teaching methodology. Their track record proves otherwise.

Education associations, federations, coalitions, and alliances are primarily interested in protecting their jobs, garnering more money from the over-burdened taxpayer, and setting the social agenda for the country. If you don't believe me, just read resolutions passed by the National Education Association (NEA).

Today's teachers are also victims of a flawed system. With the likes of Mr. McGrath in our colleges of education and with the emphasis on developing "model critical thinking skills programs for public schools and presenting strategies for reflective and rational thinking" rather than training teachers in subject matter, students in our schools of education don't stand much more of a chance than the students they are being trained to teach.

Competition must be introduced into the teaching marketplace; but as long as the education establishment possesses a monopoly on teaching jobs, there is no such incentive.

These observations are in no way intended to cast dispersion on the many good teachers who persevere in spite of the burgeoning bureaucratic paperwork and mishmash of education administrators.

John Dewey's progressive education theories of the 1930s have produced the education horror story of the 1990s. Second and third generations of social engineers have no idea that the indoctrination of today's teachers, such as espoused by Mr. McGrath, is one of the primary reasons the education system of the United States has failed.

Kramer cites the enormously increased role of the federal government in education, both financial and regulatory, with the legislature and the courts having more to say about what goes on in the schools in the past thirty years or so than in the entire previous history of the country. Its corollary is the increasing power and influence of special interest groups, each pressing for its own agenda or program.

He adds: "When benefits flow to the bureaucracies that come into being to administer these programs once they are established, it is *their* interests, and not necessarily the education interests of the children in our schools that are served.

According to Kramer, "Until a college degree guarantees the possession of some real body of knowledge, and the acquisition and transmission of knowledge is understood to be the function of educating institutions, rather than the implementation of a social/political agenda, we are lost and likely to remain so."

The Clarion-Ledger
Wednesday, March 4, 1992

Yes: Responsibility Basic As Learning the Three 'Rs'

The earlier in life a young person learns that when you do wrong you must suffer the consequence, the sooner that person will become a responsible adult. That realization is as important to one's education as reading, writing and arithmetic.

I hope that the Jackson School Board will stand firm on their expulsion of thirteen disruptive students at Provine High School. It's time that schools start to teach that rules are established for the well-being of the entire school community and when rules are broken that the punishment for such offense is speedily and unwaveringly rendered.

To do otherwise would be an injustice to the young person who has violated the rules, not to mention those young people who are serious about getting an education.

If the 13 suspended students learn the lesson that you can break the rules and get away with it, then respect for authority will be challenged later in life when the consequences are far more serious.

Yes, it is sad that the education of these young men has been threatened, but it may be a valuable lesson for them to understand that an education is a valued commodity and is not just handed out to those who are enrolled in school. Being suspended for a year may give them the opportunity to realize what they're missing and provide the resolve that when they can return to school they will do so ready to work for an education.

And a word to the black "leadership" who demanded that expelled students be put back in the classroom .... If taxpayers are going to be asked to underwrite the $1 million estimated annual cost for an alternative classroom with an armed guard for troublemakers or be faced with housing inmates at the state penitentiary, I think you have exhibited the need to improve your own education.

The Northside Sun
Letter to the Editor
Thursday, November 5, 1992

"Waste" Sign of Throw-Away Society

It is a "sad bit" that teachers must scrounge for books, but it is not because the public school systems of Mississippi are "inadequately supported."

It's because education dollars are being misspent.

Education is a big and lucrative business, especially when tax dollars are involved. With textbooks, just as in other education commodities, there's a lot of money to be made.

The textbook publishers of this country reap large profits by continually issuing "updated" editions of textbooks and the schools keep buying them. It's much like the fashion industry dictating clothing styles. Outdate the old so that the new will sell. The name of the game is called "make more money," and publishers are laughing all the way to the bank.

Basic information contained in subjects such as language, math, history and literature does not change every other year.

It's outrageous for school districts, parents and students to continually replace books before they wear out, especially when today's "new editions" are costly and not necessarily better. As in other areas of education, accountability is needed in textbook spending.

This situation is true in private schools as well.

As a private school patron who purchased each textbook used by three children, it was a rare instance for a sibling, coming just one year behind, to use the same textbook; once a book was discontinued it had practically no resale value.

Rather than citing the need for more education funding, the public should be seeking answers to why warehouses full of perfectly good textbooks and badly needed teaching materials are allowed to exist.

Why, with educational costs at an all time high are new books and teaching materials stockpiled for "debinding?'

Why, when Mississippi students in the Delta are made the stepchildren of "up east" school districts whose charitable castoffs are brought in by the truckloads?

Why when a conservation conscious nation is encouraged to recycle?

The scene of the waste in those Flora warehouses in an indictment of a throw-away society and a shame to the system that perpetuates it.

The Clarion-Ledger
Monday, July 12, 1993

America's Problem: Failing to Pass Its Moral Heritage

I doubt that any reader of *The Clarion-Ledger* was surprised to learn that "officials battle rise in youth crime," as noted in a July 4 heading on an article by staff writer Butch John.

While the story adequately points out the increase of juvenile crimes, it treads lightly on the causes. Having recently read an eye-opening and thought-provoking book, *Why Johnny Can't tell Right From Wrong,* by William Kilpatrick, I was struck by the fact that we recognize the problem but seem paralyzed to address the cause or to take corrective action.

There is no question that the increase in crimes committed by juveniles is directly related to the breakdown of the family. Also sharing the blame is an entertainment industry that glorifies brutality and a school system that produces moral illiterates.

According to Mr. Kilpatrick, one of the principal reasons for this societal breakdown is the schools' failure to provide character education.

He points to the fact that traditionally our schools used literature, history and other means to teach such values as honesty, respect, and moral courage.

In the 1960s and 1970s, most schools switched from character education to an untested model generally known as "decision-making."

In place of the stories and songs that transmitted values to generations of school children, this radical new educational theory has substituted teaching methods that foster the notion that any values system is acceptable so long as it is self-discovered and "feels right."

The schools have helped produce a citizenry unable to distinguish reasonable moral arguments from mere rationalizations.

If we really want to get serious about youth crime, reform must take place with the schools discarding "decision-making" and implement character education. Professor Kilpatrick points the way by suggesting positive steps. Included in the book is an annotated guide to more than 100 books for children and young adults that transmit moral values.

The book addresses one of America's most pressing problems – our failure to pass on our moral heritage to the young.

The Clarion-Ledger
Sunday, May 1, 1994

"GOALS 2000" Will Bind Education in Federal Red Tape

More wasted money ($647 million to be exact) will be poured into the "education sinkhole" in an effort to "reform" education with the passage of the GOALS 2000: Educate America Act.

According to an article, ("Deliver us from Clinton's schools bill," by Bruno V. Manno, former U.S. assistant secretary of education, from the June 22, 1993, Wall Street Journal), GOALS 2000, by imposing "national delivery standards" will shift from a focus of what our children *learn* to what education bureaucrats *spend.*

Who for a minute believes that when "delivery standards" are linked with a state's eligibility for federal education money that the reform will not mirror "voluntary" national standards?

There is no doubt that once federal education dollars are accepted, Washington will impose on states, communities and classrooms more federal red tape, more requirements, and more directives through rules and regulations.

Having attended numerous local school board meetings in which budgetary expenditures were discussed, I can guarantee that every federal dollar comes with strings attached. Federal dollars contribute to additional personnel required to compete for and manage grants and entitlements and to implement programs. This method removes lay control of education and defies long-standing American tradition of local school control.

Schools, rather than being temples of knowledge, are becoming daycare centers, health clinics, psychological counseling offices, and delinquent reformatories. It's no wonder teachers want more pay.

Many public schools have abandoned traditional academic instruction for Outcome-Based Education (OBE), which replaces teaching facts, information, concepts, and essential skills in reading, writing, and arithmetic with "higher order thinking skills," ignoring the self-evident truth that it is impossible to employ "higher order thinking" without a base of factual knowledge.

GOALS 2000 tightens the grip of education bureaucrats because *they* set the required outcomes, develop the curriculum, train the teachers, and judge student performance as *they* control the schools and the money. You can bet not much will change.

Education scientists are hard at work in their laboratories to assure that what children say, think and know must conform to Politically Correct ideology, attitudes, and behavior.

What children won't know will be everything else. And because they won't know the basics of reading, writing and arithmetic, they won't be able to learn anything else.

GOALS 2000 will reform education, all right, by continuing to change the three R's to the three D's: Deliberately Dumbed Down.

The Northside Sun
"As I See It"
Thursday, July 28, 1994

Latest Education Fad to Restructure America's Schools (Part I of IV)

THEY CALL IT Outcome Based Education (OBE) or sometimes performance-based education. It's the latest education fad that's supposed to "restructure" America's schools ... that is, until parents find out what OBE is and how it differs from the education they envision for their children.

Parents object to outcome based education because it's experimental and uses unproven methods. What has been proven is that in states where OBE has been tried (Kentucky, Pennsylvania, and Washington State, to name a few,) the results have been lower student test scores, increased bureaucracy, and sky-rocketing costs.

"It's not happening at my child's school." You have either said these words or had them said to you. I've even had officials in the Mississippi Department of Education tell me emphatically that Mississippi schools are not instituting OBE.

I'd like to believe them, but how long are we going to keep trusting, when they keep failing and our children end up the losers?

Say what they will, all indications point to the fact that new "state competencies" will soon affect every public school in Mississippi.

THE MISSISSIPPI Legislature has passed education bills that establish some of OBE's goals; the state Board of Education has scrapped the Stanford Achievement Test in favor of a $6.6 million contract with Riverside Publishing Co. for an open-ended performance-based system; Mississippi will be signing on to Goals 2000, a massive $647 million "education reform" package that will bring Federal bureaucracy into every school district in the state, requiring all Mississippi schools to be judged by an "accuracy of measure" based on performance outcomes.

Most would agree that there is a critical need for change in our educational system, but the restructuring currently underway won't produce academic excellence. In fact, it has the real potential to decrease student achievement.

Educators continue to use the classroom to test new education programs that continually fail. Because they have been trained in "progressive" education methods taught in almost every school of education in this country, they doggedly refuse to recognize that students in Germany, Japan, Canada and France seem to flourish in more traditional learning environments.

THEY CONTINUE to seek "new" methods when what produces literacy is the system that served this nation well until the turn of the century. It's called traditional in-put education, and it works.

Most of us were taught to read and write, learn history, math, science, biology and other subjects. OBE focuses on what the student is when he comes out of school, not what he knows.

You were tested to determine how much you had learned. OBE diagnoses behavior, attitudes, beliefs, and values, and uses strategies to change them.

You were instructed and challenged to do your best. OBE teachers monitor the group while students teach each other and become peer dependent.

You were taught national patriotism. OBE focuses entirely on global citizenship and global community.

You graduated in 12 years or when you met the required number of Carnegie Units. OBE allows graduation only when behaviors, attitudes, beliefs, and values meet vague and subjective "learning outcomes."

Businesses and educators have collaborated to produce and promote so-called "world-class education." That sounds good if "world class" means the best. But in OBE it means students will be dumbed-down so that they will work for the same low wages paid to third-world laborers, allowing American businesses to be competitive with underdeveloped countries in the world market.

WITH OBE, "success" means no one will fail. Goals are set so low that the slowest learner can claim success. High achievers are hindered because their full potential can never be met with ceilings set for under achievers.

OBE is not academic; it's psychological. It's not uplifting; it's depressing. It's a terrible invasion of privacy. It won't improve students' test scores, and "performance outcomes" will help parents know what their kids feel and think about "relevant" issues, but they won't have a measure of how much their children know.

How long will it take, and how many students will suffer, before the education establishment recognizes that parents send their children to school to be taught reading, writing, mathematics, history, geography, and science?

It's time the experimentation stops.

The Northside Sun
"As I See It"
Thursday, August 4, 1994

What Does Restructuring Mean to Schools? (Part II of IV)

MISSISSIPPI parents, good teachers, and administrators know very little about the restructuring of public education that is now underway ... education reform that has the potential to derail traditional education as we know it.

In neighboring Alabama, a glitzy education reform package called "Alabama First" met with strong opposition when the general public learned that the plan de-emphasized academics and was based on "performance outcomes," an education fad now sweeping the country.

Performance outcomes is another name for Outcome-Based Education (OBE), developed by William Spady, sociologist and former director of the federally funded Far West Regional Laboratory for Educational Research and Development, which is directing the implementation of OBE nationwide.

Everywhere it has been tried, a storm of protest has followed. Why? Because OBE is a radical form of restructuring being pushed on local schools from the top down.

It's expensive; it deals with feelings and emotions rather than academics; it robs teachers of valuable teaching time with a towering amount of paperwork; it's a top-heavy social experiment which puts the state in the business of shaping student's values and producing politically correct individuals in the name of "higher order thinking skills" to function better in an "interdependent" world.

THE STATE OF Virginia gave OBE the boot when an outraged public forced then-Gov. L. Douglas Wilder to kill the program.

In Mississippi, unfortunately, rather than one bulk performance-based education package, the reform is quietly being approved piece by piece.

In the 1994 session of the Mississippi Legislature, S.B. 3350 was passed. It states: "The State Board of Education shall, on or before July 1, 1994, implement the performance-based accreditation system which shall include school performance standards that are comparable to any standard which may be established. The system shall establish rigorous minimum standards; ... establish strict measures for those districts which fail to meet minimum standards."

Note the terminology "may be established." This bill signs a blank check for national "opportunity-to-learn" delivery standards that are yet to be established.

Many school administrators and teachers have been able to reject experimental programs, but with new performance based assessments, any school or teacher not meeting the "performance outcomes" may suddenly find their school placed on probation and subject to Corrective Action Plans (CAPs) by the State Department of Education.

DO WE REALLY want the State to dictate our educational standards?

They will. With the passage of Goals 2000, a state's delivery standards are linked to federal funding. The Feds will be telling each state how much it should spend per teacher, per pupil or per building in the name of "equity."

They say it's voluntary. Have you ever known anything that is voluntary when government money is concerned?

Goals 2000 is a nightmare of education doctrine. It mandates equal graduation rates according to racial and ethnic groups, which should be a tip-off to what happens to individual intellectual distinction.

It endorses "developmentally appropriate" early-childhood practices – a code phrase for elevating self-esteem over academic instruction.

It sets up a National Education Goals Panel, consisting entirely of politicians, who pander to the National Education Association (NEA), to review standards, curricula, and tests promulgated by, in effect, a national school board.

Excerpts from the June 1992 Mississippi Curriculum for Social Studies, published by the Mississippi Department of Education, shows just what's planned to "correctly" mold the attitudes of the young.

"Social studies ... should emphasize the development of positive attitudes, learning skills, critical thinking, decision-making skills, social responsibility, and shape positive personal and cultural values."

OBE raises the fundamental question of WHO should decide what values, attitudes and beliefs a child should be taught. Should it be the parents or the U.S. Department of Education?

Continuing: "The revised (Social Studies) curriculum encourages the presentation of controversial issues honestly and accurately within their historical and contemporary context."

Under number two of the Social Studies Goals – Primary Level: "In the study of their personal and family histories, children will learn about cultural differences and similarities through the riches of first-hand experiences and quality literature."

This assumption is an outrageous invasion of privacy. No teacher or school has any business delving into personal or family history!

Social Studies Goals – Junior High Level: number four "As they continue to develop social skills, they should develop political knowledge and skills to participate in an interdependent world."

FOR SENIOR High Level, the Social Studies Goals include:

Goal 1 "The social studies grades 9 through 12 incorporates history, government, geography, and elective economics, and the social sciences which will aid students in forming attitudes and values consistent with our democratic heritage and help them to become responsible citizens on an interdependent world ...."

Goal 2 "The curriculum ... encourages critical analysis and creative thinking, which will help students develop a historical perspective and a sense of values which will help them see more clearly the continuing development of their own nation and the interdependence that characterizes the world."

Global Education, full blown in OBE, teaches a global perspective rather than an American perspective wherein American independence is replaced with global interdependence. It trains for world citizenship and world government, population control, radical environmentalism, and government "solutions" for every problem.

Unbelievable? Yes.

It can't be happening here! Oh, but it is!

What can we do?

I offer three suggestions to parents and taxpayers: guard your wallets; weigh carefully the educrats' words because they often mean the opposite of plain language; and beware of behavior modification masquerading as solid academics.

The Northside Sun
Thursday, August 11, 1994

Education Reform Means Even More Federal Control (Part III of IV)

Do we want local control of education or Federal control? Does accepting Federal money mean more independence or less?

I think most of us know the answers. We are rapidly selling away our freedom and sadly, with the selling of our schools, the future of our nation.

The Senate Elementary and Secondary Education Reauthorization Act – improving America's Schools Act of 1994 (S1513) was passed by the U.S. Senate on August 3.

S1513 is a $12.6 billion takeover of education by the federal government that is unprecedented in our nation's history. The bill contains 834 pages of NEW federal mandates controlling education, social services, children and parents in the home.

S1513 will eventually, through implementation, mandate Outcome Based Education for every state and every local school that accepts federal or state money.

The bill gives the U.S. Secretary of Education the power to "approve a state plan (he) determines meets the requirements."

S1513 connects the "voluntary" Goals 2000 with S1513 and in effect makes adoption of federal performance standards mandatory – "Each state plan ... shall be integrated with each other under Title II of the Goals 2000: Education America Act."

In plain language, this means that in order to get the federal education dollar, our State Department of Ed must conform to what the fed prescribes for state schools.

Even though there is a federal law that prohibits it, S1513 authorizes the federal government to "support development of curriculum-based learning resources" that are "intended to be applied nationally."

This procedure would not be so troublesome if the State Department of Education had not established state "standards" that dovetail with national goals.

Number four of the five Mississippi Standards states, "School performance standards (should be established) that are comparable to any national standards which may be established."

You must be kidding! How can we sign a blank check to accept any national standard when we don't even know what they are?

Governor Kirk Fordice, in his remarks at the Neshoba County Fair, spoke of "autonomy" for state school districts. And rightly so!

Education reformers are controlled by the National Education Association (NEA), the most powerful and well-funded lobbying group in the country; and the NEA wants to control the money, the teachers, the schools and the curriculum. Nothing good will come out of Washington nor from any of the "education laboratories."

And don't think that home schoolers and private schools will be exempt.

While the House counterpart of S1513 generated a tremendous outpouring of phone calls that amended HR-6 to exempt home schoolers and private schools from federal regulation, the issue is not yet dead.

Hundreds of times the words "all children," "all students" and "all schools," are used in S1513. All paths lead to successful mastery of the state/federal tests for higher education and employment. Successful mastery means that children will have to be taught whatever is on the test, i.e., the government curriculum.

Of special concern to private schools and home schoolers is the "certificate of employability" concept (passed in a technical change bill by the Mississippi Legislature last year.) This dangerous legislation would require students to present a "certificate of employability" to an employer when state performance outcomes are achieved. These certificates would not be available for students who are not in government schools.

Can parents, teachers and administrators, as well as the general public, do anything to stop the OBE steamroller that's heading our way?

I would suggest the following:

- Know and understand what's going on. Ask questions. Don't take my word for it, but find out for yourself. Attend State Department of Education Board meetings and all public meetings where education issues are discussed.
- Local school administrators should be asking to see the federal coded handbooks that say that they will be required to monitor individuals; that there is being proposed an electronic portfolio that can transfer permanent records (of students, teachers and administrators) across state lines. Talk about "Big Brother!"
- Parents should be raising questions about parental rights. OBE will be making psychological changes in your child.
- Ask school officials to justify why your child's self esteem needs to be changed. Ask

what the risks are and what might happen if an unlicensed school psychologist practices "behavior modification" techniques without parental consent. What about liability?

- Ask to see the "performance-based" tests scheduled to begin in October. If subjective testing is done, look closely at each student learning outcome and ask: How do you measure self esteem of a child? How do you score it? How much self esteem is enough?
- How will the tests be graded? Does the student get an A B C D or F grade, or will it be a simple pass or fail? Who decides what the standard is? How will a child be remediated if he fails to meet the standards?

And probably the most important question each parent should ask: What if my standards differ from those of the state? Who has the final authority ... the parent or the state?

There is also a question of costs. According to recently departed JPS Superintendent, Ben Canada, the Jackson district will be the first in the South and the second in the nation "invited" to work with the Washington-based Council for Basic Education in developing local standards and curriculum goals. And it will be expensive.

Parents should be aware that it will take about a year to develop the "new curriculum, new programs and new schools."

JPS 2005/2010 gives a hint as to what these "new schools" will be. They won't be centers of learning, but "community centers" that will provide pre-school child care and extended day care, health clinics, senior citizen centers, and the sites for "special interest" meetings.

Dr. Canada, in referring to his "vision" for local schools asks, "What do we want? How do we do it? And how will we pay for it?"

It's up to every Jackson citizen to answer his questions by becoming involved. We will lose the game by default if we don't show up to play.

Don't be deceived. Fine sounding goals or expectations based on subjective teaching methods can never replace a traditional education which demands that a student learn a body of knowledge that has absolute answers upon which he can build outward from the base.

The Northside Sun
Thursday, August 18, 1994

Mobilized Parents Strong Force for Education
(Part IV of IV)

IF YOU'VE READ my last three articles on education "restructuring" which have appeared in *The Northside Sun*, you will understand, and I hope, share, some of the concern I feel about the future of education in Mississippi.

My greatest concern is the general void of knowledge about education issues shared by teachers and parents alike.

If you mention Outcome Based Education (OBE) to most parents, you are met with a blank stare. Most have no idea that new "standards" being proposed for local schools is the early implementation of a controversial education experiment that is meeting opposition nationwide. Rather than focusing on academics and individual achievement, OBE refocuses on shaping students' belief, attitudes, and personal behavior.

Most parents are unaware of legislation that was introduced last year in the Mississippi legislature that would allow school personnel to provide psychological counseling without parental consent to almost any child in any school and with immunity for civil or criminal charges if damage to a child results. While this outrageous proposal died in the House Education Committee, it is a foretaste of what's to come.

VERY FEW KNOW about "certificates of employability" which was passed in a technical change bill that would provide students, once "performance outcomes" are achieved, to be eligible for employment certificates while students from private schools or those home schooled would not be eligible for certification because they did not meet the criteria established by the state.

The general public is unaware of the far-reaching implications of federal legislation that would provide federal "solutions" and virtually nationalize every school in the nation that accepts federal education dollars.

Three 1994 federal bills, *Goals 2000, the Elementary and Secondary Education Reauthorization Act* (HR-6, S1513) and *Schools-to-Work*, coupled with state educational "reform" measures, will complete the transfer of local control of schools to Washington.

Marc Tucker and David Hornbeck, visionary OBE planners, said to achieve their goals ... "will require a change in the prevailing culture – the attitudes, values, norms and accepted ways of doing things .... The question is how to bring about this kind of cultural transformation on the scale we have in mind?"

That's what's at stake in our schools – the ways of living we will hand down to our children and our grandchildren.

WHILE I HAVE outlined the problem, I would be remiss if I failed to suggest some positive things that must be done now to reverse the "reformation" of Mississippi schools.

1. Be informed as to what's going on in the classroom.
2. Express your opinion to your elected representatives, both state and national; say NO to education experimentation in our schools.
3. Work to elect sound, common sense people to local school boards (in Jackson work to get an elected school board). No one should be elected who is not committed to returning public schools to institutions that train young people in the basic academic skills needed to function in life. We need school boards made up of sound thinkers who will not rubber stamp everything proposed by the education establishment.

Concerned individuals across the state of Mississippi are joining forces to keep OBE out of Mississippi schools. It will take people who care and who are willing to track education restructuring.

SCORE 100 MISSISSIPPI, a grassroots organization of concerned Mississippians, has been organized to bring education issues to the general public and actively participate in the restructuring process of public schools.

SCORE 100 MISSISSIPPI has been organized with the belief that:

- Education should be focused on academics of the highest standards, incorporating demanding curriculum that fosters motivation, promotes individualism, and rewards excellence.
- Parents rights regarding their children's education should supersede state and federal ideologies and should be the basis for education legislation.
- Public awareness should be raised concerning the critical issues confronting the education and development of Mississippi children.

SCORE 100 MISSISSIPPI is providing information to parents about specific plans for education restructuring; scheduling speakers for club programs; tracking and initiating legislation to meet positive educational objectives.

If you would like to be put on the mailing list, please send your name, address and phone number to ***SCORE 100 MISSISSIPPI***, P. O. Box 12101, Jackson, Mississippi 39236-2101.

The Clarion-Ledger
Thursday, August 25, 1994

Government Is Intending to Control All Local Schools

Gov. Kirk Fordice's proposal to allow Mississippi's public schools to "secede" from state control bears merit.

There's no question that education reform is needed. Rather than improving education, the State Department of Education may be exacerbating the problem.

State Superintendent Tom Burnham spoke volumes when he said, "I don't know ... how you spend federal dollars without guidelines and the structure *they* put in place."

As aptly stated in *The Clarion-Ledger*'s "education" editorial on August 6, "Everyone is for local control of public schools."

What few Mississippians realize is how extensive state and federal control of education has become and that "public schools" have in effect become "government schools."

On August 3, the Elementary and Secondary Education Reauthorization Act – Improving America's Schools Act of 1994 (S1513) was passed by the U.S. Senate.

It is a $12.6 billion takeover of education by the federal government that is unprecedented in our nation's history. The bill contains 834 pages of *new* federal mandates controlling education, social services, school administrators and boards, children and parents. S1513 gives the U.S. secretary of Education the power to "approve a state plan (he) determines meets the requirements of curriculum-based learning resources" that are "intended to be applied nationally."

S1513 connects the "voluntary" GOALS 2000 with S1513 and in effect makes adoption of federal performance standards mandatory.

Our state Department of Education is eager to comply. One of our state "goals" is "school performance standards that are comparable to *any* national standards which may be established."

You've got to be kidding! How can we jeopardize our schools by agreeing to *any* school performance standard that *may* be established – especially in light of what's coming out of Washington these days?

The government intends to control "all children" "all students" and "all schools" just as it intends to control every area of our lives.

Wake up, Mississippians! If we allow Orwellian education to prevail, we will have only ourselves to blame.

The Clarion-Ledger

Thursday, November 23, 1995

Chances Are, Your Child's Considered "At Risk" in State Public Schools

As more social services are provided
by the schools, less time is being spent
on reading, writing and arithmetic

During my two months on the State Board of Education, I heard frequent reference made to children who are classified as "at risk."

Curious as to how many children in Mississippi public schools fall into the "at risk" category, I raised the question with Dr. Tom Burnham, State Superintendent of Education. I was stunned by his reply. Dr. Burnham told me that "80 percent of children in Mississippi public schools are `at risk'." – 80 percent!

Before this ominous pronouncement has you reaching for the aspirin bottle, there needs to be some explanation as to why so many children are in peril.

According to the Master Plan for Services for Students At Risk from Prevention Through Remediation (U.S. Department of Education, August 19, 1988), "a student at risk is *any* student who, because of his/her individual needs, requires some kind of *uniquely designed intervention* in order to achieve literacy, graduate, and be prepared for transition from school to post-school options. Without appropriate intervention, a student is at increased risk for failing to achieve commensurate with his/her ability, for truancy, and for dropping out. Without appropriate intervention, such a student may not be able to participate meaningfully in society as a competent, productive, caring, and responsible citizen."

In order to provide "uniquely designed intervention," partnerships are being formed to link Education with the U.S. Department of Health and Human Services and the U.S. Department of Labor so that *all children* can be caught in the social-service web to turn public schools into "one-stop" community/health/training/employment centers.

Consider the Jackson 2005/2010 "vision for the district" unveiled in 1994, which addressed "conditions that hinder a child's growth, intellectually, socially, and physically (and which) should be addressed by the community."

We've all heard the oft-quoted African proverb that parallels the JPS vision, "It takes a whole village (community) to raise a child."

In my mind, raising a child takes a mother and a father, and most parents don't want the whole village butting into the raising of their children. If parents relinquish their authority to the "whole village," you can bet that the village will teach your children something you'd just as soon they didn't learn.

A tip-off to this new public school ideology is the language used nationwide in state legislation that is being introduced ... "collaborative service delivery system," "coordinated services for children at risk," "integrated service delivery initiatives," "on site, coordinated early intervention and case management services to children at risk".

Many state legislatures are cooperating with the educationists and the teachers' unions by passing bills that refer to public schools as "Community Centers" or "Family Resource Centers." As more and more social services are provided by the schools, less and less time is being spent on reading, writing, and arithmetic.

And since declining test scores indicate that schools are failing to provide the academic skills that parents expect, new tests are being developed and test scores "recentered" to convince parents, and the general public, that schools are doing their job.

Undoubtedly, there are children who come from dysfunctional families, who have no responsible parent to shape their character, who need a helping hand, but the responsibility for these children should not be placed on the school at the detriment of those pupils who have the desire and ability to be good students.

Most parents don't consider their children to be "at risk," but if your child is in a public school in Mississippi, chances are he/she is being targeted for one of many "uniquely designed intervention" programs currently on the drawing board.

And the more children designated "at risk", the *more personnel and funds* the public school system demands. The individual's desire to learn and acquire knowledge is a purposely forgotten factor in education restructuring. Rather than concentrating on the 80 percent who are 'at risk', more time and energy should be devoted to "accentuating the positive."

The goal of public education should not be to "remold" public schools into "national human resources development systems," as some social engineers have proposed, but to provide a rich and challenging academic education that will allow each student to fulfill his/her individual God-given potential.

The Clarion-Ledger
Thursday, December 14, 1995

Legislature Must Ensure Valid Phonics Program Used to Teach Reading

Mississippi educators erred when they embraced whole language as the method to teach reading.

I hope that when the gavel sounds to open the 1996 legislative session, those "new faces" will also have "good heads" filled with lots of common sense – especially where education is concerned.

It's time that the Education Committees of both Houses of the Mississippi Legislature consider education methods that are tried and true rather than blindly accepting proposals developed and promoted by the State Department of Education and endorsed by education "helpers" such as the Public Education Forum and the Millennium Group.

An example of what can happen when legislators don't look past the end of their noses is the adoption of the "Writing to Read" computer program for which the state pledged $7 million in 1989 when former Democratic Gov. Ray Mabus struck a deal with the Riordan Foundation of California.

While the Mississippi legislature was embracing this "new and inventive" computer technology, other state legislatures were turning thumbs down. There was conclusive evidence available at the time that Writing to Read was a failed program.

Most parents would be outraged to see the computer workbook (kept at school) which shows a picture of an eagle with the word "eagle" spelled "egl", or the picture of a face spelled "fas", or wheel, spelled "whel." The child not only sees the word misspelled, but *writes* the word incorrectly.

It's downright criminal! Criminal to spend tax dollars for a failed system when the bottom line is to sell IBM computers and criminal to deprive children of their right to learn to read.

I'm amazed at how people who are normally sound-thinkers take leave of their senses when influenced by so called "professionals." The education "professionals" not only manipulate legislators but dupe parents and teachers alike by leading them to believe that kids can be more creative and uninhibited if they "play with the English language" and use "inventive spelling."

Children can be creative and learn to write on the computer *correctly,* and I applaud the teachers and administrators who refuse to use Writing to Read, recognizing it for what it is – education malpractice.

And don't let anyone tell you that most public schools use phonics to teach reading. Combining the "look-say" method with "sound out" syllables is *not* systematic, intensive phonics. It's phony phonics.

Recently, a 27-member State of California Task Force reported "a crisis that demands immediate attention."

The crisis? California was ranked at the bottom-of-the-barrel in the 1994 National Assessment of Educational Progress (NAEP).

Horror of horrors! The California scores tied Louisiana's as the lowest of all states ranked. Where was Mississippi? Among the bottom four.

The California report, "Every Child A Reader," rejected the "whole language" philosophy and warned that unless reading is taught differently, "we will lose a generation of children." The report urged a kindergarten-to-university overhaul of teaching methods, textbooks, and teacher training to ensure that all children are reading independently no later than the third grade.

The report said that most children need to be systematically taught phonics, letter patterns and other "decoding" skills that enable good readers to recognize words virtually automatically.

Would Mississippi dare be so brave? Can Mississippi educators face up to the fact that they erred when they embraced whole language as the method to teach reading and admit, as California has, that it isn't working?

California children and Mississippi children deserve SIDE Phonics (Systematic, Intensive, Direct, Early Phonics). They can get it through phonics curricula, such as *Open Court; Professor Phonics Gives Sound Advice; The Spalding Writing Road to Reading, Distar; Sing, Spell, Read and Write; or Word Wise.*

All parents deserve to know the method of reading instruction used in their child's school, their child's reading score, and the total average reading score for the school compared to the state and national average.

Parent and child would also benefit from the establishment of a minimal passing score for reading. Any child who does not reach a minimum score would be retained at that grade level until reading proficiency is gained and a passing score achieved.

A bill introduced by Rep. Rita Martinson and supported by ***SCORE 100 MISSISSIPPI*** would require all school districts to offer an alternative (and more cost-effective) phonics program from approved phonics curricula.

There are many good teachers who would welcome SIDE Phonics to the classroom. Regrettably, however, the educationists, who have the ear of the policy makers, will probably never admit publicly that whole language has been a horrendous failure.

If we want to provide Mississippi children with the key to unlock the English language through intensive, systematic phonics, your elected representatives need to hear from you!

The call to action is clear. Reading – the basis for *all* learning – should be our first priority.

The Clarion-Ledger
Tuesday, January 17, 1995

Meetings in Jackson, Tupelo Will Discuss Restoring "Real" Education

The neighborhood school has virtually been replaced with "education factories" directed from a bureau.

Do you remember how good it felt to score 100 on a test? That's the feeling of achievement that ***SCORE 100 MISSISSIPPI*** wants Mississippi students to experience.

SCORE 100 MISSISSIPPI is the Statewide Committee On Reforming Education (SCORE) which has brought together concerned citizens from around the state who believe in traditional education based on academics of the highest standards with demanding curriculum that fosters motivation, promotes individualism, and rewards excellence.

SCORE 100 MISSISSIPPI believes that top grades should be based on comprehension of facts and attainment or knowledge gained through preparation and hard work. Grades should not be based on a watered-down, non-objective testing or inflated grading system, or on what a student feels rather than what he or she knows. Tests should be accurate academic measure by which teacher, parent, and pupil can gauge real learning.

Changes in testing methods and new subjective assessments based on outcomes have resulted in closer scrutiny of education objectives nationwide.

Over the last 30 years there has been a growing federal presence in public education with curriculum influenced nationally, rather than locally.

With establishment of the U.S. Department of Education in 1979 and the 1994 passage of GOALS 2000 and other major federal education legislation, intrusion into local schools has dramatically escalated. The result: Parents are losing their fundamental right to direct the education of their children.

The neighborhood school has virtually been replaced with "education factories" directed from a central bureau. Increasingly, education is becoming a big (and profitable) business.

The change in the lifestyle of the American family has resulted in many parents relinquishing the primary responsibility for their children's education to others. Taking up the slack are "education specialists" who under the banner of progressive reform are developing non-academic "standards" or "outcomes" by which students, teachers and schools are measured.

The result is not just reform, but fundamental re-invention of education. There has been a paradigm (model) shift from traditional education (educating to think) to education for change – change of all sectors of society – economic, social, and political.

In order to solve society's problems, many schools are becoming "one stop shopping centers," providing on-site access to social service agencies. Plans are on the drawing board to provide full childcare, clinical health care, psychological counseling, and employment agencies.

Additional cost to taxpayers? You betcha!

New education jargon has made it virtually impossible for teachers and parents to communicate with any certainty of understanding. Education bureaucratese is about as intimidating as the terminology used by nuclear scientists.

The emphasis in public education on "multiculturalism," "globalism," and "political correctness" at the expense of the 3-Rs has resulted in drastically lower levels of student academic achievement and declining test scores.

And don't think that children in "homeschools" or "good private schools" won't be affected by this education restructuring.

Through business and education partnerships, "workplace competencies," developed by the U.S. Department of Labor, will require "Certificates of Initial Mastery" (CIMs) to obtain employment. Unless *all* students *master government standards and outcomes*, they may not get a job.

To help parents and teachers better understand education's "new direction," ***SCORE 100 MISSISSIPPI*** is sponsoring several town meetings featuring Anita Hoge, nationally recognized author and education analyst from Pennsylvania, who has documented restructuring plans. Mrs. Hoge is highly qualified to explain Mississippi's reform plans and how they correlate with GOALS 2000.

Her Jackson appearance will be Thursday at 6:30 p.m. at Murrah High School Auditorium and in Tupelo at Itawamba Community College Auditorium at 10 a.m. on Saturday, January 21. Both meetings are open to the public and are free of charge.

An educated populace derived from a strong public educational system is vital to the future of this nation.

Let this serve as a wake-up call to Mississippians!

It's time to reject non-academic reform plans, restore tried and true teaching methods and common sense to education, and act now to reclaim our public schools.

The Clarion-Ledger
Thursday, March 29, 1995

We Must Try to Save Public Education

In a "school war" between traditionalists and modernists, I'm a devout traditionalist

America needs "Education Glasnost" in which educators and policy makers find the courage to speak the truth ... and the truth is that our education system is failing.

A 1994 Gallup poll shows only 22 percent of American public school parents are happy with the nation's public schools; only two percent of the American public would give the nation's public schools an "A," and only 20 percent give the system a "B".

Once upon a time parents and teachers were a team. But now parents see a trend away from academics to attempted reforms using values clarification, open classrooms, team teaching, new math, multiculturalism, mastery learning, and political correctness. Parents are shut out of the educational system by those who believe that only trained professionals are qualified to educate.

Educators, in turn, place the blame for education failures on too little parental support, broken homes, poor parenting, too much TV, too little discipline, and too little money.

Both parent and educator are right.

The dilemma has resulted in a "school war" between traditionalists and modernists. I'm a traditionalist.

In my mind, the primary function of schools is to provide challenging curriculum of the highest standards to develop the mind; excellence should be rewarded and individualism encouraged; schools should demand more of students rather than less; and parents' rights regarding their children's education should supersede state and federal ideologies. (And that means the right to pray in school!)

Modernists believe that no student should be allowed to fail; schools should meet the *social* needs of the child by providing health care, food, psychological counseling, and daycare to allow teenage mothers to stay in school. They also believe that no amount of money is too much to spend.

When these two very divergent views of education collide, the modernists prevail. At present, they control education legislation, schools, and the money. There is no room for any diverse opinions. Anyone who disagrees is labeled the enemy of public education.

Centralization of school control, which leads to ballooning and costly bureaucracy, has been intensified by the fact that more and more funding is coming from the state and federal government.

Centralization is being pursued with a vengeance by both Democrats and Republicans, who favor national goals and standards to which each state's public schools would have to conform (at least if they want to receive federal money).

The increase in centralization can best be illustrated by the fact that in 1945-46 there were more than 100,000 school districts in the United States. Today, there are only 15,701.

While the teacher population of the public schools increased 57 percent between 1960 and 1984, and the number of principals and supervisors increased by 79 percent, other personnel skyrocketed by 500 percent. Education is big business.

Many parents are discovering that school gets in the way of education.

At least 300,000 children and their parents in the United States, and by some estimates up to 1.5 million, have decided to educate their children at home. Home-schooling is gaining a prominence it hasn't had since the public schools were established a century and a half ago.

Rejecting the "socialization" of public schools, parents, without the help of a specially trained adult and many with little or no formal teaching instruction, are developing in their children an authentic understanding that comes from an internal desire to know. They are also instilling their own values, world view, and work ethics in their offsprings. They are not abdicating their parental responsibility to the state.

But home-schooling is not for everyone. In many homes there is no parent to be the teacher.

Many families, especially those who are financially unable to provide an alternative to public education, are trapped in the system.

Can public schools be saved? Never let it be said that we didn't try.

There are many dedicated and outstanding teachers struggling to stay in the system. But many are leaving, and very few young people make a career commitment to teaching. This situation is regrettable because it is the teacher who is the key to education. It's the teacher with his or her gifts who can influence, inspire, and instill the desire to learn in a student.

The "education" forces who became actively involved in blocking my confirmation to the State Board of Education, including among others, the MAE, the NAACP, and JPS lobbyists, made one big mistake: they underestimated my commitment to *good* education.

A position on the state board would have limited my capacity to speak out publicly and would have effectively muzzled me.

Their rejection has given me the opportunity, in my style and with a *loud* voice, to champion the right of each child in every Mississippi school, whether public or private, to become a good reader; to receive a high quality education; to have the right to enter the school building confident of having a good teacher and without fear of violence; and to guarantee parents, through local control, to determine the type education they want for their children without government control.

The Clarion-Ledger

Thursday, November 2, 1995

Despite Media Reports, Governor's PRIME Initiative Is Not Dead At All

An exciting education reform
endeavors sweep the nation, Mississippi
has the opportunity to lead the way.

Gov. Kirk Fordice's PRIME initiative has the educationists and the teachers' unions in a frenzy. Misinformation by these groups is being circulated to derail the governor's plan to affect true education reform.

The governor has been accused of using PRIME as a campaign ploy when in reality he saw the need for the people to have a say after his initial efforts to improve education went nowhere in a Legislature strongly influenced by MAE education lobbyists.

Recent newspaper articles would have you believe that PRIME is dead. Not so.

The intent was never to have PRIME on the ballot this year. Gathering the 83,345 signatures from across five congressional districts takes time. The fact that in two months more than 50,000 people have signed petitions leaves little doubt that by the October 1996 deadline, the signatures will be there.

In spite of all the red herrings, signing a PRIME petition will not radically alter our public schools. It only puts the question of local school control on the ballot. If it passes, it will be up to parents and local school personnel to determine the type schools they want for their communities.

Its purpose is to provide much needed competition, more options for parents, teacher flexibility and empowerment, and freedom from regulation and bureaucratic process.

PRIME will not provide public funds for private schools as some have claimed. Most private schools, fearing loss of autonomy, don't want state dollars because with it comes government intervention and regulation.

Even if PRIME fails to win approval, control of public schools by education bureaucrats and unions will eventually be history as more and more parents and teachers become dissatisfied with the system and seize the opportunity to roll up their sleeves, roll back regulations, and open and operate schools that will provide children with a solid academic education.

Exciting education reform endeavors, many more "radical" than PRIME, are taking place nationwide. Rarely do the local media report the following facts:

- The charter school concept is enjoying a large and growing circle of supporters. As of August, 1995, over 250 charter schools have been approved in 10 states. Nineteen states, Mississippi excluded, permit the establishment of charter schools and some states are even providing seed money to encourage their growth.

  Successful charter schools combine fundamental aspects of public schooling with the flexibility and freedom of the private sector and are evaluated on how well students achieve rather than on compliance with administrative policies and mandated budget allocations. Their focus is on the education of children rather than the preservation of the "education system."

- The Education Leaders Council, a networking group dedicated to genuine reform, includes state school chiefs from Florida, Virginia, New Jersey, Georgia, Arizona, and Pennsylvania. School officials who have joined the council have expressed the belief that the best education reforms don't involve more money but rather more local control of school and choice.
- Fife Symington, governor of Arizona, has proposed eliminating the Arizona State Department of Education, scrapping teacher certification, closing failed schools, providing private school vouchers to parents, and denying the right of teacher unions to bargain collectively.

Meanwhile, back in Mississippi ... Dick Molpus and Ronnie Musgrove, the Democrat candidates for governor and lieutenant governor, are accepting PAC money from the NEA and MAE to assure that the status quo in Mississippi public schools is maintained. During the last six months, through the "Mississippi Coordinated Campaign," the NEA and MAE have funneled more than $30,000 and $52,000 respectively into the campaign coffers of the Democrats.

Mr. Molpus, who in 1982 helped develop the education reform plan that has produced the system in place today, can't brag about his education track record when test scores are at an all-time low.

And Mr. Musgrove, as chairman of the Senate Education Committee, is in the hip pocket of the education lobby and has swallowed their propaganda hook, line, and sinker.

Both of these candidates are committed to perpetuate a failed system and the vested interests of the rich and politically powerful NEA and MAE in return for campaign contributions and votes.

As education reform sweeps the nation, Mississippi has the opportunity to lead the way.

Through PRIME, Gov. Fordice has offered a plan to re-energize our schools and return local control to the people. His aggressive and far-sighted leadership puts Mississippi on the cutting edge of future education breakthroughs. That leadership qualifies him for a second term.

And if you haven't done so, sign a PRIME petition today.

The Clarion-Ledger

Tuesday, January 21, 1997

Educators Must Realize Whole Language Has Been Tried, Found Guilty

A legislative hearing will focus on reading instruction designed to help Mississippi school children.

In 1993, I first wrote about the failure of "whole language" as a method of reading instruction. Today, four years later, the failure is even more evident in state-wide reading scores. Last year, student scores ranged from a low of 40 for ninth-graders to a high of 49 for eighth-graders. The national average, which is a national disgrace, is 50 on a 100-point scale.

The reading scores for this year have not been released, but indications are that Mississippi students still can't read; and, according to recent newspaper reports, concerns over low reading achievement continue to surface in state Board of Education meetings.

What amazes me is that the board seems to be stupefied as to the reason Mississippi reading scores are low. Also, that state Superintendent of Education Tom Burnham was asked by the board "to devise a new measuring stick, one that might become part of the state's performance-based accreditation system."

It sounds as if, and I hope I'm wrong, that if the present tests show that students can't read, the solution is to change the method of testing to satisfy the demand for higher scores. This familiar tactic is just another means by which education malpractice can be disguised.

Whole language has been tried and found guilty. How long will it take Mississippi educators to accept the verdict? How many more children will be passed through our educational system without being provided the key to unlock the English language?

Some educators are unwilling to admit their failure; but many others, like Dr. Bill Honig, former state education superintendent of California, are willing to place the blame where it belongs ... on the failure of whole language as an effective means of reading instruction.

After extensive research, Dr. Honig recognized that whole language was an ineffective way to teach reading. With California reading scores tied for the lowest in the country, he convinced California governor, Pete Wilson, and the California Legislature that most children need to be systematically taught phonics, letter patterns and other "decoding" skills that enable readers to recognize words virtually automatically.

The California report, "Every Child a Reader," totally rejected the whole language philosophy and warned that unless reading is taught differently, "We will lose a generation of children." Recognizing the problem, California has allocated more than $100 millon to return to systematic, explicit instruction in sound-letter relationships (phonics), and to add the "phonemic awareness technique" for children who are unable to learn to read with the phonics method.

And guess what. As more and more states reject whole language, textbook publishers, left with millions of whole language textbooks, are looking for a place to unload their rejectamenta ... and Mississippi is buying.

The "phonemic awareness technique" has been developed for those children who, as some claim, can't be taught phonetically because they are unable to hear the sounds.

While I don't profess to be an authority in reading instruction, I have reservations about classifying any student as unable to "hear" letter combinations such as "th" or "ng" if systematic, intensive phonics is properly taught. In fact, the verbal exercises of "sounding out" consonants used in teaching phonics would greatly improve enunciation and pronunciation, which have been lost in present-day "language arts."

In the early 1900s, the literacy rate in the United States was in the 90th percentile with phonics as the *modus operandi*. If children of that era didn't have difficulty hearing phonetic sounds, I'd like to know what terrible catastrophe has occurred to cause "deafness" in today's student.

These questions and many more will be answered by a distinguished panel in a hearing before the joint Mississippi House/Senate Education Committees this Thursday, January 23, at 12:30 P.M. on the first floor of the State Capitol. The meeting is open to the general public.

Parents interested in helping their children become readers should take advantage of this opportunity to hear what experts in the field have to say.

Leading the panel will be Jimmy Kilpatrick, of Houston, Texas, who is chairman of the Texas Educational Task Force and advisor to Governor George W. Bush, and the Texas Educational Association. Kilpatrick was also chosen as Legislative Educational Chairman for the Texas Association of Mexican-American Chambers of Commerce.

Others on the panel are Marsha Sonnenberg, an education consultant and former assistant superintendent for curriculum development at the Wharton Independent School District in Texas, and Dr. Eldo William Bergman, Jr., who is a consultant in Child Neurology and Developmental Medicine and the Executive Director of the Texas Reading Institute. Sonnenberg has instructed school superintendents and school districts on designing and implementing early childhood language and reading programs.

The meeting should be of highest priority for every member of the State Board of Education and members of local district school boards from across the state.

It would behoove Dr. Burnham, state superintendent of education; Dr. Gerald Hasselman, associate state superintendent in charge of academic education; Jo Prather, early childhood director for reading (K-12); and Johnny Franklin, director, office of instructional development, to also be in attendance.

Excuses for failing to teach Mississippi children to read can no longer be accepted.

The Clarion-Ledger
Letter to the Editor
Tuesday, April 8, 1997

Melton Only Attempting to Bring Order Out of Chaos

I've always admired Frank Melton for putting action to his words. Instead of just talking about problems, he tries to do something about them.

Trouble at the Capital City Alternative School? Students using profanity and being out of control? Parents and teachers asking for help? Thank goodness Melton is willing to take the bull by the horns to help school officials bring order out of chaos.

His involvement resulted in twenty-four students being arrested for disorderly conduct and abusive language, and putting everyone on notice, including 175 other students, that inappropriate behavior would not be tolerated.

Interim Superintendent Dan Merritt shouldn't be "puzzled" by Melton's motives. I believe that Frank Melton sincerely wants the best for the kids of Jackson and as a member of the State Board of Education has the authority to visit any school in the State of Mississippi unannounced at any time.

For a JPS School Board member to say Melton's visit to the school "wasn't a nice trick" leaves me once again questioning the leadership of Jackson Public Schools.

One of the reasons we have children unable to function in a normal classroom environment is vividly illustrated by the statement made by the mother of one of the 13-year old students arrested on Tuesday. In *The Clarion-Ledger* report, "JPS officials question TV executive's tactics," she is quoted as saying "It was a plot" (to involve her child in their scheme.)

While I don't know this mother personally, I would be willing to bet that she is a single parent with an out of control son, (if he weren't he wouldn't be at the Alternative School).

**If there is a father in the home, then he should have been at the Alternative School to take his son in tow. All* children need an authority figure to lay down the rules; and if they don't have one at home, they need someone like Frank Melton.

If they don't have a Frank Melton, then the next authority figure to appear on the scene will probably be a judge sentencing their out-of-control child to prison. Somewhere, at sometime, children must learn respect for authority; and in order to teach this important lesson, parents need all the help they can get and should be supportive and appreciative of those individuals who care enough to step in and take control.

*Omitted when published.

The Clarion-Ledger
Tuesday, August 26, 1997

Do MAE Members Really Support the Ideology, Agenda of the NEA?

Lobbying has worked effectively in state Legislature

How many of the 8,000-plus teachers holding membership in the Mississippi Association of Educators (MAE) endorse and support the goals of their national affiliate, the National Education Association (NEA)? Do MAE members know or even care about NEA ideology, or does the desire for higher pay drive their support of the nation's most powerful union whose goal is to control U.S. education, school curricula, access to the teaching profession, and even the nation's political agenda?

Gathered in Atlanta over the Fourth of July weekend for the annual NEA convention, 8,923 delegates and 5,469 registered non-delegates, celebrated the "gains" made in the 104th and 105th (Republican) congresses: Those "victories" include the largest single increase ever in *federal* education funding $3.5 billion, surpassing even Clinton's budget request.

The National Education Association, called by some the National Extortion Association, takes credit for defeating the Parental Rights and Responsibilities Act, all efforts to curtail Goals 2000, School-to-Work, affirmative action, and all school choice voucher bills.

The NEA's non-academic, ultra-left political agenda includes funding for the National Endowment for the Arts, statehood for the District of Columbia, ratification of U.N. treaties on women and children, tax-funded education of children of illegal immigrants, a national holiday honoring Cesar Chavez, and a new initiative to revive and ratify the Equal Rights Amendment (ERA).

According to convention watchers, gay and lesbian activists have become the most influential single group within the NEA convention. The NEA Gay Lesbian Caucus (NEA-GLC) celebrated its 10th anniversary this year with numerous caucuses and convention events and succeeded in weaving its agenda into about a dozen resolutions approved by delegates.

Last year, a resolution drafted by NEA-GLC and adopted by delegates said that "education should increase tolerance" (of the Gay/Lesbian lifestyle). This year, "tolerance" was changed to "acceptance."

Candace Gingrich, lesbian sister of Newt, spoke at the NEA-GLC's caucus dinner on July 5 and a lesbian caucus featured a 90-minute video entitled "It's Elementary, Teaching About Gay Issues in School."

Whether or not one agrees or disagrees with what goes on at NEA conventions, the shenanigans of the "educators" are definitely educational (though not in the academic sense), having not a whit to do with reading, writing and arithmetic.

The wealthy NEA maintains government relations field teams to work directly with state affiliates and NEA members "to enhance their effectiveness in political activities and legislative advocacy."

The NEA political affairs program wages what it calls "effective, unified campaigns to elect leaders, from the school board to the White House, who are committed to public education." – i.e., the NEA political agenda.

Their lobbying program has worked effectively in the Mississippi Legislature. The MAE "grass-roots network" turns out in droves for the "cause of education and the nation's children."

When the Senate Education Committee, chaired by "Mr. Education" himself, then-Sen. Ronnie Musgrove, set the time and place for the committee hearing on my appointment to the State Board of Education, the MAE knew about it before I did and turned out in force to voice their opposition. They made sure that no diverse opinions on education initiatives would be tolerated!

The NEA convention's Fourth of July celebration featured a choir of young black singers who sang two religious songs as part of their program. One selection, *What a Mighty God We Serve,* received a standing ovation at the conclusion of the choir's outstanding performance. The next day, NEA President Bob Chase apologized from the platform for the two religious songs and stated emphatically that they had not been cleared by the NEA.

My question is: Do Mississippi teachers who belong to the MAE support the policies of the NEA? If not, why do they remain silent?

And for those who really care about public education, it's time for your legislative voice to become louder than that of the MAE/NEA which now holds sway over the Mississippi Legislature.

The Clarion-Ledger

Tuesday, March 5, 1996

Mississippi's School-To-Work Could Have Dangerous Consequences

To their credit, not all businessmen support the new labor/education agenda.

Have you been asked if you want your child put on track for vocational training through the Workforce and Education Act of 1994?

Have you heard of the career development proposals recommended by the Mississippi School-to-Work Planning Council for public education in our state?

I'm not opposed to vocational training or student career development, but I am concerned that some of our education leaders who maintain a strong legislative lobby at the state capital are promoting programs formulated by federal legislation – GOALS 2000, CAREERS, Workforce Development Act, and the Schools to Work Opportunities Act – which could be detrimental to our children and the future of our state and nation.

To understand this national industrial/education agenda is to compare it to the life-management, government-knows-best philosophy of the health care plan developed by Hillary Clinton. The general public caught on to that scheme but knows little about an equally dangerous idea formulated by Mrs. Clinton and her cohorts to provide "human capital" for the emerging technological, global workplace of the 21st century.

The 1990 Ira Magaziner/Hillary Clinton report, "America's Choice: High Skills or Low Wages!" provides us with the Clinton blueprint for the work-based learning model for American schools which is to be implemented through the Secretary's Commission on Achieving Necessary Skills (SCANS) of the U.S. Department of Labor. Secretary of Labor Robert Reich is a longtime Outcome Based Education (OBE)/dumbing-down advocate.

Additionally, GOALS 2000, in linkage with other enactments, notably School-to-Work, implements much of the Clinton agenda. In the plan, a National Skills Standards Board would develop performance standards that "will be applied to all youth" and "would incorporate apprenticeship/work-based learning models and guidelines for granting skills standards and certificates of mastery."

Sound familiar?

Through federally approved state plans, School-to-Work would dictate how schools are to certify workplace competencies for all children and would integrate work-based learning into the curriculum and track students into specific occupations at an early age.

The 1996 Mississippi School-to-Work Transition Planning Council Report to the governor recommends "linking content curriculum and competencies to national education goals and to SCANS skills and knowledge areas."

It's the "linking" that concerns me.

The industrial/education reform plan is being pushed nationwide by the Business Roundtable, an organization of the CEOs of the 200 largest corporations in the country who, needless to say, have a vested interest in gaining cheap American labor to compete with cheap labor of Third World countries. The theory they espouse is that schools should concentrate less on knowledge and literacy and more on work place skills and state formulated social attitudes.

To their credit, not all businessmen support the new labor/education agenda. As one top executive expressed it, "What we need is more attention to the basics of education, not less. You can train people to do various operations in anybody's plant, but in order to succeed at anything, you must first have a good basic concept or reading and writing. That's what our schools are failing to provide."

In August of 1995, a *Clarion-Ledger* news article reported results from student testing in the three-year-old Mississippi Tech-prep program. It showed that students in the Tech-prep program are weak in academic skills.

So weak, in fact, that while they out-scored the nation on the performance tests in seven of the eight occupational skills; they were below the national average on the written academic portions of the test in all eight areas.

And we all know that the national average is nothing to brag about.

The article stated that Superintendent of Education Tom Burnham was concerned about the problem of academics in the program. And well he should be.

With new emphasis on integrated workforce skills being added to school curricula and with performance-based testing replacing standardized tests and literacy exams, there will soon be no true gauge of determining real academic achievement.

Other concerns with Mississippi School-to-Work:

- Many young people don't always decide on a field of work, much less a specific industry, while still in high school. School-to-Work seems to anticipate forcing them to make an early choice or to have the system make it for them.
- Few employers have the time or money to offer work-based learning slots for student job training.
- After training students to specific jobs, will there be jobs available?

Robert Holland, in his book, *Not With My Child, You Don't,* asks: What is the primary purpose of education? Is it to:

(a) Enable students to develop their intellects to the utmost of their capacity and to become independent-thinking individuals in a free society, or is it to ...

(b) Train youngsters to be competent, well-socialized, customer-serving workers in the high-performance workplace to meet the needs of big business?

And who decides whether its liberal arts or workplace indoctrination?

(a) Patrons of the school, who pay the taxes and provide the children, or ...

(b) Corporate chiefs with big bankrolls in partnership with elitist coalitions, education/social engineers, and the federal government.

If you answered (a) to both questions, go to the head of the class!

The Clarion-Ledger

Tuesday, August 17, 1999

2000 Is Year State Supposed to Reach Educational Goals

The miracle year, 2000, is just a little more than four months away. That's when all those lofty educational goals were supposed to be met. The goals of 2000 proposed by educators, legislators and regulators somehow failed to meet the target date even though reform promises were made, billions of dollars were spent and new, innovative programs introduced.

During the administration of Ray Mabus and his "Mississippi BEST" education reform bill, Mississippi bought into IBM's computer whole language reading program, "Writing to Read." The cost was $13 million – $6 million from the Riordan Foundation and $7 million from state funds – to put computers in "every kindergarten and first grade in Mississippi."

Still below average

Six years later, in 1995, a *Clarion-Ledger* article reported there were 317 "Writing to Read" computer labs in 286 Mississippi elementary schools, with another 24 schools applying for the summer of 1996. IBM trained 1,700 Mississippi teachers and administrators to use "Writing to Read."

And what have we gotten?

According to National Assessment of Educational Progress "1998 Reading Report Card for the Nation and the States," released in March, Mississippi ranks below the national average in grades four and eight. And the national average? 215 on a scale of 0 to 500.

No matter how you figure it, Mississippi receives a failing grade in teaching children to read. The good news is that the obvious failure of whole language is finally forcing educators nationwide to reevaluate the methods used to teach reading.

In 1996, in an unprecedented action, 40 professors of linguistics and psycholinguistics from Harvard, MIT, Brandeis, Northeastern University, University of Massachusetts, and Boston University took a strong stand against mandating whole language as a standard of reading instruction and openly sided with systematic phonics instruction.

At the annual meeting of the Southern Regional Education Board (SREB) in July, two reading specialists addressed classroom instruction and teacher education. They strongly support expanded, intensive course study for *teacher* training, focusing on phonemic awareness in lower grades and requiring certified classroom teachers to be retrained to teach reading phonetically.

In Mississippi, we need to be asking how well our colleges of education prepare future teachers to teach reading. How can teachers be held accountable if they're being taught a failed method of instruction?

What are we waiting for?

Professional development efforts should focus on the following:

- Teaching specific phonemic awareness skills in undergraduate coursework.
- Strong mentoring programs for student teachers.
- Opportunities for teachers to learn from experts who can demonstrate effective teaching strategies in the classroom.

In California, the Sacramento City Unified School District uses a phonics reading program called "Open Court."

Since its inception several years ago, reading scores have risen from the 35th percentile for first-graders two years ago, to the 54 percentile last year, to the 62 percentile this year.

In a column of August 1993, I wrote: "Open Court," far and away one of the best phonics programs ever developed (and also cost effective) has been placed on the approved list for Mississippi schools. What are we waiting for?

And six years later, with thousands of Mississippi children still unable to read, I'll ask the question again.

What are we waiting for?

The Clarion-Ledger
Monday, October 18, 1999

What Do You Know About School Health Clinics?

A controversy has been raging in California over passage of a school health clinic bill that would increase the number of health clinics located on school campuses and the expansion of the types of services offered students.

More than two thousand parents converged on the California State Capitol to protest the passage of the bill, prompting Governor Gray Davis to veto it on October 6.

What made these parents angry?

The bill was a clear threat to parental authority, allowing clinic personnel to provide "confidential medical services without (parental) consent." The medical services would provide "comprehensive" primary and mental health services, including prescribing and dispensing drugs, mental health assessment, pelvic exams, diagnosing and treating sexually transmitted diseases, prescribing, dispensing and referring children for birth control, treatment for substance abuse, weight control, even acne. You name it; the new clinics would have provided it.

In effect, the bill would allow children whose parents drop them off at school for academic instruction, to participate in unlimited medical and/or mental health services during classroom hours without mom or dad ever finding out.

I started thinking about the highly touted school based health clinics established by the Jackson Public Schools and now being expanded to other areas of the state. How much do we really know about these clinics?

Do we know:

What sort of medical services are provided in the school-based clinics?

Is parental permission received for each individual treatment and not just one blanket permission form signed at the beginning of the school year? (An example would be a parent signing a form for a physical for PE that would allow all treatment by the clinic to be automatically approved.)

Are teachers allowed to refer students for treatment?

Do the clinics prescribe drugs? If so, what drugs?

Are students counseled about or allowed to leave campus for "reproductive" services, including abortions?

Where does funding for the clinics come from? Are they privately funded, or does the taxpayer foot the bill? Are the parents' insurance companies billed for any of the services?

Can each health-care clinic establish its own parental consent policy, or is this determined by state law? If determined by law, what does the law say?

Can children sign themselves up for "confidential" medical services?

Are parents allowed access to the medical records kept by school-based health clinics?

In California, schools now allow children 12 years and up to sign up for mental health counseling and apply for Medi-Cal to pay for the services.

Once students are signed up, parents no longer have the right to review their children's medical records. In other words, no one will tell them anything about what the student is being treated for, his progress or lack thereof.

No wonder parents in California are outraged.

When the school based health clinics were established by the Jackson Public Schools, I don't recall that any questions were raised.

Maybe it's time we started asking some.

(After this article was published, I was invited to Johnson Elementary in Jackson to see their school health clinic. I must admit that I was impressed with how well the school and clinic were run. Some of my questions were answered and concerns addressed. However, this was a well-run program. What about schools that lack the management and over-sight of Johnson? I still contend that it is the parents responsibility for the health care of their children ... and not the schools.)

The Clarion-Ledger

Tuesday, November 2, 1999

Candidates Can Learn from Public Academy Success

Which of the two candidates for governor can make a difference in education?

Ronnie Musgrove is the fair-haired child of the MAE and the heir of the William Winter/ Ray Mabus era of education reform.

Musgrove points with pride to increased teacher pay, more computers in classrooms, air conditioning of public school buildings, and equalization of funding between the state's richer and poorer schools.

But what has he done for academics and the acquisition of knowledge by Mississippi children in the classroom? If Musgrove takes credit for improved education during his eight years in the Senate and four years as Lt. Governor, why aren't his successes showing up in higher test scores?

Parker agenda confused

Mike Parker seems confused about his education agenda. In Congress, he voted for two terrible bills, GOALS 2000 and the 1997 Employment, Training and Literacy Act, both of which increased federal control of the classroom.

To his credit, Parker supported tax-free education savings accounts, charter schools, private school vouchers for low-income families, and home schooling. He also voted to abolish the U.S. Department of Education.

That record means he was right on some issues, wrong on others.

A myth has been perpetuated that children from low-income, disadvantaged backgrounds cannot learn as well as "rich kids" in private schools.

How long will we accept this excuse when the real reason for failure is the lack of a challenging curriculum and responsibility on the part of educators?

The television show "60 Minutes" recently spotlighted two successful public middle schools, KIPP Academies in Houston, Texas, and Bronx, New York.

Despite large class sizes (35 per classroom in one school) and shoestring budgets, Kipp students are aspiring to superior academic achievement. Let me repeat ... these are PUBLIC schools.

At the Houston KIPP, the 95 percent low-income student body scored in the 61st national percentile for reading and the 81st for math. At the Bronx KIPP, low-income students tested in the 69th percentile in reading and the 81st percentile in math.

Freedom, flexibility key

The key to the success of KIPP Academies is freedom and flexibility. Principals who refuse to tolerate failure are given the freedom to decide how to spend their money, whom to hire and what to teach.

KIPP creates an atmosphere of success, holding teachers accountable for student achievement.

Teacher quality supersedes seniority. Principals are given the freedom to recruit the best instructors they can find and give them the freedom to adapt their individual styles to the needs of their students. In return, the principals demand results ... and get them.

The articulate, enthusiastic, happy students and teachers interviewed at KIPP left little doubt that these schools are working. Many of these "poverty" children have a bright and promising future because of the many scholarships earned for academic achievement.

I doubt that Musgrove could ever support a program like KIPP because he's tightly tied to the educationists who are unwilling to relinquish control of Mississippi public education.

Parker could prove himself if he works to loosen bureaucratic control for initiatives such as KIPP, uses a lot of common sense rather than dictates from the education establishment, and rewards educators who focus on results and not dollars.

One can only hope that voters will make the better choice.

The Clarion-Ledger
Tuesday, March 7, 2000

Early Childhood Programs Just A Big Boondoggle

The push is on for another education initiative that will cost the taxpayers millions and probably do nothing to provide a better education for Mississippi children.

It's called "early childhood development" or "prekindergarten" aimed at 3-and 4 year olds.

After considerable debate last week, the Mississippi Senate approved SB 2302, which provide voluntary prekindergarten for 4-year olds.

Seems to be a wonderful idea to get more tax dollars in the name of education, set up additional government bureaucracy, and provide free babysitting.

A necessity?

The idea is being promoted nationally by the crowd who thinks "universal preschool is no longer a luxury, but a necessity for our children and our society."

They're the ones who believe that government and government schools know better how to run our lives and raise our children than we do.

Consider the Head Start program, which was founded as a federally subsidized, early intervention, preschool program.

Since its inception in 1965, approximately 15 million children have participated in the national Head Start program, which has cost the U.S. taxpayer $35 billion.

We've had more than enough time and spent enough money to determine if such programs work.

So how successful have early intervention programs been?

No lasting benefits

A CATO Institute policy analysis by Darcy Olsen reviewed 35 years of preschool programs and found that there is no evidence that early childhood programs provide any lasting benefits.

In fact, any initial gains that lower income children make in Head Start disappear entirely within a few years after they exit the program.

Both the General Accounting Office (GAO) and the Department of Health and Human Services have found that the Head Start program "had no lasting impact on the cognitive or socioemotional test scores of enrollees."

And Edward Zigler, director of Child Development and Social Policy at Yale University and a cofounder of Head Start, states: "There is also evidence that middle class children gain little, if anything, from preschool. Those who argue in favor of universal preschool education ignore evidence that indicates early schooling is inappropriate for many 4-year-olds and that it may even be harmful to their development."

I grieve for today's child

The author of *The Hurried Child,* Dr. David Elkind, of Tufts University, finds: "There is really no evidence that early formal institutionalization brings any lasting benefits for young children. By contrast, the risk to the child's motivation, intellectual growth and self-esteem could well do serious damage to the child's emerging personality."

What an injustice to children, to put them "on track" at such an early age.

By the time they reach first grade, many will be bored with the prospect of learning.

Some will be inattentive, hyperactive, classified as learning-disabled and perfect candidates for Ritalin.

I grieve for today's child who is robbed of the carefree days of childhood; deprived of learning from an at-home, caring mother and attentive father, and rushed into the nanny state of Big Brother.

Mississippi legislators who desire to "do something" for young children should be tempered by the facts and think long and hard before throwing more money into the "education" abyss.

The Clarion-Ledger
Letter to the Editor
Friday, October 13, 2000

Leave Students Out of Flag Debate

My hat's off to School Superintendent Jerry Baird for having the wisdom and exhibiting the leadership to keep the state flag issue out of the DeSoto County public schools. ("Official: Flag flap too hot for kids," Sept.3)

With all due respect to the 17-member Advisory Commission on the Mississippi State Flag and State Superintendent of Education Richard Thompson, I believe that the proposal to involve students in this controversial and very political issue is a bad idea.

William Winter, commission chairman, has stated that he opposes allowing the people of the state to vote on the flag issue because it's "divisive."

According to my dictionary, *divisive* is defined as "creating dissension or discord." Why would we want that in our schools?

One would have to be blind to fail to see how children are used and exploited by educators (and politicians) to promote a given agenda.

With public education promulgating political correctness and the rewriting of history, does anyone doubt that divisiveness will flourish in classrooms across the state as essays and poems are written and the state flag redesigned?

Just what we need for Mississippi's future!

The Clarion-Ledger
Tuesday, June 5, 2001

"No Child Left Behind" Ed Bill Major Disgrace

The No Child Left Behind Act (H.R. 1), passed the U.S. House by a vote of 384 to 45 on May 23, was to reverse thirty years of failed federal education policies.

The bill was crafted to reflect the campaign promises of George W. Bush to promote academic excellence, consolidation, flexibility, accountability and choice, thus providing opportunities for children left behind by the current system

Instead of freeing schools from the failures of heavy handed government and ironclad mandates, H.R.1 lays out a growing federal presence in education.

The bill authorizes $22.9 billion in spending for next year alone, $3.5 billion more than Mr. Bush requested.

Funding staggering

The amount of money being allocated to the U.S. Department of Education is staggering. It will increase the department's spending by 22 percent or $9.2 billion.

This in spite of an investigation that has been launched to determine what has happened to $450 million in "misplaced" funds received by the Department of Education over the last three years.

NBC News recently reported that the department had misappropriated funds to purchase expensive sports cars and equipment, misused credit cards – spending $200 million in unauthorized purchases and double-paying a $250 million dollar grant.

Some call it Potomac Fever, that strange malady that infects members of Congress who become overwhelmed by the power of their office and giddy with the prospect of spending someone else's money. But for any member of Congress to vote increased federal dollars to a governmental agency that can't account for $450 million, makes me think that our representatives need to be provided with sick leave and brought home for a strong dose of common sense.

And forget consolidation. The original 900-plus page education bill contained 38 federal education programs that grew like Topsy to 50 before passage. Authorization to fund programs with "such sums as may be necessary" will add additional dollars during appropriations. It's estimated that the consolidated 50 programs under H.R. 1, if fully funded, will cost taxpayers more than $22 billion.

Local control fading fast

And instead of flexibility, the regulatory language that will emanate from each government bureaucracy identified in the bill will add enough "shalls," "wills," and "musts" to eliminate any possibility of returning schools to local control.

In spite of the glowing report from Education and the Workplace Chairman, John Boehner, and the willingness of the White House to "go along to get along," H.R. 1 offers no substantive education reform.

But the fat lady has yet to sing. As H.R. 1 moves to the House-Senate conference committee, there is still hope that the Potomac Fever will break and sound thinking will prevail. If the federalization of education is not curtailed, one wonders how long public education can survive before the death knell is sounded.

As someone on Capitol Hill said recently, "In Congress nowadays you have a choice between the evil party and the stupid party. And when a proposal moves forward that is BOTH evil and stupid, we call it bipartisanship."

In the interest of bipartisanship, the Republicans have caved, the federal education bureaucracy flourishes, the taxpayers get fleeced, and children will continue to be left behind.

The Clarion-Ledger
Saturday, June 30, 2001

Mississippians Benefit from SREB Program

Advocating doctoral degrees among minorities goal

The Southern Regional Education Board (SREB) was founded in 1948 at the request of Southern leaders in business, education, and government. It is an alliance of fifteen states that work together to improve every aspect of education – from early childhood education to doctoral degrees and beyond.

It was my pleasure to stand with other Mississippi delegates led by Governor Ronnie Musgrove to recognize the accomplishments of two Mississippians who received special recognition at the annual meeting in Atlanta recently.

This year marks a milestone for the SREB Doctoral Scholars Program created in 1993 to address the long-standing national shortage of minority faculty. The program was created to increase the number of minority scholars who earn Ph.D.s and assist those who seek to become faculty members at colleges and universities.

This highly successful SREB program claims key accomplishments, which include the following:

- 100 program graduates and more than 200 scholars progressing toward their doctoral degrees;
- A 90 percent retention and graduation rate – more than double the national rate for minority Ph.D. scholars;

- A 70 percent placement rate of program graduates on campuses as faculty, administrators or postdoctoral researchers – more than one-third greater than the national placement rate for minorities; and
- The Presidential Award for Excellence in Math, Science, and Engineering Mentoring.

Mississippi is proud to have six SREB Doctoral Scholars: Dr. Patricia Logan, Dr. Jennifer Riley and Dr. Jeanetta Tankson, Mississippi State University (MSU); Dr. Samuel Shingles, University of Mississippi; Dr. Valerie Simpson, University of Southern Mississippi and Dr. Voletta Williams, Jackson State University.

Recognized at the SREB annual meeting was Dr. Jeanetta Tankson, from Rolling Fork, who was the first African-American female to receive a Ph.D. in animal physiology from MSU, Poultry Science Department.

She was also a recipient of the 2001 Mississippi Agricultural and Forestry Experiment Station Graduate Student Research Award of the Year.

Receiving special recognition as the 100th graduate of the SREB program, Dr. Riley, from Tylertown, received her degree in Industrial Engineering-Ergonomics and Human Factors from MSU.

Dr. Riley summed up the feelings of those who have received Ph.D.s through the scholars program when she said, "The SREB Doctoral Scholars Program, for many talented and motivated persons interested in faculty positions, eliminates the major obstacle of a lack of financial means to reach goals that might otherwise be unattainable."

The SREB program lives up to its promise of being "more than a check and a handshake."

It has provided deserving students with a support network that reduces feelings of isolation; makes doctoral degrees more affordable and attainable by strengthening scholar skills and credibility; expands diversity of college faculty by attracting and retaining promising minority scholars; and helps students develop scholarly habits to meet the challenges of graduate study and college teaching.

Congratulations are in order for Mississippi's SREB Doctoral Scholars and for the progress and promise of the SREB State Doctoral Scholars Program.

The Clarion-Ledger
Tuesday, August 14, 2001

Both Teachers, Students Need Some Basics

At a recent meeting of the Southern Regional Education Board, I was privileged to hear Dr. Marilyn Whirry, National Teacher of the Year 2000.

Dr. Whirry is of the old school – from an era of education professionals who believed in challenging curriculum, academic excellence, and discipline.

While her credentials are impressive (she holds a master's degree, studied at Harvard, raised two children, and earned her doctorate in contemporary literature), I was most impressed by the fact that she has taught English at Mira Costa High School in Torrance, California for 33 years.

Remember the basics

Dr. Whirry is a teacher *par excellence,* and fortunate the students who sit under her tutelage.

She minced no words in evaluating the nation's education system based on her yearlong travels to schools across the United States. Here, in condensed form, is what she said:

Teachers – need to be re-educated. Too many think it's OK to be bad.

Schools of Education – need to cut out the "fluff" and concentrate on a solid (5 year) course study in English, math, science, and history. An essential to retraining is professional development.

Reading – A child should be reading by the end of the first grade. No child should be passed to a higher grade until he can read.

Technology – Schools don't need more technology in the classroom until teachers know how to incorporate technology into learning.

Are you listening, Governor?

Curriculum – Math is essential in a student's senior year. Physics needs to be taught early to coincide with algebra. Biology should come later, preferably in the last two years of high school.

Students – should know college requirements before entering high school. Often students planning to attend college graduate from high school only to find that they lack the courses necessary for college level work.

She observed that high schools want to teach college level courses while colleges are having to offer remedial courses to make up for the poor preparation of students for college work.

While I lack the credentials of Dr. Whirry, I know what it takes to be a good teacher and would offer a few suggestions from the school of common sense.

If you think you'll make lots of money teaching school, you've chosen the wrong profession. The true wealth in teaching comes from the joy of knowing you've planted knowledge and the satisfaction of realizing that it's taken root.

Keep priorities straight

Take seriously the fact that to some children you are the most important person in the world.

Set and expect high standards, and you'll reap big dividends.

The best teachers are always remembered, but so are the worst. Be the best!

In her novel, *Anne of Green Gables*, author Lucy Maud Montgomery aptly describes the one-room schoolteacher of Avonlea in these words: "In the teacher, Anne found another true and helpful friend. Miss Stacy was a bright, sympathetic young woman with the happy gift of winning and holding the affections of her pupils and bringing out the best that was in them mentally and morally."

As classrooms open for another year, may each pupil find a teacher waiting at the door who is a true friend, a strong disciplinarian, and a skilled, dedicated professional.

The Clarion-Ledger
Thursday, May 30, 2002

Jackson Prep Grads Living Up to Potential

The high school seniors of 2002 have graduated. Final grade point averages have been calculated, diplomas handed out and scholarships awarded.

The Class of 2002 produced many outstanding students who distinguished themselves with exemplary academic records.

I had the opportunity to meet two such students recently: Brent Livesay and Robert Stranghoener, of the senior class at Jackson Preparatory School. Between them, these two young men have earned more than $150,000 in scholarships to further their education over the next four years.

That's no small piece of change.

Parents, teachers matter

No doubt, both students possess high intellect ... a little gray matter never hurts in doing well in school. But as Brent told me, he took advantage of educational opportunities to stretch his mind. He applied himself; he listened in class; and the result was that he scored 36 on the ACT, the highest score possible.

Credit should be given to Jackson Preparatory School for its high academic standards and accelerated courses of study that prepare students for university level work. The staff and faculty strive to produce well-rounded individuals with a solid educational base for whatever future endeavor the student may choose.

In the past ten years, five Jackson Prep students have walked away with the STAR student of the year award that recognizes top students in the state. Jackson Prep has produced more National Merit finalists than any other school in Mississippi. This year, $2,160,630 in merit based scholarships was accepted by Prep seniors with 87 of the 140 graduates each earning an average of $24,835 in scholarships.

This is not to say that some other schools, public as well as private, aren't academically challenging. This year's second place STAR student, David Newman, attended Murrah High School.

Unquestionably, teachers and parents play a major role in the educational development of a good student.

Parents should be the primary motivators and facilitators of an environment that is conducive to producing academic excellence.

Individual desire crucial

Many parents make sacrifices to provide the best possible education for their children. Just the tuition at a school like Jackson Prep ($6,500.00 per year and rising) can put a strain on most family budgets.

And what is the teacher's responsibility?

Here's how Star Student Brent Livesay's described Barbara Travers, the STAR Teacher that he selected as having contributed the most to his academic achievement: "From the very first day you could tell from her presence that it would be no nonsense when it came to work."

He describes her as spontaneous with intensity in her teaching style that expects a response. "She knows when to cut back to hold the classes' attention, and class time passes rapidly. Everything that comes from her mouth is wisdom."

But even with dedicated parents, the best schools and the most gifted teachers, the successful student must choose to work to his full potential. It's a choice that not all students are willing to make.

Both Robert and Brent chose to take the hardest courses rather than the easiest. They sought challenging curriculum and demanding teachers to help discover their capabilities and to be pushed to their fullest potential.

But it was their choice and self-motivation that allowed them to succeed.

May their tribe increase!

The Clarion-Ledger

Thursday, August 8, 2002

"Patriotism" Now Required Subject in State Schools

An outstanding education bill, passed and signed into law by the governor, went into effect July 1, just in time for the start of a new school year.

As legislation goes, Senate Bill 2321 will probably be considered by some as about as insignificant as the bill designating the Teddy bear the state toy. It requires all public schools to teach patriotism.

Patriotism, you say? Ah, yes. Those old fashioned ideas about the duties and obligations of citizenship … Americanism.

What the bill requires

The bill requires the following:

That the flag of the United States be displayed in close proximity to the school building, on a proper staff, and in each public school classroom at all times when school is in session;

That the Pledge of Allegiance to the United States Flag be recited at the beginning of the first hour of class each day (excusing anyone who objects from participating without penalty);

That school districts provide student instruction in respect for, and proper display of, the flag.

You may be saying to yourself, "I thought that was already part of a student's education. It was done when I was in school."

Yes, good schools still make patriotic education part of every school day; but some schools have allowed global education, multicultural education, and environmental education to replace the teaching of patriotism.

SB 2321 has made patriotism a required subject. And in light of the recent ruling of the 9th U.S. Circuit Court of Appeals in regards to the Pledge of Allegiance, very timely legislation indeed.

The Daughters of the American Revolution (DAR), a national women's service organization, promotes patriotic education. In Mississippi, there are approximately 4,500 women in 79 chapters across the state who would welcome the opportunity to assist local school districts in this endeavor. The DAR publishes an excellent pamphlet on the U.S. Flag Code; can provide instruction on flag etiquette, including flag retirement ceremonies; and is a good resource for classroom flags and patriotic materials.

Flag etiquette creativity

Educators have an opportunity to be creative in teaching flag etiquette. Why not let students be responsible for raising and lowering the flag from the flagpole each day? Allow individual classes to select students to serve as a color guard and rotate the honor. High schools may have Junior ROTC units capable of handling this responsibility.

The bill makes it the duty of the school boards of each school district "to provide for the flags, proper flagstaffs and their proper display."

School boards need to be aware that the size of the pole determines the size of the flag. The length of the flag should be at least one-fourth the height of the pole. For example, a 40 foot pole requires a 6x10 foot flag or larger. Don't put a postage stamp sized flag on a large pole.

Also, caution is advised in accepting architectural plans for mammoth poles at new schools. A large pole requires a large flag; and while attractive, large flags are hard to handle and expensive to replace.

A big thumbs up to the following senators who sponsored SB 2321: Little, Burton, Robertson, Jackson, Minor, Stogner, Smith, Carmichael, Chaney, Dearing, Dickerson, Gordon, Hewes, Johnson (19th), King, Kirby, Moffatt, Posey, Ross, Thames, White (29th), Hyde-Smith, Jordan, Gollott, Furniss, Chamberlin, Hamilton, White (5th), Harvey, Canon, Harden, Ferris.

If one of them represents you, express your appreciation.

The Clarion-Ledger
Letter to the Editor
Friday, March 14, 2003

Stringfellow's Support of Ed Exec Pay Hikes Is "Off Base"

Just when I thought Metro columnist Eric Stringfellow had come to his senses, he proves me wrong. His column ("Education not cheap, so don't cut execs' pay," March 9) was so off base it demands a response.

I've followed education for many years; as a parent, as an observer and critic of JPS and its administration, as an unpaid, citizen-lobbyist, as a 3-month Fordice appointee to the State Board of Education, and as a member of the Southern Regional Education Board (SREB). So I know wherewith I speak.

And one thing I know for certain is that education is top-heavy with bureaucrats.

Since the establishment of the U.S. Department of Education and the Mississippi State Department of Education has education improved? No. Has spending gone up? You better believe it!

Mr. Stringfellow states: "The Legislature has no business micromanaging education." Who's he kidding?

A state agency with a huge budget, filled with bureaucrats who love to spend and a full-time lobbyist to keep the coffers full, requires a lot of oversight and accountability.

By the way, that **department of education* lobbyist has just received a $23,000 pay hike ... more than many classroom teachers earn per year.

With 62 cents of every tax dollar going to education, state department budgets being cut to fund education, and the state budget strained to the breaking point, it's a moral outrage to grant salary increases of $40, 000, $90,000, and $100,000 to educationists.

And please, Mr. Stringfellow, don't say that "governing boards" should set salary caps. Most education boards rubber stamp proposals coming from the education elitists who think nothing of padding their own pockets.

*Omitted when published.

The Clarion-Ledger
Thursday, August 7, 2003

Education Dip Did Not Begin Just Yesterday

How many times have we heard that Mississippi has received a failing grade in public education?

State Superintendent Henry Johnson is preparing us for more bad news when nationwide test scores are released in September. The projection is that fewer than 100 of Mississippi's 880 public schools will meet federal student progress requirements.

When schools fail, we try to find somewhere to place the blame. We blame the tests, the teachers, the administrators, the parents, and even the students when in reality the demise of public education has been a long time in the making.

Long time in the making

Education "reform" became a national objective in 1983 when the Reagan administration's National Commission on Excellence in Education reported that the country's education system was "being eroded by a rising tide of mediocrity that threatens our very future as a nation and a people."

We've suffered through one reform program after another: BEST, PRIME, GOALS 2000, No Child Left Behind, and have experimented with new math, whole language, Outcomes Based Education (OBE), Multiculturalism, Global Ed, School to Work and CAREERS. Sadly, twenty-years and billions of dollars later, there has been little or no advancement in student academic achievement.

Public education in the United States began its downward spiral just after World War I when Progressive Education theorists James Cattell, John Dewey, and Edward Thorndike, influenced by the new behavioral psychology of Wilhelm Wundt, of the University of Leipzig, developed new theories that would virtually destroy our educational system.

The new learning techniques were designed to de-emphasize attainment of literacy and to teach "social skills" to assure that students would "fit" into society.

The metamorphosis was gradual. It took years to train an army of new teachers and superintendents and for the teachers and superintendents of the "old school" to retire or die off. But by the 1970s, it became apparent that the United States was facing an education crisis.

Money perpetuates failure

The education theorists who today call themselves "social constructionists" continue to permeate every aspect of public education. They control university schools of education where future teachers are indoctrinated to the progressive-humanist-behaviorists philosophy. They write the textbooks, curricula, and professional journals, and exert a powerful influence in the political arena.

Until that changes, there is little possibility that public education can achieve any degree of academic excellence.

And no amount of money will change a failed education system. **More money only empowers the educationists, textbook publishers, curricula developers, and the many contractors who feed off the education system.* More money means perpetuating continued failure and declining literacy.

On June 19, the annual National Assessment of Education Progress (NAEP) released nationwide test scores in reading. Out of a possible score of 500, Mississippi fourth-graders scored 203 (14 points below the national score of 217) while eighth-graders scored 255 (8 points below the national score of 263.)

The next day, a *Clarion-Ledger* headline heralded Mississippi's improvement in reading scores. Improvement? When Mississippi students are below the national average and 36 percent of U.S. fourth-graders can't read at what the test defined as a "basic" level?

Whom are we kidding?

**It reminds me of some of the self-esteem programs promoted in public education. Our children can't read, but we sure feel good about it.*

*Omitted when published.

The Clarion-Ledger
Thursday, January 15, 2004

Teachers Must Train Children to Use Phonics

Tat-a-Tat-Tat, Tat-a-Tat-Tat – I'm still beating the drum for phonics!

But guess what? More and more folks are joining the band, and I hope others will pick up the beat.

Claiborne Barksdale, director of the Barksdale Reading Institute, has suggested to the State Board of Education that schools of education train prospective teachers in how to teach children to use phonics to read.

The board will be meeting today to consider requiring schools of education to beef-up reading instruction courses. The proposal, supported by the University of Mississippi Education Deans' Council, would increase the number of required hours in reading instruction to five courses, or 15 college hours. Barksdale has asked that 3 of those hours be in phonics training.

Evidence overwhelming

In my opinion, the decision to approve his proposal should be a no-brainer. The overwhelming evidence from research and classroom results indicates that the cure for the disease of illiteracy is the restoration of the instructional practice of intensive, systematic phonics.

Phonemic awareness not only gives a child the key to unlock the English language but it also greatly improves verbal communication.

Have you ever noticed how many children speak as if they have a mouth full of mush? The practice of "sounding out" words when learning to read phonetically not only strengthens reading skills but also helps with enunciation – the ability to pronounce with distinctness and articulation.

Educators in general are slow to admit failure. But with Mississippi's reading test scores in

50th place nationally, it should be obvious that educators have been doing something wrong.

The something wrong is failing to stress phonics and relying too much on whole language. The whole language or "look and say" method teaches reading by memorizing or guessing at words in context by using initial letter or picture clues.

Recognize the problem

Former Gov. Ray Mabus' BEST education reform act gave us the whole language computer program, "*Writing To Read,*" at a cost of $7 million in tax dollars and brought Mississippi classrooms "creative writing through inventive spelling."

Any common-sense thinker who looks at a first grade "*Writing To Read*" workbook would instinctively recognize education malpractice.

For example, an exercise would show a picture of an eagle, and the student is instructed to write and say "egl". Is it any wonder that when the picture prompt is removed and the student sees the word "eagle," he doesn't have a clue? Multiply that one word by hundreds of other words and you'll understand why children can't read.

Teachers have told me that the correct spelling of a word can be taught at a "later" time. Later? Does that mean in a remediation class?

The sad reality is that once a failed program is adopted, it just won't go away.

That's why, in my opinion, it's imperative for the Board of Education to accept the recommendation of those who have done the research, recognized the problem, and taken a step in the right direction.

Mississippi schools of education should be required to provide future teachers with more semester hours of reading instruction, solidly grounded in phonics.

The Clarion-Ledger

Thursday, April 1, 2004

School Funding: Just How Much Will Be Enough?

The sky is falling! The sky is falling!

Just as the sky didn't fall on Chicken Little, the school-house doors won't close if the Mississippi Legislature fails to "fully fund" education.

Every year the education lobbyists descend on the state capitol with demands for increased funding for public education; but no matter how much money legislators earmark for education, it will never be enough. And with the state scraping the bottom of the budget barrel, you can bet there's a tax increase on the horizon.

Billions being spent now

Of course, public education should be adequately funded. But at no time in history has so much money been spent on education.

Billions of dollars come from federal, state, local and private funding sources with little, if any, results in academic improvement.

Unfortunately, much of the money never makes it to the classrooms but goes to education bureaucrats, top-heavy school administrations, and education profiteers who make a killin'on contracts for school construction, textbooks, portable classrooms, testing, curriculum development – you name it.

The land acquisition-dirt deal for the new $23 million Brandon High School now under investigation by a public-corruption task force and the Federal Bureau of Investigation, is a good example.

Speaking of tax increases, the Madison County School District is presently testing the waters to see if Madison County residents will support a school bond issue.

I love the way this bond proposal is being pitched: "It's less than $5 a month, or 15 cents a day." Whom are they kidding?

While the exact amount of the proposed tax increase has yet to be determined, projections are being based on a $100,000 house and $15,000 car, which school officials say is a $58 a year tax increase.

Statistical data sets the cost of an average home in Madison at $189,700, and there are more than a few homes in the $500,000 and up price range. Many cars on Madison County roads cost a lot more than $15,000, and what family this day and time can manage with just one car?

Public forums packed

Public forums are being held to get input and gage support for the bond issue. I attended the first one at the new Ridgeland High School. The room was packed with parents and school personnel who support the bond proposal because they want a football stadium, performing arts complex, and field house for female sports.

In that partisan crowd, anyone speaking in opposition to the bond proposal would have had to be a brave soul indeed.

The press has lambasted Flora mayor, Jw Richardson, for speaking against the bond issue at the second forum. He spoke the truth when he said, "Somewhere along the line we've got to look for income other than taxpayers to finance this growth. We can't stand to pay that much more in taxes."

An editorial in this newspaper said his position was "unfortunate and, sadly, shortsighted." ("School bond: Flora would benefit from it, too," March 24). And a Madison paper's lead editorial asked the question, "Will Richardson's legacy be the Flora mayor who opposed a 2004 school bond issue that began Madison County's downward spiral in growth?"

That's a laugh!

If anything, Mayor Richardson will attract folks to the community of Flora. I'll be first in line.

The Clarion-Ledger
Saturday, May 14, 2005

Barbour Right to Deny Excess Ed Spending

Governor has sought fair 4 percent increase in spending for schools

I applaud Governor Haley Barber's call for an open and honest dialogue on funding education. Too bad his appeal will fall on so many deaf ears.

The idea that Mississippi must "fully fund" education at a time when this state is facing a budget crisis is ludicrous.

Education spending in Mississippi is at an all-time high, as 62.44 percent of the 2005 budget will go to fund education. There has been nearly a 50 percent increase in education spending in the last five years, and Mississippi ranks 3rd in the nation in funding increases.

What the governor proposes in his education plan is a 4 percent increase in spending; yet he and others who oppose a tax increase so that education can get a bigger cut of the pie are now accused of being against public education. That's untrue and unfair!

Instead of continually demanding more money, educationists need to look at ways to cut excessive education spending.

One huge savings could be achieved with district consolidation. Mississippi has 149 school districts – far more than necessary. More school districts mean more administrative costs and employees.

According to a study done by the Mississippi Center for Public Policy, there are 62 percent more assistant principals and "supervisors" overseeing 12,000 fewer students than ten years ago with every category of K-12 spending except one growing at least 31 percent ahead of inflation during the same time period.

Even with schools operating with fewer state dollars than they say they need, the legislature gave huge salary increases to school superintendents last year. The average raise was $3,900, but 18 superintendents received an annual increase of $10,000 or more with two superintendents receiving salary increases of over $20,000.

When was the last time the average Mississippian got that kind of raise?

A bundle could be saved on travel expenses. Administrators, principals, school board members frequently attend education meetings like the one to be held in June at the Beau Rivage Casino. **When money is tight, you don't take vacations.*

And printing expenses could be cut. I mean expensive, slick paper, full-color materials produced by the state department of education and local districts. Most of it is unnecessary and the money could be better spent in the classroom.

Legislators don't have the backbone when it comes to trimming fat from the education budget. The education establishment, led by the State Department of Education, the superintendents and school board associations, teachers unions and others who feed at the education trough, represents a huge and powerful lobby.

A new low was reached this year when school children were used in letter-writing campaigns and booed the governor from the steps of the state Capitol.

The scare tactics need to cease. The schoolhouse doors will be open next year, and teachers will still have jobs – without increasing the education budget.

In addition to education, there are other budgetary obligations that must be met, such as maintaining our highways, prison system, hospitals, and debt retirement. Belt-tightening is in order and education is no sacred cow.

*Omitted when published.

Submitted to *The Clarion-Ledger*
Letter to the Editor
Unpublished

School Attorneys Stand to Lose Education Dollars

As reported in *The Clarion-Ledger* article "School attorneys take aim at PRIME", the Mississippi Council of School Board Attorneys is opposed to Governor Fordice's PRIME education plan.

Should anyone be surprised?

Many in this group have raked in staggering amounts of legal and lobbying fees over the past decade from the ballooning budgets and bloated bureaucracies of local school districts, especially in the larger districts.

Because passage of the PRIME initiative would likely trim down the legal grab bag of public funds that have been used to stuff the coffers of several large law firms, it is not surprising that school attorneys are opposed to any change in the present system.

The scare tactics being employed by those who stand the most to lose from PRIME make me believe it's the best thing going to significantly impact the education system of Mississippi.

It is, after all, up to the people of Mississippi and not the employed school attorneys with personal interests at stake to evaluate and determine the merits of the Governor's plan.

Unpublished and undated
Spring 2005
Summing up all that's wrong with education ....

Fully Funding Education – Will It Produce Results?

How much money will it take to "fully fund education"? It will take all the gold in Fort Knox, and then some.

When John Stossel aired an ABC documentary in January of 2005 suggesting that public education has plenty of money but is squandering it, the network was bombarded with hate mail from the ones who benefit the most from those education dollars... primarily, the National Education Association (NEA).

According to Stossel, if you divide the U.S. Department of Education's figures for total spending on K-12 education by the department's count of K-12 students, it works out to about $10,000 per student or $250,000 per classroom of 25 kids.

Since the passage of the 1965 Elementary and Secondary Education Act, which concentrated unprecedented authority over American education by the federal government, education spending has ballooned from approximately $25 billion in 1965 (adjusted for inflation) to more than $108 billion in 2002 with the money being channeled through dozens of government agencies and hundreds of programs. And if President Bush's FY2007 budget proposal is approved, education funding for programs under No Child Left Behind will have increased 40 percent ($17.3 billion to $24.4. billion) since he took office.

When evaluated by using academic results, the strictures of the U.S. Constitution, and plain common sense, the federal government has no place in education. The U.S. Department should be abolished, and education should be returned to parents and local control with more dollars directed to the classroom.

While federal funding is growing like kudzu, there are tremendous increases in the amount put into the education pot by state, local, and private entities. Some estimates put education spending in the U.S. at $600 billion last year, and what has it accomplished?

National academic performance has not improved; math and reading scores have stagnated; graduation rates have declined; and researchers have shown numerous billion-dollar programs to be failures.

Since 1980, when I first became interested in education reform, one factor became apparent: it's not how much money is spent, but *how* the money is spent.

The oft-sited example of how NOT to improve academic performance is the Kansas City, Missouri "experiment." According to the Stossel report, in 1985, Judge Russell Clark ordered the government to spend additional billions on the city's predominately black schools. The bureaucrats renovated school buildings and added enormous gyms, an Olympic swimming pool, a robotics lab,

TV studios, a zoo, a planetarium, and a wildlife sanctuary. They added intense instruction in foreign languages and were so lavish in spending that instead of busing they paid for 120 taxis to transport more white kids to the city's schools.

The result? The schools got worse. In 2000, five years and $2 billion later, the Kansas City school district failed 11 performance standards and lost its academic accreditation for the first time in the district's history.

If increases in per pupil expenditures result in better test scores, why is it that Washington, D.C., that spends $8,393 per student scored dead last on every standardized national test, while students in the state of Utah, which spends $3,969 per student, scored close to the top every time? On the ACT, Washington, D.C. students scored 17.8, while students in Utah scored 21.5. But topping them both were U.S. home schooled students who scored 22.8 on the ACT ... and cost the taxpayer nothing.

The least expensive schools in the U.S. are the Catholic schools. A study by two professors at the Hoover Institution compared public and Catholic schools in three of New York City's five boroughs. Parochial education outperformed the nation's largest school system "in every instance," and it did it at less than half the cost per pupil.

The U.S. spends more on schooling than the vast majority of countries that outscore us on international tests. Japan spends half the amount we do on public education, 2.6 percent of GDP versus our 5.2 percent. Japan's classrooms are two to three times larger than those in the U.S. with 60 students in a class; yet 8th graders in Japan scored 105 points higher than our 8th graders in math. Only 6 percent of U.S. citizens have taken calculus compared to 86 percent of the Japanese population.

Don't be conned into believing that school failure is the result of the lack of funds. The facts just aren't there.

So, why can't public schools do better? And where does the money go?

The American Association of School Administrators reports that the average U.S. school district now spends 81 percent of its budget on personnel, including teachers, support staff, and administrators.

In Mississippi, there are 62 percent more assistant principals and supervisors overseeing 12,000 fewer students than ten years ago. And the Mississippi Legislature gave nearly three-fourths of the state's 149 local school superintendents a hefty raise just last year.

Why do we need 149 school districts, anyway? It has been a recognized fact for years that school district consolidation could result in huge savings in education expenditures, but the subject has become a political hot-potato with legislators lacking the backbone to address the issue.

In a 2004 press release, the Mississippi State Department of Education sited a huge expenditure in the department's budget ... busing. Schools transport 95 percent of the students in

Mississippi with buses traveling 53 million miles per year. Those buses are usually only half full ... the ones passing my house usually have 8 or 10 students on board ... yet no one seems to be making an effort to see what can be done to reduce the cost of busing. With gas prices rapidly approaching $3.00 per gallon, or higher, the cost to Mississippi taxpayers will be astronomical this school year.

School boards share some of the blame for inflating school budgets by rubber stamping most of the unnecessary and non-essential spending requests from school superintendents and department personnel. Also, feeding at the education trough are text book publishers, curriculum developers, and testing groups.

The education establishment wields a big stick and maintains full-time lobbyists at the state capitol to watchdog any attempt to slow the gravy train. While they're in session, your state legislators hear daily from the associations of school boards, school administrators, and teachers, as well as lobbyists from the state department of education.

Jeanne Allen, of the Center for Education Reform, describes the education industrial complex as more than 200 groups, associations, federations, alliances, departments, offices, administrations, councils, boards, commissions, panels, organizations, herds, flocks, and coveys with their own agendas, bureaucracies and power over education. "As a whole they are maddening in their resistance to change. They always talk about change, but rather more like quicksand, or a tar pit, the ideas slowly sink out of sight, leaving everything just as it had been."

While many educators seem well-intentioned, they seem incapable of grasping the fact that no matter how much money is poured into the education sinkhole, unless serious changes take place and drastic overhauls are made in the classroom, nothing's going to change.

And change seems to be what educationists resist most.

Classroom instruction today reflects the philosophy of the progressive education movement introduced by John Dewey in 1930. For the past seventy-five years, America's classrooms have been used by psychologists, sociologists, educationists, and politicians as a giant laboratory for unproven, untried theories of learning.

Thomas Sowell, a scholar in his own right who understands the failures in American education, wrote an insightful article on education dogma. He points to what he believes has been wrong for so long in our schools and sites a 2005 opinion poll among professors of education as an example of education malpractice.

In the poll, the question was posed, should teachers be "conveyors of knowledge who enlighten their students with what they know"? Or should teachers "see themselves as facilitators of learning who enable their students to learn on their own"?

Ninety-two percent of the professors of education said that teachers should be "facilitators" rather than engaging in what educators call "directed instruction"... or in simple terms, just plain good teaching.

On the question of the teaching of math, the professors of education were asked what is more important in math, that children "know the right answers to the question" or that they "struggle with the process" of trying to find the right answers? 86 percent chose "struggling" over "knowing."

The idea that children will "discover" their own knowledge rather than have teachers pass on to them the knowledge that took scholars and geniuses decades or even generations to produce is truly astounding.

And when it comes to discipline problems, fewer than half of the professors of education considered discipline "absolutely essential" to the educational process.

Thomas Sowell summed it up when he said: "By their fruits ye shall know them" may be an ancient adage, but results take a back seat to dogma when it comes to the education establishment. That is why there has been so little to show for all the additional billions of dollars poured into American education during the past three decades."

No wonder teachers struggle to measure up to acceptable academic classroom standards. If they're taught that the teacher should be "a guide on the side," and not "a sage on the stage" (the fashionable phrase among educators today), is it any wonder our education system is failing?

The Barksdale Reading Institute, an Oxford based think tank devoted to reading instruction, successfully persuaded (because of the money behind their initiatives) the State Board of Education to require schools of education to increase the number of required hours in reading instruction to five courses. Three of the fifteen hours had to be in phonics instruction.

In my opinion, this should be a no-brainer, with overwhelming evidence from research and classroom results indicating that the cure for the disease of illiteracy is the restoration of the teaching of phonological awareness and decoding (phonics). Yet our tax-funded public universities with schools of education were reluctant to allow even three hours of teacher training in phonics.

Obviously, what has been tried in education reform throughout the last thirty years has not worked. Why, then, do we continue to let the same people with the same education philosophy control our schools? It's a vexing problem, and one not easily solved.

There's no question that public schools are faced with challenges like no other time in history. How do you teach parentless children who come to school hungry, having never had a story read to them or been taught their ABCs? And how do you handle heavily medicated children who have been diagnosed with Attention Deficit Disorder (ADD) or kids who are discipline problems? I can imagine the frustration of teachers whose hands are tied in dealing with out-of-control brats for fear of being sued.

According to a recent article in the Wall Street Journal, the world of education reform may soon change. A group of families filed a class action lawsuit in Chancery Court in Newark, N.J.

asking for an immediate and meaningful remedy for 60,000 children trapped in failing schools – by transferring control over education funds from bureaucrats to parents.

The plaintiffs in **Crawford v. Davy* ask that children be allowed to leave public schools in which fewer than half of the students pass the state math and language literacy assessments that measure educational proficiency and that the parents of these children be permitted to take the *pro rata* share of the public money spent on their children to seek better opportunities in other public or private schools.

Thus far, court challenges of this sort have only produced massive increases in spending as judges see money as a means to fulfill state constitutional mandates for "equity" or "adequacy". The outcome of the New Jersey lawsuit bears watching.*

Can public education be saved?

If the stranglehold of the education bureaucracy can be broken, it may happen. But I doubt that it will.

The future of education rests with the development of a market-driven education system that gives parents control over how their children's share of education funding is used. The development of alternative schools, such as charter schools, is essential to future success by providing a choice in education resources.

Additionally, new schools of education must be established. Public funds should be diverted from state universities and colleges unwilling to change and reinvested in schools of education that will retrain veteran teachers and instruct prospective teachers in the "old school" tradition where discipline is applied, academic excellence promoted, and achievement rewarded.

Providing a good education, strong in basics and aimed toward academic excellence, is essential to the future of our nation. It is our responsibility to see that children have the opportunity to learn, whether in public, private, charter or home schools so that they will be able to fulfill their God-given potential.

*A decision on *Crawford v. Davy* is expected to be handed down from the Appellate Division soon. (August 2009)

CHAPTER XI

This and That
and a Few Gripes

Always keep your words soft and sweet,
just in case you have to eat them.

The Natchez Democrat
Lifestyle
Wednesday, October 3, 1990

DAR Celebrates 100 Years

Fire the cannons! Hoist the flag!

The DAR is 100 years old!

Not its members, mind you, even though there are some that age, but the National Society Daughters of the American Revolution (NSDAR).

You've heard of a woman scorned? Well, that's how it all started. Back in the summer of 1890, four women – mad as wet hens – banded together to form a patriotic society.

Discrimination was the reason. Women had been excluded from membership by the Sons of the American Revolution (SAR), and they were determined to prove "that anything you can do, we can do better".

And did they ever ... The SAR has never fully recovered from their faux pas ... being outnumbered today by ten DARs to every one SAR.

Forget your perception that DARs are little old ladies in tennis shoes .... As a Washington, D.C. cabbie, who ferries the ladies around the capitol city observed, "They sure do liven up the place, and do they have a good time." The DAR owns a whole city block of buildings near the White House – real estate valued at $41 million. The three-building complex houses the DAR Library, one of the finest genealogical libraries in the country; the DAR Museum containing more than 33 period rooms and 40,000 objects of early Americana; the administrative offices, where business is conducted; and a 3800-seat auditorium built to house the annual convention, Continental Congress, and which until the opening of the Kennedy Center, was the only public auditorium in D.C.

Any woman is eligible for membership in the DAR "if she is 18 years of age, directly descended from a man or woman who, with unfailing loyalty, aided the cause of American Independence."

A prospective member must be able to prove her lineage back to an ancestor who served the American cause during the American Revolution.

Believe me; this is not easy to do. Anyone who has dug for her "roots" will tell you that it's difficult to trace a line over two-hundred years. I would have never been able to join the DAR if a professional genealogist in the family had not done my digging.

Not everyone is eligible for membership in the DAR. Historical circumstance prevents many "Johnny Come Latelies" from joining the society because they descend from immigrants arriving in this country after the Revolutionary War. These descendants account for 40 percent of the population of the United States.

It's like some of those organizational memberships that I've always aspired to, but never quite attained.

... like being a Phi Beta Kappa. You have to have the credentials.

The first president general of the DAR was Caroline Scott Harrison, wife of President Benjamin Harrison. It's not surprising that with 730,000 women admitted to membership over the 100-year history of the DAR that nine have been First Ladies.

Other notable members include Clara Barton, founder and president of the American Red Cross; artist Grandma Moses; Susan B. Anthony, well known suffragette; and Dr. Anita Newcomb McGee, who directed the NSDAR effort to assist the United States Government during the Spanish-American War to alleviate the shortage of male nurses by examining and certifying applications of 4,000 nurses for the war effort. These nurses became the nucleus of the Army Nurse Corps.

The society's objectives are three fold ... historic preservation, promotion of education, and the fostering of true patriotism and love of country.

It would take volumes to relate all that the DAR has achieved in its first century, but suffice it to say that the members do more than just have tea parties and wave the flag.

Notable in the area of historical preservation, consider the following:

- In 1971-74, a national project furnished the Council Chambers and the Assembly Committee Room at Independence Hall in Philadelphia, Pennsylvania.
- In 1974-77, the society commissioned and funded the ceiling murals in the East-Wing corridor of the United States Capitol as a bicentennial gift to the Nation.

- Between 1928 and 1929, Madonna of the Trail monuments (each statue is eighteen feet high and depicts a pioneer mother and her two young children) were placed in each of twelve States across the country from Maryland to California along the National Old Trails Road.
- More than $516,000 was contributed to the Statue of Liberty restoration in observance of the 100th birthday of "Lady Liberty."
- $200,000 was donated to the restoration of Ellis Island where a "Wall of Honor" was erected listing the names of DAR ancestors who entered the United States as immigrants.
- Hundreds of historic buildings and sites have been purchased and maintained. Countless graves of Revolutionary War patriots have been located and marked.

In the area of education:

- The DAR supports two schools in the Appalachian region – Kate Duncan Smith DAR School in Alabama and Tamassee DAR School in South Carolina, both accredited by the Southern Association of Colleges and Schools.
- DAR contributes to four other schools, including clothing, gifts and scholarships. More than a million dollars is sent to the six schools.
- The American Indians Committee of NSDAR assists American Indians with approximately $100,000 in financial and scholarship aid.
- More than a third of DAR committees work with and for young people.
- The DAR sponsors Constitution Week and American History Month Essay contests in elementary and secondary schools.
- Junior American Citizen Clubs, a citizenship training program for boys and girls kindergarten through high school, promote dependability, service, leadership and patriotism.
- Good Citizenship and ROTC Medals are awarded in secondary schools, colleges, and universities.
- DAR scholarships in the amount of $8,000 are awarded annually in American History to a graduating high school senior. Other scholarships are given in the fields of nursing, occupational therapy, political science, government, and economics. A monetary award is presented annually to the Outstanding Teacher of American history.
- Books, periodicals, brochures, and pamphlets are published by the DAR. The *DAR MAGAZINE* has been published since 1892 and has 42,495 subscribers.

In patriotic endeavor:

- The first, and only resolution of the first NSDAR Continental Congress in 1892, was to honor and respect the Flag of the United States of America.
- Since the beginning of this century, the DAR has presented a Flag of the United States

to the Senate and House of Representatives for use at the rostrums of the President of the Senate and the Speaker of the House.

- In 1937, the Flags at the United States Naval Academy, Dahlgren Hall, were given by the DAR.
- The DAR promotes correct Flag usage by providing thousands of Flags and Flag Codes (many in Braille) to youth groups, schools, libraries and naturalized citizens each year. It also makes available to the deaf, The Pledge of Allegiance to the Flag of the United States of America in sign language.
- Since 1910, the DAR has assisted immigrants to become naturalized citizens. In addition to assisting in naturalization courts and citizenship classes, the DAR, with government permission, began a program of occupational therapy for the women who came through Ellis Island. The program was so successful that the DAR was asked to extend the plan to include the U.S. Marine Hospital on Ellis Island. It continued for 28 years after immigration duties ended. Much of the occupational therapy work that is carried on in government hospitals today is the result of this DAR-initiated activity.
- Since 1920, the *DAR Manual for Citizenship* has been given free to anyone seeking American citizenship. More than 10 million copies have been distributed.
- The DAR initiated American History Month (February) and Constitution Week (September) as special observances.
- Since 1908, DAR annually gives awards to honor graduates of the five service academies and three other military schools.
- The Memorial Bell Tower and Carillon at Valley Forge was built to honor American heroes, living and dead, of all wars.
- DAR members donate thousands of hours of volunteer service in 166 VA Medical Centers and 11 non-VA hospitals in appreciation of the service rendered by the men and women of the Armed Forces.

In 1905, the Mississippi Society of the DAR awakened the interest of the general public to preserve and restore the Old National Road, known today as the Natchez Trace Parkway. Because of the diligence and foresight of the DAR, the once famous artery of travel was preserved and eventually paved from Natchez to Nashville. Fifteen historical sites on the Parkway have been marked by the DAR.

The Mississippi Society purchased and maintains Rosalie, an antebellum home in Natchez, recently designated a National Historic Landmark by the U.S. Department of the Interior.

Mississippi has also provided the National Society with a President General. Mrs. Richard Denny Shelby, of Beulah, was elected to the top office of DAR and served from 1980-83.*

Little old ladies in tennis shoes having tea parties. Hardly!

As many of the 203,000 DAR members gather on October 11, 1990, in Washington, D.C. and in approximately 3,128 chapter meetings in all fifty states and around the world for DAR's Centennial Celebration, they won't be resting on their laurels!

These Daughters of the American Revolution will be rededicating themselves to the DAR Motto of "God, Home and Country." They will be perpetuating the memory and spirit of those men and women who gained American Independence – looking forward to the many opportunities that await them in a second century of service to the Nation.

*Georgane Ferguson Love Easley of Hattiesburg and Vicksburg was the second Mississippian to be elected NSDAR President General and served from 1992-1995.

(As you read this chapter, you'll find a few "gripes". We all have them and I'm sure you can relate.)

The Clarion-Ledger
Tuesday, August 27, 1996

Hey, If You Want Both Instant, Modern Service You've Gotta Wait for It

My question is why? Why do customers have to be treated like automatons rather than human beings?

Has anyone out there tried to call BellSouth, Delta Airlines, or Entergy lately? If you have, you'll know what I mean when I say it can be a maddening experience.

When you call, you'd better be prepared to get a busy signal, or if you should be one of the lucky ones to get through, you'll sit on the line listening to music or repeated messages to stay on the line for a service representative.

Service? Not the kind I'd like to have.

I detest those automated messages, "Press one if you want new service," "Press two if you want to discontinue service," "Press three if you want to report a problem," "Press four ...."

I've called BellSouth several times during the last few weeks. A recorded message tells me to enter my phone number.

That seems reasonable. I press in the phone number and I'm informed that the number is incorrect. After the third try, entering the correct number, trying it with and without area code, and still being told that I'm entering the number incorrectly, I'm ready to rip the phone off the wall.

I fell for a credit card pitch from a BellSouth representative who assured me that I would save 20 percent on area calls served by BellSouth. When the Visa card arrived ... I was instructed to call a number to activate the account.

And who was on the other end of the line? That familiar "service" representative with the message to ... "Press in your phone number," "Press in your account number," but when the order came to press in my Social Security number, I balked. I don't give out my Social Security number to just anyone ... especially a machine.

When I refused to comply, an operator came on the line and informed me that the account could not be activated without it.

"Fine", I said, "just cancel the account."

By that time I had already decided that the deal wasn't all it was cracked up to be since the 20 percent savings was limited to calls made on the credit card and not dialed from my home number.

Her reply? "Sorry, the account can't be cancelled without authorization from the person whose name is on the account." Since the phone is in my husband's name, I called him to the phone.

He was informed that he would have to give his Social Security number to cancel the account. He refused to do so but suggested to verify that he was the person in whose name the account was carried, she should call back to the telephone number listed in his name.

She asked for the phone number, which he gave, only to be informed that it wasn't the correct number.

He then asked what number she had listed, and she repeated the number that he had just given.

After a few comments from him about inane corporate red tape, she hung up. Click.

We were both angry and determined that never, never, would another telephone solicitation receive anything but, "Thank you, we're not interested." Click.

Then there's Entergy ....

A malfunctioning air-conditioner required three trips by a serviceman before it was finally determined that the power-saving device, installed on the unit by MP&L (now Entergy), was malfunctioning and cycling the unit off.

Trying to avoid the "press one" routine, I called the power company executive offices for relief.

I was informed by a real person that we didn't have such a device because "that program was discontinued some years ago."

Having replaced an air conditioner motor and paying for three service calls to reach this point, I was getting a little testy.

I won't repeat what I said, but the energy-saving device that I was told "I didn't have" was removed the next day.

And Delta Airlines? I'll save that for another time.

It's not that I dislike BellSouth, Entergy, Delta, and other corporate giants who provide services that I need, but it seems that the more mechanized we become, the more frustrations grow.

My question is why? Why do customers have to be treated like automatons rather than human beings? Why does blood pressure have to go up before someone listens? Don't they realize that it's rude to leave customers hanging on the phone for hours waiting for service?

I've been told that it's a sign of age, that I'm just "too old" to fit into the modern-day mode of doing business in this fast-pace, automated world. That's a sorry excuse.

The truth is, I'm old enough to remember when service was a company's number one priority; when the customer was always right, and when competition was the name of the game.

If modern technology has brought us to this point, I hate to see where future "progress" will take us.

(While this article mentioned several major corporations, the problem has been exacerbated to the point that only under emergency conditions do I try to reach a service representative by phone. If I have no alternative but to use the phone, I allow at least 3 hours of wait time to resolve the problem.)

The Northside Sun
Thursday, October 10, 1996

Northsider Finds Beloved Wandering Pet

There's nothing better than a dog story ... especially one with a happy ending.

It began on Saturday of the Labor Day Weekend, when unbeknownst to us, Maggie, the family cur, decided to take off with Mustang, a personable neighborhood beagle. The siren call of the Pearl River had beckoned the pair before; but this time, it was to prove an almost fatal attraction.

When Maggie didn't show up for supper, we were concerned, but thought she would be waiting at the door the next morning. Just off on a lark, we reasoned.

After two days and no Maggie, we were frantic.

Anyone who has ever lost a pet knows the feeling .... Had she been dognaped? Was she dead at the side of the road, the victim of a passing car?

My inner fear was that she was trapped or snagged by her collar in the underbrush of the vast and isolated river basin ... crying pitifully to be released while slowly dying from lack of food and water.

I had sleepless nights; we patrolled the streets; my husband and I walked the paths leading to the river; the dog pound and Mississippi Animal Rescue League were checked; Farmer Jim put Maggie on Pet Parade; an ad was placed in the "lost and found" of the newspaper; signs were posted at major intersections ... all to no avail.

My hopes were continually dashed as few calls came in and leads failed to pan out.

After a week, we felt within our hearts that the family pet, a loved member of the family, would never be seen again.

I blamed myself for allowing Maggie the freedom to roam; for not having adequate identification on her collar; for not taking immediate action when we discovered her missing.

And then the break that we'd been hoping for ... a ray of hope, but at the same time a sense of dread. Mustang's owner had seen one of the signs posted in the neighborhood and called with information that their dog had been found on Labor Day in Flowood in the vicinity of River Oaks Hospital.

Flowood! That's across the Pearl and miles from our home. Maggie may not be the smartest dog I've ever known, but she sure knows how to travel!

Somehow the dogs had crossed the river, and it was evident that Maggie had strayed too far to find her way back home without some help. Five days had passed, and even the possibility that she would still be in the same vicinity seemed remote.

Every sign that had been posted in Northeast Jackson was removed and taken to Flowood. Fliers were left at police stations; calls were made to the Rankin County Sheriff's office and the Brandon Animal Control; streets were cruised.

Maggie had on a collar, but the ID tag had been lost and we had failed to replace it ... dimming our hopes even more that she would ever be found.

On Sunday night, nine days after Maggie's disappearance, a young woman, later identified as Jennifer Mallory, called to say that she had seen a sign for a lost dog. Could the dog that she had taken in belong to us?

Jennifer had seen a dog wandering in the apartment complex in which she lives just off Lakeland Drive. She had befriended her ... feeding, bathing, and loving her, until a friend agreed to take the dog to provide a permanent home.

Was it Maggie? Yes!

A call to Phyllis Armstrong, who lived in Morton, turned up the vagabond which had caused our family a week of anxiety and heartache. Maggie had journeyed far but seemed to have learned little from the experience.

After all, she's just a dog.

But what about her master?

The lesson learned is that we human beings must exercise the higher intelligence with which we're endowed, to provide the proper environment and care for those animals for which we are responsible. It's a shame that we continually pay the price for our own stupidity.

Other lessons learned ...

- Never allow a pet to roam unattended.
- Always have pets properly identified, especially if you want the peace of knowing that if a tragedy should occur, you can be contacted.

- Be kind to strays. A stranger who appears at your door may be someone's beloved companion.
- Perseverance pays off.

Maggie is home and presently asleep at my feet. I'm eternally grateful to all who made it so.

To Ingrid, Mustang's master, to Jennifer and Phyllis, to Helga at the Brandon Police Station, to the unnamed gatekeeper at Sanderson Farms, Inc. in Flowood, to the kind officers at the Flowood Police Station, and to the many understanding friends who listened, consoled, and yes, even prayed for Maggie's return; a great big "thank you."

This story could have had a tragic ending; so I'm glad that it just provided some valuable lessons. In all things, we can learn from experience and try to do better.

The Clarion-Ledger
Tuesday, March 11, 1997

It's Not Always Safe to Appear in Print, But At Least It Is "Educational"

Participation in *The Clarion-Ledger*
Reader Editorial Board
is a learning experience.

It hardly seems possible that two and a half years have passed since *The Clarion-Ledger* Reader Editorial Board was established. From this writer's perspective, it has been a most enjoyable experience to appear on the op-ed page on a regular basis.

Having one's views in print can produce interesting repercussions, requiring a certain thickness of skin, and in some instances, the use of a bullet proof vest.

Being a columnist also develops certain notoriety that, when being introduced, often results in the conversation beginning with ... "You're name is so familiar. Haven't we met somewhere before?"

It can also be a little disconcerting when a stranger recognizes you from the column mug shot. When asked, "Are you Dot Ward?", I never know whether to admit that I am or pretend that I'm not ... especially if the person is with JPS, the State Department of Education, or from Bennie Thompson's office.

Since appearing in print, I've been amazed at how many times I've arrived for an appointment with a public official to find that there's someone sitting in to serve as a witness. Whoa!

I've been approached from time to time by folks wanting me to write a column on a particular subject *they* feel strongly about. I've always declined to be a "ghost" writer because I believe that in order to be an effective writer of letters to the editor or Op-ed columns, one must have the inspiration that comes from the need to express the writer's own opinion and the courage to state it publicly.

I've made some wonderful friends because of the Reader Editorial Board. One friend in particular, while confined to a hospital bed, never once failed to call me bright and early on the morning my column ran. One day last spring I received an Easter card from that friend, only to be shocked and saddened several days later to read his obituary in the paper. I miss hearing that early morning greeting, "I like your column."

Of course, not everyone does, and I hear from them, too. Like the classroom teacher who, following my recent column, "*Whole Language tried, found guilty*", wrote to say, "You shouldn't `through' stones at the public schools." I rest my case.

One poignant letter came from a Vietnam veteran who responded to a column I wrote on patriotism in which I suggested that God rules in the affairs of men and that we owe our liberty to those patriots who, "with a firm reliance on the protection of the Divine Providence, sacrificed their lives, fortunes, and sacred honor."

The letter painted a vivid picture of the horrors of war as the writer described how three men in his command were lost, and twenty others wounded, in a skirmish with the North Vietnamese. According to the writer, the experience taught him that "you and I cannot, must not, rely on some external god to do things for us." I was admonished never to write of freedom unless I "give credit where credit is due ... to those who have paid the price for liberty, alone and without supernatural assistance, for to do otherwise would cheapen the price that was paid."

This man, a graduate of a Baptist seminary with a master's degree in religion, not only fought for his country, but lost his faith in a Vietnam jungle.

I try to respond to each person who writes, but in this case, words were hard to come by.

The initial introduction of *The Clarion-Ledger's* Reader Editorial Board set forth the premise that the stated intent of the newspaper in creating a reader board was to develop a forum for the exchange of ideas and opinions. Little did I know that some ideas and opinions would create a hail storm of controversy resulting in a real lambasting on the editorial page.

The board was to be "voices of diversity" so that "we would [collectively] grow as human beings by being exposed to new ideas." That aim was a pretty high-minded challenge and presented a tall order for the Reader Editorial Board to fill.

My editor recently wrote the board to thank us for "sharing our knowledge, insight and wisdom" through our columns and comments.

While I don't know how much knowledge, insight, and wisdom my columns have provided, being a member of *The Clarion-Ledger* Editorial Board has deepened my understanding, enriched my life, and broadened my horizons.

The Clarion-Ledger
Thursday, May 15, 1997

Know Difference Between Voluntary Service, Involuntary Servitude?

Volunteering should stem from personal motivation, not orders from the government.

Are we feeling good about ourselves yet?

Have you called your local "America cares" recruiter to sign up for your volunteer stint?

A general, four presidents, one vice-president, five first ladies, and several thousand other participants gathered at the Presidents' Summit for America's Future to give Americans the "unprecedented opportunity" to reach a new level of commitment to our nation.

As if we don't already fulfill a commitment to our country by coughing up a huge portion of our income each year to pay the tax obligation assessed by Uncle Sam!

Please don't misunderstand. I think volunteerism is great! In fact, I'm a full-time volunteer, and countless others share the same commitment. That's why it's difficult to criticize the "call to help America's children."

The problem with the highly visible national initiative is that it's typical of many feel-good programs hatched by politicians to improve their image and to enlist the help of well-intentioned individuals who don't know the difference in voluntary service and involuntary servitude.

No doubt many of the Summit participants are sincere individuals who truly want to make a difference by volunteering. Others have ulterior motives.

What the Clinton Administration has in mind goes far beyond volunteering. The President has called for high schools across the country to make community service part of the curriculum, to give students credit for "volunteer" hours, and to make community service mandatory for graduation.

Lynn Steirer, a student in Bethlehem, Pennsylvania, fought her school's mandatory service program that required 60 hours of "volunteer" service in order to graduate. Already a Meals on Wheels aide and involved in numerous Girl Scout service projects, Lynn contributed hundreds of hours to her community, at her own initiative, but refused to submit her hours to the school for credit.

In her last semester, Lynn was told that she would be allowed to graduate if she would agree to report her volunteer hours for school credit.

But her resolve was strengthened when a school official asked the question, "What is more important, your values or your diploma?"

Lynn chose to give up her diploma, eventually obtaining a graduate equivalency degree instead.

She has no regrets about her decision because, in her own words, "Volunteering is important, but in a country that values its liberty, we should make sure that student "service" is truly voluntary."

A bill designed to overhaul public housing would require residents to contribute eight hours a month in community service. The idea raised the rancor of some Democrats who charged that it would be unconscionable to "force' anyone to work without pay. Jesse Jackson Jr., even went on record to say that it would be "treating welfare recipients as if they were indentured servitude."

Mandatory community service projects make "indentured servants" out of welfare recipients but "volunteers" out of students.

Figure that one out.

President Clinton has called for adult volunteers to teach children to read. What in the world are we paying teachers to do?

My objection to the national preoccupation with volunteerism is that it will do more to harm than to help the American spirit of volunteerism. Americans are the most giving people in the world and have always done their part to lend a helping hand, share a talent or ability, and give back to their communities through volunteer service.

Such volunteerism should stem from personal motivation with the individual determining how best to channel time and talent into effective community service. Americans don't need to be coerced or manipulated by political opportunists. Neither do they need to be given a guilt trip based on the premise that a national "crisis" exists and that the efforts of a volunteer force and expanded government programs will cure what ails us.

A participant on a recent *Crossfire* television broadcast, referring to the media hype being given the Presidents' Summit, remarked that the Bible teaches us to "Be careful not to do your `acts of righteousness' before men, to be seen by them. If you do, you will have no reward from your Father in heaven."

Something to think about.

The Clarion-Ledger
Letter to the Editor
Thursday, December 18, 1997

Writer Is Mistaken About Backing for Women's Monument

I think that Vickie Felton, in her Nov. 11 letter, "State can still back women's monument," jumped to an incorrect conclusion.

She seems to have a feminist chip on her shoulder in pointing out Mississippi's lack of support for the monument to the Women in Military Service for America (WIMSA) and obviously didn't research the facts.

The flag of our state was presented in a ceremony at the WIMSA Memorial by the Mississippi Society Daughters of the American Revolution (DAR) representing participation and support of the 4,800 Mississippi members.

The DAR honors the memory and spirit of men and women who have served their country in all wars ... beginning with the American Revolution.

The Mississippi flag that was presented will be permanently displayed in the Flag Hall at the WIMSA Memorial.

If Ms. Felton had taken time to read the WIMSA dedication program in which major sponsors were listed, she would have seen former U.S. Rep. Sonny Montgomery, U.S. Sen. Trent Lott, and U.S. Rep. Chip Pickering acknowledged as contributors.

Rather than wasting time criticizing our elected officials for their lack of support, Ms. Felton could have told all Mississippians how they can help recognize the significant contributions made by women in the military.

A computer registry at the memorial lists the names of women who have served.

What better way to honor the memory of a family member or friend than to be sure that the name is written there?

To be eligible, a woman must have served in the military or with the Red Cross, United Service Organizations, Special Services or Cadet Nurses, and must have been employed overseas in direct support of our armed forces during conflict.

Of course, monetary contributions to the WIMSA Memorial are needed. The address is WIMSA, Dept. 560, Washington, DC 20042-0560.

The Clarion-Ledger

Tuesday, December 23, 1997

Too Great A Fixation on "To be Jolly" Leaves Ho, Ho, Ho Lot of Letdown

Commercialization of

Christmas as a time to buy, buy,

buy too often leads to the blues.

In all its gaiety and tradition, the holiday season can produce some of the highest highs and the lowest lows. The documented rise in serious depression and the increase of suicides from Thanksgiving to New Year's Day leaves little doubt that the "Christmas blues" are real and something to be reckoned with.

I'm not referring to serious, clinical depression and I don't profess to have any special insight into the cause and effect, but I can share some observations based on personal experience and common sense.

We do it to ourselves.

Somewhere along the line we've gotten the perception that Christmas is beautifully decorated homes, loads of presents (with lots of money to buy 'em), bountiful tables of scrumptious food, happy families. Picture perfect.

The problem is very few of us live picture perfect lives, and when our expectations are unfulfilled, it causes us to feel inadequate and unhappy.

These feelings are intensified during the holidays because of stress and fatigue, too much food and drink, so much to do and too little time to get it done, and the commercialization of the holiday as a time to buy, buy, buy.

It doesn't help that the "season to be jolly" keeps getting longer and longer. It used to start after Thanksgiving – now it's Halloween. And don't forget "Christmas in July."

I've heard that the older you get the faster it rolls around. In this fast-paced world, it seems like just last month that Christmas was here and now it's time to do it all over again.

If we're truthful, most of us would confess that at one time or another we've allowed ourselves to be caught up in that picture perfect vision of Christmas. It's not altogether our fault because the culture of our day dictates that we deserve the good things of life while at the same time denying the source from whom all true blessings flow.

To escape the Christmas blues, we must learn what C.S. Lewis called the goodness of being ordinary. Our vision of perfection needs to be adjusted to be the perfection of the one whose birth is the cause of celebration.

Be reminded that the King of Kings was not born in a palace, but in a lowly stable ... a building for beasts to lodge and feed in. It can't get any more ordinary than that.

He came not to be served, but to serve. Instead of self-centeredness, our joy should be found in service to others.

When I get caught up in the desire for more things, I often think of the story of the young woman who was despondent because she didn't have money to buy a new pair of shoes until she met a happy young woman who had no feet. How shallow is the happiness and contentment found in worldly possessions.

If this Christmas your holiday decorations fall short of the Martha Stewart standard; if your family is dysfunctional; if the neighbor's dog grabs your Christmas turkey off the grill; if the only present under the tree is another outlandish necktie just like the one you got last year; or even if you don't have a Christmas tree, don't despair!

Kiss the Christmas blues good-bye and find peace and joy in being ordinary ... the kind of ordinary that is the reason for the season.

The Northside Sun

Thursday, September 17, 1998

Flying the Friendly Skies Can Be An Exhausting Experience

Have you flown "The friendly skies" lately? If you have, you know that they're not as friendly as they used to be.

If you're lucky enough to get a seat on a flight, don't count on getting much to eat.

On my last trip, Delta didn't even offer coffee. My choice was lemonade, punch, or water.

I asked for coffee, and the flight attendant said that she would bring me a cup "if she had time after cabin service is completed."

According to a recent ABC News report on air travel, meal service has been scaled back by 25 percent, staffing decreased by 10 percent.

That's not all ABC reported. There's been a 14 percent increase in passenger complaints.

Frequent flyers report long lines at ticket counters, oversold flights, crowded, cattlecar conditions on board, ticketing restrictions and penalties, cancelled flights. Even pilots are complaining that they are being forced to fly more hours than should be required.

Flying in or out of Jackson International is an added measure of misery.

The construction presently underway at the airport, (seems as if it has been underway for the past 10 years) makes pick-up and delivery of arriving and departing passengers a nightmare.

On a recent trip, I had to pay for the privilege to park in the back-forty of the west parking lot. I was exhausted and wringing wet by the time I, with bag in tow, made the uphill trek to the terminal in the mid-day, 100 degree heat.

Upon my return, I planned to beat the system by retrieving my car before picking up my luggage. That was a mistake.

There was no way to even get near the terminal in a car! The one traffic lane open to the lower level baggage area had a least a hundred other cars trying to queue up for incoming passenger pick-up.

After waiting in line for what seemed like an hour, I reached the baggage claim area only to find that there was no place to park. After making the loop a second time, I defiantly pulled into a restricted zone.

I think the traffic cop sensed that I was on the verge of "road rage." He looked the other way as I illegally parked. By this time I was willing to risk a ticket or car-tow. Anyhow, I reasoned that there was no way a tow truck could get within a mile of my car.

Upon entering the terminal, I found the baggage claim in total chaos. At least two other flights had arrived, and weary travelers were falling over each other trying to claim their luggage from the baggage carousels.

While this particular instance was an exception rather than the rule, there is no question that air travel in general has deteriorated in recent years. Just ask any frequent flyer.

My neighbors had been scheduled on a 3:20 p.m. departure from Albuquerque, arriving Jackson at 9:30 p.m. Their flight had been cancelled, and the only other flight to Jackson was through Atlanta at 1 a.m. They had to reclaim their checked luggage and kill 10 hours in the Albuquerque airport before flight time, arriving Atlanta at 6:00 a.m. to kill another three hours before connecting with the flight I was on.

And I thought I had it rough.

That's when the old joke "if you want to get to heaven, you have to fly through Atlanta" ceases to be funny.

I'm always glad to see companies make a profit. But airlines are obviously pocketing the $600 million profit reported this year at the expense of passenger comfort, convenience, and perhaps, even safety.

The worst part is that air travel is expected to increase by 50 percent in the next 10 years.

Think I'll gas up the car 'cause flying sure "ain't fun no mo'!"

The Clarion-Ledger
Tuesday, April 30, 1996

Mississippi State Society DAR Is Celebrating "100 Years of Service"

Recounting 100 years of DAR accomplishments and achievements is a reason for celebration.

You may never have heard of the Daughters of the American Revolution (DAR), but for approximately 5000 Mississippi Daughters in 81 chapters across the State of Mississippi, May 5, marks a very important anniversary.

On that date, in 1896, the Natchez Chapter DAR held an organizational meeting at Monmouth, the 1818 plantation home of General John A Quitman, an early Mississippi governor. The meeting was the founding of the Mississippi State Society Daughters of the American Revolution (MSSDAR).

Next weekend, Mississippi Daughters will make a pilgrimage to Monmouth for a re-enactment of that first DAR gathering.

Prior to the meeting at Monmouth on Sunday, the Mississippi Daughters and their guests will enjoy a Saturday night Centennial Gala at Rosalie, the Natchez antebellum home owned and maintained by the Mississippi State Society. The event will feature dinner under a gigantic tent in the Bicentennial Garden on the bluff of the Mississippi River and special entertainment by an ensemble of the Mississippi Symphony Orchestra and mezzo-soprano, Lester Senter. Guy Hovis will act as Master of Ceremonies.

Recounting 100 years of DAR accomplishments and achievements is a reason for celebration.

Early in the history of the Mississippi State Society, the Mississippi Daughters made a lasting public contribution to our state. From 1909 until 1933 the MSSDAR placed historical markers in 14 counties to mark the original path of the Natchez Trace. The Daughters worked tirelessly to awaken public interest in preserving the natural beauty and historical significance of the Trace, leading to the reconstruction of the Natchez Trace and the eventual development of a great scenic parkway from Nashville to Natchez.

Recognizing the significant contributions of the men and women who have served in the defense of our nation, Mississippi Daughters have given thousands of hours in volunteer service at the Veterans Administration Medical Centers in Biloxi, Gulfport and Jackson.

Sadie McLemore of Jackson was recently recognized by the National Society DAR for having given an incredible 19,283 hours (you read it right ... 19,283 hours!) in volunteer service at the VA Medical Center in Jackson over the last 15 years.

DAR members assist immigrants to become naturalized citizens by providing free copies of the *DAR Manual for Citizenship* and actively participate in naturalization ceremonies.

Always promoting respect for the flag of the United States of America, the Daughters provide flags to schools, scout troops, and public facilities. Braille flags are made available for the visually impaired.

As a special MSSDAR Centennial gift to the state of Mississippi, two flagpoles and flags were dedicated in a ceremony at the Mississippi Governor's Mansion, and a U.S. Flag was presented to *The Clarion-Ledger* at the opening of its beautiful new facility, compliments of MSSDAR.

In addition to supporting two DAR schools in remote mountain areas of Appalachia, the Mississippi Daughters:

- Promote American History Essay Contests for students in grades 5th through 8th.
- Recognize an outstanding Mississippi teacher of American History with an annual monetary award.
- Actively participate in community literacy programs.
- Sponsor citizenship training for boys and girls, kindergarten through high school, in Junior American Citizens Clubs.
- Award ROTC medals to outstanding cadets in high schools and colleges.
- Provide training in leadership and patriotism through sponsorship of chapters of Children of the American Revolution.
- Recognize outstanding students with DAR Good Citizenship awards.
- Sponsor DAR scholarships in the fields of nursing, occupational therapy, political science, history, government and economics.

Rosalie was purchased by the Mississippi State Society on April 25, 1938. In keeping with the

DAR objective of historic preservation, the house and gardens were lovingly preserved and restored. In 1989, Rosalie was designated a National Historic Landmark and is today a major tourist attraction.

Not being deterred by the mistaken image of "little old ladies in tennis shoes," the DAR offers its members (many of them "Junior Members" under the age of 35) an opportunity to meet new people with similar interests, develop friendships, and to join with others who cherish the priceless heritage enjoyed by all, while promoting the ideals of patriotism and love of country.

During 26 years as a member of the Daughters of the American Revolution, I have personally reaped the benefits of outstanding educational information provided through the National Defense Committee and NSDAR Resolutions. While the DAR is non-political, non-partisan and does not lobby, members receive a wealth of information on current issues that affect our families and our nation. DAR members learn the importance of responsible citizenship and strive to support and defend the United States Constitution and maintain our Republican form of government.

As the Mississippi State Society Daughters of the American Revolution looks back over its first 100 years, it also looks forward to beginning a new century of service to God, Home and Country.

Is there reason for celebration? You bet!

The Natchez Democrat
Letter to the Editor
May 1996

State DAR Gives High Marks to City of Natchez

The Mississippi State Society Daughters of the American Revolution recently held a two-day celebration in Natchez to commemorate its centennial which began with the organizing of the Natchez Chapter in 1896.

The city of Natchez rolled out the red carpet for the Mississippi Daughters and their guests, and I wish to commend the Natchez Convention and Visitor Bureau for the invaluable assistance it provided in coordinating and overseeing every aspect of the event.

Rene Adams and Laura Godfrey put in many hours and much hard work to see that everything ran smoothly.

While many people in Natchez helped make our celebration a success, I especially wish to thank the administration of the City of Natchez, Historic Natchez Foundation, Pilgrimage Garden Club, Natchez Garden Club, Monmouth Plantation, First Presbyterian Church, the Great Mississippi River Balloon Race, Natchez Pilgrimage Tours, the Ramada Hilltop Inn, Lady Luck River Park Hotel, and Natchez Eola Hotel, Entergy, and Callon Petroleum Co.

Because the Mississippi State Society DAR owns and maintains Rosalie, Mississippi

Daughters consider Natchez a second home. We're grateful to our many friends and neighbors who pitched in to help us have a wonderful 100th birthday party.

Dot Ward

MSSDAR State Regent

The Clarion-Ledger

Tuesday, June 1, 1999

"Wired World" Full of Things to Drag Us into Oblivion

Technology is fast out-pacing man's ability to keep up.

Tom Brokaw in a recent address to graduates at the College of Santa Fe said that technology has become one of the most ruthless instruments of oppression.

He said it is not enough to wire the world if you short-circuit the soul.

He's right, you know. We've come so far so fast that all of us are affected to some degree. And we haven't even experienced the turmoil expected with Y2K.

Americans enjoy the highest standard of living in the world; we are leaders in advanced technology.

Void looms

Yet with unbelievable advancements in just the past 10 years, there seems to be a void, a nagging uncertainty, that we're being deprived of the quality of life that brings inner peace, security, and happiness.

Our lives are becoming more complicated because of the very technology that is suppose to make life easier.

Take for example what use to be the simple process of receiving mail.

Now when you check the mailbox, you also have to check the fax machine, e-mail, and voice mail.

And the telephone, once in a stationary location, now goes with us in the car. Cell phones are carried in pocket or purse and calls can be received or made from just about anywhere.

Upscale new homes are designed with the latest technology ... computerized sprinkler systems, alarm systems.

We even have the ability to automatically turn on lights, open and close drapes, or start supper cooking with the touch of a button.

We're beeped at by microwave ovens, shrilled at when security is breached, and talked to by answering machines.

It takes a genius to figure out how to program the VCR or to operate the varied remote controls that come with modern day television sets and music systems.

We're a society obsessed with things.

Things that weigh us down and complicate our lives.

We either have too many things or not enough things. And when things don't work or break down, we experience stress and frustration.

Downsizing

This was brought home to me after a recent move to the suburbs from a house that my family had occupied for 29 years.

In an effort to downsize, we made a concerted effort to dispose of the many things we had accumulated over the years, only to be faced with acquiring more things to outfit the new home.

If Y2K turns out to be as bad as some of the doomsday prophets predict, it may do more to improve our lives than the technology of recent years.

Once again, family members will be conversing rather than sitting stupefied in front of a television or computer screen.

Creativity will flourish as we find new and innovative ways to provide the creature comforts to which we've grown accustomed.

And without the disturbance of telephones, computers, televisions, and fax machines, if only for a few days, mankind may be able to free itself from the ruthless instruments of oppression and find the opportunity to become reacquainted with his Creator.

The Clarion-Ledger
Saturday, June 12, 1999

Is Waiting on Doctors A New Health Care Rule?

If you haven't been for
an office visit lately, expect
to wait for awhile.

It happens sooner or later.

Favorite topics of conversation – weather, politics and religion – are replaced with talk of ailments, the latest surgery, or what the doctor has to say.

From what I've heard lately, I've concluded that physicians need to swear to a new Hippocratic Oath: "If we're going to keep them living longer, we need to treat them better."

The "treatment" is not the "doctoring" but how patients are worked through the system. That is, if you can get into the system.

Unless your condition warrants immediate attention, the first available appointment is usually weeks and sometimes months, away.

And when your appointment time finally arrives, more often than not, you'll cool your heels for a good while in the waiting room. If you're a "work-in," plan to take your lunch.

Based on various opinions as to how well a doctor handles his practice, the consensus is that medical practitioners, especially large medical groups and clinics, need to periodically evaluate office management beginning with the waiting room.

How long are patients kept waiting – both in the waiting room and examining room?

If they are not seen within a reasonable length of time, front desk personnel should offer some explanation for the delay and allow the patient to decide if he wants to continue to wait or reschedule the appointment.

Every physician has emergencies or delays, which patients understand, but if it's common practice to keep patients waiting for indeterminable lengths of time, changes should be made in office management.

Once upon a time, doctors made house calls. Now, it's virtually impossible to talk with one on the phone unless you have M.D. behind your name. If you're lucky, you may reach a nurse, but often a return call won't come until the end of the day.

The "herd treatment" is also offensive to patients.

Being lined up and run through like so many cattle makes one feel less than human.

It's also helpful to be clothed when first seeing the doctor rather than wrapped in a paper sheet.

Many doctors' offices are kept so cold that if you're not sick when you get there, you soon will be.

I've been told that temperatures are kept frigid to retard the spread of germs. Sounds reasonable, but it doesn't do much for patient comfort.

In recent years, physicians have been forced to modify their medical practice because of an increase in the number of patients, the paperwork generated by Medicare and medical insurance, threats from a sue-happy public, and sky-rocketing medical costs.

The changes have had a detrimental effect on both physician and patient.

Of course, the issues I've raised do not apply to all physicians; but more and more as the conversation turns to medicine, there is a shared opinion that these situations are becoming the norm rather than the exception.

With an aging population enjoying a longer life expectancy, applying the Golden Rule to patient "treatment" will go a long way to improve the practice of medicine.

The Clarion-Ledger
Friday, November 10, 2000

Marine Corps Deserves Our Thanks

Today is a special day for the United States Marine Corps, which celebrates 225 years of service to the nation.

Call it tradition or esprit de corps – whatever it is, the United States Marines have it!

From the Halls of Montezuma, to the shores of Tripoli, to the Battle of Trenton to the Argonne, to Guadalcanal and Iwo Jima, from Inchon to the Korean Armistice, to Lebanon and the Dominican Republic, from the opening battles in Vietnam to the Mayaguez Rescue, and in Operation Desert Shield and Desert Storm, to relief operations in Northern Iraq, Somalia, Rwanda, and Haiti, Marines have distinguished themselves in war and peace.

Since being established by the Continental Congress on November 10, 1775, to fight in the Revolutionary War, the United States Marine Corps, our "ready force," has defined the standards of military prowess and efficiency.

It's like President Ronald Reagan said, "Some people spend an entire lifetime wondering if they made a difference. The Marines don't have that problem."

In 1921, General John A. Lejeune, 13th Commandant of the Marine Corps, issued a directive that the honorable service of the Corps be celebrated throughout the globe on the Birthday of the Corps "so long as the eternal spirit which has animated our Corps from generation to generation and has been the distinguishing mark of the Marines ... continues to flourish."

On this, the 225th Birthday of the Corps, men and women worldwide, in large groups and small, will be gathering to celebrate the glories of the Marine Corps' illustrious history and to honor the memory of those who have borne the name Marine. Many paid the ultimate sacrifice of their lives for freedom's cause.

As Americans join you in celebrating, remember that a grateful nation cherishes your service, stands in awe of your accomplishments and achievements, applauds your spirit, and salutes your honor, courage and commitment.

To the few, the proud, the Marines ... Happy Birthday!

The Clarion-Ledger
Saturday, March 9, 2002

Cancer Diagnosis Puts Life in Perspective

We take so much for granted – family, health, life itself

What a way to celebrate New Year's Eve – flat on my back in a hospital bed recovering from unexpected major surgery!

An additional shock came when I learned that I was joining approximately 1 million other people in the U.S. who received the diagnosis of cancer in 2001.

Never having experienced more than a rare bug or cold, I always figured that when I did get sick, I'd do it up right. Like every experience in life, you handle it. Actually, you don't have much choice. And fortunately for me, the prognosis is very good that I will live to a ripe old age so I can keep bugging the liberals with my conservative columns.

Being sick saps your strength, changes your schedule, exposes your weaknesses. But in all things, I believe that we have an opportunity to learn and to grow. Here are a few things I've learned:

We take so much for granted. Good health, friends, and family top the list. Suffer a little adversity, and you'll find out just how much family and friends mean.

I won't expound on family, but mine has been terrific! And friends, literally from all parts of the country, many I've never met, are praying for me, and I'm appreciative because I believe in the power of prayer. Call it heaven-sent or just a coincidence that Jannie Johnson, a fellow columnist, phoned the day I came home from the hospital. She'd seen my name while thumbing through her Rolodex and was prompted to call. When she heard the news, her spontaneous and beautiful prayer was so heartfelt and uplifting that God had to sit up and take notice.

Have you ever thought about how much "comfort" we receive from food? Well, I've been comforted real good with enough gourmet meals in my freezer to last six months.

And the many calls, notes, get-well cards, and emails have done much to lift my spirits.

I learned that in selecting get-well cards, always pick one that's upbeat – even if the circumstance is dire. The one I enjoyed the most announced, "I hope you get better soon!" The inside said, "... but if you don't, can I have all your stuff?" I'm still laughing, and laughter is good for the soul.

But the attention and caring has also reminded me of those who suffer without family and friends. I know there are many people who face a life-threatening disease alone; so I've made a commitment to pray for them each day.

And I'm learning about the bonding of fellow sufferers, those who have gone through chemotherapy, radiation, or other cancer treatment. They lend support to newly diagnosed cancer patients.

One new and special friend introduced me to "comfy caps," which she makes to give to other cancer patients. I liked mine so well I passed the pattern on to a friend in Maryland who has just received the "C" diagnosis.

I found a real friend in Sharon Busby, who coordinates "Look Good…Feel Better" program at Baptist Medical Center. I couldn't have made it through my first chemo treatment without her help.

I've always wanted to be a redhead, and she made it possible by sending me home from the hospital with two wigs (and one of them is red!).

Having cancer allows you to relate to the experiences of other cancer patients. I particularly enjoyed the recent ("Larry McCool – optimist calls faith, focus key to healing." Feb. 18).

Larry's upbeat attitude and undaunted spirit in fighting cancer is great.

Cancer is a serious business. It reminds you of your own mortality.

One thing we human beings share in common is that we're going to die. Ready or not! But like the country preacher, I don't have to worry because "I've already got my glory bags packed."

And the most important thing learned thus far is to thank God for every day I have, including the bad ones, for without the valleys I'd never appreciate the mountaintops.

The Clarion-Ledger
Thursday, December 19, 2002

Phyllis Schlafly Remains Worthy of Much Praise

Words of praise and admiration often come as eulogies, too late for the person for whom they're spoken. That's why, when Ann Coulter used her column and book to champion Phyllis Schlafly, I said, HEAR! HEAR!

It's not that Phyllis Schlafly is an unknown. She was named one of the Ten Most Admired Women in the World by Good Housekeeping Magazine for 15 consecutive years and one of 100 Most Important Women of the 20th Century by Ladies Home Journal.

Schlafly is credited with virtually single-handedly stopping the passage of the Equal Rights Amendment (ERA).

Schlafly, a capable leader

There is no doubt that she's brilliant.

Schlafly is a Phi Beta Kappa graduate of Washington University, received her Juris Doctor from Washington University Law School and her Masters in Political Science from Harvard.

She has written 20 books. Her first, *A Choice Not an Echo,* published in 1964, sold more than three million copies. She has testified before more than 50 Congressional and legislative committees; published a monthly newsletter, *The Phyllis Schlafly Report,* for 36 years; writes a weekly syndicated column, and has a radio talk show and commentary heard on 460 radio stations.

In 1972, Schlafly founded Eagle Forum and serves today as its president.

She's successful at whatever she undertakes, including a happy marriage and raising six children, an accomplishment that causes feminist groans and teeth gnashing.

My path crossed Schlafly's in 1986 when I was appointed resolutions chairman of the National Society Daughters of the American Revolution (DAR). Phyllis was national defense chairman.

For six years I had the opportunity to work with Phyllis Schlafly. The experience proved to be the equivalent of earning a college degree.

I was impressed with her indefatigable energy, capable leadership, broad influence, and in-depth knowledge of issues.

But by far, the most impressive thing about Phyllis was the way she interacted with an average housewife from Mississippi.

She treated me as an equal, asked my advice, and included me in every event she planned. She saw to it that I was seated on the stage of Constitution Hall in Washington, D.C. for National Defense Evening and at the head table for the National Defense Luncheon.

Tireless, fearless worker

I was introduced to many of her friends ... Chief Justice and Mrs. Warren Burger, Elizabeth Dole, Jack Kemp, Pat and Bay Buchanan, Bill Bennett, Jesse Helms, Pat Robertson, Henry Hyde, Dr. Edward Teller (father of the hydrogen bomb), and Ollie North.

She was always in the picture…literally, and saw to it that I was, too. Her radiant smile makes her a natural before the camera. Her pictures make her look at least fifteen years younger than she is. Doggone it!

Phyllis Schlafly will be 79 years old on her next birthday. She has been a national conservative leader for 40 years, and she's still going strong.

On January 5 she will be on CSpan2 talking about her latest book, *Feminist Fantasies.* Later that month she will be honored by the Conservative Political Action Conference (CPAC) in celebration of the 20th anniversary of the defeat of ERA.

Ann Coulter called Phyllis Schlafly "brilliant, beautiful, principled, articulate, tireless and absolutely fearless."

She's that and so much more. Truly a remarkable woman indeed.

The Clarion-Ledger
Thursday, May 22, 2003

Historic Home's Preservation Stalled by Lease

Is it historic preservation
vs. the Mississippi Supreme Court?

As the result of a recent Mississippi Supreme Court decision, a famous historic landmark may be removed from public access.

The case involves the validity of a current lease on the Stephen D. Lee Home built in 1847 on a tract of 16th Section land in the city of Columbus, Mississippi.

It was home to the first president of Mississippi A & M College, now Mississippi State University, and remained in the Stephen D. Lee family for seventy years until the Lee heirs conveyed their interest in 1916 to the City of Columbus for use as a school site.

The school was built adjacent to the Lee home and used until a fire destroyed the school and severely damaged the home in 1959.

Foundation operates site

The school district opted for a new school location with plans to demolish the damaged Lee Home, that is, until a group of civic-minded citizens stepped in. They recognized the importance of preserving the historic old home and with the full blessings of the city and the school district formed the Stephen D. Lee Foundation, a nonprofit corporation, to restore and operate the home.

To facilitate this commitment, the school district executed a lease to the foundation in1960 at a nominal rental of one dollar per year.

In good faith and reliance upon the agreement and lease, the foundation took possession of the home and expended hundreds of thousands of dollars in restoration costs.

The home now houses an educational museum filled with irreplaceable period furniture, art works, historical documents, clothing, and glassware.

Hundreds of school children tour the home each year as an "eyes on history" enhancement of their educational experience.

The Lee Home is a major Columbus tourist attraction with docents giving thousands of volunteer hours to staff the home.

Now, more than forty years after the foundation restored the home with private funding and opened it to the public, the secretary of state contends that the foundation's lease is invalid.

Will doors be closed?

In the suit prosecuted by Eric Clark on behalf of the State of Mississippi, the lower court found in favor of the S.D. Lee Foundation; the Mississippi Supreme Court has reversed the lower court. The decision, now under reconsideration, could open the door for the secretary of state to demand additional large annual lease payments beyond the financial means of the nonprofit foundation, raising the likelihood that the doors of the S. D. Lee home would have to be closed.

In my mind, there is something terribly incongruous about this.

The Mississippi Legislature has authorized millions of dollars for the preservation of historic sites through the Mississippi Landmark Program. Yet an agent of state government is spending thousands of taxpayer dollars to sue a nonprofit organization that is struggling to preserve and maintain, at its own expense, a Mississippi historic site.

If Mr. Clark prevails, the future of the S.D. Lee Home is uncertain.

It would be a shame for Columbus to lose the benefits of this historic home and an injustice to those who for years have invested their dollars and sweat equity in preserving part of the history of their state and community.

Submitted to *The Clarion-Ledger*
Unpublished

The Telephone Company You Can't Reach By Phone

Have you tried to call your local telephone company lately? I'm talking about the one that advertises itself as the "Number One Service Provider"; the Baby Bell that now serves nine southeastern states.

I've never called that I wasn't informed by an automated voice that "we are experiencing extremely high call volume at this time. Call back later when call volumes are lower."

I wish someone would tell me when that is.

I've called at all hours of the day, five days a week, and always get the same message.

I've tried using the Right Touch Service, the company's automated information service, but with little success. The menu of eight options never seems to fit the problem I'm calling about so I enter "0" to speak to a service representative.

That's when I'm told how long I'll have to wait. "All of our service representatives are busy. Your wait will be approximately fifteen minutes?" What they really mean is you'd better pack a lunch.

And they call this service?

What are advertising agencies thinking when they use "service" as a come-on to attract new customers?

Take for example this statement from the company's website: "Ranked No. 1 in local telephone customer satisfaction by J.D. Power & Associates for three years since study was initiated in 1996." I wonder if J.D. ever sat with a dead phone to his ear waiting for service.

Or the catchy slogans – "Listening - Answering" used in full-page newspaper advertisements.

I know they're not answering; so I doubt that they're doing much listening.

And a logo from the side of a service truck, "Connect and create something."

That's a joke. If I had to wait to be connected by this company to create something, I'd thrown in the towel a long time ago.

Way back in 1966, I wrote an opinion column expounding on the lack of service and my frustration in using telephone menus in doing business.

When the column ran, I received a call from a phone company executive, saying that they were working hard to correct the deficiencies in their phone menu and improve customer service. He gave me his private number and said that if I ever had a problem in getting through the calling system to just call his office.

I would never abuse his offer, but over the years I have often found it necessary to seek his assistance when the service department wasn't answering the phone.

If service doesn't improve soon, I might just have to share his number with you folks who share my frustration.

CHAPTER XII

Patriotism and Citizenship

Put none but Americans on guard tonight.

George Washington

The Northside Sun
"As I See It"
Monday, July 4, 1988

Holiday Applauds Fathers of Freedom

JULY 4, 1988, marks the 212th birthday of the independence of the United States of America. On this day Americans will celebrate the signing of the Declaration of Independence, which was adopted by the Continental Congress on July 4, 1776.

Founders of our nation felt that it was an important occasion for celebration. John Adams said: "I am apt to believe that it will be celebrated by succeeding generations as the great anniversary festival. It ought to be commemorated as the day of deliverance, by solemn acts of devotion to God Almighty. It ought to be solemnized with pomp and parade, with shows, games, sports, guns, bells, bonfires, and illuminations, from one end of this continent to the other, from this time forward for evermore."

Independence Day was first observed in Philadelphia, Pa. on July 8, 1776. When bells were rung, bands played, the Declaration of Independence was read and the people rejoiced. It was not until 1941 that the United States Congress declared July 4 as a legal public holiday.

A NEW NATION WAS BORN WHEN 13 British colonies won their freedom and independence from Great Britain. Colonial troops clashed with British soldiers at Lexington, Mass., to begin the Revolutionary War on April 19, 1775. Fighting was to continue for eight years, but ties between the colonies and the mother country were permanently severed when the Second Continental Congress adopted the Declaration of Independence in 1776.

France recognized the independence of the United States in 1778 and became an active ally. Spain declared war on Britain in 1779, and Holland did so in 1780.

Faced with so many enemies, Great Britain gave up all hope of conquering the American patriots whose forces rarely exceeded 15,000 men, and on Sept. 3, 1783, recognized the new republic in the Treaty of Paris, formally ending the Revolutionary War.

THE MEN WHO won independence for this country and pledged to each other "with a firm reliance on the protection of the Divine Providence, their lives, fortunes and sacred honor" paid a tremendous price for their dedication to freedom.

Of the signers of the Declaration of Independence, five were captured by the British as traitors and tortured before they died. Twelve had their homes ransacked and burned. Two lost their sons in the Revolutionary Army. Nine of the 56 who fought died from wounds or the hardships of war.

HISTORY records that John Hart was driven from his wife's bedside as she was dying. Their 13 children fled for their lives. His fields and grist mill were laid waste; and for more than a year he lived in forests and caves, returning home after the war to find his wife dead and his children gone. A few weeks later, Hart died from exhaustion and a broken heart.

When British forces took over the residence of Thomas Nelson, Jr., to use as their headquarters at the Battle of Yorktown, Nelson urged Gen. George Washington to open fire, totally destroying his home. Nelson died in bankruptcy.

Carter Braxton of Virginia, a wealthy planter and trader, lost his ships to the British navy; sold his home and properties to pay his debts, and died in rags.

THOMAS MCKEAN was forced to keep his family in hiding during the war. He lost all his possessions for the cause of freedom yet served in Congress without pay.

The men who signed the Declaration of Independence were merchants, farmers, lawyers, jurists, and plantation owners. Most were men of means and education, and they knew that if the colonial cause failed they would be executed. Such was their dedication to the cause of freedom.

Today, the Fourth of July filled with family gatherings, fireworks displays, flag waving and celebration should also serve as a time of reflection. In the words of Lyman Abbott, "He who looks with pride upon the history which his fathers have written by their heroic deeds, who accepts with gratitude an inheritance which they bequeathed to him and who highly resolves to preserve this inheritance unimpaired and to pass it on to his descendants enlarged and enriched, is a true American ...."

AS WE celebrate yet another birthday of the United States of America, let us perpetuate the memory and spirit of those men and women who achieved American independence and rededicate ourselves to the cause of liberty.

The poem "God Bless America" by Helen Steiner Rice expresses it best:

"America the Beautiful"
May it always stay that way,
But to keep Old Glory flying
There's a price that we must pay.

For everything worth having
Demands work and sacrifice,
And freedom is a gift of God
That commands the highest price ...

For all our wealth and progress
Are as worthless as can be
Without the faith that made us great
And kept our country free!

Have a wonderful Independence Day 1988!

The Northside Sun
Thursday, September 14, 1989
"As I See It"
Articles on the U.S. Constitution also appeared in
The Clarion-Ledger, September 17, 1989 and September 13, 2003.

Week Celebrates U.S. Constitution

WHEN PRESIDENT George Bush signs the proclamation designating September 17-23 as Constitution Week, he will be the eighth United States President to do so.

The tradition began in 1955 when Gertrude Carraway, President General of the National Society Daughters of the American Revolution, submitted a tentative resolution to the National Chairman of the NSDAR Resolutions Committee designating the week as a time to bring the Constitution of the United States and the importance of its preservation to the attention of the American people. The subsequent resolution was adopted April 21, 1955, by the DAR Continental Congress.

Members of Congress received copies of this DAR resolution; and on June 7, 1955, at a flag presentation to the Senate by the DAR Executive Committee, this resolution about Constitution Week was discussed.

ON JUNE 14, Senator William F. Knowland, of California, introduced Senate Concurrent Resolution 140, authorizing and requesting that President Eisenhower follow the DAR example by proclaiming September 17-23 as Constitution Week.

Following passage of this resolution by both houses of Congress, President Eisenhower issued his Proclamation on August 19, 1955.

The first observance of Constitution Week was so successful that on January 5, 1956, Senator Knowland introduced a Senate Joint Resolution to the President designating September 17-23 annually as Constitution Week. This resolution was adopted on July 23 and became Public Law 915 on August 2, 1956.

THE PURPOSES of the observation and celebration of Constitution Week are to emphasize the responsibility of protecting and defending the Constitution and preserving it for posterity; to understand that the Constitution is our great heritage and the foundation of our lives; and to study the historical events which occurred during September 1787.

DAR members across the country are instrumental in seeing that Constitution Week is brought to the attention of all Americans by asking that the Flag of the United States be flown during the week; by erecting displays in banks, libraries and other public buildings; and by providing radio and TV stations with public service announcement on the Constitution.

The Commission on the Bicentennial of the United States Constitution has asked for the DAR's help in encouraging participation in "Bells Across America – A Ringing Tribute" on September 17, the 202nd anniversary of the signing of the U.S. Constitution.

THE RINGING tribute will start at 4:00 P.M. (EDT) or 3:00 P.M. our time, and coincides with the time at which the Constitution was signed in Philadelphia in 1787. Individuals and groups across the nation are asked to simultaneously ring bells for up to 202 seconds. The tribute can be made with bells, chimes, and carillons.

Each year the DAR sponsors the Constitution Week Essay Contest for eleventh and twelfth grade students. This year the contest is co-sponsored by the Commission on the Bicentennial, which has designated 1990 as the Year of the Judiciary as part of the five-year Bicentennial commemoration period.

Because the Supreme Court sat for the first time on February 2, 1790, the theme for the national contest is "*Why Are Independent Judges Important in the Preservation of Our Constitutional System of Government?*" National winners and their teachers will gather in Washington, D.C. as guests of the Bicentennial Commission. The national winner will also receive a monetary award of $1,000 from the DAR.

IN JACKSON, Mayor Kane Ditto has issued a proclamation designating September 17-23 as Constitution Week. Rebecca Cravat Chapter DAR is offering free copies of the U.S. Constitution in Braille to the visually impaired.

The Braille edition is provided by the Nation Braille Press, Inc. and the Bicentennial Commission and will be distributed by Radio Reading Service of Mississippi. Free pocket-size copies of the Constitution will also be available at the Northside Library.

The five Jackson area DAR chapters are actively involved in marking this very special event and will provide interested individuals with patriotic material, copies of the U.S. Constitution, essay contest information, speakers for school and club programs, a list of mail-order manuscripts, slide and video programs, as well as a book list for suggested reading on the United States Constitution.

DOES CONSTITUTION WEEK have any significance to you? Ask yourself ....

Do you know why the United States Constitution is the fountainhead of our great liberties – religious, political, and economic?

Do you know how our Constitution enables the United States to grow and prosper, becoming the most powerful country in the world, while at the same time preserving individual freedom?

Do you know what is in our Constitution that caused these happy results and made us the envy of the whole world?

If you know the answers to the questions, Constitution Week is the time to share your knowledge with others. If you don't know the answers, then you have an opportunity – indeed a duty – to study the Constitution to gain a new appreciation of its genius.

THE CONSTITUTION by itself cannot guarantee freedom. It can only secure freedom so long as we, the people, understand its precepts, guard its principles, and insure its perpetuation.

As President John Quincy Adams said in a speech on the Constitution fifty years after it went into effect ... "So may your children's children ... after another century of experience under our national Constitution, celebrate it again in the full enjoyment of all its blessing."

Constitution Week provides us with this opportunity!

The Northside Sun
Thursday, June 29, 1989

Creed Gives Americans Recognition

"I believe in the United States of America as a government of the people, by the people, for the people; whose just powers are derived from the consent of the governed; a democracy in a republic; a sovereign Nation of many sovereign States; a perfect Union, one and inseparable; established upon those principles of freedom, equality, justice and humanity for which American patriots sacrificed their lives and fortunes.

"I therefore believe it is my duty to my country to love it; to support its Constitution; to obey its laws; to respect its flag; and to defend it against all enemies."

These words were written by William Tyler Page in 1917 as the result of a nationwide contest for the writing of a national creed which would express in the briefest possible form an expression of American political faith reflecting the fundamental principles most distinctive in American history and tradition.

PAGE WAS a student of history and was familiar with the great historical documents of the United States as well as the famous statements made by many great Americans. He used phrases from those writings and statements in composing *The American's Creed.*

- He borrowed from the Preamble of the U.S. Constitution, "the United States of America";
- From Abraham Lincoln's Gettysburg Address, he used, "A Government of the people, by the people, for the people."
- From the Declaration of Independence, he took, "Whose just powers are derived from the consent of the governed."
- From Article IV of the Constitution, "A sovereign Nation of many sovereign States."
- From the Preamble to the Constitution, "A perfect Union."
- From Daniel Webster, "One and inseparable."
- From the Declaration of Independence, "Established upon those principles of freedom, equality, justice and humanity for which American patriots sacrificed their lives and fortunes."
- In substance, from Edward Everett Hale's *The Man Without a Country,*" he took, "I therefore believe it is my duty to my Country to love it."
- From Article VI of the Constitution, he used, "To obey its laws."

COMING HOME from church on a Sunday in May, 1917, William Tyler Page determined that the creed he would write would be fashioned along the lines of the Christian or Apostle's Creed. In March, 1918, Mr. Page received word that his entry in the contest, which was one among more the 3,000 entries, had been chosen the winner.

On April 3, 1918, Mayor James H. Preston, of Baltimore, presented the award of one-thousand dollars to Page. This award was made in the House of Representatives Office Building in Washington, D.C. as The American's Creed was officially accepted on behalf of the United States by the Commissioner of Education and by the Speaker of the U.S. House of Representatives. The complete proceedings of the official acceptance of the American's Creed may be found in the Congressional Record, No. 102, April 13, 1918.

Three days later Mr. Page purchased Liberty Bonds with the prize money and gave them to his church.

A DESCENDANT of President John Tyler, Page served almost 61 years at the United State Capitol, beginning as a page in 1881 at the age of thirteen. In 1919, he was elected Clerk of the U.S. House of Representatives and held that office until December, 1931, at which time a new post was created for him – Emeritus Minority Clerk – which he held for the remainder of his life.

The last public appearance of Page was on a Sunday evening, October 18, 1942, when he was a guest of the Daughters of the American Revolution at the 50th Anniversary Celebration of the Pledge of Allegiance to the Flag of the United States held in DAR Constitution Hall in Washington, D.C. On this occasion, he led the recitation of the American's Creed.

The next day, October 19, 1942, Mr. Page passed away. On the same day, the House of Representatives adjourned in honor of his memory.

In the words of Page, "The American's Creed is a summing up, in one hundred words, the basic principles of American Political faith. It is not an expression of individual opinion upon the obligations and duties of American citizenship or with respect to its rights and privileges. It is a summary of the fundamental principles of American political faith as set forth in its greatest documents, its worthiest traditions and by its greatest leaders."

HAVING WITNESSED on television throughout the past weeks the tragic plight of the Chinese people living in a totalitarian state, I am reminded anew of the blessings of liberty that are ours in the United States of America.

As we celebrate yet another birthday of this great nation, the words of The American's Creed should give voice to what we as Americans believe and provide us with a clearer recognition that it is "our duty to our country to love it, to support its Constitution; to obey its laws; to respect its flag; and to defend it against all enemies."

Can we do less?

The Clarion-Ledger
Monday, July 8, 1991
Related article *The Madison County Journal*, July 9, 1998

Independence Day Thanks Should Be Directed to God

The editorial referenced is "Independence! Spectacular 4th display is expected" was appropriate for the day, it missed the mark for the reason and manner in which we should celebrate.

Founding Father John Adams, who was quoted in the editorial, said that he believed that the day would be celebrated by succeeding generations with "pomp and parade, with shows, games, sports, guns, bells, bonfires and illuminations." In the sentence preceding this statement, he said: "It (Independence Day) ought to be commemorated as the day of deliverance, by solemn acts of devotion to God Almighty."

In the move to secularize our society, it has become fashionable to omit any reference to God. How sad that the Lord God, who is truly "our guardian, guide and stay," should be forgotten!

Deuteronomy 8:19,20 (NIV), plainly tells us that "if you ever forget the Lord your God and follow other gods and worship and bow down to them, I testify against you today that you will surely be destroyed. Like the nations the Lord destroyed before you, so you will be destroyed for not obeying the Lord your God."

Lest we forget, when Americans sound the "bells" in celebration, the thanks and awe should be to God, who has blessed our land with freedom and peace.

The Northside Sun
"As I See It" Thursday, November 4, 1993
Related article *The Clarion-Ledger,* November 11, 1993

11th Hour, 11th Day, 11th Month Fitting

November 11, 1993, commemorates the 75th anniversary of the Armistice of World War I, a day of unique significance in the history of the United States.

Seventy-five years ago, the cease-fire agreement of World War I was signed, ending a four-year conflict that took the lives of 126,000 Americans. The armistice was signed on the 11th hour of the 11th day of the 11th month (November 11, 1918) and fittingly, in 1919, President Woodrow Wilson proclaimed November 11 as Armistice Day to remind Americans of the tragedies of war.

A law adopted in 1938 made the day a federal holiday and in 1954, Congress changed the name to Veterans Day to honor all United States veterans of all wars.

We in Mississippi have always held in high esteem those who have served and died in service to their country.

A fitting monument to the soldiers of Mississippi, who served valiantly in the vanguard of their country's wars, was built in 1939-40 "to the memory of those who fell in the service of this country by land and by sea ...." and stands today next to the Old Capitol on North State.

The War Memorial Building, designed by E. L. Malvaney, is built around an open courtyard, containing a symbolic tomb which was erected in tribute to "the ideals and purposes for which gallant Mississippians suffered and died" and as an inspiration "to shield forever the fragile quality of liberty."

Under a flag flown at half-staff, the tomb stands as a silent memorial. The inscription at its head reads, "Time will not dim the glory of their deeds."

Time does have a way of letting us forget ... those Mississippians who gave their lives ... 704 in World War I, 4185 in World War II, 409 in Korea, and 637 in Vietnam and 18 others unaccounted for in Southeast Asia. Many who survived the wars of this nation have lived with physical disabilities that forever altered their lives.

It is because of their faithful service to our nation that the National Society Daughters of the American Revolution on the 75th anniversary of Armistice/Veterans Day, is asking all Americans to join in a special salute to the men and women of the Armed Forces whose extraordinary contributions and personal sacrifices helped preserve the blessing of freedom for future generations.

On Veteran's Day, fly the flag and at the "eleventh hour of the eleventh day of the eleventh month" join with other Americans by observing a moment of silence in schools, workplaces and homes, followed by the ringing of bells in churches and public buildings to let our veterans know that we, a grateful nation, have not forgotten.

The Clarion-Ledger
Tuesday, November 8, 1994

Don't Stay at Home Today, Because One Vote Can Make A Difference

The most important civics lesson of all is that of responsible citizenship within these great United States.

Today, Election Day 1994, millions of Americans will go to the polls to vote. Many millions more will stay home.

Forfeiting ones' voting privilege is a puzzling phenomenon in view of the fact that most impediments to voting, such as literacy tests, poll taxes, residency requirements and burdensome registration, have all but disappeared.

Where, then, have all the voters gone?

Could it be that many citizens stay home because they feel that one vote makes no difference? If so, consider the following:

In 1645, one vote gave Oliver Cromwell control of England; in 1649, one vote caused Charles I of England to be executed; in 1876, one vote gave Rutherford B. Hayes the presidency of the U.S.; in 1923, one vote gave Adolph Hitler leadership of the Nazi Party; and in 1941, one vote saved the Selective Service – just two weeks before Pearl Harbor was attacked.

Does voter apathy exist because we think that none of the candidates represents our views?

It's been said that our nation is a "government of the people, by the people, and for the people." In reality, we have a government only "of the people" who vote. The results are that our elected officials often represent only the special interests of the people who voted for them.

If one finds good candidates in short supply, it could be that "we the people" must share some of the blame. By allowing our own personal standards to decline, we accept diminished personal standards in those whom we elect to leadership positions.

If this nation is to survive and prosper, we need able men and women of high personal character and integrity to seek public office. They should be encouraged to run and then be enthusiastically supported because the moral character of our leaders dictates to a large degree public policy.

If we allow pessimism to override our concern for the future of our nation and the preservation of our American heritage through non-participation in the electoral process, we in effect contribute to the nation's decline.

Participation in the democratic election process requires knowledge of how the election process functions, how candidates are nominated and elected, and in-depth information on candidates and issues.

An effective voter must know which district, ward, or precinct he or she is in and be prepared before arriving at the polling place to know who and what is on the ballot.

At times, the ballot can be complex and even intimidating. In order to cast an intelligent vote, some energy must be exerted on the part of the electorate. Let's face it. A lot of folks are just too lazy to make the effort.

Even our schools often fail to adequately prepare young people for the task of self-governing. In a rush to teach kids global citizenship, schools neglect the most important civics lesson of all, that of responsible citizenship within these great United States.

We *all* need a refresher course on the value of the ballot and to learn again that a high price has been paid for the privilege of self government.

If you ever get complacent or decide to stay home on Election Day, just ask any citizen of Soweto Township or the former Soviet Union if he thinks voting's worth the effort.

A wise man once said: "The United States has become a great nation, not so much by reason of what government has done for us, but by reason of what government has left us free to do for ourselves."

Make no mistake about it; if you forfeit your citizen's right to participate in the process of self-government, pressure groups and selfish interests will gladly fill the vacuum.

We enjoy a freedom in this country that is unequaled anywhere else in the world. The responsibility that comes with that freedom is the never-ending challenge to participate in the process of self-government in order to secure good government.

The Clarion-Ledger
Tuesday, July 4, 1995

We Must Remember Why Nation Really Celebrates Independence Day

Who will remember the words
acknowledging dependence upon
Almighty God if we fail to repeat them?

I admit it! I'm so patriotic that the blood in my veins runs red, white, and blue!

I come by this patriotism honestly. Generations ago, my great, great, great, great, grandfather, Nathaniel Tucker, served in the Continental Army during the American Revolution in order to establish American independence.

This nation has been blessed with many patriots who not only believed in the United States of America but who were also willing to fight for the cause of independence. That patriotism is why we celebrate.

According to one of our Founding Fathers, John Adams, the celebration of our independence "would be celebrated by succeeding generations as the great anniversary festival" and "ought to be commemorated as the day of deliverance, by solemn acts of devotion to God Almighty."

He went on to say that it ought to be solemnized with pomp and parade, with shows, games, sports, guns, bells, bonfires, and illuminations, from one end of this continent to the other, from this time forward for evermore.

Today, this statement by John Adams is often revised to leave out any reference to God. How sad that we fail to recognize the source from which all freedom comes.

The men who won independence for this country pledged to each other "with a firm reliance on the protection of the Divine Providence, their lives, fortunes and sacred honor."

The personal sacrifice of the signers of the Declaration of Independence is well documented but rarely recalled. Five were captured by the British as traitors and tortured before they died. Twelve had their homes ransacked and burned. Two lost their sons in the Revolution and nine of the 56 signers who fought, died from wounds or the hardships of war.

Independence Day, filled with its family gatherings, fireworks displays, flag waving and celebration, should also serve as a time of reflection. In the words of American Congregationalist preacher and editor Lyman Abbott, "He who looks with pride upon the history which his fathers have written by their heroic deeds, who accepts with gratitude an inheritance which they bequeathed to him and who highly resolves to preserve this inheritance unimpaired and to pass it on to his descendants enlarged and enriched, is a true American .... "

That's why I'm concerned when I see the history of our nation being revised. How will future generations be able to "look with pride ... upon heroic deeds" if we fail to "preserve this inheritance unimpaired?" Who will remember the words acknowledging dependence upon Almighty God if we fail to repeat them.

Why is it that we, Americans living in the greatest nation on earth, fail to recognize the source of our greatness? Outsiders seem to understand better than we do.

Brigadier General Carlos P. Romulo, of the Philippine Islands, was one foreigner who loved the United States. He served with General Douglas McArthur in World War II and was later ambassador to the United States from the Phillipines.

When he returned to his home to become president of his alma mater, the University of the Philippines, he made the following address:

"I am going home, America, farewell! For 17 years I have enjoyed your hospitality and have visited every one of your 50 states. I can say I know you well. I admire and love America. It is my second home.

"What I have to say now is both a tribute and a warning: Never forget, America, that yours is a spiritual country.

"Yes, I know that you are a practical people. Like others, I have marveled at your factories, your skyscrapers, your arsenals. But underlying everything else is the fact that America began as a God-loving, God-fearing, and God-worshipping people, knowing that there is a spark of the divine in each of us. It is this respect for the dignity of the human spirit which makes America invincible. May it always endure.

"And so I say again in parting, thank you, America, and farewell. May God keep you always, and may you always keep God."

As we celebrate yet another birthday of the United States of America, let us acknowledge our reliance upon God; perpetuate the memory and spirit of those men and women who achieved American independence; and rededicate ourselves to the cause of liberty.

The Clarion-Ledger
Tuesday, July 2, 1996

Freedom Is A Two-Edged Sword; Let Us Remember So This 4th of July

We have flung off one external restraint after another, but we have not learned how to restrain ourselves.

Arthur Gordon in his outstanding book, *A Touch of Wonder*, relates the story of being present at a Fourth of July gathering in which the speaker extolled the virtues of freedom.

As the applause died at the conclusion of the speech, a young man's voice rose from the crowd: "Why don't you tell them the whole truth? Why don't you tell them that freedom is the most dangerous gift anyone can receive? Why don't you tell them that it's a two-edged sword that will destroy us unless we learn how to use it, and soon? Why don't you make them see that we face a greater challenge than our ancestors ever did?

"They only had to fight for freedom. We have to live with it!"

In reflecting on the young man's remarks, Mr. Gordon points out that perhaps we have a misguided concept of liberty. That we are using the freedom of choice gained for us by our forefathers to choose the wrong things.

Mr. Gordon believes that we have pushed the concept far beyond freedom from tyranny or oppression until now the freedom we claim has come to mean freedom from all unpleasantness: from hardship, from discipline, from the stern voice of duty, from the pain of self-sacrifice.

We have flung off one external restraint after another, but in the process we have not learned how to restrain ourselves.

Or as a wise man once said: "A man's worst difficulties begin when he is able to do what he likes."

We seem to have difficulty in knowing what it means to be an American.

It's almost as if we're ashamed of Americanism. We apologize for being too nationalistic and stress our global interdependence rather than our national independence.

We teach our children to be citizens of a global community rather than teaching allegiance to one nation – the United States of America.

Our schools fail to teach American History; and when it is taught, it is distorted by politically correct revisionism.

We try to disguise the fact that we are Americans by hyphenating. Some citizens would rather be called African-American, Spanish-American or Native-American. Multiculturalism accents our diversity rather than our unity.

We've even divorced ourselves from the English language by accommodating bi-lingual education. And through the use of some 265 government documents, printed in hundreds of languages represented in the American melting pot, we have diluted the common language that maintains our identity as Americans.

We've placed leaders in authority over us who are corrupt, dishonest, and immoral; some of our judges, through their decisions, are re-writing the law rather than abiding by the United States Constitution.

We've lost our moral compass by allowing our culture to be corrupted by dirty books and smutty movies. Television has robbed our families of hours, even years, of high quality time together.

We say that we're committed to putting "children first" while killing millions of unborn children in their mother's wombs.

In the words of Arthur Gordon, "We begin to tolerate, than accept, than condone, and then openly endorse ... so subtlety, we have lowered the flag of righteousness."

Americans need to look squarely at some of the ugly areas in our national and personal lives and ask ourselves to what extent these things stem from a distorted concept of freedom which leaves us free to be selfish, lazy, ignoble, and weak.

The freedom that we enjoy in this country is unequaled anywhere else in the world. But with freedom comes responsibility – responsibility to preserve the heritage of freedom that was given us by our forefathers; responsibility, as stewards of freedom, to govern ourselves, to keep and strengthen the Republic, and to pass on to future generations a heritage that is enlarged, enriched, and unimpaired.

The Clarion-Ledger
Saturday, June 14, 1997
(Related articles on Flag Day were published in *The Clarion-Ledger* June 14, 1995, June 14, 2002, June 14, 2003, and *The Northside Sun*, June 9, 1988.)

Let Flag Day Today Begin A 21-Day Salute to the Flag of the United States

The day was cold and blustery. The bone-chilling wind made the walk to Fort McHenry a brisk one, but the experience that awaited was to be the kind that warms men's souls when the fire of patriotism is ignited.

It was at the site of Fort McHenry, now a National Monument and Historic Shrine near Baltimore, Maryland, that a young American patriot, Francis Scott Key, wrote the stirring words which would eventually become our national anthem.

Key, detained aboard a British ship in the harbor, penned the words "by dawn's early light" on September 14, 1814, when he saw the stars and stripes of "Old Glory" still waving over the fort after a 25-hour British bombardment.

The flag that Key saw was of gigantic proportions. It was 30 feet high by 42 feet wide and contained some four hundred yards of wool bunting. It had been made by Mary Pickersgill at the direction of Major George Armistead, Commandant of Fort McHenry, with instructions "to have a flag so large that the British will have no difficulty in seeing it from a distance."

Mary Pickersgill's flag, which today is displayed at the Smithsonian Institution in Washington, D.C., survived an estimated 1,800 bombs, rockets, and shells fired at the fort by the British fleet.

The history and heritage of our nation's anthem and the flag that inspired it are preserved for future generations by the National Park Service in a film presentation at the Fort McHenry visitor's center.

As the film concludes, the audience is told to face the right wall where a curtain is slowly drawn back to reveal a breath-taking view of our flag flying high above the Fort as the voices of young cadets from the U.S. Naval Academy Choir fill the auditorium with the stirring words of *The Star-Spangled Banner.*

It was a special time. A patriotic fervor filled us with love for that flag, pride in our nation's accomplishments, gratitude for those who preserved it; and, I might add, left nary a dry eye in the room.

Today, on Flag Day, we honor that flag – the Flag of the United States of America.

The first national observance of Flag Day was on June 14, 1877. President Woodrow Wilson issued a proclamation in 1916 calling for a nationwide observance of Flag Day to be held each year on June 14. In 1949, Congress gave the holiday permanence by resolving "That the 14th day of June of each year is hereby designated as Flag Day ...."

Flag Day is not a legal holiday, but it's a good time to focus attention on the proper use and display of the flag as outlined in the United States Code. Rules governing the flag are often neglected, not because of intentional disrespect but from lack of knowledge.

Did you know that ....

- The flag, when it is in such condition that it is no longer a fitting emblem for display, should be destroyed in a dignified way, preferably by burning.
- The flag should never be used as wearing apparel, bedding, or drapery.
- The flag should be displayed only from sunrise to sunset on buildings and on stationary flagstaffs in the open, and may be displayed twenty-four hours a day *if properly illuminated during the hours of darkness.* (This means, it's not to be a decorative fixture on the front of one's house unless illuminated during the night.)
- The flag should not be displayed on days when the weather is inclement except when an all-weather flag is displayed.
- The flag should never touch anything beneath it, such as the ground or the floor.
- The flag should never be used for advertising purposes in any manner whatsoever. It should not be printed or otherwise impressed on paper napkins or boxes or anything that is designed for temporary use and discarded.
- Each star on the American flag represents a state and has a specific location on the blue field determined by the order in which the state it represents entered the Union. Mississippi is 20th, which puts our star in almost the center of the flag – at its heart – fourth row, third from the left.

The Flag Code, like the U.S. Constitution and other important American documents, contains information for effectual American citizenship.

Let Flag Day be the first day of a 21-day Salute to the Flag of the United States of America by flying "Old Glory" every day beginning today and ending on Independence Day, July 4.

The Clarion-Ledger
Tuesday, July 1, 1997

Test Yourself on How Much You Know About Being An American Citizen

This quiz can test your IQ and determine your eligibility for American citizenship.

This Friday, Americans from all walks of life will be celebrating the 221st birthday of the United States of America. Independence Day, the 4th of July, is the day to revel in our Americanism.

Most of us are natural born citizens, having no requirement for citizenship other than the fact that we were born within the borders of this country. Those who are foreign-born and wish to become American citizens are required to pass a test before being granted that privilege.

The citizenship exam required by law and administered by the Immigration and Naturalization Service of the United States Department of Justice tests the knowledge of the applicant for those qualities deemed necessary for responsible citizenship.

Those of us who have been given a free ride because of our American birthright should be required to take the same test to see if we measure up.

In 1920, when it became apparent that aliens arriving on our shores needed help in preparing for citizenship, the Daughters of the American Revolution (DAR), a patriotic women's organization, printed the first *DAR Manual for Citizenship.*

The citizenship manual met a "long-felt need" to provide the information necessary for responsible citizenship. During the first year, 75,000 editions were printed in Italian; 50,000 were printed in English, Spanish, Hungarian, Yiddish, and Polish. Each year, the manual's popularity increased, and by 1952 the *DAR Manual for Citizenship* was printed in English and 19 foreign languages.

The foreign language editions were discontinued that year when the law was changed to require applicants to speak English. The Naturalization Service supported the change, believing that it is just as much a part of citizenship to teach English as it is to teach the principles of Americanism. The DAR agreed.

For more than 75 years, the *DAR Manual for Citizenship* has been made available to Naturalization Courts for distribution to foreign-born immigrants who apply for citizenship or for use in Americanism classes. To date, more than 12 million copies have been furnished to applicants by the DAR free of charge.

The Naturalization test requires basic knowledge of U.S. history, law, and government. And to help the applicant prepare for the examination, the manual contains a 50-question sample test.

Listed below are 15 of the questions which can test your IQ and determine your eligibility for American citizenship. You must answer at least 12 questions right to pass.

1. What kind of government does the United States have?
2. What is the highest law of the land?
3. How many branches are there in our government?
4. How many terms can a President serve?
5. How many justices on the Supreme Court?
6. How many senators are there in Congress?
7. How many representatives are there in Congress?
8. Name the senators and representatives from your state.
9. How many amendments are there to the Constitution?
10. What are the first ten amendments to the Constitution called?

11. What document declared the 13 colonies to be free and independent States?
12. When was it signed?
13. Name the war in which we won our independence from Great Britain.
14. Who was the greatest general of this war and what office did he afterward hold?
15. How many stars are there on the American Flag? And what do they represent?

The test should be a no-brainer for most Americans. Sadly, it won't be.

If you answer all 15 questions right, you're a patriot. If you failed to achieve a passing grade, just be glad that you're already a citizen of the United States and not on the outside trying to get in!

Answers to the Quiz: 1. A republican or representative form of government; 2. The Constitution of the United States; 3. Three - Legislative, Executive and Judicial; 4. Two; 5. Nine, the Chief Justice and eight Associate Justices; 6. One Hundred; 7. The number is determined by the population of the State. There are presently 435 members of the House; 8. Senators: Cochran and Lott, Reps. Parker, Wicker, Thompson, Pickering, Taylor; 9. Twenty-seven; 10. The Bill of Rights; 11. The Declaration of Independence; 12. July 4, 1776; 13. The American Revolution; 14. George Washington - first President of the United States; 15. Fifty - the Union of fifty states.

The Clarion-Ledger
Tuesday, December 14, 1999

We Need Leaders Like Washington Today

Two-hundred years ago today, on December 14, 1799, George Washington died at his beloved Mount Vernon.

As a tribute to the Father of Our Country, it is fitting to commemorate his life on this anniversary by remembering his service and leadership to our nation.

George Washington was chosen by his peers as general and commander-in-chief of the united colonies in the war for independence from England. He led the Continental Army for eight difficult years before the ultimate victory at Yorktown.

As President of the Constitutional Convention held in Philadelphia at the conclusion of the war, he helped write the basic law that would govern the new nation.

After the Constitution was ratified by the states and took effect, Washington was unanimously elected to serve as the first President of the United States. He served for eight years, having been re-elected unanimously to a second term.

Washington was a man of integrity and character. He was dignified, reserved, dependable, modest, and honest.

He was God-fearing, describing his own role in the American Revolution as a "humble agent of a favoring Heaven." He began and ended each day kneeling with a Bible opened before him. As President, he said: "God will mark the path so plainly that I cannot mistake the way."

President John Adams, at the time of the official announcement of the death of George Washington, told the U.S. Senate: "His example is now complete; and it will teach wisdom and virtue to magistrates, citizens, and men, not only in the present age, but in future generations, as long as our history shall be read."

In a day when heroes are Hollywood celebrities and sports figures, how America needs a George Washington to raise a standard by which to measure. Let us learn the lessons of wisdom and virtue from George Washington's exemplary life that made him "First in war, first in peace, first in the hearts of his countrymen."

Companion Piece from:
The First Epistle
First Presbyterian Church, Jackson, MS
Thursday, December 16, 1999

George Washington
"First in War, First in Peace, First in the Hearts of His Countrymen"

Two hundred years ago on December 14, George Washington, the "Father of our Country," died at his beloved home, Mount Vernon. In commemorating this date, it is fitting for all Americans to remember the life of George Washington and to recall his words and deeds.

Washington began each morning and ended each evening kneeling with a Bible open before him. While many of his public prayers are well know, it was the earnestness of his private devotions that reveals the depth of his faith.

Written in his own hand from his personal prayer book, George Washington prayed one Sunday evening ... "O most Glorious God, in Jesus Christ my merciful and loving Father, I acknowledge and confess my guilt, in the weak and imperfect duties of this day. I have called on Thee for pardon and forgiveness of sins .... Let me live according to those holy rules which Thou hast this day prescribed in Thy holy word; make me to know what is acceptable in Thy sight, and therein to delight, open the eyes of my understanding, and help me thoroughly to examine myself concerning my knowledge, faith and repentance, increase my faith, and direct me to the true object, Jesus Christ the Way, the Truth and the Life. Bless, O Lord, all the people of this land, from the highest to the lowest, particularly those whom Thou has appointed to rule us in church and state.

"Continue Thy goodness to me this night. These weak petitions, I humbly implore Thee to hear, accept and answer for the sake of Thy Dear Son, Jesus Christ our Lord, Amen."

The Washington Monument, in Washington, D.C. stands more than 555 feet. Engraved on the metal cap atop the monument are the words: "Praise be to God."

The Clarion-Ledger
Tuesday, October 23, 2001
Reprinted: *The National Defender*, Vol. 44, No. 1, Sept. 2002

America Has Lacked Love for God, Country

As the Sleeping Giant awakes, it has been gratifying to see Americans unite in a common cause that has rekindled religious fervor and reenergized our patriotism.

But why has it taken a September 11 to rout us from our indifference and complacency?

Why is the flag suddenly in vogue and patriotic exercises stressed in our schools?

And why do we suddenly seek God for comfort and protection?

Could it be we've been found wanting?

America is vulnerable and we feel apprehension – if not outright fear – that the American way of life will never be the same again. It can no longer be business as usual.

Rededication to values

The wake-up call we've received should serve to strengthen and revitalize this nation. It will do so if we seize the opportunity. Let September 11 mark the beginning of a rededication to those principles that have made our nation great, the values and beliefs upon which this nation was founded.

And let's be sure we have our priorities right.

John Adams, our second President, had his right when he said: "It must be felt that there is no national security but in the nation's humble acknowledged dependence upon God and His overruling providence."

And as we get right with God, we need to take a refresher course in Americanism 101.

Begin by examining the documents that are the framework of our government – the Mayflower Compact, the Declaration of Independence, and the United State Constitution.

Take to heart the words inscribed on our national monuments and the buildings that house our seats of government.

Learning U.S. History

Keep Old Glory flying! But show it respect! Familiarize yourself with the U.S. Flag Code, which sets forth the existing rules, customs and etiquette pertaining to the display and use of the flag.

Study our history and learn about our patriotic customs and symbols.

All school children should know which star on the blue field of the United States flag represents Mississippi. It's the 20th star (because our state was the 20th admitted to the Union) and can be found on the fourth row, third star from the left. "Our star" is the top star of four at the center of the flag. It's at the very heart!

And when we place our hand over our heart to recite the Pledge of Allegiance to the flag, don't let it be without meaning and understanding. Do you know why our flag stands for a "republic" rather than a democracy? And just what does "indivisible" mean?

And don't forget the service of the men and women of our Armed Forces or the millions of American veterans who have paid the ultimate price for freedom.

Honoring veterans

November 11 is Veteran's Day. In attending ceremonies in recent years honoring our veterans, I've been disappointed that so few people attend. It seems most are too busy to take time from leisure activities to recognize the service of our vets and to say a simple "thanks." That too, should change.

Join with fellow Mississippians at 9:30 a.m. Saturday, Nov. 10, on the grounds of the Woolfolk Building across from the state capitol building in downtown Jackson as the Mississippi Veterans Monument is dedicated.

Perhaps September 11 happened at just the right time in our nation's history.

The First Epistle
Vol. 36, No. 26, Thursday, July 3, 2003
Reprinted in *The First Epistle*, June 29, 2007

Faith of Our Fathers

As the Declaration of Independence was being signed, Samuel Adams declared: "We have this day restored the Sovereign to whom all men ought to be obedient. He reigns in heaven and from the rising to the setting of the sun, let His kingdom come."

As words of faith are rapidly disappearing from our textbooks and revisionists are intent on rewriting history to remove the truth about our country's Christian roots, we should be mindful that God blessed the birth of this nation because of the faith of our Fathers.

Did you know that 52 of the 56 signers of the Declaration of Independence were orthodox, deeply committed Christians? They recognized the importance of prayer and sought the guidance of Almighty God in their actions and deliberations.

The first official act of the Continental Congress on September 7, 1774, was a call to prayer. The 35th Psalm was read, and many in the body knelt as they "turned imploringly to Heaven for Divine interposition."

The patriot, Patrick Henry, didn't just say the famous words, "Give me liberty, or give me death." He also said in the same speech: "An appeal to arms and the God of hosts is all that is left us. But we shall not fight our battle alone. There is a just God that presides over the destinies of nations."

On July 4, 1821, John Quincy Adams, the 6th President of the United States, declared: "The highest glory of the American Revolution was this; it connected in one indissoluble bond the principles of civil government with the principles of Christianity."

Let this Independence Day be a time of rededication to the Christian principles exemplified in the lives of our forefathers. Let us be found on our knees before God thanking Him for blessing this land with abundance, prosperity and peace.

The Clarion-Ledger
Thursday, October 23, 2003
Reprinted in *The National Defender*, Vol. 46, No. 3, November 2004

Statesmen, Not Politicians, Are Sorely Needed

In his play, *Knights,* the Greek writer of comedy, Aristophanes, wrote, "You have all the characteristics of a popular politician: a horrible voice, bad breeding, and a vulgar manner."

That was back in 424 B.C., and while I wouldn't go so far as Aristophanes, I'm certain that some would say that's an apt description of some politicians of 2003.

In a little more than a week, voters will choose the next leaders of our state.

Why do I feel so uninspired?

Parties wielding power

Of course I'll vote because I believe it is the first priority of good citizenship. But more often than not, especially in recent years, I find that I'm voting for the lesser of two evils. By this attitude, I don't mean evil in the literal sense; it's just that most candidates don't exhibit the dignity, character, and integrity that I would like in a leader. To put it simply, they are politicians when what we need are statesmen.

Forgive my political incorrectness for referring to both men and women as statesmen. While I fully support women who wish to run for public office, if any female candidate insists on being called a "stateswoman," she won't get my vote.

The two major political parties, Republican and Democrat, contribute their share to the general disillusionment of many voters.

"The Party" holds the purse strings to campaign funds, forcing many candidates (and later officer holders) to dance to the party's tune or lose party support. And many "party people" become so focused on power and control that they put the good of the party before the good of the country.

Political campaigns have become nothing more than name-calling slugfests with political strategists plotting ways to destroy the opposing candidate. Harry Truman may have taken the heat in the kitchen, but today's kitchen is so hot that it's probably a disincentive to attracting qualified would-be candidates.

Many good people are simply unwilling to subject themselves and their families to the negative campaign rhetoric and mud slinging, or to have their buried skeletons (most of us have them) held up for public scrutiny.

Campaign costs too high

The cost of running for public office, especially for a state or national office, requires big bucks. The amount of money it presently takes to wage a successful campaign is downright obscene, and I don't see any change on the horizon.

To raise campaign funds, most candidates are forced to get in bed with special-interest groups who, once the candidate is elected, expect a payback with largesse and votes favorable to their cause.

But as most people would say ... that's politics! But it's also the reason many voters stay home on Election Day.

Alexander Pope, the noted English poet and satirist of the early 1700s, knew a statesman when he saw one. His definition should be the inspiration of each man or woman who seeks public office:

Statesman, friend to truth! of soul sincere,
In action faithful, and in honor clear;
Who broke no promise, served no private end,
Who gained no title, and who lost no friend.

May our political system be blessed with more statesmen and fewer politicians.

The Clarion-Ledger
Saturday, June 12, 2004

Help City to Retire Old U.S. Flag on Monday

Do you have big plans for Flag Day? If you're like most folks, I doubt it.

This rarely celebrated holiday is just a blip on the calendar ... no day off from work ... just another day.

But all of that is about to change.

While I can't promise a day off, Flag Day 2004 promises to be more than just another Monday. There will be a flag burning in Jackson.

The only time most of us see the U.S. flag burned is when rabid anti-American demonstrators appear on TV. While this type burning is done to defile the flag and all it stands for, there is a way to burn the flag that is altogether right and proper.

Section 176(k) of the U.S. Flag Code states, "The flag, when it is in such condition that it is no longer a fitting emblem for display, should be destroyed in a dignified way, preferably by burning."

If you've never attended a flag retirement ceremony, avail yourself of the opportunity to join with city officials and other patriotic citizens who will gather at 11:00 a.m. Monday at the flagpole in the Josh Halbert Gardens at City Hall. It will be a memorable occasion, one not soon forgotten, to see the old flag retired from service as Taps is played.

And to make the day even more special, the beautiful, new flag that will replace the one being retired is being presented to the City of Jackson in honor of Jackson firefighters and emergency service personnel.

Who among us can forget the heroism of the 343 men and women of the New York Fire Department who died on September 11, 2001, or the image of their fellow firefighters raising the U.S. flag in the rubble of the World Trade Center?

According to Carolyn Best, regent of Rebecca Cravat Chapter of the Daughters of the American Revolution (DAR) that is sponsoring the Flag Day event, "There could be no better time to honor the flag of our country and to recognize the service and dedication of our own firefighters and emergency service personnel."

As part of this Flag Day observance, take a look at your own flag. (I certainly hope you have one.) Does it need to be retired from service because it is faded, tattered or torn? To fly a flag that is no longer fit for display shows disrespect for the flag.

If your flag is in need of retirement, bring it to the Flag Day event, or drop it off at any municipal fire station during Flag Week, June 13-19, for proper disposal.

Join with other Americans in giving Old Glory a 21-day salute by flying the flag everyday, weather permitting, from Flag Day through Independence Day. And if the flag is left up after dark, remember to have it well illuminated.

On Monday, round up the kids, close the shop, take either a late coffee break or early lunch hour, and join us at 11:00 a.m. at the flagpole at City Hall in downtown Jackson.

Make this Flag Day a day to remember!

The Clarion-Ledger
Wednesday, July 4, 2007
Reprinted: *The National Defender*, Vol. 50, No. 2, September 2008
The Gazette, Galax, Virginia, October 20, 2008

Let's Rededicate Ourselves to American "Principles"

Now is the time for all good men to come to the aid of their country!

Now, as never before, we need men and women who understand that being an American is more than living in America. Being an American is a concept based on a set of values and ideals. It's a burning patriotism that believes that this country is the best in the world, inferior to no other nation, with no apology.

As we celebrate this Independence Day, I have great concern for the future of the United States of America and wonder if that "City on the Hill" will survive for our children and their children's children.

My disquiet stems from many serious changes taking place today.

We have elected politicians rather than statesmen to govern us. We are becoming a bilingual society, with only half of the candidates running for president believing that English should be the official language of the United States. American jobs are vanishing as U.S. companies close plants and outsource to locations overseas or south of the border. The Rule of Law is being eroded by a government that refuses to enforce our laws and gives amnesty to millions of people who have entered the U.S. illegally. Political correctness has stifled freedom of expression and common sense. Judicial supremacists are attempting to remake America into a society that rejects traditional marriage, banishes the Pledge of Allegiance, the Ten Commandments and the Boy Scouts.

Where once there was integrity, honesty, and decency, we have lowered the flag of righteousness by allowing moral decay to eat away the very fiber of American society.

U.S. sovereignty is being threatened by an agreement called the Security and Prosperity Partnership, which if approved by Congress next fall, will bring us closer to the North American Union. The union would in effect erase the borders between the U.S., Mexico, and Canada, allowing free migration of peoples between countries. This move toward globalism will be a giant step to One World Government or a "new world order," and the United States of America will fade into oblivion.

Taken individually, the problems we face are not insurmountable; but collectively the life threatening condition plaguing this nation may prove to be fatal unless immediate action is taken to reverse our direction.

On this Independence Day, my prayer is that God will never remove his protective hand from our nation and that all Americans will rededicate themselves to the principles and ideals that made this country great.

The Clarion-Ledger
Saturday, June 14, 2008

June 14 Is Flag Day, So Wave and Honor the Red, White, Blue

George M. Cohan expressed my sentiments exactly when he wrote the lyrics of *You're A Grand Old Flag* in 1906 for the musical *George Washington, Jr.*. His tribute to the U.S. flag is as popular today as it was 100 years ago and in simple verse sums up the affection patriotic Americans have for the flag.

Old Glory is a "grand old flag!"

Birthed in 1777 at the Second Continental Congress, the flag of our country has a long and distinguished history. It has undergone many changes over the years, but the basic design of red and white stripes with stars on a field of blue has remained the same.

And even in our nation's darkest hours, Old Glory has been "a high flying flag" that brought hope to its people – the hope that "forever in peace may it wave."

Let us not forget that our Grand Old Flag

- Crossed the Delaware with George Washington.
- Inspired Francis Scott Key to pen our National Anthem, *The Star-Spangled Banner,* in 1812 as he saw, "by dawn's early light" that "our flag was still there."
- Was carried in triumph by Andy Jackson in New Orleans and prevailed at Appomattox, and San Juan Hill.
- Saw Belleau Wood in World War I.
- Witnessed the attack on Pearl Harbor; was proudly raised at Iwo Jima; and flew from the mast of the U.S.S. Missouri when Japan surrendered to end World War II.
- Survived the battles of Pork Chop Ridge and the Chosin Reservoir in Korea and was present at the negotiations at Panmujom.
- Followed the Ho Chi Minh trail and was aboard the last helicopter out of Saigon.
- Waved over the burning sands of Desert Storm.
- Arose like the Phoenix from the rubble of the World Trade Center.
- And today maintains a presence in Iraq and Afghanistan.

How proud we were to see The Stars and Stripes planted on the surface of the moon and how our hearts swell with pride when the U.S. Flag is raised at award ceremonies recognizing U.S. medalists at the Olympics.

And our hearts break to see the flag covering the caskets of American heroes or handed to weeping widows or other family members at graveside services.

General Douglas MacArthur said of Old Glory: "The flag of the American Union is a visible symbol of the ideal aspirations of the American people. It is the one focus in which all unite in reverential devotion. We differ in religion; we differ in politics; we engage in violent disputes as to the true meaning of the Constitution, and even challenge the wisdom of some of it provisions; but through the sanctifying folds of the flag, the collective intelligence of the Nation rises superior to the wisdom of its parts, and thus endures the perpetuity of the Republic."

Old Glory is "the emblem of the land I love," and accordingly President Woodrow Wilson issued a proclamation in 1916 for a nationwide observance to honor the Flag of the United States and President Harry Truman signed legislation in 1949 making June 14, Flag Day, a national observance.

So let "ev'ry heart beat true 'neath the red, white and blue" as we celebrate that grand old flag!

Acknowledgements

My grateful appreciation to those who helped make this book possible:

Sandra Scott of The Type Shop

For her patience, diligence and outstanding efficiency.

Richard B. Wilson, Jr.

For designing such a snazzy book cover

Marshall Ramsey

For being Marshall and sharing his talent with me

Evelyn North

For spending hours proofing and keeping me from misplacing modifiers

Friends and Family

For their encouragement and enthusiasm

About the Author

Dot Ward is the recipient of the Patrick Henry Medallion for Patriotic Achievement awarded by the Military Order of the World Wars; the George Washington Medal awarded by Freedoms Foundation at Valley Forge; the Eagle Award from Eagle Forum; Strong Woman Award for Leadership from Mississippi Baptist Health Systems; and DAR Community Service Award. She was named twice to Outstanding Young Women of America.

For more than twenty-five years her newspaper columns and letters-to-the-editor appeared in local newspapers. Her outspoken columns on education resulted in an appointment by Governor Kirk Fordice to the State Board of Education and a 4-year term on the Southern Regional Education Board.

She held leadership positions in the Daughters of the American Revolution – 2-term national chairman of the NSDAR Resolutions Committee; Vice President General NSDAR; and State Regent of the Mississippi State Society. She was a charter member of the Board of Directors of the Metropolitan Crime Commission; and is on the Board of Directors of the Natchez Trace Parkway Association, presently serving as Association president.

She lives in Madison, Mississippi with her husband, a retired attorney. They have three grown sons, a granddaughter and grandson.